THE PEOPLE NEXT DOOR

KERI BEEVIS

First published in 2021 by Bloodhound Books.

www.bloodhoundbooks.com

Print ISBN 978-1-914614-54-5

ALSO BY KERI BEEVIS

PSYCHOLOGICAL THRILLERS

Deep Dark Secrets

Dying To Tell

Trust No One

Every Little Breath

CRIME THRILLERS

M for Murder (#Book 1)

D for Dead (#Book 2)

For Trish
Fellow author, partner in crime, and true friend.
Here's to many more years of plotting, beta reading
and creating fab stories.

PROLOGUE

It was gone seven when he finally pulled into his driveway and the house was immersed in darkness. That was his first clue that all was not right. There should have been one light on at least.

He thought back to earlier that morning before he had left for his meeting. The anger, the accusations, the threats and the violence. Even though it was hours ago that she had struck him, he could still feel the sting of her hand on his cheek.

If he could have cancelled his plans he would have. He would have spent the day reassuring her and trying to make things right. He would have taken the time to show her just how much he cared about her. Instead, when he left, she was locked in the bedroom, and he had no idea what her mood was going to be like when he returned. Would she still be mad, unwilling to listen to reason, or would she have calmed down enough for them to have a civil conversation?

He unlocked the front door, calling out a greeting as he reached for the hall light, his unease growing when he was met with silence. Nothing looked out of place, but the house was cold, the heating off, and a stale stiffness clung to the air. A curious old scent reminiscent of body odour and faeces and rotting meat.

Something was very wrong.

Heart thumping, he took the stairs two at a time, fear clogging his throat when he saw the bedroom door ajar, screaming her name before he entered the room, before he saw her.

She was sat in the chair in front of the dresser, head slumped forward and blood soaking through the ropes that were holding her in place.

Anger, panic and despair blinded him as he rushed to her, slipping in the puddle of red pooling on the rug beneath her, and then he was on his knees, tears streaming down his face as he tried to make sense of what had happened, a howl of anguish ripping through him as he cupped her cold cheeks, raising her head to look into sightless eyes.

She was gone.

He loved her and would have done anything for her. In that moment he would have even killed for her.

As his head pounded, the rage building with his need to avenge her, the floorboards creaked behind him.

Raising his head, he stared at the figure silhouetted in the doorway, at the knife still red with blood, and he froze, a cool clammy shiver caressing his back as he tried to comprehend what he was seeing, the realisation of what had happened while he was gone, shocking him into a stunned silence.

Several seconds passed before he managed to speak, his voice little more than a whisper when the words finally came.

'What did you do?'

PART I

BEFORE

1

The bang that came from upstairs immediately halted conversation, all eyes looking towards the ceiling.

'What was that? You don't have a ghost, do you?'

'Not that we're aware of.' Ellie Summers glanced at Roxanne, whose red lips were painted in a smirk, then across the table at her boyfriend. Ghosts? It wasn't something they had even considered when they had bought the place. Ash wasn't a believer and neither was she. At least she didn't think she was. As the floorboards creaked and what sounded suspiciously like footsteps moved directly above where they were sitting, she reconsidered.

'Someone's up there.' That was from Roxanne's husband, Pete, stating the obvious, his voice dropping to a whisper.

Ash shook his head. 'It's an old house and it creaks and groans. It's probably nothing.' Still, he pushed back his chair, getting up from the table. 'Stay here, I'll go check it out.'

'Pete, maybe you should go with him,' Roxanne urged, her tone also hushed and her smirk now gone.

'But Ash said to wait here.'

'What if someone's broken in?'

While Pete dithered, seeming reluctant to move, Ellie got to her feet. 'I'll go. You two finish your dessert.'

Neither of her friends protested too much as she stepped out into the hallway, hurrying after Ash, who had already disappeared up the stairs.

She cautiously followed him, annoyed that her shoulders had tensed and her legs were trembling. This was her new home. She refused to be afraid of it.

But what if someone has broken in?

Although she tried to dismiss the question, the nagging voice had her moving faster.

If anything happened to Ash...

No, she was over-reacting. Roxanne and Pete's concern was getting to her.

Ash was right. Old houses made noises. He should know. After all, he did design buildings for a living.

Still she climbed the stairs quietly, fearful of making too much noise, freezing to the spot with her heart jumping, when she stepped on a creaking floorboard.

'Ash? Where are you?' Her tone was hushed as she peered both ways down the long landing. The noise had come from above them, so she headed left towards their bedroom, wondering if she should have brought a weapon.

For what? This wasn't a movie.

But if someone had broken in...

Which was ridiculous. They were in the middle of nowhere.

She thought of *Crimewatch* and the remote properties that were often ransacked. The location of their new home, which had been a selling point for both of them, was suddenly now less appealing.

Ghost or no ghost, there had definitely been footsteps and the idea there could be a stranger in the house was actually a hell of a lot more frightening than anything supernatural.

'Ash?'

Her heart was thumping now. Where was he?

Ellie took the last tentative step towards the bedroom, annoyed she was scared to enter a room that should be her sanctuary. The shape that suddenly blocked the doorway, barrelling into her, broke that train of thought and she screamed.

'Jesus, Ellie. Don't sneak up on me like that,' Ash hissed, seeming as startled as she was.

'I didn't know you were in here.'

Something between them growled and Ellie stepped back, spotted yellow eyes glaring up at her.

A cat?

'What the hell? Where did she come from?' She assumed it was a girl, given the pink glittery collar.

The feline hissed and Ash scratched behind her ears in an attempt to calm her. 'The window I guess.' His eyes glinted, teasing. 'That's what happens when you leave them all open. Things get in.'

Annoyingly, he was right. It had been a stifling hot day and Ellie had earlier opened all of the upstairs windows in an attempt to cool the house down, despite Ash telling her the pond in the garden below their bedroom balcony was a breeding ground for mosquitoes. She glanced at the long curtains billowing at the French doors and hoped the cat was the only thing that had come in. At least a blessed breeze had finally picked up, which should offer some relief through the night.

'See, nothing sinister.' Ash hooked his free hand around Ellie's waist, pulling her close and pressing a kiss against her nose. 'Just a cute little cat.'

'She is cute. I wonder who she belongs to.'

'Probably the neighbour.'

'Maybe.' Ellie followed him down the stairs and through to where Pete and Roxanne were sat.

'Here's your ghost.' Ash grinned, holding up the fluffy black bundle.

Pete had the good grace to look a little sheepish, while Roxanne's eyes widened. 'You got a cat?' She glared accusingly at Ellie. 'You never said.'

'She's not ours.'

'Where did she come from then? Yours is the only house around here.'

'Not quite. There's a neighbour behind us.' Ash pointed out, going to the front door. 'She probably belongs to them.'

'But what if she doesn't? You can't just turf her out.'

'She's a cat. She was obviously outside exploring and decided to be nosy when she saw the open window.'

'She could be a stray!'

'Does she look like a stray?' She's not skinny, her coat is shiny, and look, she's wearing a collar. She'll be fine.' Ignoring Roxanne's glare, Ash opened the door and put the cat down on the front step.

'Ellie!'

'She's not ours, Roxanne. We can't just keep her.'

When Roxanne mumbled out a protest under her breath, Pete covered her hand with his and shot her a warning look. Roxanne wasn't an animal lover and her protests were likely more an excuse to have a dig at Ash.

Ellie had really hoped they were past this.

Luckily the cat didn't seem keen to hang around, darting off across the front garden and into the bushes to the side of the property.

'See.' Ash closed the door, a goading smile on his face as he stepped back into the room. 'Not ours and she didn't want to be ours,' he told Roxanne.

'Who wants more wine?' Ellie asked, jumping in quickly before Roxanne could respond.

'That sounds like an excellent idea,' Pete answered for his wife before draining his glass. His cheeks were already rosy from the couple of bottles the four of them had polished off over dinner.

Like Roxanne he was generally a mellow drunk and easily distracted by the promise of more alcohol. Ellie planned to fill Roxanne's glass and move her on to a different subject. As she gathered the empty dessert dishes, she shot a look at Ash. 'Can you go grab another bottle?'

She followed him through into the kitchen, dumped the dishes on the counter.

'Don't wind her up, okay?'

'I'm not winding her up. Roxanne reacts too easily.'

He was right, but that wasn't the point.

'She does and you know that, so don't bait her.' When Ash's mouth curved into a sly smile, she snuck her arms around his waist, pulled him close so her hips pressed against his, and kissed him lightly on the lips. 'Please. For me.'

He rolled his eyes dramatically, but the smile widened to a grin as his hands settled on her arse. 'Okay, for you. Roxanne-baiting is one of my favourite hobbies though.'

'I know.' Ellie pulled herself free. 'Now wine.'

'Can't we just stay in here for a little longer?'

'And ignore our guests?'

'They won't notice. Roxanne is still probably whining about the bloody cat.'

'They have empty glasses and think we're going to fill them.' When Ash made no attempt to move, Ellie selected a bottle of Malbec from the wine rack herself. 'Come on.'

'You're no fun,' he grumbled as he followed her.

Roxanne held her empty glass up. 'So have you met your new neighbours then?' she asked, appearing to be over cat-gate.

'Not yet. But we've been busy unpacking the last couple of days. I'm sure we will bump into them soon enough.'

'I still don't get why you moved all this way out into the sticks, especially when you work from home, Ellie. Aren't you going to be lonely?'

'We wanted to be out of the city.' Ellie finished uncorking the bottle and topped everyone up. 'Yes, this is a little further out than we intended, but we got it for a steal. It needs some work, but we can put our own stamp on it.' She shared a brief affectionate look with Ash, recalling some of the ambitious plans they had been making. 'And no, I won't be lonely. There are plenty of jobs to do around here while Ash is at work.'

'Are there even any shops close by?'

'There's a Spar in the village and Tesco is only a few miles away.'

'And we have a pub,' Ash added.

Pete raised his glass. 'Now you're talking. In stumbling distance?'

'Call it more a brisk walk.'

Roxanne had out her phone and was tapping into Google. 'Four pubs apparently. Oh no, ignore that. Three of them are no longer there.' She scrolled some more, teeth biting into her bottom red lip. 'Okay, you have a church. You can go praise the Lord.'

'I'm sure they will both love that, especially Ash. Though I don't think they let sinners in.' Pete sniggered at Ash, who grinned broadly.

'I can behave myself when I want to.'

'Hold up. My bad. The church is closed too.' Roxanne arched a regal brow. 'Corpusty is officially dead.'

'We didn't move here for a big social scene. We wanted somewhere quiet.'

'Clearly, Ellie. Well, it looks like you got that.'

'It's a really pretty village.'

'Hey, isn't it here that they do the big bonfire thing?'

Roxanne scowled at her husband. 'What bonfire thing?'

'Google it. I'm sure they do a big procession for Guy Fawkes.'

'That's just one night of the year.'

Ellie exchanged another look with Ash. Roxanne was clearly in one of her picky moods. She discreetly glanced at the slim rose-gold watch Ash had bought her for her last birthday and wondered what time Pete and Roxanne planned on calling a taxi.

It wasn't that she wanted rid of them. Pete was Ash's best friend and Ellie and Roxanne went back years, but the last few days had been exhausting and what was supposed to be a fun night with friends was beginning to drag a little. Roxanne was hard work when she was like this and the thought of waving her and Pete goodbye then leaving the dishes and collapsing into bed was all too appealing.

'Oh, okay. This looks interesting, as in interesting in a totally fucking creepy way. Did you two realise you had moved to Summerisle?'

'To where?' Ellie questioned.

Roxanne was too busy scrolling to answer, so Ash did on her behalf. 'It was the island in *The Wicker Man*. You've seen it, right?'

'I've heard of it. Don't think I've seen it though. We're not on an island though.'

'Oh, Ash, mate. You have to sort this,' Pete interjected, adding to Ellie. 'It's a cult classic. You need to watch it.'

'Okay.'

That was one of Pete and Ash's things: movies. They were a

pair of geeks when it came to quoting their favourite lines at each other.

'Actually, this does look pretty cool.' Roxanne held up her phone so they could see pictures of a parade, some people dressed up, as they walked down the street holding batons of fire.

'Wow, that happens here in Corpusty?'

'Apparently so. They have a big procession to light the guy.' Roxanne showed Ellie another picture of the huge bonfire. 'Pete, we might have to come back for this.'

'See, not such a bad place after all.'

Roxanne shot Ash a look then turned back to her phone.

'Anyone fancy playing a game?' As Pete and Roxanne seemed in no hurry to call a taxi and Roxanne was now engrossed in her phone, Ellie figured she should try and lift the mood.

'Poker?' Pete suggested.

'I think we have some playing cards. Ash, check the drawer in the cabinet behind you.'

'Okay, this is interesting.'

'What?' Ellie asked Roxanne bluntly. Her friend was still scrolling through her phone and making no attempt to join in.

'Do you remember Naomi Tanner?'

'No.'

'The girl who went missing about five years ago. Her mother was found murdered and she just vanished from her bed.'

'It rings a vague bell.'

'I remember.' Pete nodded. 'The police thought her dad killed her, though they could never prove it. What about her?'

Roxanne's eyes widened dramatically. 'She came from Corpusty.'

'Nice.' That was from Ash who couldn't have sounded less interested. He hadn't been in the UK at the time, having only moved here three years ago. 'Are we going to play poker?' he asked, shuffling the playing cards he had found and seeming keen to change the subject. 'Put your phone away, Roxanne.'

She pouted at him, but finally placed it down on the table, picking up her wine glass and taking a long sip. 'Didn't she live out in the sticks on the outskirts of the village?' she asked Pete coyly. 'In a house a bit like this?'

'You didn't even realise she came from here until a moment ago,' Ash pointed out. 'And now you know what type of house she lived in?'

'I'm just saying. The details were a bit murky, but they're coming back to me.'

'What's your point, Roxanne?' Even Pete sounded annoyed.

'There is no point.'

'Then let's focus on the game.' He picked up the cards that Ash had dealt.

Roxanne left hers on the table, choosing instead to run her finger around the rim of her glass. 'It just had me thinking. There can't be that many houses here. What if this was the one where she lived?'

Oh for fuck's sake.

Ellie managed a smile, though it was through gritted teeth. 'I hardly think we're living in a house where a murder took place... if that's what you're insinuating.'

Roxanne smiled sweetly. 'I'm not insinuating anything.'

'Then let's play cards,' Ash pushed.

'I'm sure if anything had happened here, the estate agent would have said something when we bought it,' Ellie said.

'I'm sure they would have.' Roxanne smirked. 'Right, Ash?'

He scowled back at her, though didn't say anything. Like Ellie, he had clearly had enough.

Roxanne picked up her hand, glanced at it. 'Okay, let's play.'

2

They shouldn't have worked and on paper probably didn't. Ash was impulsive, didn't take life too seriously and, before he had met Ellie, had been known for having a roaming eye, while Ellie was calm, organised and had her life mapped out.

Even the stars were against them, Roxanne had pointed out, though Ellie didn't believe in any of that crap.

It had been at a dinner party that Roxanne and Pete were hosting that their paths had first crossed. Ellie had been lured there unknowingly for a blind date. At thirty-four she wasn't getting any younger, Roxanne kept telling her, and maybe it was time she started looking for someone to settle down with.

Ellie wasn't bothered about meeting anyone. Work kept her busy and she had a good social life. No family (she was an only child and both parents had died when she was young, while her grandmother, her last remaining living relative, who had taken care of her all of her life, had passed away when Ellie was in her early twenties). She had plenty of friends though. She was independent, happy and although she had a shocking relationship history – several loser boyfriends followed by five years of celibacy – she wasn't looking for love.

Roxanne had been determined to set her up with Colin, a colleague, and after meeting resistance from Ellie, who simply wasn't interested, had lured her to dinner, hoping the pair of them would hit it off.

They didn't.

Colin was pleasant enough, but frightfully dull, and there was no spark there at all. Even trying to make conversation with him was hard work and the night had steadily gone from bad to worse, as Roxanne refused to accept her matchmaking attempt had failed.

They were midway through eating her Sri Lankan curry, when an unexpected visitor had crashed the party and things had suddenly taken a turn for the better.

Roxanne had been annoyed when the doorbell rang, dispatching Pete to get rid of whoever was daring to bother them. When he didn't return immediately, sounding pleased to see the caller, Roxanne had sighed deeply and rolled her eyes, before thumping her cutlery down dramatically and going to sort out both her husband and whoever he was talking to.

Ellie and Colin were left to make awkward small talk which consisted of Colin announcing, for the third time that evening, that he wasn't good with spicy food and that his delicate stomach was going to pay the price later, then, when Roxanne's raised voice carried through to the dining room, his eyes went bug wide and the flush the food had put in his cheeks disappeared, as his face drained of colour. 'Uh-oh, she doesn't sound happy.'

Not for the first time, Ellie suspected that Colin was a little afraid of Roxanne, and she wondered if he had been bullied into coming to dinner tonight. She recalled Roxanne had snapped at him to eat the food she had cooked when he had been dubiously pushing it around his plate.

As the pair of them fell into an uncomfortable silence, Roxanne's heels clacked on the hardwood floor of the hallway. 'Apparently we have another dinner guest.'

She didn't look impressed, her red lips drawn in a tight line and the rosy glow of anger in her cheeks suggesting that she and Pete had exchanged words. As she stomped through to the kitchen, slamming cupboard doors, and plates and cutlery onto the counter, Pete stepped back into the room with the newcomer, whose eyes locked with Ellie's, and as his smile widened into a crooked grin, her world spun right off its axis.

As introductions were made, Ash pulled up a chair next to Ellie, and Roxanne returned from the kitchen, slapping down a plate of curry in front of him.

Ellie had heard about Ash Brady, mostly unpleasantries from Roxanne who wasn't a fan of her husband's best friend, but their paths had never crossed, and he was not at all as she imagined. In her head she had pictured him as an arrogant player who was constantly competing with Roxanne for Pete's attention. Ellie had already decided she wouldn't like him, but now realised that Roxanne's description might have been slanted.

Ash had grown up with Pete in Australia and the pair of them had been thick as thieves until Pete's family had relocated to the UK. Now it seemed he was living and working over here himself and in, what she would learn was true Ash style, he had spontaneously decided to travel to Norfolk and call in on his friend, overnight bag in tow.

There had been a connection right from the start and it was more than just physical. Yes, Ellie was drawn to those fascinating whisky-coloured eyes that shone with enthusiasm when he spoke and that wide appealing mouth, and his face was so expressive and open. It went beyond attraction though. He was funny, making her laugh, and so easy to talk to. As the evening progressed, their chairs had gradually moved closer together, Ash's leg casually brushing against Ellie's, and their conversation became more one on one. Colin didn't seem to mind, and almost appeared relieved that the matchmaking pressure was off. He seemed more relaxed, chatting away to Pete about politics, while Roxanne mostly sat and scowled.

She made a point of pulling Ellie to one side shortly before her taxi arrived and warning her off. 'It's all an act, you know.'

'He seems really nice, Roxy, and genuine too.'

'Ha, that's what he wants you to think. Trust me, he is charming the pants off you right now because he wants to get you into bed. He will tell you anything you want to hear. But once he's slept with you, he will lose interest. Don't be fooled by him. You're just another conquest.'

'You haven't seen him in ages. Maybe he has changed.'

'He hasn't. Believe me, I know.' Roxanne's expression had softened slightly. 'I'm only looking out for you, Ellie. You're not the best judge of character and I don't want to see you get hurt. You need a man who is dependable, safe and solid.'

Not the best judge of character? Ellie's hackles had risen. Okay, so she'd had some lousy boyfriends, but that didn't mean she was a bad judge of character, and she was quite capable of looking out for herself. 'You mean I need a man like Colin,' she said sarcastically.

Roxanne arched a brow. 'You could do worse.'

Perhaps it was partly out of annoyance with Roxanne, but when Ash walked out with Ellie to the taxi later and asked if he could have her number, she was quick to hand it over.

Maybe he hadn't changed and did only want to get her into bed, but she was a grown woman and had never had a one-night stand. Perhaps it was time she started living a little.

Much to Roxanne's chagrin, Ellie and Ash did go out on a date. Several in fact. Ash was based in Cambridge, though was willing to make several trips to Norfolk to see Ellie and after they had met up a handful of times, she took the plunge and went to stay with him in the flat he was renting.

Despite Roxanne's warnings, Ash didn't dump her after they had slept together and if anything they became closer. It was after a year of commuting, of long lazy weekends, of accompanying Ash on a handful of business dinners, lots of passionate sex and the odd heated row (they both had a bit of a temper) and a week tucked away in a remote cottage in Scotland, where it had rained relentlessly and they had really been given the time to get to know each other and gauge how well they would live together, that he casually mentioned the role that had opened up in the firm of architects in North Norfolk, and suggested relocating.

Initially he moved in with Ellie, but her place was tiny. Figuring they were both ready to make their relationship more permanent, they decided to get on the property ladder. They both had decent jobs. Ash's work was more reliable than Ellie's, but it was still two incomes. She did have savings though, a bitter bonus of being orphaned young, which she dipped into to put down a sizeable deposit.

And now here they were. The dream home in the countryside.

Okay, so maybe it was more a dream vision at the moment. The house was in dire need of some tender loving care, but it was structurally sound and just needed someone to restore it to its former glory. Ash was certain that he and Ellie could do most of the work themselves. If there was anything they couldn't deal with they would hire in outside help.

Right now, standing in the middle of the back bedroom that she planned to eventually use as a studio, all Ellie could see was where the fading wallpaper had fallen away from the wall and how it badly needed plastering, the hole in the ceiling where the light fitting had been ripped out, the broken floorboards, and the cracked and mouldy window.

It was like this all over and was going to take forever to fix. Had they bitten off too much and bought themselves a money pit? It was Ash's first day back at work and here alone, after three solid hours of clearing rooms so work could begin, Ellie was overwhelmed.

Maybe they should have picked something that needed a little less work.

Running her fingers back through her hair in frustration, she drew in a sharp breath and stepped over to the window, stared out at the garden below, and in that moment remembered exactly why she had wanted this house.

The garden was beautiful.

Two acres of mature trees and bushes with a large pond and little stone paths that cut across the lawn. She wanted to stake solar lights along them, hang more lights, maybe lanterns, in the trees, fill the pond with colourful fish, and could imagine barbecuing on the generous patio area, then eating steak and sipping cold bottles of lager with the man she loved, as they overlooked their own slice of paradise.

She wasn't afraid of hard work and never had been. Yes, they were going to have to work their socks off, but it really would be worth it.

Motivated, she turned on the radio, tied her sweaty blonde hair back into a ponytail and went to work with the steamer. It was time to find out how much damage was hidden under the wallpaper. Once they knew exactly what they were dealing with, they could come up with a plan of action.

She worked late into the afternoon, drinking her way through two litre bottles of water, as the hot August sun blazed through the windows, dampening her T-shirt. She forgot to stop for lunch, and it wasn't until she did eventually pause for a break, her throat parched again and desperate for a cup of tea, that she remembered they were out of milk. Out of most things, she realised, peering into the fridge.

She wasn't up for a big shop, but they at least needed basics, and tempting as it was to message Ash and ask him to stop on his way home, Ellie really wanted that cup of tea.

Damn it. She was going to have to go to the Spar shop.

It was a fifteen-minute walk, but only a few minutes in the car, and lazy as that was, she was keen to get back, have her cup of tea, then get cracking on with the wallpaper stripping.

Not bothering to freshen up, figuring she would be in and out of the shop inside two minutes, she shut all of the windows, grabbed her purse and keys, and locked up.

Her car was a furnace and she cranked up the air conditioning, pulling out of the driveway on to the country road that led into the village. Although the house fell within Corpusty's boundaries, it was actually a bit further out in the countryside and, apart from their neighbour, there were no other properties for at least a mile. As she slowed to follow the twists and dips in the road she toyed with what to get for dinner. Something easy to prepare. Ash had been working all day and Ellie was knackered. Neither of them would want to mess about cooking an elaborate meal.

She was debating buying a couple of pizzas and some bits to throw a simple salad together when the animal ran out in front of her.

Ellie had no time to react, slamming her foot on the brake a second too late. She wasn't travelling fast, but the impact as her car ploughed into whatever it was, created a sickening thud.

Ohmigod, ohmigod, ohmigod.

She peered through the windshield, tried to see over the

bonnet, but the creature was out of sight. Was it a young deer or a fox? Running shaking hands over her face, she took a moment to draw a couple of deep breaths, released her seatbelt and stepped from the car.

Was it dead? She had never killed anything before. Never even been in any kind of road accident.

A low pitiful whimper broke through the silence, cutting straight through her. Oh God, she had hurt it and it was dying. That was worse than dead.

She hurried forward, gasping out loud when she realised the animal on the road in front of her car was a dog. There was blood, so much blood, and though it was barely moving, it managed to lift its head slightly, looking up at her with mournful brown eyes.

'Oh fuck. Oh baby, I'm so sorry.'

She wanted to cry, wanted to sit her shaking legs down and sob for the poor creature. That wasn't going to help either of them though. He... she even... was still alive, which meant Ellie had to try and find someone who could help.

Bending down, she touched the blood-matted fur, tried to reassure the dog. She was going to be sick. It was her fault. She had done this.

Think, Ellie. Damn it. Pull yourself together.

Where was the nearest vet? Her phone would tell her. She had left her bag in the car.

'I'll be right back,' she soothed. 'I promise.'

The pitiful whimpering echoed around her head as she grabbed her phone, did a quick Google search. The nearest vet was about five miles away.

Ten minutes later she had managed to lift the dog onto the back seat of her car. It was cold and shivering, and she covered it with an old blanket she had in the boot, tried to reassure it that everything was going to be okay, just hoped she could make it to the vet in time for them to help.

She wanted to fall apart, but forced herself to get behind the wheel, knew, as she fastened her seatbelt again, that falling apart was not an option. Instead, she glanced over her shoulder at the whimpering pitiful bundle of fur sprawled on the back seat.

'We're going to go get you some help. It will be okay, I promise.'

3

There had been no sign of Virginia when Benjamin Thorne left to take their cat, Miss Moneypenny, for her annual check-up at the vet.

He knew she had been in her favourite spot in the conservatory that looked out over the garden and from the angry streaks of paint on the canvas, he suspected his sister was in one of her moods, which meant he would probably suffer for it later.

As he made the short drive with the cat mewing in her basket beside him, he pondered over his volatile sister. She was so angry with him and just didn't seem to understand the consequences of her own actions. She was his burden and he had accepted that. Knew that because of how she was, he would be shackled to her until the day he died.

It was tough for her, he got that, and he knew how lonely she was, but he also knew that Virginia didn't always play well with others.

He suspected that she was aware of the new neighbours and that bothered him. He didn't want her causing them any trouble.

He had seen the couple briefly from a distance, heaving boxes from a van, but he had kept away. He never liked to intrude.

His late mother had once told him that a good neighbour was friendly, but never over-friendly, and he did his best to follow her advice. He had to admit though, he was intrigued to know more about the newcomers. The last owner had never lived there, choosing to sublet it, and the tenants he rented to never stayed long. There were long periods of time when the property had stood unoccupied.

It was a shame as it really was a beautiful house, despite the tragedy that had happened there. It had just been neglected over the years. Hopefully the new owners had plans to do some work to it.

Parking outside the vet, he lifted the cat carrier, taking Miss Moneypenny inside, ignoring her plaintive cries to let her out, and smiled warmly at Jill, the receptionist.

'Our favourite lady is looking forward to her check-up I see.'

'No matter how often I bring her, she never gets used to it.' Benjamin set the carrier on the counter while Jill checked him in and made a fuss of the cat through the bars, earning herself a hiss. 'Now, now, Miss M. Behave yourself.'

'She's in a feisty mood today.' Jill laughed. 'I'm sure I can find a treat to win her over once Trevor has seen her.'

'She will like that.'

'Do you want to take a seat? He won't be long.'

Benjamin glanced at the small waiting area, selecting the chair nearest to the reception desk. As he was the only one there, he placed Miss Moneypenny's carrier on the seat next to him.

'So how are you, Jill? Are you keeping okay?'

'Can't complain.'

'Is your hip giving you any aggravation since your operation?'

'It's steadily improving. I think this warm weather helps.'

'Ah, yes. It's good for the bones. We've been very lucky this summer.'

'We have, and long may it–' Jill broke off as the bell sounded and a blonde woman spilled through the door.

Benjamin's eyes widened with shock as he took in her appearance, saw that she was covered in blood. In her arms she held a dog. The poor thing was not moving and he wasn't sure if it was dead or alive. But then he heard a whimper.

He was off his seat in an instant, was aware of Jill stepping out from behind the reception desk.

'He was in the road. I couldn't stop. I tried.'

'It's okay, love. It was an accident.' Jill glanced at the dog, her expression giving nothing away. 'Give me two seconds. Trevor?' She raised her voice. 'Trevor, we need you out here now.'

The woman was wild-eyed, frantic, and it took Benjamin a second to realise that he knew her, though he couldn't quite place how.

'It's going to be okay.' He tried to soothe her, even though he knew that was very probably a lie. 'Trevor is an excellent vet.'

The door opened at the back of the surgery and Trevor came running through, followed by one of the young nurses who worked for him. 'What have we here?' he asked, going straight to the dog.

'It was an accident. I didn't mean to hit him.'

'Her.' Trevor smiled kindly at the woman. 'She's a girl. Only a few months old by the looks of it.' He nodded to the nurse. 'Okay, Maria, let's get our young friend here through to the consulting room and see what we're dealing with.'

'Would you like me to come back?' Benjamin asked. He was in the way here. The dog was an emergency. Miss Moneypenny could wait.

'It's kind of you to offer, Benjamin, but let's just see what we're dealing with here. If you're happy to wait, that is.'

'Of course.'

Trevor and Maria lifted the dog from the woman's arms, the poor animal letting out a yelp, and when the woman went to follow them, Jill caught hold of her arm. 'You can't go in there with them, love.'

'But I did this. It's my fault.'

'Trevor will take care of her. There's nothing you can do to help in there. You'll just be in the way. Now why don't you come with me and let me take a few details. Then you can go home and I can call you if there's any news.'

'I'd rather wait.'

'What's your name, sweetheart?'

The woman blinked. 'Ellie... um, Elisabeth Summers. Everyone calls me Ellie.'

'Okay, Ellie.' Jill gently pushed her onto a seat in the waiting area and poured her a drink of water from the cooler machine, pressing the paper cup into her hand.

'Thank you.'

'Now, have you called the police or the RSPCA?'

'No... I'm sorry, I didn't think. I just knew I needed to get help. I suppose I should have done that.'

'It's okay, Ellie. You were worried about her and you reacted. A lot of people would have done the same. The important thing is she is here now and we can try to help her.'

'We need to find her owner. Oh God, what will they think? I hit their dog.'

'It was an accident, love. You mustn't blame yourself. You leave finding the owners to us.'

Jill was good with her, Benjamin mused as he took his seat again beside Miss Moneypenny and watched as the woman, Ellie, went through everything that had happened.

Ellie, short for Elisabeth. Personally he preferred the lengthened version of her name. Elisabeth was prettier and more traditional.

She was younger than him, maybe by eight to ten years, and though frazzled by what had happened, she was pretty too. And oh-so familiar. She glanced at him, with wide green eyes and managed a small smile, and he realised why he recognised her. She was his new neighbour. He recalled seeing her outside, a large box in her arms, as he drove past.

He almost said something, but then he worried she might think he had been spying on them, when, of course, he had been doing nothing of the sort. Instead, he smiled back.

'I'm sorry to hold your appointment up,' she said as Jill paused their conversation to answer a call. Ellie was a little calmer now, more focused as she sipped her water, though still glanced anxiously at the closed door where Trevor had taken the dog. The blood on her T-shirt and jeans was drying and she had a smudge of it on her cheek.

'It's okay. I had no plans this afternoon, so it's not a problem to wait or come back.' He peered into the front of the cat carrier. 'We don't mind, do we, Miss Moneypenny.'

'James Bond fan, eh?'

'Oh yes. I've seen all of the movies many times.'

'Who is your favourite Bond?'

Benjamin straightened, smiled, pleased that she was showing an interest. 'Roger Moore. You?'

'Has to be the original for me. Sean Connery.'

He was about to ask her what her favourite Bond film was when her mobile rang. Ellie jumped as though she had forgotten it was with her and quickly pulled it from her bag, glancing at the screen. 'Excuse me, please. I need to take this.'

Benjamin nodded, watching her as she headed towards the door, talking in hushed tones. She was probably speaking to the man he had seen her with back at the house. Her husband, he assumed. He was trying not to listen, but it was difficult in such a small room. To distract himself he opened the cat carrier and pulled Miss Moneypenny out for a cuddle. She had calmed down now as she often did once she was in the vet's and was happy for the fuss.

'I need to stay here,' Ellie was saying. 'I can't just leave her.'

Was Benjamin imagining it or did she seem a little agitated?

Whatever, she was determined to be here for the dog, hanging up the call and returning to her seat, a frown on her face. Benjamin just hoped the animal pulled through.

She studied her hands, lost in thought, rubbing at where the blood had dried, and he didn't like to disturb her, so he stayed silent.

Was she thinking about the dog or the conversation she'd had with her husband?

After ten minutes or so had ticked by, and as though feeling the weight of his stare, she glanced up, eyes the colour of a stormy sea, and for an awful moment he thought she was going to tell him off for eavesdropping, but then her scowl softened to a smile as she spotted the cat.

'I know who she is.'

'I'm sorry?'

'Your cat, Miss Moneypenny. I recognise her pink collar.'

'You do?'

'She paid us a visit the other night. You must be our new neighbour.'

Benjamin narrowed his eyes slightly and pursed his lips, trying to appear momentarily confused as he considered her words. He thought he pulled it off.

'We just moved into Hazelwood Cottage,' Ellie prompted. 'I'm Ellie Summers.'

'Oh, yes, yes, of course. I thought I saw activity when I drove past the other day.' That was good. He would hate for her to think he was some kind of busybody. 'Nice to meet you, Ellie. I'm Benjamin Thorne. I hope our little madam here wasn't any bother. She does like to wander.'

'No, no bother at all. It was a warm night and we had the windows open. She must have been curious and wanted to explore.'

'How are you settling in?'

'Okay, thanks. We're mostly unpacked. A lot of work to do, but...'

She paused, her face paling as Trevor stepped out of the examination room.

Seeing Jill on the phone, he headed straight over to where Ellie and Benjamin were sat.

Ellie was already on her feet. 'How is she?'

'She's lost a lot of blood, but I think she will pull through. I'm going to need to amputate her front left leg though.'

'What?' Ellie looked devastated. 'Is there nothing you can do to save it? Money isn't a problem. I can pay for whatever she needs.'

Benjamin sat quietly and listened as Trevor explained the dog's condition, telling her that the front leg was shattered beyond repair. He advised her to go home and get some rest, promising either he or Jill would call with an update in the morning, before turning to Benjamin and apologising for his wasted trip.

'Honestly, Trevor, it's no problem. This is an emergency.'

'Speak with Jill and she will sort another appointment for Miss Moneypenny.'

As Trevor disappeared back through to the examination room, Benjamin glanced at Ellie. She appeared to be in shock. Was she going to be okay to drive?

He was wondering if he should offer to give her a lift, when the bell sounded and a man walked in. Although he wore sunglasses, Benjamin had recognised him before he pushed them up onto his head, knew he was Ellie's husband.

'Ash?' She sounded surprised that he was there, though went straight to him.

'Are you okay?'

'They have to amputate her leg. It's all my fault.' She had been so brave up to this point, but now her face crumpled and, even though she was covered in the dog's blood, he took her into his arms without hesitation.

As he held her, stroking her hair and telling her it wasn't her fault, Benjamin studied them together.

Although he wore jeans, Ash was smartly enough dressed for Benjamin to assume he had been at work. Obviously somewhere that didn't require a suit, though the shirt and clean trainers suggested he hadn't been doing manual work. Ellie was actually the scruffier of the two, her hair tied back in a messy ponytail and her jeans ripped in places. Even without the blood, her T-shirt looked grubby, and he guessed she had been at home prior to hitting the dog.

Had she taken time off work to help sort the house or was she perhaps a housewife?

Benjamin knew not many women stayed at home these days, preferring to earn their own way in the world, and he respected that.

He had tried to push Virginia to find a job at one point, though she hadn't really been interested. Although she had been limited in the type of work she could do, he believed it would be good for her to mix with other people. Challenging too. She wanted to be an artist, but truth was, her paintings were never going to sell. Of course, he never told her that, he didn't want to break her heart. Instead, he allowed her to keep painting, and he ensured she had all the tools she needed. Anything to keep his little sister content.

Benjamin's mother had always told him he was a people pleaser. She had said he should look after himself first instead of worrying about others. Truth was, he couldn't help it. He hated seeing anyone in distress, and right now he wished he could do something to take away Ellie's pain. She was inconsolable over the dog, blaming herself, and even though he barely knew her, it was still upsetting to see. It wasn't his place, though, to interfere.

Jill was with the couple now, offering tissues, and talking quietly to Ellie's husband, and a few minutes later he was guiding her out of the door. He must have agreed with Jill to leave Ellie's car at the surgery and pick it up later, as they drove off in his SUV.

Benjamin stroked Miss Moneypenny, affectionately tickling behind her ears and musing over the afternoon's events, as Jill returned to the reception desk. It had certainly been an unusual way to become acquainted with his new neighbour and Ellie had disappeared from the surgery as abruptly as she had arrived.

'That poor girl. She was beside herself,' Jill commented. 'What an awful thing to happen.'

As Benjamin nodded, murmuring his agreement, his gaze slid over to where Ellie had been sitting and the mobile phone that was on her vacated seat.

It must have slipped out of her bag.

Jill glanced over, spotting it at the same time. 'Oh, she forgot her phone.'

Benjamin slipped Miss Moneypenny back into her carrier, locking the door. He went over and retrieved Ellie's mobile from the seat.

'I suppose I had better put it somewhere safe for her,' Jill said.

'Aren't you supposed to be calling her tomorrow?'

'Well, yes, but...' The penny dropped. 'Oh... we won't be able to give her an update.'

'It's okay. She's my new neighbour. I can drop the phone off on my way home.'

Jill's eyes widened. 'New neighbour? You mean she's living in Hazelwood Cottage?'

'That's right. They moved in a few days ago.'

'I can't imagine why anyone would want to live there... not after what happened.'

'It's just a building.' Benjamin smiled, though it was a little forced. People did like to dwell on the past. He preferred fresh starts and was a firm believer in moving on. 'Just bricks and mortar. It's been standing empty for a while now and the tenants who have lived there before haven't really appreciated it. I think it will be nice to see the place loved again.'

'Well, it was a beautiful house,' Jill agreed, though she still looked a little unsure.

'And it will be again. I have high hopes that they will return it to its former glory.'

'Do they know? About what happened?'

'I honestly have no idea. I only met Ellie for the first time today and she was a little preoccupied.'

'She was. Poor love. Will you ask her?'

Benjamin shook his head. 'Unless she says something, I won't mention it. It was a few years ago now and if they don't know what happened then perhaps it's kinder to them that it stays that way.'

4

Benjamin took Miss Moneypenny home before walking back down the long driveway that led to Hazelwood Cottage. He had seen the SUV was in the driveway so knew his new neighbours were back home and as he neared the house he spotted a couple of the upstairs windows were open. It really was a beautiful afternoon, the heatwave that had already lasted much of August showing no signs of abating.

Of course, the one negative was the garden. The dry grass and wilting flowers were desperate for water and he reminded himself that he must put the sprinklers out after he had dropped off the phone.

The wooden front door was in need of a good varnish and he expected that would be on the list of chores for Ellie and her husband once they were settled. It was a lovely house, despite its grisly history, and it would be so nice to see it brought back to life again.

As he lifted his hand to the brass door knocker, raised voices came from inside, and he paused, immediately a little on edge. He wasn't good with confrontation and really didn't want to intrude on a domestic situation. He debated whether to knock, as the shouting continued, straining his ears to hear.

One voice, not two, and it was male. Why would Ellie's husband be yelling at her? Was he angry about her hitting the dog?

He had seemed sympathetic in the vet's, comforting her when she became upset. Had that just been an act? Benjamin's mother used to say that you could never tell what went on behind closed doors and he knew how true that was, recalling poor Naomi, and the abuse he knew she had suffered at the hands of her father.

Remembering it made Benjamin feel a little sick. This had been Naomi's home. Was the pattern of abuse now repeating itself with a new family?

He was tempted to walk away, reminding himself that whatever was going on with Ellie and her husband was none of his business. He needed to return the phone though. He had promised Jill he would drop it off, so Ellie would have it for when they called her in the morning. Besides, he was probably over-reacting. It was because of what had happened to Naomi that he was now automatically suspicious. He still felt guilty that he had known what her father was like, yet had turned a blind eye for so long.

Before he could change his mind, he rapped the knocker loudly against the door, then stepped back, straightening his shoulders, his chin up. He wouldn't draw any attention to the yelling. He would simply pretend he hadn't heard it.

There was no immediate answer and he stood waiting, shoulders dropping slightly, mouth dry, and Ellie's phone clutched tightly in his hand, as he debated whether to try again.

He knew they were home and they would have heard his knock on the door. Were they purposely ignoring him, perhaps embarrassed that he had heard the shouting?

Benjamin knocked again. If they didn't answer this time he would leave. He could always return later and put a note through the door. He wouldn't drop the phone through the letterbox. It could get damaged. Jill had trusted him with it, so he wanted to hand it over personally.

He was debating doing just that when the door suddenly opened, taking him by surprise.

Ellie's husband stared out, a scowl on his face. 'Yes?'

'I... er, hello, I'm Benjamin Thorne.'

Despite Benjamin's smile, the scowl on the man's face didn't thaw.

'Um, Ellie...'

'What about her?'

'We met at the vet's.' Benjamin held out her phone. 'She dropped this.'

Ellie's husband glanced at the phone then back at Benjamin, his eyes narrowing suspiciously. 'She gave you her address?'

'We're neighbours. I mean I'm your new neighbour. I wanted to drop it off.'

Finally the scowl softened. 'You live behind us?'

'I do. Ellie recognised Miss Moneypenny and we realised we lived next door to each other.'

'Miss Moneypenny?'

'My cat. I understand she paid you a visit on Saturday night. I'm sorry about that. I hope she was no trouble.' Benjamin cursed himself under his breath. *Stop apologising.* It was a bad habit of his, continually telling people he was sorry when he had done nothing wrong.

'She was fine.' Hazel eyes studied him, assessing. 'I'm Ash. Ellie's boyfriend.'

Benjamin shook Ash's offered hand, as his mind processed that piece of information. *Boyfriend, not husband.* He shouldn't be surprised. Lots of couples live together before marriage these days. He supposed he was a little old-fashioned like that, assuming people to be married.

'Is Ellie okay? She was quite upset.'

Ash nodded. 'She's fine, mate. Bit of a shock, but she's dealing with it. She's tougher than she looks.'

He had an accent. Now he was giving more than brief answers, Benjamin could pick up on it. He was Australian. Not from around here then.

'Is she about?'

It was an unnecessary question and Benjamin cursed himself the second the words were out of his mouth. He had no reason to see Ellie, didn't want her boyfriend to think there was anything going on, which, of course, there wasn't. Ash had already looked suspicious that Benjamin knew the address though. Benjamin suspected he might be one of those possessive types. Ellie was a pretty girl and Ash probably didn't like her getting close to other men.

'She's in the shower.' Ash nodded at the phone in Benjamin's hand. 'You came to return that?'

'I did.' As he had no reason to hold on to it, Benjamin handed it over. 'Please pass on my best to her.'

'Will do.' Ash started to close the door and Benjamin turned to leave. 'Hey, Ben.'

Irritation crawled over his skin. 'It's Benjamin.'

Ash nodded, the corner of his mouth curving. 'Benjamin.' He held up Ellie's phone. 'Thanks for dropping this off. Appreciate it.'

Benjamin smiled tightly. 'No problem.'

He told Virginia about the new neighbours during dinner. As had been the case most evenings since the heatwave began, the

French doors were open. Some evenings there was a blessed breeze, but tonight it was still, the muggy heat clinging to the air. Benjamin suspected they were due for a storm.

Talking about Ellie and Ash helped him realise that there was something about them that was niggling him. On the surface, Benjamin wasn't sure what it was, but dig a little deeper and honestly he was mildly concerned about Ellie.

It was stupid really. He had met her for all of half an hour and he'd only encountered Ash briefly. They had argued on the phone, though, and then Ash had shown up at the surgery unexpectedly, almost as if he was checking up on Ellie. That coupled with the yelling Benjamin had heard when he went to drop the phone off and Ash's initial cool reception, had him all kinds of paranoid and most likely jumping to conclusions.

Perhaps he had just caught Ash on a bad day.

It was because he was thinking about Naomi again, he realised that. There were new people in the house, and it was making him remember what had happened.

Benjamin pushed the vegetables around on the plate with his fork. He didn't have much appetite. He was thinking about Naomi, still so sad about what had happened. He recalled the night the police sirens had cut through the air, the lights flashing at the end of the driveway.

'There was so much blood.' That was what Eileen Symonds had said when Benjamin saw her in the Spar shop a few days later.

Of course, Eileen hadn't seen it first-hand, but her cousin's boy was a paramedic and had been one of the first on the scene.

John Tanner had been a terrible husband, an awful father. He was the only one guilty. Benjamin knew that, so why did he continue to blame himself?

It was in the past now and he really needed to try and move on. He speared a piece of carrot and forced himself to eat.

'Ellie seems nice. I think you'll like her.'

His comment was met with silence. Virginia had never had much to say, but these days Benjamin just talked to himself. Still, he kept trying, hoping things would change and she would come around.

He sipped at his water as he stared out at the garden. 'I need you to promise me, Virginia, that you will leave them alone, okay? No spying on them or trespassing on their property.'

Feeling her anger, Benjamin softened his tone. 'I know you're curious and I know you get lonely, that you don't have visitors, but they're our new neighbours and we have to respect their boundaries. You don't want to make them feel uncomfortable, do you?'

That worry that she might cause them trouble stayed with him after dinner was finished and he had cleared the table. He stared out from the kitchen window as he washed up, looking towards the small orchard where Virginia liked to wander.

He was glad she had the garden, and he kept the generous space filled with colourful flowers and trees, wanting her to have somewhere pretty she could go and lose herself. Growing up, she had always loved to take her easel in the garden and spend the afternoon outside painting.

This was how he tried to picture his sister when he felt her wrath, remembering how she had once been happy and content in the beautiful garden he had created for her.

He had just finished drying and putting everything away, when he glanced out of the window again, thought he saw a brief flash of her dress as she darted behind a row of conifers.

Was she heading towards the neighbouring property? He had specifically asked her to stay away.

He strained his neck to try and catch a glimpse of her, the muscles in his stomach tightening. 'Please, Virginia. Please leave them alone.'

Although he spoke the words aloud, he knew that no one was listening.

5

Ash dropped Ellie off at the vet early Tuesday morning to pick up her car. They weren't yet open and she looked anxiously through the window, wondering how the dog was.

'They said they'd call with an update as soon as they have news,' he reminded her through the open window.

'I know, I just...' She trailed off. Knowing they were going to call didn't help with the waiting.

'You have your keys?'

He had asked that already, before they had left the house, knowing how forgetful Ellie was. She patted her pocket, found a smile for him. 'Right here. What time will you be home?'

'I have a late afternoon meeting, so probably not until about seven.' He pushed his sunglasses up onto his head and studied her for a moment. 'You going to be okay?'

Ellie nodded. 'Plenty at home to keep me busy.'

When he continued to stare at her, seeming unconvinced, the morning sunlight picking out auburn highlights in his unruly dark hair and flecks of green in those golden eyes, she added, 'I'm fine, honest. Go to work. You'll be late.' She leant through the window, kissed him full on the lips. 'I'll message you when I hear from them, I promise.'

Finally, seeming satisfied with that, he put his sunglasses back on and left her to it.

According to the sign on the door it was only another forty minutes until the surgery opened and she was tempted to wait. But she decided there was no point in torturing herself. She would go home, get on with stripping the wallpaper and try to take her mind off the dog. Ash was right. They would call her when they were ready.

She stopped at the Spar shop on the way home and picked up enough groceries to see them through the next couple of days. At some point she would head down to one of the bigger supermarkets and do a full shop, but not today, not when she was distracted and on tenterhooks waiting for news.

After putting everything away, she busied herself with more wallpaper stripping. The previous owners had been fans, it seemed, of geometrical patterns and bright colours. Nothing wrong with making a statement, but Ellie favoured a softer classic look, more in keeping with the traditional style of the cottage.

She had filled three bin liners when the call came from the veterinary surgery. Trevor told her that the operation had gone well and the dog was recovering.

Ellie had let out the sigh of relief she hadn't realised she was holding, boosted further when he went on to say the animal was microchipped and they had made contact with the owner. Then her heart sank again as he explained the woman she belonged to no longer wanted her, and that the dog, a golden-retriever-cross-collie called She-Ra (Ellie might have actually laughed at the name if not for the gravity of the situation) had been turned over to them to be rehomed. They were currently making calls to try and find her a place in a shelter.

She thanked him for the update, WhatsApped Ash to tell him the news, and received a message straight back.

As in Princess of Power She-Ra?

A smile tugged at the corners of her mouth as she replied.

I guess so. I don't know any other She-Ras, do you?

Ash responded to that with a sick face emoji.

Setting her phone to one side, Ellie tried to put She-Ra out of her mind as she threw herself back into work. Despite the fact she had the radio playing and she was humming along, her mood gradually dipped and she couldn't help blaming herself for the dog's predicament. If she hadn't hit her, if her leg hadn't been amputated, then she would still have a home. Even a midday call from Ash to check she was okay couldn't lift her spirits.

Still, she threw herself into her task, filling more bin bags and working up a sweat as the sun blazed through the window, pausing only to chug at her water bottle. Eventually she stopped for a break. She was surprised to find it was nearly four thirty and she hadn't had any lunch. She realised that was a mistake when her belly rumbled loudly.

It was too late to eat now, but she took the break anyway, heading downstairs and making a cup of tea, grabbing a Hobnob from Ash's stash to take the edge off her appetite. Munching on the biscuit, she took her tea outside. There wasn't much respite. The humidity clinging to the air made it just as warm in the garden as it was upstairs, but out here, away from the dust and the grime, she could breathe the heady scents of the overgrown jasmine and clematis bushes.

Inside was a priority, but she was already mapping out plans for what she wanted to do with this lovely outdoor space. Conscious that her muscles would stiffen if she sat and drank her tea, she wandered along the pathway with her mug, going over her plans and trying to visualise how everything would eventually look, in an attempt to lift her mood. As she neared the bottom of the garden, she spotted a gap in the conifers with a direct view through the criss-cross fence into the neighbouring garden.

Benjamin's garden.

Curiosity had her pushing forward.

She had liked what she had seen of her new neighbour, appreciating his kindness in the veterinary surgery and that he had taken the trouble to return her phone, and although the two properties weren't on top of each other, they were remote enough from the rest of the village that she hoped they would get along well.

Even though they probably wouldn't bump into each other that often, Ellie liked the idea of having someone close by who she could trust in case of an emergency.

She peered through the fence into Benjamin's garden. It was a sizeable plot, bigger than the one Ellie and Ash had, filled with mature plants and trees that all looked lovingly maintained. Benjamin appeared to care for his property. Always a sign of a good neighbour.

In the distance she could see his house. A large pale-grey building with a wide chimney set in its dark roof, and shuttered windows. It wasn't exactly what she would call a pretty house, but it had plenty of character, and history, too, she suspected. It was grand and... masculine.

Ellie had never sexed a house before, her lips curving even as she realised what she had done. She was right though. If houses had a gender, this one was definitely male.

Did Benjamin live here alone or was he married with a

family? They had only spoken briefly and all Ellie really knew about him was that he liked James Bond movies and owned a cat.

She suspected he was a few years older than her, maybe early forties. This wasn't a bachelor pad-type house though, so there was probably a Mrs Thorne, maybe some children too.

As though thinking about his wife conjured her up, a woman stepped out from behind a row of conifers and into Ellie's line of sight. As she did so, she glanced up in the direction of the fence and the pair of them made eye contact.

Ellie took a sudden step back, aware she had been snooping, her cheeks burning as the woman stared at her. She had been caught out, so had no choice but to own it.

'Hi. Sorry, I was just being a bit nosy and admiring your lovely garden. I'm Ellie by the way, your new neighbour.'

When the woman continued to stare, but made no response, Ellie shuffled her feet, uncomfortable. 'Are you Benjamin's wife?'

She looked younger than him, though not young enough to be his daughter, her light-brown hair hanging in a cloud of loose curls that fell around her shoulders, and, dare Ellie say it, she was a little bit frumpy. The floral long-sleeved maxi dress that fell around her ankles had lost its shape and the sun was reflecting off the thick unattractive glasses she wore, so Ellie couldn't see her eyes. She wrung her hands together, almost childlike in manner as she watched Ellie, though didn't respond to her question.

Okay, this was getting a little weird. 'Well, it's nice to meet you. I'd better get back up to the house.'

Ellie didn't wait for her to react, turning and heading back up the garden to the patio, where she finished her tea as she considered Benjamin's wife, because that, she decided, was who she had to be. What a strange lady. Nothing at all like Benjamin, who was open and friendly.

Back in the house, she rinsed her mug, setting it on the drainer, then went upstairs, figuring she would finish the room she was working on then think about dinner. Ash usually did most of the cooking, was better at it if she was honest, but Ellie had told him she would sort meals while she wasn't working.

The room was going to be a guest bedroom. Not that it would get much use. Ellie had no family and Ash's parents and brother were in Australia. She hoped they might come visit at some point, though, and she wanted to have a warm, welcoming space for them to stay. As she worked the putty knife under the strip of paper she had sprayed, she toyed with colours for the room, tried to imagine it in a subtle shade of pale blue or grey, maybe with a wooden bed frame and cream furniture. She could visualise it with a vase of flowers picked from the garden on the dresser. She would google some ideas later and get Ash's input.

Thinking of the garden had her thoughts sliding back to Benjamin's wife and the strange encounter. The woman hadn't seemed angry that Ellie had been snooping through the fence, but then she hadn't really seemed anything at all.

Perhaps Ellie should take a bottle of wine round, a thank you to Benjamin for returning her phone. That way she could find out what the deal was with the wife.

Maybe tomorrow, she decided, peeling the paper away from the wall. As she did, she realised there was something underneath. It was writing. A childlike scrawl.

There was a mark and beside it was a name. Naomi, along with the words 'age twelve'. As the paper peeled further, it revealed more marks, with Naomi's name again and the various ages she had been.

A height chart.

Naomi must have been a child who had lived here at some point and this had been her bedroom.

Ellie finished stripping the wallpaper, cleared up her

rubbish and dragged the bags down the stairs and out to wheelie bin. She would have a quick shower then get some dinner together for when Ash returned from his meeting.

It wasn't until fifteen minutes later when she was standing under the warm spray, feeling it lick against her aching muscles, that she recalled the conversation from Saturday night and what Roxanne had said.

Naomi. The girl who had gone missing.

6

Ellie dropped Naomi Tanner's name into casual conversation over dinner that night. They were eating on the patio, taking advantage of the heat that still clung to the air, while trying to ignore the annoying flies that kept buzzing around the table.

After finding the height chart, Ellie had been tempted to message Roxanne. Although she remembered fragments of the conversation from Saturday, she had been annoyed with her friend at the time and hadn't taken in too many details. She recalled the girl had been called Naomi, though, and that she had disappeared. What she couldn't remember was who had died. Was it the girl's mother? And she couldn't remember what Naomi's surname was.

In the end, she decided against going to Roxanne. She would gloat and Ellie did not want to give her the satisfaction of knowing she was right about the house. Instead, she turned to Google.

Even with her vague criteria, it hadn't taken much effort to find Naomi and learn the full tragic details of what had happened to her family.

From the various news articles she read, Louise Tanner had been stabbed to death and her seventeen-year-old daughter, Naomi, had disappeared. Initially police had thought it was a burglary gone wrong. Then attention had shifted to Naomi's on-off boyfriend, Callum, before switching closer to home and onto John Tanner, who had eventually been arrested for the murder of his wife. John had been away on a business trip at the time but had no witnesses to vouch for his whereabouts on the night in question.

The police held him in custody, but they didn't have a strong enough case to file charges, and he had eventually been released. No other arrests were ever made and it was widely believed that John was guilty, even if the police couldn't prove it. He had moved away a few months later, still protesting his innocence, and Naomi's whereabouts remained unknown.

It took a little more digging, but Ellie found a picture of the family home.

Although she already had suspicions, a ball of dread still knotted in her stomach as she recognised the front door and canopy that John Tanner was standing in front of. The antique door knocker with the cherubs moulded into the brass was visible just over his shoulder. It had charmed Ellie when she had first seen the house. Now it made her feel sick.

How had they not known they were moving into a house where a murder had taken place?

Surely the estate agent would have said something when showing the property. They had an obligation to let people know stuff like this, didn't they?

As she considered calling them, a message popped up from Ash saying he was on his way home. She realised she had spent longer than intended googling the Tanner family and in doing so had completely forgotten about dinner. Not that she had much of an appetite after her discovery, but Ash would be hungry, plus she had skipped lunch and needed to eat something. Knowing she didn't have much time, she settled on a simple pasta dish.

As she crossed the hallway to the kitchen she glanced at the staircase and the spot at the bottom of the steps where Louise Tanner's body had been found.

Louise's husband had called the police after returning from his alleged business trip. She had been lying there dead in a pool of blood for close to twenty-four hours.

Dicing the chicken fillets and throwing them into the heated pan, Ellie contemplated again whether she should contact the estate agent. Deciding she would mention it to Ash first before going in all hot-headed, a horrible nagging doubt wormed its way into her brain.

What if Ash had known?

It was a silly, groundless thought and he had done nothing to deserve her distrust. Still she couldn't help thinking that something like this probably wouldn't bother him. Ash was all about present and future and he erred towards the practical. As an architect his brain was more scientifically programmed than Ellie's creative one, and she could almost hear him now, telling her that yes, all buildings have history, but that they are bricks and mortar, and nothing within them can affect the here and now.

And Ellie would, for the most part, agree he was right. She liked to consider herself sensible, and aside from that one doubting moment on Saturday night when Miss Moneypenny had given them a scare, she didn't buy into ghosts or the idea that the past could hurt the present. She did, however, believe that houses were more than just bricks and mortar and that they gave off a vibe, as stupid as that may sound. So far, those vibes had all been good, but now knowing the secrets that were hidden within the walls of their new home, everything felt different.

If Ash had known the truth about the history of the house, was it possible he might have kept it to himself, knowing it was liable to freak Ellie out?

They had been lucky to get the house for a steal, Jeremy Fox of Dandridge & Son Estate Agents had told them when their offer was accepted.

Ellie remembered that Ash had asked a million questions about the place, to the point that Jeremy had been a little irritated with him. She got the impression that Jeremy liked to do as little as possible to secure a sale. Of course, the one question Ash hadn't asked, because seriously, who would think to ask it, was had any murders taken place in the house.

No, Ash would never have thought to ask and Jeremy certainly hadn't disclosed it. Ellie was wrong even to consider that Ash might know about the history of the house and be keeping it from her.

But as she put the pasta on to boil, that same nagging voice reminded her again of Roxanne's odd comment on Saturday night, after Ellie had pointed out that the estate agent would have said something if anything bad had happened in the house.

I'm sure they would have. Right, Ash?

At the time, Ellie had assumed Roxanne did it to get a rise out of Ash, but now she wasn't so sure.

'Not hungry?' Ash asked now, looking at her mostly full plate where she was absently pushing her pasta around with her fork.

'Not particularly.'

'You're still worrying about the dog?'

'She-Ra. She has a name, Ashton.'

'And I refuse to use it, Elisabeth.' Ash's eyes crinkled at the corners as he grinned. 'Anyone who calls their dog She-Ra should be sectioned and banned from keeping dogs.'

'I think she should be banned from keeping dogs for abandoning hers at the vet,' Ellie muttered, switching her fork for her beer bottle and taking a drink. 'Seriously, what kind of person does that?'

'The woman's an idiot, Ellie. Honestly, she doesn't deserve her. The dog's better off being rehomed. At least they can find someone to love her.'

'I guess.'

'So is it just the Princess of Power pissing you off? You've been testy ever since I got home.'

'Testy?'

'Yeah, testy. A bit snappy, your mind elsewhere, and you just called me Ashton. You only do that when you're annoyed with me or have your serious head on. What's up?'

'Nothing's up.'

'You're sure?'

'I'm sure.'

'Okay.' Ash turned his attention back to his food, scooping another huge forkful of pasta up and shovelling it in his mouth. Subject over, just like that.

Ellie slammed her beer bottle down on the table. Well, not exactly slammed, but she definitely landed it hard enough to have his head snapping back up as he looked at her, his golden eyes wide. 'Did you know about Louise and Naomi Tanner when we bought the house?'

She hadn't intended to blurt it out, knew she shouldn't make assumptions or accusations, but she certainly had Ash's attention, though his expression was for a moment unreadable before he creased his brow in confusion.

'Who?'

'The previous occupants of this house. Louise Tanner who

was stabbed to death in our hallway and her daughter, Naomi, who vanished from her bed five years ago.'

'What? That happened here?'

'Don't look so surprised, Ash. Roxanne was talking about it on Saturday night.'

His face darkened. 'I try not to pay too much attention to what Roxanne says.'

'I'm quite aware of that. It's not what I'm asking though. Did you know what had happened before we bought the house? Did the estate agent tell you?'

Ash stared at her for a moment before answering. 'No, Ellie, I didn't.' He put his fork down, hands clasped and elbows on the table, and continued to hold eye contact, the green sparks of his irises flashing bright against the gold with annoyance as he waited for her to react.

Was he telling the truth? She didn't know whether to believe him.

'So Jeremy said nothing?'

'No, he didn't.' When Ellie pouted at that, he quickly added, 'Do you seriously think I would keep something like that from you?'

Would he? She realised she wasn't sure.

How could he not have known?

You didn't know.

Ellie pushed the irritating little voice of logic to one side. She didn't know because she hadn't been the one with all the questions.

'You spoke to him loads, though, before we put in an offer. He was getting sick of you asking him stuff, remember?'

'Yes, about how long it had been on the market, why it was being sold, what work had been done. I think I would remember if he had said someone had been killed here.' Ash raked his hands back through his hair. 'Jesus, Ellie. I thought you trusted me.'

'I do. I...' She trailed off, aware she didn't have an argument, still didn't have any logical reason to doubt him. Ash had always been upfront with her, right back from the moment they had met. He wasn't the sort of person to keep secrets from her.

'I'm sorry.' She let out a frustrated sigh, annoyed with herself for reacting the way she had. She wasn't generally a suspicious person, but the discovery had thrown her. 'Look, I do trust you and I shouldn't have doubted you. I guess I freaked out a little when I found out and... God. Damn it, Ash. How could we have bought this place and not have known?'

The look he gave her before answering was measured and she suspected what was coming, knew what his stance would be. 'Is it really that big a deal? It's just a house.'

'But someone died here. Horribly.'

'In the past. What happened then doesn't affect anything that happens now.'

'But–'

'Do you think this place is haunted? I thought you didn't believe in ghosts.'

'I don't.'

'So why does it bother you so much?'

'I don't know. It's just horrible knowing it happened here, in our home.'

'Okay, that's fair enough, and I get that what happened was tragic.' Ash reached across the table and caught hold of Ellie's hand. 'But you know that's probably why this place was within our budget.'

'Which is why Jeremy should have told us!'

'Yeah, he should have, but if he had told us and you then dismissed the place without looking at it, we would have missed out on a great opportunity.'

Ellie narrowed her eyes. 'To live in a murder house?' she asked dryly.

Ash's lips curved, though his eyes remained sober. 'Do you feel unsafe here?'

She considered the question, gave him an honest answer. 'No.'

'And you know this place is just a shell, that it's what we do to it that will make it our home, right?'

'Yes.'

'Something awful happened here, but we have the chance to make it a happy place.'

'I guess.' Why was he making everything sound so bloody reasonable? Ellie pouted a little as he talked her round, and deep down a part of her realised that everything he said made perfect sense. Could she put what had happened here behind her? Until she had learnt about the Tanner family, she had counted her blessings and considered they had been lucky, and yes, she had been in love with the house.

She could move past this, or at least she would try.

That's what she promised Ash that night and she meant it, though she still took her frustration at not being told out on Jeremy Fox the following morning, calling Dandridge & Son Estate Agents as soon as they opened and ranting down the phone at him for ten minutes.

It didn't achieve anything. Jeremy smarmed his way through the conversation, telling her that the seller hadn't disclosed the murder and pointing out – a little too smugly she thought – that he hadn't been under any obligation to research the history of the house himself, so she had no legal ground to stand on.

Ellie worked some of her frustration out on the house, putting in a solid three hours of manual labour before stopping for a break. Ash was right. They would ignore the history of the place and claim it as theirs. The sooner they could put their own stamp on it, the better.

Downstairs, waiting for the kettle to boil, she stared out over the garden, towards the Thorne house, recalling her odd encounter with Benjamin's wife. She wondered if either of them was home. She still had to thank Benjamin for returning her phone.

She had been working hard on the house over the past couple of days and could do with a break. Besides, she really wanted to know what the deal was with Mrs Thorne.

Maybe it was time to find out.

7

The neighbouring driveway was sheltered by overhanging trees, their branches intertwining to offer a tunnel of shade from the heat of the midday sun, though they did nothing to help with the humidity. Ellie had showered and changed into a cotton sundress before leaving the house, but a trickle of perspiration was running down from her neck into the back of the dress, and the bottle of white wine that had been cool when she took it from the fridge was already damp in her hand.

As she approached the Thorne house she stared in wonder, pushing her oversized sunglasses up onto her head, amazed at how big it was. From the angle she had seen yesterday, it had looked a decent size, but not like this. It was enormous.

And immaculately maintained. The light-grey exterior of the house looked well cared for and the roof in good condition, given that it must be several hundred years old, while the windows were clean, appearing freshly painted, and the ivy growing up trellises around the door, trimmed and healthy.

Although she had only just moved in next door, Ellie was a little embarrassed. It was obvious that the Thornes were house-proud people and she didn't want to be the one letting down the neighbourhood.

She glanced at the first-floor windows, wondering how many bedrooms the house had. Unless the rooms were huge, then there had to be at least six or seven bedrooms up there, possibly more.

Did Benjamin Thorne have a big family?

As she continued to stare, Ellie realised there was someone at one of the upstairs windows looking down at her and heat rose in her cheeks. Here she was with her mouth agog just gawking at their house. What the hell must they think?

Knowing she had been caught out again, she raised a hand, smiling as she waved.

Hopefully it was one of Benjamin's children. That wouldn't be quite so bad.

But as she neared, the face against the glass became clearer, the cloud of scruffy hair and the thick glasses familiar, as she recognised the person standing there was Mrs Thorne.

Great. She's going to think I'm spying on them.

Ellie couldn't turn back now though. The woman had seen her approaching the house. No, she would just have to shrug it off, tell Benjamin's wife what a beautiful home she had and admit she was admiring it as she approached.

Still, there was a flutter of anxiety in her belly as she used the brass knocker (much grander than the one on her own front door. This one had a lion's head snarling at her) and waited.

Benjamin had seemed like such an unassuming man and she had pictured him in a neat, but modest cottage, not somewhere that looked like it could house the von Trapp family.

She ran her fingers over her head, hoping to smooth down any stray hairs that had escaped her ponytail, glad she had changed out of her scruffy work clothes, even if it was just into a cheap Primark dress. She wondered why Benjamin's wife hadn't come downstairs to answer the door.

There was no sign of Benjamin himself, though it was a weekday, so he was quite possibly out at work. She had no idea what his job was. And there was no car in the driveway, though there was a double garage to the side of the house.

Ellie was pondering what to do, a little uncomfortable that his wife knew she was there, but was choosing to ignore her, when noise came from the other side of the door.

She gripped the bottle of wine tighter, had a smile ready as the door swung open, expecting it to be Mrs Thorne. She was a little surprised when she found herself face to face with Benjamin.

'Ellie, how nice.'

He had a beaming smile on his face, seeming happy to see her, and she relaxed a little.

'I thought I'd just pop round and say thank you for the other day, for returning my phone.'

'It was honestly no trouble. You were on my way home.'

'I brought you a little something.' Ellie held out the wine. 'I hope you like white.'

'That's very thoughtful of you. Why don't you come on in?' He took the wine from her then pulled the door back to allow her to enter, and even though Ellie had only planned to drop the wine off then leave, she was curious to know what the house was like inside.

She stepped through the doorway, finding herself in a spacious hall with wood-beam ceilings and a wide staircase. Beyond that was a room with an Aga that she assumed was the kitchen. Narrower passageways led off in both directions and she suspected the house was something of a rabbit warren.

The house was old, and had plenty of character and charm about it. A faint whiff of polish clung to the air, and she guessed the house was as tidy and clean inside as it looked from out front. A bit like Benjamin, who was casually, but smartly dressed in pressed chino-style trousers and a short-sleeved white shirt, his hair neatly combed and his face clean-shaven.

It struck Ellie that he was at odds with his wife, with her cloud of curly hair and her shapeless dress, but then she felt bad judging the woman's attire. Mrs Thorne had been in the privacy of her own garden and Ellie had only seen her because she had been snooping. Given the mess Ellie had been in herself while she'd been working, it was hardly fair to cast stones.

'I was just about to have some lemonade,' Benjamin told her. 'Do you fancy a glass? It's home-made. An old family recipe. Too hot for tea or coffee at the moment, don't you think? Though, of course, I can put the kettle on if you prefer.'

'Lemonade is fine, thank you.'

Ellie followed Benjamin through to the room beyond the staircase, trying not to gawk at the enormous kitchen, as he placed the wine down on the counter then fussed about getting the drinks.

'You'll have to excuse the clutter in here. I haven't had a chance to tidy up.'

Clutter? She glanced about the immaculate room. There was some paperwork on the counter, but other than that the kitchen was spotless, the surfaces gleaming and filled with expensive appliances.

'Have you lived in Corpusty long?'

'All of my life.' He poured the cloudy lemonade and handed her a glass. 'This house has been in the Thorne family for generations.' He sounded proud and understandably so.

'It's a beautiful house,' she told him, and meant it.

'Thank you. It needed quite a lot of work doing to it when I inherited it from my parents, but I'm gradually getting on top of everything.'

'Is it just you and your wife living here?'

'Wife?' Benjamin's face filled with surprised amusement as though she had just asked something ridiculously funny. 'Oh, no. I'm not married.'

'Sorry, I saw a lady at the upstairs window and assumed–'

'Shall we go and sit in the garden? It's far too nice a day to be indoors.'

The words were spoken a little sharply, Benjamin already leading the way before Ellie had a chance to answer. A crash from above had him halting and she saw his face tighten. 'What the hell's she broken now?'

He said the words good-naturedly, but the lines around his mouth had tightened and he didn't look happy.

'Who's upstairs?' Ellie was downright curious now and didn't care if she was being nosy.

'I live with my sister.' Benjamin shook his head. 'Would you mind waiting here please?'

He was gone before she could answer and Ellie heard the sound of his footsteps on the stairs moments later as she stood in the cool kitchen, the glass of lemonade in her hand, processing the information she had just learnt.

So, the woman in the garden was Benjamin's sister.

Ellie hadn't been close enough to get a good look at her, but guessed the woman was maybe in her late twenties or possibly early thirties. A little younger than herself.

It was an odd arrangement living with her brother, but then Benjamin had said the house was passed down through generations. Maybe it was a family tradition, all living together under one roof. It's not like there wasn't enough space.

As she waited and sipped at her lemonade, voices came from above. At first, they were muffled, but then one was yelling and it sounded too high-pitched to be Benjamin. A little uncomfortable, Ellie was wondering whether she should head out into the garden, when a door slammed, making her jump.

Yes, she should go outside. The last thing she wanted to do was get caught up in the middle of a family argument.

She stepped out of the kitchen door, found herself on a patio that spanned the length of the back of the house, with views over Benjamin's stunning garden. Did he tend to all of this himself or did he have help? It really was quite beautiful.

She was admiring a display of coloured flowers, some of which she recognised, but many others she didn't, thinking she would need to get some tips off Benjamin before attempting her own garden, when he rejoined her.

Ellie didn't miss the slightly flustered look on his face, the colour rising high in his cheeks.

'Sorry about that.'

'It's no problem,' Ellie lied. 'Is everything okay?'

'Yes, yes. Just the bloody cat knocking a vase over. It's sturdy though, so luckily didn't break.' He nodded to himself, sipped at his lemonade, and looked as if he was debating whether to say something else, so Ellie waited patiently.

'I did ask Virginia to come downstairs and join us,' he said eventually, before elaborating, 'Virginia's my sister.'

'That would be nice.' Another lie. Well, part of one. Ellie was getting the impression Virginia didn't particularly like her, though she was still curious about the woman.

'I'm not sure if she will. She's in one of her moods.'

'Well, perhaps I'll meet her another time. This garden is lovely, Benjamin. Do you do all of this yourself?'

'What? Yes, yes.' He had been distracted, probably still thinking about his sister. 'I used to have a chap come in once a week, but now it's all me.' He sounded proud. 'I find gardening very therapeutic. I've always liked tending to and looking after things.'

'You'll have to give me some tips.'

'Of course, I can do that. I tried to get Virginia interested in helping me. She appreciates the garden, but not the work involved though.' He laughed softly. 'She's not had it easy, my sister.'

Oh? Ellie was curious, though she remained quiet, waiting for him to continue.

'She has... she has difficulties.' He didn't elaborate on what type of difficulties, leaving her imagination to run riot. 'Did Trevor give you an update on the dog?' he asked, changing the subject abruptly.

Ellie had been about to ask more about Virginia and the switch in conversation threw her for a moment. 'Umm, yes, he did. She's going to be okay.'

She didn't offer any more details. Benjamin didn't need to know that She-Ra's owner had abandoned her at the vet's.

'That's good news. Good news indeed.'

They wandered the garden for a bit as they drank their lemonade, Benjamin pointing out different flowers and shrubs, seeming genuinely flattered that Ellie was interested.

She wondered how much company he had if it was just him and his sister. He hadn't mentioned anything else about Virginia and what her difficulties were and although Ellie had a hundred questions, some of them were personal. She decided she would wait until she knew him a little bit better before prying.

She assumed Virginia lived with Benjamin because she needed him to look after her. He hadn't mentioned work, so Ellie was unsure what he did for a living. Was he Virginia's full-time carer? If so, it must be lonely for him. The house and garden were picture perfect, but they really were in the middle of nowhere. She decided she would invite Benjamin and Virginia over for dinner one evening. She would mention it to

Ash tonight before she asked, though was sure he wouldn't mind.

'I can give you some cuttings if you like?'

Benjamin's voice interrupted Ellie's train of thought. 'Sorry?'

'Some cuttings for your garden? I suppose, though, you probably have your hands full with fixing up the house. Maybe next summer.'

'No, that's very kind of you. Thank you.' Ellie hesitated. Benjamin had lived here his whole life. 'Did you know them? The people who lived here before us?'

If he was surprised by her question, he didn't show it. 'The tenants? No, not really. They were private people, kept to themselves. I waved a couple of times if I was passing, said hello, but I never had a conversation with them.'

'What about the family before? The Tanners?' She immediately regretted asking the question, could see the tightening of his mouth and the colour warming his cheeks, though it was out there now. No taking it back. They had been neighbours and if he had known them well, it could be difficult for him, having the past raked up. Plus, of course, it made Ellie appear nosy. Which, okay she was, but she didn't want to broadcast it.

When he didn't respond immediately, she tried to take it back. 'I'm sorry, I'm prying. You don't have to answer that.'

Benjamin shook his head. 'No, it's okay. I should be better at talking about it by now. It's been what? Five years? Damn tragedy what happened to that poor family.'

'Were you close?'

'I didn't know John very well. He was away a lot, but Louise and Naomi were good people.' He was silent for a moment, staring across the garden towards Ellie's house. 'I was home the night it happened, but I never heard a thing. That bothered me for a long time, knowing I had been so close, but had been unable to help.'

'It wasn't your fault though.' Ellie didn't push for further details, could tell it was painful for him to talk about. She shouldn't have raked the memories up.

'Does it bother you?' he asked quietly.

'Living in the house?'

'Yes, knowing what happened there.'

'It's just bricks, just a shell.' She painted on a smile that was perhaps a little too bright, as she quoted Ash. 'It's our job now to fill the house with happy memories.'

Benjamin studied her for a moment, as if he didn't quite believe her, but he didn't call her out on it. 'I guess that's one way to look at it.'

'Do you think he did it? John Tanner.' Ellie's voice was not much more than a whisper. She hadn't meant to say the words aloud.

Benjamin gave her a sober look before he answered. 'Yes, I think he probably did.'

8

Virginia's bedroom was at the front of the house and, although Benjamin had offered on several occasions over the years to move her to a room with a garden view, she preferred to stay put.

His sister had always been about the routines and familiarity, so he got that, just as he understood that her room must remain untouched. He had offered to redecorate it on many occasions, but knew Virginia sought comfort in the pastel pinks of her childhood and in the collection of dolls on the ottoman at the foot of her bed.

Personally, Benjamin hated the dolls. He had always found them a little creepy, disliking the way their eyes followed him around the room. Now, as he leant against the doorjamb facing the bed, he was aware of them watching him, judging, as they always did when he stood here and spoke to his sister.

'I think you would really like Ellie.' He waited for an answer, but there was only silence. 'I told you she's nice. I think she has a good heart.'

He wished Virginia would stop giving him the silent treatment, that she would just say something. Anything. The silence had always been annoying, but he guessed it was preferable to when she lost her temper. That was often exhausting, with Benjamin left to clear up the mess.

No, the silence was better.

As he started to close the bedroom door, he was aware of her shifting on the bed behind him.

'Are you worried about Ellie?' he asked, though kept his back turned. 'You really do have nothing to fret about. I'm just being friendly, neighbourly.'

A sliver of concern snaked its way into his gut. 'Ellie isn't a threat to you. You know that, right?'

Her continuing silence did nothing to reassure him.

'She's not like the others. I want you to promise me you will leave her alone.'

He waited but could tell she had already closed him out. The discussion – or rather, lack of it – was over.

'I'm going downstairs to get dinner ready,' he told her, keeping his tone light, but as he pulled her door shut and headed back downstairs, the familiar dread gnawed at him, and he couldn't help worrying that it was all about to happen again.

9

'Are you really going to stay living there?'

Roxanne screwed her nose up, seeming disgusted by the idea, and Ellie was already regretting telling her she had been right about the house.

They had met in Norwich for a morning of shopping followed by lunch. It had been Roxanne's idea and Ellie had initially said no, before changing her mind. She had worked hard on the house all week and deserved a break.

'We've already bought it.' Ellie shrugged, before wheeling out the line about new memories she had borrowed from Ash and had already used on Benjamin. With practice she thought she was beginning to sound believable, and with time, maybe she would even convince herself.

'But that's downright creepy. The woman didn't just die in your house, she was murdered there. And no one knows what happened to her daughter.'

'It's in the past though. It happened over five years ago.'

'Doesn't it bother you at all?'

'No!' Ellie said the word a little too sharply, quickly following it up with a smile. Of course it bothered her, but if she told

Roxanne that, her friend would run with it. She picked up her menu, pretended to study it, even though she had already decided on the spicy chicken salad, and rolled her shoulders to relax them.

She was an idiot and shouldn't have said anything. Roxanne had already been anti the idea of her moving in with Ash and Ellie had just given her more ammunition.

'Have you decided what you want to order?' she asked, to change the subject.

Roxanne pursed her lips, looked like she was going to say something else, but then thankfully looked at her own menu. The reprieve was short-lived though, as she clicked her fingers at the waiter and ordered eggs Benedict and another pot of tea, before looking expectantly at Ellie.

Ellie smiled at the waiter and gave him her order, before thanking him and handing over her menu. 'What?' she demanded, as Roxanne studied her, a smirk on her face.

'I bet he knew.'

'What?' Ellie repeated, though her heart sunk. She knew exactly where this was going and mentally kicked herself again.

'It would be typical Ash, finding something like that out, and going ahead without telling you.'

'He didn't know. He was as shocked as I was.'

'Well, of course he is going to say that. He's not stupid.' Roxanne rolled her eyes. 'You know, it wouldn't bother him in the slightest living in a house where someone had been murdered. And if he thought he was getting a bargain. You did say you were surprised you got the house at such a low price. Ash is manipulative, but he isn't stupid. He would have questioned why.'

She was talking in that slightly smug way as if she knew Ash best, which irritated Ellie. Ash was her boyfriend and yes, okay,

Roxanne may have known him longer, but it didn't mean she knew him better.

'What did you mean on Saturday night?'

'What did I mean about what?'

'When I said about the estate agent disclosing the murder, you smiled at Ash and made a comment, as if you knew something.'

'Did I?'

'Yes, Roxy, you did. It was of course they would, wouldn't they, Ash?" or something like that.'

'I don't remember, but I was probably fooling around. You know what I'm like when I've had a few drinks.'

Was Ellie imagining it or was Roxanne looking a little uncomfortable?

'So, are we going to head back via Next and you can get those sandals you liked?'

The abrupt change of subject threw Ellie and immediately made her suspicious. She was tempted to push Roxanne on the comment she had made, but equally was grateful for the subject change.

'I don't know. They weren't cheap and I don't really need any new shoes.' Ellie was about to add that she and Ash had enough expense with the house, but stopped herself, not wanting to bring it up again.

'Just whack them on your credit card. That's what I do.'

Which Pete then settles, Ellie thought. She had heard Pete moaning to Ash about his wife's out-of-control spending habits. Besides, she wasn't like Roxanne, preferring to be careful with her money.

Ellie's job as an illustrator brought in regular enough work and paid for her to have a comfortable lifestyle and Ash had a good job, plus Ellie had savings put away, but she wasn't going to dip into them for a pair of sandals she didn't need.

Instead, she enjoyed her lunch, letting Roxanne prattle on about whether she should have her hair cut into a bob or invest in hair extensions, conscious that over the last couple of years, the two of them had grown apart. Since she had been dating Ash, Ellie realised. And she wasn't sure it was a bad thing.

Roxanne had always been a little catty, but it was more noticeable with her constant digs about Ash, and Ellie was beginning to see she was also quite self-centred.

Of course, the friendship would continue; Pete was Ash's best friend, but Ellie might try to cool it a little.

She spent another hour after lunch wandering around the city centre shops with Roxanne, didn't buy the sandals, though did pick up fish and a bloomer loaf from the market, figuring that would take care of dinner. As she was making her way back to her car, she glanced at Facebook, pleased to see she had finally had some interest in the old washing machine that had been left at the house. Ash had wanted to take it to the tip, but Ellie was convinced they could get fifty quid and had insisted on advertising it, knowing it all helped towards their refurbishment budget.

After agreeing the sale and telling the woman that she could pick the machine up on Saturday morning, she let Ash know, then drove back to Corpusty. She tried to talk herself out of stopping for a bottle of white wine. It would go well with the mussels she was planning on; but she and Ash had been drinking most nights since moving in and really should cut back.

As she approached the village she figured, 'Fuck it, it's Friday' and pulled over by the Spar shop. Inside, she debated between two bottles, before deciding to get them both.

'Excuse me. You're the lady who moved into Hazelwood Cottage, aren't you?'

Ellie was waiting in line to pay and turned to face the voice coming from behind her, a woman who was maybe in her mid-sixties, with auburn hair feathered around her face.

'Um, yes. We moved in a couple of weeks back.'

'I'm Christine Jameson. I live on Horseshoe Lane. I thought I recognised you. Are you settling in okay?'

'Yes, there's a lot to do, but we're getting there, thanks. I'm Ellie Summers. It's nice to meet you.'

'It's a lovely house. Shame the last owner didn't take care of it. Often the case with rental properties though. I guess you're planning on staying there and fixing it up? Living there yourself?'

'Yes, that's the plan.' Well, it had been before Ellie learnt about Louise Tanner's murder. Although it didn't bother Ash, she was still getting her head around the idea of living there.

'A family home then,' Christine mused. 'Plenty of room to raise kids.'

Ellie smiled but didn't respond. She had only just moved in with Ash. They hadn't ever discussed kids. If it happened, it was a long way down the line. She wondered if Christine would be the sort to frown if she knew Ellie and Ash weren't married.

Although living together was commonplace these days, Benjamin had seemed surprised. Maybe it was something people living further out in the countryside were less familiar with.

'Have you lived in Corpusty for long?' she asked, changing the subject.

'Coming up for twenty-three years this October. You'll love it here. There's a real sense of community. I run the local Slimming World group.' Christine glanced Ellie up and down, as if deciding whether she was worth inviting, and Ellie self-consciously held the bottles of wine in front of her. 'Louise Tanner used to attend my sessions.'

Before Ellie had a chance to comment on that, Christine

continued. 'Poor woman, she lost all that weight and was looking marvellous, and then she went and died a few weeks later, before she had the chance to really show it off.' She studied Ellie again, narrowed her eyes. 'I take it you know about the Tanners. They lived at Hazelwood Cottage a few years back. Before that man and his tenants moved in.'

'I've heard about them and what happened.'

'Not sure I could live there myself, not after that, but you're right, it will make a lovely home. Nice and quiet too. Only the one neighbour.'

'Do you know the Thornes?'

'Of course. Everyone knows each other around here. Benjamin Thorne is a lovely man. Always has plenty of time for everyone. I do feel sorry for him, though, having to deal with that sister of his.'

'Virginia?'

'That's her. Stares at you a lot, never has anything to say for herself.'

'I've seen her, but not to speak to.'

Oh, she won't speak to you. She has tantrums, you know. Benjamin sometimes has to send her away. He can't cope, poor thing. It must be difficult for him.'

'What is actually wrong with her?' Ellie felt a stab of guilt that she was asking Christine and not Benjamin, but she was curious, and Benjamin hadn't seemed like he wanted to say too much about his sister. She had sensed he was a private man.

'Complications going back to her birth. She's never been quite right. After her parents died Benjamin became her legal guardian. If you ask my opinion, she shouldn't be living there with him. I think she should be in a home where they can better care for her needs and are better prepared to deal with her outbursts.'

Ellie smiled and nodded, still uncomfortable that she had

asked. She was relieved when the queue moved forward and it was her turn to be served, exchanging just a friendly goodbye with the woman after that.

As she headed back to the house, she mulled over the conversation, recalling her visit to the Thornes. She had heard raised voices after Benjamin went to investigate the dropped vase. He had told Ellie the cat had knocked it, but if Virginia was having one of the tantrums Christine had spoken about, had she done it?

Virginia hadn't wanted to meet Ellie, had ignored her that afternoon in the garden. She had struck Ellie as aloof and a little odd, but was she aggressive or just misunderstood?

Perhaps inviting her and Benjamin to dinner was a bad idea. Ash had been cool with it, but if Virginia was likely to be a problem, perhaps dinner was best swerved.

Except she had wanted to do it for Benjamin, concerned that he was lonely, and unfortunately, she couldn't invite him without his sister.

Sod it. She would invite them both. It was one dinner. How bat-shit crazy could Virginia be?

After putting the fish and wine in the fridge, she locked up again and headed back down the driveway to the Thorne house, figuring she would see if Benjamin was in and whether he and Virginia fancied coming over for dinner on Sunday evening. No sign of his car again, but there hadn't been last time either, so it was quite possible he was home.

She knocked on the door, waited, then knocked again.

Perhaps he was out.

After trying one more time without success, she fished in her bag for her pen and tore a piece of paper from the back of her diary. She scribbled a quick note letting Benjamin know she had stopped by and asking about dinner, popping her mobile number at the end so he could call or text to let her know, and pushed it through the letterbox.

It was only Friday, so plenty of time to get food in if he accepted the invite.

Heading back down the driveway, Ellie was oblivious to the curtain twitching in the upstairs bedroom and the eyes that watched her until she disappeared from sight.

10

Ash had messaged to say he had some work to finish up and was going to be late home, so Ellie frowned when she heard a car pulling to a halt in the driveway. She was in the kitchen slicing chunks of bread to go with the mussels, a glass of white wine on the go, and set down the knife, wiping her hands on a tea towel before heading through to the hallway.

It wouldn't be Pete or Roxanne. Benjamin possibly? Though surely he would come by foot.

She opened the door, stepping out into the driveway, didn't recognise the white van or the two men who climbed out, her stomach knotting, aware she was home alone. Maybe they just had the wrong address.

'Can I help you?'

They were younger than her, though not by much. Late twenties maybe, both lanky in build. They had to be here by mistake.

'You're Ellie?' That was from the taller of the two, his bald head red on top from where the sun had caught it. His friend stared at her, a smile on his bearded face.

'Yes.'

No mistake then.

'We're here for the washing machine.'

Oh. 'I thought Claire was coming in the morning. That's what we agreed.'

'Something's come up. She sent us to get it tonight.' His accent was pure Norwich.

'Well, my boyfriend isn't home yet. It's still in the cellar. We were going to bring up later.'

She cursed herself the moment the words had left her mouth. Why the hell had she told them Ash wasn't home and she was here alone?

Stupid, Ellie, stupid.

Baldie glanced at his friend then back at Ellie. 'That's not a problem, love. We can manage it between us.'

'I'm sorry, but now's really not a convenient time to collect.'

'Look, so here's the deal. Claire never told us any of this. Her kid has been rushed into hospital and she asked us if we would help her out. She never said anything about that it had to be tomorrow, but I guess her head is all over the place, so she wasn't thinking straight.'

'I'm really sorry to hear that.' Ellie tried to ignore the stab of guilt. 'I just...' Damn it, she really didn't want to let them in. 'As I say it's just not convenient.'

'We could be really quick. In and out. We won't be in your hair.' Baldie chanced a smile and she wavered slightly. They seemed nice enough and if what they said about Claire was true then would it really hurt?

'Barry, mate. Come on. It's not a good time.' That was from the friend who still stood by the van.

Baldie... or Barry, as he was called, let out a reluctant sigh. 'I understand, love. Don't worry, we'll let Claire know. We're working tomorrow so can't come back, but we'll ask her to contact you if she's still interested.'

Damn it. Maybe she was over-reacting.

'Wait.' Both men looked at her and Ellie found a smile for them. 'Okay, come on in. You're here now, so you might as well take it.'

She opened the door wide and let them in, hating that her spider sense tingled as they stepped past her. Was she making a mistake?

'It's in the cellar,' she told them. 'As I say, we didn't expect you tonight, so I'm afraid you'll have to bring it up yourselves.'

'Not a problem. Lead the way.'

Ellie didn't like having them behind her, especially when she heard them whispering to each other. As she led them into the kitchen, her gaze slid to the knife she had been using to slice the bread. It was on the chopping board in clear view, next to her phone.

If either man grabbed it.

They won't. You're over-reacting.

Still, she wished Ash was here. She couldn't even message him without it looking obvious what she was doing.

'Nice house you have here,' Barry's friend was saying. 'Must have cost a bob or two.'

Oh God. Were they going to rob her?

Ellie quickly stepped across the room, annoyed her hand was shaking as she closed it over the knob to the cellar door. 'It's down here.'

She tried to keep her tone confident, not wanting to let on that they were unnerving her, flipping on the light, and holding the door wide so they could step inside.

They didn't.

Instead, Barry stopped in front of her, eyebrows raised expectantly. 'After you.'

What?

'I'm busy. You can just go on down and get it. If you turn left at the bottom of the stairs you can't miss it.'

For a moment Ellie thought he was going to challenge her, but instead, he exchanged a look with his friend before glancing back at Ellie and nodding. 'Sure. Come on, mate.'

Ellie watched them disappear down the stairs, annoyed she still felt shaken.

She could still hear them muttering to each other, their voices low enough that she couldn't make out what they were saying, and she didn't like it. What were they whispering about that they wouldn't want her to hear?

She went back to where she had been working, slid the knife out of sight and picked up her phone. It wouldn't hurt to let Ash know they were here.

She fired off a quick message.

What time do you think you'll be home? There are two men here to pick up the washing machine. They came a day early. X

Ash's reply didn't take long.

Please tell me you didn't let them in the house. I'm on my way home now. Twenty minutes tops. xx

Oops. She was about to break it to him that they were in the cellar when Barry called up to her.

'Ellie, can we borrow you for a minute?'

Shit.

Her heart raced as she dithered, debating what to do. Should she leave the kitchen, pretend she hadn't heard them? But then it was too late because Barry was calling her name again and this time she heard his footsteps on the stairs, didn't have time to disappear from sight before he appeared in the doorway.

'Can you come down here for a moment, love.'

'Oh? Is there a problem?'

'Come down and I'll show you.'

Fuck!

She had no choice but to follow him through the door, angry with herself that they had even managed to get in the house in the first place. Ash was going to kill her. Well, if Barry and his mate didn't do it first.

Damn it, Ellie. Don't go there.

She reached the bottom of the stairs, though held onto the banister, ready to scarper at the first opportunity. 'What did you need to show me?'

'You see this here?'

The way he had positioned himself, she couldn't see anything, so was forced to step closer to see what he was talking about.

'What?'

'This.'

He was pointing to the old hearth that the previous owner must have ripped out from the living room. Ellie wasn't sure what exactly that had to do with the washing machine.

She was conscious of Barry's friend moving from her peripheral vision and adjusted her position slightly, not liking that he was now standing between her and the stairs.

It was cool in the cellar but sweat had beaded on her forehead and under her arms, and her belly was twisting with nerves.

Despite their lanky build, both men were bigger than her. She was a bloody idiot letting herself get caught in this situation.

'What about it?' She tried to keep her voice calm, annoyed at the slight tremor in it.

'Well, it's just sitting here, so I assume you don't want it. Would you take twenty quid?'

The nerves eased slightly.

'Yeah, sure. If you want it.'

Ellie glanced back towards the stairs and at Barry's friend hovering by them. Would he let her past?

He grinned at her, showing off a bad set of teeth, and she wondered if he realised he was scaring her. Enjoying it perhaps.

'You lived here long?' he asked, making no attempt to move from the stairs.

'A couple of weeks.'

'Boyfriend at work, is he?'

'He will be home any time now.'

'Right.'

'I should go back upstairs.'

Ellie headed towards him, ready to barge past.

'Wait!'

She forced herself to stop. 'What?'

'Don't you want your money?' Ellie looked at Barry and the wad of notes he was holding out. 'Sixty, right? That's forty for the washing machine and twenty for the mantle.'

'It was actually fifty for the washing machine.'

'Was it?' Barry glanced at the appliance. 'There are a few dents in it.'

'Which were covered in my ad.'

He sighed, though smiled. 'You drive a hard bargain. Okay, fifty for the machine and twenty for the mantle.' He pulled another tenner from his wallet, handed the wad to her.

Ellie quickly took it, shoving the money in her pocket.

'Thanks. I'll be upstairs.'

This time neither of them stopped her and she quickly made her way up the steps.

'Ellie?'

The scream she had held in finally escaped as the figure

stepped into her path and she almost lost her balance, gripping onto the banister.

Benjamin looked as startled as she did, eyes wide and a gasp on his lips as he took a step back. 'Ellie!' he repeated.

From down below came Barry's voice. 'Everything okay up there?'

'Fine. Just a friend. He made me jump.'

Ellie tried to gather herself together, sucked in a breath to slow her heartbeat. 'Benjamin. What are you doing here?'

'I'm sorry.' Benjamin pushed his glasses up the bridge of his nose. 'I didn't mean to make you jump. I knocked, but... well, the door was open. I was worried.'

'It's okay.' She found a smile for him, reached out to pat his arm. 'I'm sorry I scared you.'

'I brought you some cuttings for the garden. Remember, I promised.' He held out a bag, his expression earnest. 'I'm sorry if this isn't a good time. If you're busy I should go. I didn't realise you had company.'

'No, no, please stay.' Ellie pushed him further into the kitchen. 'I'd like you to.'

'Is everything okay?' Benjamin glanced past her at the cellar door.

'Yes, well, I think so.' She told him about the two men who had shown up unexpectedly, keeping her voice low. 'I'm sure everything's fine, but Ash isn't home yet, and I would rather not be alone with them in the house.' Although there were two of them and only one of Benjamin, she would feel safer with him here.

'Of course I will stay.' His brow creased. 'I'll give you my number then if you're ever in this situation again, call me and I will come over. I'm an accountant and work from home, so I'm often there.'

'Thank you.' Ellie glanced at her wine glass. Although her

heartbeat had steadied, the whole incident with Barry and his friend still had her nerves on edge. 'Would you like a drink? I have some wine open, or I can put the kettle on if you prefer tea.'

'Tea would be nice, thank you.'

Benjamin put the bag of cuttings down on the kitchen table and pulled up a chair as Ellie filled the kettle. While she waited for it to boil, she grabbed her glass and took a sip of her wine. It had warmed in the early evening heat, but still soothed her raw nerves.

'I'm not a big drinker,' Benjamin told her conversationally. 'Occasionally with dinner or for a special occasion.'

'I should probably cut back a bit.' When he raised a brow, Ellie hurriedly added, 'I don't get drunk, but Ash and I have been having a drink most nights since we moved in.'

She made the tea, topped up her wine glass, then moved to sit at the table with him.

'I actually stopped by to see you earlier.'

'You did?'

A loud bang came from the cellar and they both looked towards the door. Moments later, Barry's voice followed. 'Sorry. Just knocked it against the wall.'

He backed into the kitchen, face red with exertion, and sweat beading on his forehead, as he hugged onto the washing machine. His friend was on the other side and didn't appear to be lifting his fair share of the weight. They dumped it on the floor and Ellie winced at the impact, grateful that the kitchen was still in a mess, and in need of new tiles.

'It's heavy,' Barry muttered to her, before staring at Benjamin, who sat sipping his tea.

'It is,' his friend agreed.

'I'm surprised you noticed, Kelvin. I might as well have carried it up myself.'

'You know I have a bad back.'

'Yes, you remind me, every time we have to lift stuff.'

The friend, Kelvin, gave a guilty smile, but didn't dispute the point. 'I'll go grab the mantle,' he told Barry, disappearing back down the stairs.

It took another ten minutes of faffing, but eventually Ellie closed the door on them, relieved they were finally gone, but also chiding herself for over-reacting to the whole situation.

She had pocketed seventy quid though, which all helped.

'You said you stopped by earlier,' Benjamin reminded her as she returned to the kitchen. He had obviously been thinking about it.

'Yes, I guess it would have been around three thirty. I did knock, but I assumed you were out as your car wasn't in the drive.'

'That's because I keep it in the garage. No, I was home all day. I've been in the garden, though, this afternoon, so I guess I never heard the door. I'm surprised Virginia didn't answer. Maybe she was asleep. She sometimes takes a nap in the afternoon.'

Going by Ellie's previous encounter with her then what Christine Jameson had said, it didn't surprise her that Virginia hadn't answered. 'It really doesn't matter. I had just stopped by to invite you and your sister over for dinner on Sunday evening if you're free.'

Benjamin's face instantly brightened. 'Really? That's so kind of you, Ellie. Thank you. We would love to come.'

'Excellent. Is there anything either of you don't eat? I was thinking I'd roast a pork joint.'

'No, no, pork is great. We both eat anything. Roast pork is actually one of my favourites.'

He seemed absolutely thrilled at her invitation and Ellie was pleased she had asked him. As she waved goodbye to him twenty minutes later, he thanked her again.

'I'm really looking forward to it,' he told her.

'It will be nice,' Ellie agreed, closing the door behind him. This time she made a point of locking it. Although the Barry and Kelvin situation had turned out to be nothing, it had highlighted to her the isolation of the house. And while that had initially been a selling point for her, as she loved the idea of her and Ash having their own space and privacy, now she was aware that, during the days while Ash was at work, if anything unsettling happened, she would be all on her own.

11

Benjamin was pleased he had taken the cuttings round to Ellie. He didn't want to make a habit of dropping in unannounced, but she had been so taken with his garden, he had been eager to share his plants with her. He hadn't expected his visit to result in a dinner invitation and he mused over this as he walked back up the driveway to his house.

On the one hand he was thrilled he had been asked, but Virginia posed a problem. Although he had hinted to Ellie that there were issues, she didn't know the full story or understand quite how difficult the whole situation with his sister was. And it was family business.

Their mother had raised them not to air their dirty laundry in public. Ellie simply couldn't find out the truth. It would bring shame on the family and Benjamin would be mortified.

He unlocked the front door and let himself inside. The place was so silent that for a moment he thought he was alone. But the slight creak of a floorboard towards the back of the house suggested otherwise.

'Virginia? Are you here?'

There was no answer, but that didn't surprise him. Maybe

she was in the conservatory. He knew she liked to lose herself in her art. He guessed it was her escape. Given her state, she couldn't go out in public, and painting offered her sanctuary.

As he wandered towards the conservatory, though, he realised he was right, could see the canvas on her easel. It had been blank earlier, but now it was a mess of pinks and reds, the quality worthy of a young child.

Of course, he would never tell her that.

'That's a pretty picture,' he said instead. 'My new camellia.'

It wasn't a question, but Virginia wouldn't have responded anyway. She seldom did.

And Benjamin was being kind, as in truth the painting didn't resemble flowers.

He sat down in one of the wicker chairs and heaved out a sigh as he studied the canvas. 'Ellie has invited us to dinner on Sunday night. I honestly don't know what to do. I told her yes, that we would be there, but we both know that's not going to be possible.'

The silence, being treated as if he wasn't even there, was starting to get to him. He had tried so hard to make things right for his sister, but she just wouldn't cut him any slack, constantly taunting him as she flitted about the house, pointedly letting him know that she was trapped there with him and that she wasn't happy with the situation, though stubbornly refusing to discuss it in a calm and rational manner. There was nothing he could do to change things for her. Her condition made it impossible. If he could give her what she wanted, he would do so in a heartbeat. But this, this limbo for want of a better word, it was unbearable. Having her there with him, but being constantly ignored, it was making him so lonely.

That was why he clung desperately to the hope of a making a new friendship. If Virginia would no longer talk to him, he needed to form new alliances. Anything to break up the monotony.

'Please, Virginia. How long are you going to keep this up?' His voice cracked, a tear escaping down his cheek, and he lifted his glasses, wiped it away. 'Are you going to hate me forever?'

He thought about the institution. She had been a frequent visitor there for much of her life. Sometimes for short spells, other times for much longer. She would cry and scream when it was time to go there, but the family had been given little choice. When she lost control she became a danger to others, as well as herself.

If only he could send her there this time. Unfortunately, though, it was no longer an option.

And that was a worry.

At the moment she was behaving herself. Well... behaving herself as well as Virginia ever could. Her tantrums targeting just Benjamin. And while that was awful, he could just about handle it.

But if things changed, and he was terrified they might, then he really didn't know quite what he would do.

Because when Virginia was really bad, God help anyone who got in her way.

12

Ash arrived home later than he had promised, and Ellie was cursing his name when she eventually heard his key in the lock then the front door open. It closed again, though he didn't immediately come to find her, and she was irritated enough by his lateness that she wouldn't go to him. Instead, she sipped at her second glass of wine, savouring the pleasant buzz it gave her, while putting the pan of mussels back on the heat.

A couple of minutes later she heard his footsteps, squealing in surprise as he came up behind her and caught her in a hug.

'Something smells good,' he told her, mouth close to her ear. A delicious shiver going through her when he gave her lobe a playful nip with his teeth.

'It was ready an hour ago,' she grumbled, easing herself out of his embrace. As nice as it might feel, he didn't get off that lightly.

'Yeah, sorry about that. Things took a little longer than I was expecting.'

'You said twenty minutes.'

'I did, and I really am sorry. Will you forgive me if I tell you I brought you a present.'

'Maybe. It depends. What kind of present?' Ellie picked up her glass, gulped down the rest of the wine.

'Are you drunk, Ellie Summers?'

'I may have had a couple of glasses of wine while I've been waiting for you.' She raised her chin defensively. 'If you had been home when you said you would...'

'I know, I already apologised twice.'

'If Barry and Kelvin hadn't been genuine–'

'Who?'

'You weren't here. It's a good job Benjamin showed up when he did.'

'Whoa, hold on. Backtrack. Who are Barry and Kelvin?'

Realising the wine had made her tongue loose and she had said too much, Ellie pulled a face, shrugging her shoulders at him.

Ash's eyes narrowed. 'Did you let those guys in to get the washing machine?'

'We would have lost the sale if–'

'Damn it, Ellie. I told you not to let them in the house.'

'You weren't here, and they were really persistent. Benjamin showed up and he stayed until they had gone.'

'New neighbour Benjamin?'

'Do you know any other Benjamins in Corpusty?'

Exasperated, Ash raked his hands back through his already messy hair. 'No, I don't, but that's not the point.'

Ellie shrugged again, this time chancing a smile. 'At least we don't have to lug it up the stairs now.'

He didn't have an answer for that, and, as he stood there looking so adorably frustrated with her, she couldn't help but start laughing.

'You're not funny,' he grumbled, but she could tell he was beginning to thaw, the heat in those amber eyes of his starting to cool. The corners of his generous mouth twitching and threatening to betray him.

A noise came from the other side of the house. Scratching followed by what sounded like a yelp.

Ellie's laughter stopped, her eyes widening. 'What was that?'

'What was what?'

'I heard a noise. Ash, I think someone's in the house.'

'I never heard anything. Maybe you imagined it.'

'No, I definitely heard something. It sounded like...' She trailed off, studied him, the telltale giveaway when he rubbed his hand across the back of his neck, refusing to meet her gaze. 'What are you up to?'

'Nothing.'

'Ashton!'

Now he looked at her, amusement lighting up his eyes, and he held out his hand. 'Come on, I think it's time to give you your present.'

Ellie had assumed he had bought her flowers or a bottle of gin. A sorry gift for being late. Now she was a little wary. Still, she took his hand, let him drag her out of the kitchen and across the hallway to the small second living room that Ash was planning on using as an office.

'Close your eyes.'

'What? Why?'

'Just do it, okay. Trust me.'

'Hmm, I don't know about that.' Ellie gave him a measured look, though did as requested. As the door creaked open, she heard a whine followed by a bark, and she immediately opened them again.

What the hell?

Sat on a blanket on the sofa, was the dog she had hit. The stitches where her front leg had been, still looked raw, and she was on the skinny side, but she was alive and seemed pleased to see Ellie, looking up at her with beseeching brown eyes, her golden tail thumping.

A wave of different emotions hit all at once. Guilt at what had happened, relief that the dog was okay, but confusion at why she was here. Combined with the wine, it was all a little too much and Ellie burst into tears, going to the little dog, and crouching down, wrapping her arms around her, and burying her face in her soft fur.

'Oh, baby. I'm so sorry for what happened.'

The dog whined again, but her tail still thumped as she attempted to shift position so she could lick at Ellie's face.

'You okay?'

Ellie glanced at Ash, still not understanding. 'What is she doing here? Did Trevor let you bring her to see me?'

'She's ours, Ellie.'

'What?'

'Her owner didn't want her, and she was going to be put in a rescue shelter. I figured we could adopt her.'

Ellie sniffed, swiping at her wet cheeks as his words sunk in. 'That was a pretty big decision to make by yourself, Ash.'

'You don't want her?'

'I never said that. I just think it's something you should have run past me first. A dog is a big commitment.'

'I'm aware of that. I grew up with dogs.' He sounded a little irritated and Ellie wondered if she was making too big a deal about it. 'I wanted to surprise you though. You felt so shitty about the whole situation. We can give her a good home.'

'We can.' Ellie got up, went to him, looping her arms around his neck. He had done it with the best of intentions, wanting to make her happy. 'I love that you want to give her a home and I know you wanted to surprise me. I'm touched, I really am. You know that. You just saw me blub all over her. But going forward, we're a team, and we decide things together, okay?'

'Okay.' Ash's golden eyes blazed in challenge. 'But we're still keeping her.'

'Yes, I want that too.' Ellie rose on tiptoe, pressing her forehead against Ash's, hugging him closer. 'And thank you.'

Behind them, the dog whined, barking as they parted slightly, both turning to face her.

'Okay, She-Ra.'

'There is one other thing.'

Ellie looked at Ash again. 'There is?'

'We're changing her name.'

'We are? But isn't she used to the one she's been given?'

'She's young and Trevor says she'll soon adjust. Besides, I am not introducing her to people as bloody She-Ra.'

Ellie moved to the sofa to sit beside their new addition, who immediately snuggled up to her. 'What's your name, little one?'

'Ruby?'

'No, she doesn't look like a Ruby.'

'Mia?'

'No, she's not a Mia either.'

'Cookie?'

Ellie studied the dog, dismissing it. 'That's not right for her.'

'Okay, well, do you want to help me out here, Ellie, because you're saying no to everything I suggest, but you're not coming up with anything yourself.'

'Don't pressure me. I'm thinking.'

'Well, don't take all night about it,' Ash grumbled, as he sat himself on the floor by the sofa, reaching up to tickle under the dog's chin. 'Our little pop needs a name.'

'Pop?'

'Princess of power.'

Ellie was quiet for a moment as she considered what he had just said. 'That's it. That's her name.'

'Princess? Sorry, Ellie, but no fucking way. She's not having a pink collar either.'

'No, not Princess. Poppy. That's who she is.'

Ash studied the dog, didn't seem appalled by the idea.

'It suits her,' Ellie pushed. 'In fact it's perfect for her. And I like that the first three letters stand for Princess of Power.'

'Poppy.' Ash tried out the name. He nodded. 'Okay, I can go with that. I'll speak to Trevor tomorrow and get them to change the name on her paperwork. She still needs to go back for regular check-ups, but he said she'll soon adjust to walking on three legs.'

'We need to get her some stuff.'

'I already picked her up some food and a couple of bowls, and Trevor lent me a harness we can use for now. We can go get her whatever else she needs over the weekend.'

'She's probably hungry, aren't you, Poppy? Do you want something to eat?' Ellie smoothed her hand over the dog's silky ear, then she suddenly remembered that she'd left her own dinner unattended on the stove. 'Shit, the mussels.'

She jumped up, rushing through to the kitchen, relieved to find the food was salvageable.

As she was taking the mussels off the heat, Ash wandered through with the bits he had bought, Poppy limping behind him, and Ellie ignored the stab of guilt. They had given the dog a home and they would love her, make sure she had a good life. Once she got used to walking on three legs, she would be fine.

Ellie busied herself dishing up the food, while Ash fixed Poppy's dinner, neither of them spotting the puppy disappearing.

'Poppy?' Ash set the food dish down on the floor, filled the second one with water. He glanced around for the dog. 'Poppy? Ellie, did you see where she went?'

'No, I...' Ellie trailed off, spotting the open cellar door at the far end of the kitchen. 'Ash?'

He was already heading towards it, Ellie hot on his heels, when Poppy barked.

They found her sitting just inside the doorway at the top of the stairs. She paused her racket for long enough to look at Ellie and Ash, then let out a whine followed by another barking fit.

What the hell was up with her? And how had she even managed to get through the door?

It had been closed. Ellie was sure of it.

'Poppy?'

When the dog refused to listen to Ash, he scooped her up, carrying her back into the kitchen and closing the door behind him. She wasn't happy though, continuing to sit there after he had shut it.

'You need to keep that door shut until she's used to walking on three legs,' he told Ellie, managing to finally distract Poppy with her food bowl. 'Those stairs are steep. If she fell, she would hurt herself, or worse.'

'The door was shut.'

When Ash raised his eyebrows, clearly disbelieving her, Ellie questioned herself. It had definitely been shut, hadn't it? She remembered closing it after Barry and Kelvin left and she'd had no reason to open it since. 'I'm not lying, Ash.'

'I never said you were lying, but how did it get open?'

Ellie stared past him at the door. The way it clicked shut when it was closed meant there was no way it could spring open by itself. Someone or something had opened it, and that was unnerving.

13

Benjamin couldn't remember the last time he had been invited to dinner. Of course, there had been the occasional work thing over the years, and when he was younger there had been the odd romantic meal out. But he hadn't dated in years: most women had not accepted his situation with Virginia, and that was before things had taken a turn for the worse.

He understood their reluctance, even though he didn't like it, knew that being sole carer for his volatile sister had made him a less than desirable partner. Gradually he had come to realise that going out actively looking for love just wasn't worth the hassle or the disappointment. Virginia needed him and he couldn't abandon her. After their mother had died, his sister had become his responsibility and his burden to bear.

He hadn't completely given up on the idea of love though, still holding onto the idea that the right woman would show up eventually and that he could make it work.

As he made his way down the driveways between the two houses, Benjamin considered, not for the first time, that if Ellie wasn't with Ash, maybe there would be a chance for him. She was so soft and pretty with her expressive sea-green eyes and warm smile, and Benjamin was certain that on more than one occasion, there had been a spark between them. He had felt it and she must have too. Ellie was more in tune with her emotions than other women he had known, and empathetic as well. She had a gentle soul, was more likely to be understanding about the Virginia situation.

It was all irrelevant though. Ellie was with Ash, and their relationship was clearly serious, as they had bought a house together.

Benjamin would have to settle for her friendship, even if he did secretly wish for more.

He had debated over what to wear. The work dinners he attended were usually stuffy formal affairs, and he knew that dinner at Ellie's house would definitely be more casual. Still, he didn't want to get it wrong and turn up underdressed, so he had eventually settled on a pair of light-brown chinos and a casual short-sleeved shirt, taking his time ironing both to make sure they were crease free.

Virginia had made her disapproval known; her bedroom door slamming shut shortly before he left. Benjamin had flinched, almost dropping the bottle of wine he was getting out of the fridge to take for his hosts.

Not being much of a drinker, he wouldn't normally take wine, but flowers seemed inappropriate in case they gave Ash the wrong impression, and he knew Ellie liked the bottle he had picked. He had seen her drinking it on Friday evening when he had taken her the cuttings, and he had gone out to buy it specially.

Now as he approached the house, he was nervous. There was a lovely breeze that had picked up, but it was still a warm evening and sweat was beading on his back and under his armpits.

Ash hadn't been overly friendly towards him when they had

previously met, and Benjamin hoped things wouldn't be uncomfortable with him tonight. He would have preferred it if it had just been him and Ellie, but, of course, that wasn't going to happen. Then there was Virginia. He hadn't told Ellie that his sister wouldn't be joining them, as he couldn't quite come up with a suitable excuse, and he was feeling guilty about that, knowing that the table would be prepared for four, that she would have cooked more food than required.

He had decided it was easiest to tell Ellie and Ash that Virginia had thrown a tantrum. Not exactly a stretch of the truth. It would explain her late cancellation.

Benjamin had considered pulling out of the dinner altogether. It would certainly be easier. But damn it, he wanted this. He wanted that friendship with Ellie and the opportunity to pretend his life was normal, even for just a little while.

As he knocked on the door, he was reminded as always of Louise and Naomi. They had never invited him for dinner, but the three of them had struck up an easy friendship.

With John working away a lot, Louise had sometimes called him in if there was a problem. Used to living in an old countryside house, Benjamin knew about faulty pipes and leaking roofs and he was usually able to patch things up until they could be properly fixed. In return, Louise had sometimes invited him to stay for coffee.

Now, five years on, he still found it hard to comprehend what had happened and he struggled, knowing that they were no longer here.

Caught up in his thoughts, he jumped when the door opened, relieved to be greeted by Ellie and not Ash.

She had on a long, vivid blue dress. It was casual, but elegant, her blonde hair loose and falling in waves over her shoulders. Benjamin relaxed, knowing that his shirt and chinos didn't look out of place.

'Hi, Benjamin, come on in.'

Ellie peered past him, looking for Virginia.

He coughed, a little embarrassed. 'I'm so sorry to let you down this late in the day. Virginia, she– she was being difficult.'

'It's okay. I understand.'

Was it his imagination or did Ellie look a little disappointed? That wasn't good. He didn't want to disappoint her. 'I really am sorry. I know you've cooked food and gone to trouble. I should have called and let you know sooner.'

'Honestly, it's no bother. Come on in.'

Benjamin followed her through to the kitchen, the waft of roasting pork, stuffing and apple sauce reminding him he hadn't eaten since breakfast. He wasn't a bad cook. Not a natural talent, but years of practice meant he could get by. This though... this smelt amazing.

'She gets into these tantrums sometimes and when she does there is no reasoning with her. It's all so... frustrating and, well, I guess I should have never agreed she would come. I'm sorry. I really do feel bad about messing you around.'

'Stop apologising. Is Virginia okay home alone when she is like this? She won't harm herself, will she?' Ellie's wide eyes were full of concern and Benjamin's heart squeezed. She really did have so much compassion, caring more about Virginia than her ruined dinner.

'She's fine,' he assured her. 'I gave her something, a sedative, to help her relax. She will be too sleepy to do anything to hurt herself, or the house.' He let out a little laugh at his own pathetic joke when Ellie's brows raised, adding, 'We've just had a couple of broken plates this week. Nothing too terrible.'

'Has she eaten? She will probably be hungry when she wakes. I can plate her up some dinner for you to take back. You can heat it up for her later.'

'That's very kind, but I really don't want to put you to any more trouble.'

'It's fine. We have plenty.'

There was nothing accusing in her tone, but still Benjamin kicked himself. He should have let her know sooner. 'I brought this,' he told her, showing her the wine. Although it hadn't long been out of the fridge, the bottle was already warming up.

'Oh, thank you. I like this one.'

He smiled at that, but said nothing, glad that he had pleased her. As he handed it to her, he spotted a nasty bruise on her arm and couldn't help but gawp. It was on her forearm, big and ugly, the black centre tinged with yellow.

Ellie noticed him staring and her cheeks turned pink with embarrassment.

'That looks nasty.'

She smiled, but it appeared forced. 'Oh this? It's nothing. I bruise like a peach.'

Was it really that innocent? Benjamin couldn't help but think back to Naomi and the bruises he had seen on her. He was being foolish. This was a different situation and Ellie was a grown woman, not a vulnerable teenager. History was not repeating itself.

Still, it unnerved him. Had Ash done that to her?

'Did you want a glass of wine?' Ellie's voice broke through his thoughts. 'We have red and white already open. Or a beer perhaps?' she asked, as she put the bottle he'd brought into the fridge.

'No, no alcohol for me, thank you. A glass of water will be fine.' It wasn't that he was completely averse to drinking, but tonight was new territory for him and he didn't want to mess anything up. It was better he kept a clear head, especially around Ash. Benjamin was unsure about him.

'If you want non-alcoholic, we have some apple juice or Coke.'

'Okay, apple juice then, please.'

He glanced around the homely kitchen while she poured his drink. Although it needed work and Ellie had told him they were planning a full refit, she had still made it look nice, the kettle and microwave matching her tea towels and potted plants on the windowsill.

'Where is Ash? Is he about?' he asked, hoping she would say no and disappointed when she nodded.

'He's in the garden with our newest member of the family.'

'Oh?' Benjamin's heartbeat quickened, for a moment wondering what she meant. Had they adopted a child?

But then she nodded towards the bowls on the floor, and then he understood.

'You've bought a dog.'

'Well, not bought exactly. And not just any dog.' Her eyes were shining. Against the dress, they looked more blue than green, and it actually took his breath away how pretty she was. Not that he hadn't already realised it. But before she had always been dressed in scruffier clothes. Her decorating clothes, he guessed. And her hair had been tied back, her face make-up free. Not that she was wearing much now.

Benjamin didn't know much about women's cosmetics, but her lips were pinker and looked glossier, her lashes longer too, he thought. And whatever scent she wore was intoxicating. A light peachy fragrance that toyed with his senses.

'Well, aren't you going to ask which dog?'

He had never seen her this way before and when she spoke, it threw him for a moment, made him feel foolish that he hadn't been paying attention.

'It's the dog I brought to the vet,' she told him when he stared at her gormlessly. 'The one I hit.' She winced a little bit when she said that, and Benjamin realised just how raw the incident still was, and how deeply it had affected her.

'You've adopted her? That's wonderful, Ellie.'

'Well, it was Ash who arranged it.'

He listened as she told him about the surprise and all he could think about was that John Tanner used to arrange surprises for Louise and Naomi, that he would use them as a bartering tool to win his way back in after a fight.

Ellie had a nasty bruise on her arm and Ash had surprised her with the dog. Was it really a coincidence?

The thought stayed with him when Ash joined them, the three-legged puppy hopping along behind him. Ellie was besotted with the dog, Poppy they had called her, and it was clear Ash was besotted with Ellie. But was it obsessive?

If Benjamin was right and he was hurting her, he wouldn't be the kind of man who would let her leave. Or perhaps he had it wrong. He was paranoid after the Tanners and maybe that had him looking to find fault where there was none.

Still, he was wary of Ash.

'So Ellie says you're an accountant,' Ash was asking him now, as he poured more wine into his own glass. He had offered some to Benjamin, but alcohol really wasn't a good idea and he had declined.

He sipped at his apple juice as Ash studied him across the table, asking questions about his job, getting the impression the man was equally as suspicious of him.

Which was silly of course. Benjamin was completely harmless.

Why would Ash possibly view him as any kind of threat? It was ridiculous.

'Yes, not the most exciting profession, I know. But the work is regular and now I'm self-employed I can set my own hours.'

'You work from home then?'

'I do.'

On the floor beside Ash, Poppy whined, hinting for food. The dog had glued herself to his leg, seeming to have chosen him as her human. Benjamin felt sorry for Ellie, knew she deserved to be the one who bonded with the dog.

Life could be unfair sometimes.

The questions continued through dinner, about his work and his interests, and then about Virginia. Ash was very upfront in his approach, while Ellie was seemingly oblivious, taking it that the pair of them were getting along, but Benjamin could sense Ash's hostility. He knew Ellie's boyfriend had probably only gone along with this dinner because Ellie had insisted. Or maybe because he had seen him as competition and wanted to check him out.

The idea of that made him feel a little bit sick.

He had looked forward to this dinner, to the opportunity to get out of the house and the prospect of new friendships, but it wasn't as enjoyable as he had hoped.

Ellie had been wonderful, but then, Benjamin had always known that would be the case.

Ash, though, was the one who played on his mind as he later made his way back up the drive, the cling-filmed plate of pork, veg and trimmings in his hand.

A tragedy had unfolded with the Tanner family and Benjamin held himself responsible, because he hadn't acted soon enough. If the same thing happened to Ellie, he wasn't sure he would ever be able to forgive himself.

As he let himself back into the house, he was grateful that he had left the bedroom windows open. The through-breeze should make it easier to sleep.

Virginia wasn't around and for that he was grateful too.

He went to the kitchen, placed the plate of food in the fridge then pulled up one of the kitchen chairs and sat down, his mind turning over as he pondered his dilemma.

Minutes ticked by before he heard the creak of the floorboard behind him. Realised she was there. He kept his back turned, even when acknowledging her.

'It's happening again. I'm scared he is going to hurt her, and I don't know how to help. Last time I tried to intervene... well, you know how that worked out. I can't stand by and watch it happen again, but I don't know what to do, Virginia.'

He could feel her watching him, her eyes burning into the back of his head, but she didn't say anything.

'Ellie is a good person and I like her a lot. If he does anything to her... I can't let him. I simply can't bear the thought.'

The dilemma was still playing on his mind as later, he climbed into bed, rested his head on the pillow. He would monitor the situation, try to keep tabs on Ellie and make sure she was okay. There was a way forward. He understood that now, and if he felt her life was truly in danger, he knew exactly what he had to do.

14

Ash had taken the week off to help Ellie with the renovation and the pair of them worked hard on the house, clearing, stripping, plastering, and painting, while taking a little time out for long walks, pub lunches, and getting to know Poppy.

She was still adapting to being on three legs, so they took it slow with her, leaving her home when they went out, but making sure they were giving her plenty of time in the garden.

By the end of the week, they had managed to finish work on the master bedroom and Ellie's studio. Ash had mostly fitted the new suite in the main bathroom. For the first time since they had moved in, Ellie knew they were making headway and it was starting to feel like a home. There was still a long way to go, but they had made a dent in the work, and she was happily content, able to clearly see the future with the man she loved and the dog she was already smitten with.

She was also worrying less about the history of the house. Although she hadn't said anything more to Ash, it had continued to bother her, knowing that a murder had taken place there, and the search history on her phone was filled with news articles about the Tanner family and their tragic circumstances. She was a fool really, should have let sleeping dogs lie, but her curious nature (Ash called her nosy) meant she couldn't stop herself.

And Poppy hadn't helped. Her initial obsession with the cellar freaking Ellie out a little. The puppy had been desperate to get in there, and despite Ash and Ellie keeping the door closed, she sat whining and barking by the door for the first couple of days.

Ash thought nothing of it, but Ellie's over-active imagination hadn't been so sure. As they worked on modernising the house, though, putting their own stamp on it, she understood he was right. That this was their home now and nothing from the past could change that. There was nothing sinister here.

It was Saturday morning when that belief was firmly shaken, pushing Ellie right back to square one.

Ash had gone to the tip and Ellie was painting the coving in one of the front bedrooms, her position on the stepladder giving her an elevated view of the country lane the house was set back from.

It was such a peaceful location, a mile out of the village, with just the Thornes for neighbours and an uninterrupted view of fields beyond the lane. Radio X was keeping her company, playing a medley of indie tunes from the nineties that were bringing back childhood memories and giving her all the feels as she sang along, while Poppy snoozed contentedly in the strip of sunlight blazing through the open window.

The car caught Ellie's attention first. There wasn't much traffic on the lane and nothing worth slowing for unless it was someone going to either of the houses. Ellie wasn't expecting anyone, and Benjamin seldom had visitors, so when the car crawled at a snail's pace past her driveway, her curiosity was piqued.

Who was going to see him?

Like her, he had no family, apart from Virginia, and she had learnt that while he had plenty of acquaintances around the village (it seemed everyone knew him and he was highly regarded) he didn't really have any actual friends.

She found that a little sad. He was such a nice person, so down to earth and welcoming, and she was glad that they had struck up a friendship of sorts. He had seemed so flattered that she had invited him to a simple dinner, and it was a nice feeling, knowing that she probably helped make his day.

Maybe it was someone to see Virginia. Benjamin still hadn't elaborated what was exactly wrong with her and Ellie hadn't yet pried. Although she was dying to know more about the girl, she figured he would tell her in his own time.

When the car reappeared moments later, slowly reversing into the entrance of the field opposite, blocking the gate, Ellie's mild curiosity turned to full-blown intrigue, then when the male driver got out of the vehicle and stared down the driveway at the house, intrigue turned to mild concern.

There was no reason for anyone to stop by. Unless it was to do with Ash. Had something happened? A car accident, maybe? He had been gone a while, but Ellie hadn't been unduly concerned, knowing that, as it was the weekend, the tip was probably busy.

She set down her paintbrush, grabbing her phone, shocked when she saw he had been gone far longer than she realised. Almost two hours. Even if the place was rammed, it should have only taken him forty minutes, an hour, tops. She called his number, her heart fluttering madly in her chest when it went to voicemail, and for a moment she thought she might be sick.

If something had happened to him...

No, you mustn't think like that. You're over-reacting. Ash is fine and the car has nothing to do with him.

She was over-reacting. If something had happened to Ash, surely it would be a marked car, not a red saloon. And why hadn't the man parked in the driveway? It was plenty big enough.

He hadn't even approached the house. Simply stood there in the road staring. And it was starting to unnerve her.

Had Ash locked the door when he'd left? Ellie couldn't remember, but knew they had both been a little lax with security since moving out into the countryside.

She climbed down from the ladder. It wouldn't hurt to check.

Poppy opened one eye, raised her head slightly, but stayed where she was, her sunny spot too appealing to leave, as Ellie hurried from the room and downstairs. She went straight to the front door, relieved when she found it locked.

She checked the door into the garden as a matter of course, was glad she had when she found it ajar. She pulled it shut and bolted it, was heading back down the hallway to the stairs, when she saw a flash of black pass the front living-room window, and she froze.

It was him, the man. He was in the driveway, though hadn't yet approached the front door.

Who the hell was he and what did he want?

She crept into the living room, kept her back close to the wall until she reached the window, then peered cautiously round the curtain, her mouth dropping open as he half turned, taking off his sunglasses, and she caught a full-on view of his face.

John Tanner. She had googled enough pictures of him to be sure, immediately recognising his salt-and-pepper wavy hair and close-set eyes.

Why was he back here and what did he want?

A small part of her was tempted to storm outside and ask

him that, find out why he was trespassing and sneaking around the property, but she didn't, aware that the only reason he wasn't serving time for his wife's murder and daughter's disappearance was because the evidence hadn't been strong enough to convict him.

Instead, she watched him like a coward from behind the curtain, her heartbeat quickening when he disappeared from view, wishing to hell Ash would hurry up and get home.

After a couple of minutes he reappeared, looked like he was about to approach the front door, then seemed to change his mind, heading back onto the road and towards his car.

Ellie remained rooted to the spot, didn't step away from her hiding place until she felt sure the coast was clear. Dashing upstairs, she went to the bedroom window to see if he was still there and was relieved that his car had gone.

When Ash returned fifteen minutes later her worry had bubbled over into anger.

'Where the hell have you been? I tried to call you!'

'Did you? My phone was in the car and I never thought to check it before I left the tip.'

'You've been gone for two hours!'

'Yeah, sorry about that. I ran into a mate from the office, and we were chatting.'

He was so bloody laid-back about the whole thing, as though it was no big deal, and it only served to wind Ellie up further.

'I was worried about you, Ash. I thought something had happened.' Her voice had grown louder, her tone higher in pitch, and he looked at her then, hazel eyes wide.

'I'm fine. You're over-reacting just a little bit, don't you think?'

'NO! I don't think I am.'

He stared at her, seeming to finally register that she was really upset, and she could see him assessing the situation, trying to decide whether he should get out of her way or try to calm her down.

'Okay, I was gone longer than expected,' he said eventually. 'I should have let you know I had bumped into Martin and I was running late. I'm sorry. But is this really just about me being late back from the tip or is something else going on?'

'John Tanner was here!'

'Who?'

'John Tanner. The guy who used to live here. The one who murdered his wife, probably killed his daughter too. He was here, Ash. At our house.'

'You spoke to him?'

'No, I didn't open the door. Not that he knocked. He didn't even pull into the driveway. He parked out on the road and stood staring at the house.'

Ash looked at her as if she was crazy. 'Are you sure about that?'

'Are you seriously doubting me?' Ellie had raised her voice again, though she didn't care. 'I saw him with my own eyes.'

'But you have no idea what he wanted?'

'Of course I don't.'

Ash was silent for a moment and she could tell he was weighing up what she had told him. 'Look, I know you've been a bit freaked out since you found out about the murder, but are you sure it was really him?'

Seriously? He was still doubting her? 'I'm sure,' Ellie confirmed, her tone icy.

'He hasn't lived here in five years, though, and you don't even know him. Why are you so certain?'

'Because I've googled him, okay. I've seen enough damn pictures of the man to know he was standing outside our house a short while ago.'

Ash shoved his hand through his hair, let out a sigh. He

looked frustrated, annoyed even. 'I thought you had moved past this?'

Yes, she pretty much had, but that was irrelevant now, given that John Tanner had been trespassing on their property. 'No, you told me to move past this. I didn't exactly have a choice.'

'Well, you aren't going to move past it if you keep googling the guy. Jesus, Ellie!' Ash's voice was raised now, his tone heated.

'I googled him because I deserve to know what had happened here. It's not fair expecting me to live in a house and not know the full facts about what happened.'

'But why? How does knowing what happened help you? Does it make you sleep any easier at night? No. It's making you paranoid. For fuck's sake, Ellie. You're not going to get over this unless you leave it in the past where it belongs.'

'I'm not paranoid.'

'You could have fooled me.'

Frustration burned at Ellie's gut. 'So you don't believe me then?'

'Please, just listen to yourself. You expect me to believe he was here, conveniently while I was out. That he came into the driveway and stood staring at the house, but he never knocked on the door? Can't you hear how crazy that sounds? Why on earth would he come back here? It makes no sense.'

'I need to get out of here. I'm going for a walk.'

'Ellie!'

When he reached for her, Ellie shoved his hand away. Angry tears burned at the back of her eyes. Why didn't he believe her? She yanked the door open, yelping in surprise as she walked headlong into Benjamin, who stood on the front step, almost knocking the box of apples he was carrying out of his arms.

'Hi, what are you doing here?'

'I– I was just... I hope this isn't a bad time.' He shoved his glasses up the bridge of his nose, a gesture Ellie was starting to recognise as a nervous one, shuffling his feet as he peered cautiously past her into the house.

He had heard her and Ash fighting, she was certain of it, and the idea of that, knowing that he could possibly have been standing on the doorstep listening, wound her coil just a little bit tighter. 'I'm sorry, Benjamin. I'm just on my way out.' She tried to keep her tone even, though it was a struggle. 'Ash is indoors, though, so go on in.'

'Oh...'

Ellie didn't wait for his response to that, marching past him and down the driveway to the road. Part of her wished she had brought her car keys, knowing it would have been easier to get away. She could have driven into Aylsham, grabbed a coffee somewhere and chilled herself out.

That wasn't an option, though, and she picked up her pace, keen to get away from both Ash and Benjamin, wanting her own space so she could think straight.

Luckily neither of them came after her and she spent an hour wandering around the outskirts of the village, following a little footpath that she had walked with Ash earlier in the week.

She had expected him to be supportive, certainly to take her word that she had seen John Tanner and share her concerns.

Before moving to Corpusty, she'd had a vision in her head that living in the countryside would feel safer. Certainly she hadn't envisioned hiding in the house from the former owner who had murdered his wife.

And Ash thought she was making it up.

As she walked and her head cleared, she recalled how she had jumped all over him when he had arrived home later than expected and realised that she had behaved exactly like one of those panicky suspicious women she had promised herself she would never be.

No, he hadn't believed her, but was that partly her own fault? She had behaved rather hysterically.

When she had calmed enough, she turned back home. She knew she owed Ash an apology, though she hoped he would also have one for her.

She didn't condone some of the things he had said. He was going to have to take her word for it that the man outside the house had been John Tanner. And Ash was going to have to deal with the fact it had taken her a little time to get used to living in a house where a murder had taken place. But equally, she should have been more rational and certainly shouldn't have stormed out on him.

As she turned into the lane that led down to the house, her stomach dropped, and her legs stopped working. There in a lay-by up ahead was the red saloon.

John Tanner's car.

What was he still doing there?

She glanced at the front window, but with the sun bouncing off of it, it was impossible to see if he was sitting inside.

Ellie realised she had a choice. She could turn and walk further out into the countryside, try and find a different though much longer route back to the house or she could walk past the car and hope he wasn't sitting inside.

The first option wasn't appealing, especially knowing she was just half a mile from home, and she cursed herself, wishing she hadn't left the house empty-handed. She didn't even have her phone with her, so couldn't call Ash.

Drawing in a deep breath, she slowly stepped forward, knew she would have to take a chance and walk past the car.

Was he waiting for her? She had hidden inside the house earlier, but he hadn't knocked.

Did he know who she was? That she lived in his house now?

And what exactly did he want?

It's probably completely innocent. You're over-reacting.

Still she kept her eyes on the car, relieved when she was near enough to avoid the reflection and could see that the car was empty.

Unless he was lying down on the seat.

Don't go there.

Ellie told herself again that she was over-reacting. Although she couldn't explain Tanner's reasons for visiting the house, there was nothing to suggest he had a sinister motive. And maybe he had just pulled over here for a break from driving and had gone to stretch his legs.

It was certainly a plausible explanation.

As she levelled with the car, her attention was drawn to the meadow beyond, and she spotted movement by an old oak tree.

It was him, his profile to her. Strong roman nose and pointed chin, his head bowed as he studied the ground. He was just standing there as if he was in a trance.

Ellie kept her movements slow, tried to make as little noise as possible, though kept her eyes on him as she passed the car.

Almost home. Not far to go.

She was about to look away, pick up her pace for the home stretch, when he glanced up and towards the car, locking eyes with her.

Ellie froze, barely daring to breathe.

And then she spotted something glinting in his hand.

Was it a knife?

She didn't wait to find out, running quickly toward the house.

15

Benjamin was unable to settle for the rest of the weekend.

The situation with Ellie was bothering him more than he cared to admit, and he had a horrible suspicion that things were worse between her and Ash than he had initially suspected.

He hadn't meant to eavesdrop on their argument. Well, eavesdrop wasn't quite the right word. He hadn't been able to make out what they were fighting about, but he had heard Ash's raised voice and when the door had opened it was obvious that Ellie was upset. Her pale skin was heated and she looked on the verge of tears.

She had been a little brusque with Benjamin, but he understood it was the heat of the moment and that she just wanted to, needed to, get away from Ash.

Unfortunately, she had left Benjamin in an awkward position, as Ash knew he was there, and he couldn't very well go home without dropping the apples off. Uncomfortable, he had poked his head inside the house, wilting when he received a scowl from Ash.

'I've been picking apples.'

'So I see.'

'We've had a bumper crop this year. Far too many for me to do anything with, so I thought you might be able to use some. They would be lovely in an apple pie or crumble.'

For a moment he didn't think he was going to get a response, but then Ash let out something that sounded suspiciously like an annoyed huff and reached out for the box. 'Thanks.'

'Is, um... is Ellie okay?' It was a bold question Benjamin had no place asking, especially as they both knew he had overheard Ellie and Ash fighting.

Ash's golden eyes heated and Benjamin was certain he was about to get a taste of the man's wrath, but instead, he nodded curtly. 'She's fine.'

And then Benjamin was being guided back towards the front door.

'Thanks for stopping by.'

To be honest, he was relieved. He had already decided he didn't particularly like Ash, finding him too abrupt and a little intimidating. What Ellie saw in the man he didn't know.

He had hurried back to the house, tried to lose himself for an hour or so doing some gardening, wondering if he should have gone to find Ellie, check if she was okay. She had left the house on foot and couldn't have wandered far.

She had wanted to be alone, though, that much was clear, and tracking her down might make Benjamin seem a little too interested. He wasn't a stalker and certainly didn't want to give Ellie the wrong idea about him.

So, instead, he pondered and fretted, not liking one bit that Ellie was trapped in that house with Ash.

Why on earth had she agreed to buy the place with him? Had he pressured her into it, maybe hidden his true colours, charming her until they moved in?

Benjamin had read about this kind of thing before. Toxic relationships they called it.

He spent some time on his phone googling the signs while he waited for dinner to cook, even more convinced of the bad situation Ellie was in, knowing that he had to help her.

The person being manipulated often doesn't realise it, excusing the behaviour, and often accepting the blame for things themselves.

Yes, that was it exactly.

Ellie was blinkered and couldn't quite see the trouble she was in, that Ash was very bad for her. It was history repeating itself. John and Naomi Tanner all over again. The only difference was that Naomi had feared her father. In this case, Ellie was being controlled by her boyfriend. A man she could go on to marry if someone didn't stop her, make her realise what a terrible mistake that would be.

Benjamin had failed Naomi. He wouldn't make the same mistake with Ellie.

Of course, he would have to be careful though. Whatever happened, Virginia could not find out under any circumstances that he was planning to help.

She had always been a jealous girl, and nothing had changed there. If anything she was now even more of a danger. Her reaction when he had tried to help Naomi still troubled him and he couldn't risk her trying to punish Ellie.

No, if Benjamin was going to help Ellie, Virginia could not find out.

16

With hindsight, Ellie wished she hadn't reacted so quickly in fleeing from John Tanner. She had been freaked out at the time, fearful he might come after her, but he hadn't. He had remained in the field simply staring at her as she passed by.

She should have slowed down just a bit, at least enough to take in the details. Some kind of evidence that she could use to prove to Ash that she wasn't making the man up.

Frustratingly she didn't have her phone, so hadn't been able to take a picture, but the red saloon was there, and she could have memorised the number plate.

They had both calmed down by the time she arrived back at the house, Ellie going straight to Ash, who had pulled her into a tight hug, as he whispered apologies into her ear.

It helped that they were both quick to temper, but also easy to forgive. No sulking, no holding on to grudges. In most cases once the fight was over, the subject of it was put behind them. On this occasion, though, Ellie got the impression that Ash still didn't believe her about John Tanner.

Yes, he was sorry they had argued, as was she, but even

though he made all the right noises, he was still doubting her, she was sure of it.

Calling him out would cause another fight, one she didn't have the energy for, and after a lovely week together, she didn't want to end things on a sour note, so she decided to stay quiet. It hurt though. He was the one person she needed to believe her.

Tanner hadn't returned and hopefully Ellie wouldn't see him again. She vowed to keep her phone on her, though, and to get evidence if he did show up.

They worked hard on the house over the weekend, delayed only when Pete and Roxanne paid an impromptu visit on Sunday afternoon. Pete was excited to meet Poppy, while Roxanne had wandered around like a building inspector, her totally inappropriate high heels clacking against the bare floors, her nose sneered up as she offered her unasked-for opinion on everything they had so far done.

Of course, she disliked the colour Ellie had painted her studio. Apparently the soft sage-green was too drab, and she should have gone for something more vibrant. And the withering look she gave the new bathroom suite didn't need any words to make it clear she didn't like it.

Ellie had made tea and took it outside then spent forty minutes humouring Roxanne, listening to everything they should have been doing to the house. Further down the garden Ash and Pete had a catch-up as they threw a ball for Poppy.

'Wouldn't you have been better off getting one with four legs?'

'What?' Ellie drew her attention away from the dog and had to stop her mouth dropping open.

'I know you feel guilty because you ran her over, but that's not really a reason to adopt her. She's never going to be able to run about like a proper dog.'

'Yes she will.'

'Really, because look at her hobbling around. She looks pathetic. It's cruel, Ellie. The vet should have put her down.'

'No, he shouldn't have.' Ellie struggled to keep the anger out of her tone, wondering yet again why she was still friends with Roxanne. They had nothing in common. 'Given that she only recently had the operation, she's doing brilliantly. And she's so sweet-natured. Ash and I love her to bits.'

'Do you really, though, or are you just saying that because you feel bad?'

'No. I'm saying it because it's true. She's the perfect fit for us and I'm glad we went for *one* with three legs.' Ellie scowled across the table at Roxanne before getting up and gathering their empty cups. 'Now if you're done insulting my dog I need to get back to the decorating.'

'There's no need to get snotty about it,' Roxanne called after her. 'Friends should be able to speak honestly.'

'Yes, honest, not insulting. They should be supportive too.'

Ellie had stepped inside the house, so didn't quite hear Roxanne's reply to that. No doubt it was something sarcastic, as she always had to have the last word.

When she glanced out of the window, she saw Roxanne had wandered down to talk to Pete and Ash, pointedly ignoring Poppy when she brought her ball to her.

Ellie left them to it, heading back upstairs to finish painting. She heard them in the house again a short while later and shouted down goodbye to Pete when he called up the stairs. She didn't tell Ash what Roxanne had said when he came up a few minutes later, Poppy on his heels. Her friend's words would hurt him as much as they had her. Instead, she used the excuse that she had wanted to get on.

How dare Roxanne say Poppy wasn't a proper dog and insinuate that Ellie had adopted her out of guilt?

~

When Ash returned to work on the Monday, she spent extra time bonding with their new addition and after a morning of labour, Poppy contentedly chewing one of the toys they had bought her, while Ellie did the finishing touches to her new studio, the pair of them took an extended lunchbreak in the garden.

The heatwave showed no sign of abating and Ellie had to encourage Poppy to drink from the water bowl she had brought outside. After playing ball for a while, they wandered down to a sunny spot at the end of the garden and flopped on the grass. Poppy panting away as she snuggled closer, resting her head on Ellie's stomach.

This was going to be the perfect place for lazy warm weekends with a blanket to lie on and a good book. And it was nice and secluded, too, surrounded by thick shrubbery. Maybe she might swap the book for Ash.

Ellie closed her eyes, stroking Poppy's soft fur, the sun heating her face as she daydreamed. She didn't mean to doze off, but when Poppy growled, shocking the hell out of her, she awoke with a start, taking a second to remember where she actually was.

Poppy was already up on her three legs, her growl having turned to barks, and Ellie leapt up as the puppy took off on a lopsided hop-run towards the house. Although the garden was enclosed, something was bothering her, and that in turn bothered Ellie.

It wouldn't be that difficult to open the side gate or climb over the fence, and although the front door was locked, the French doors that led into the garden were wide open.

As she caught up with Poppy who was now completely

agitated, managing to grab hold of her collar, Ellie caught a flash of something, or rather, someone, up ahead.

Realising whoever she had seen was inside the house, she froze, dread causing her stomach to drop.

Fuck!

Her first thoughts were that John Tanner had returned and honestly, that idea terrified her, but then the figure became clearer, and she realised it was Benjamin's sister, Virginia.

She was wearing the same dress she'd had on when Ellie had seen her before, her hair still knotted and tangled (did Benjamin ever comb it for her?) and the sun reflecting off her glasses.

What the hell was she up to?

Ellie knew that the girl was unwell and also that she was prone to fits of rage, but seriously, what was she doing wandering into the house uninvited? Benjamin couldn't realise she was here. Ellie knew he wouldn't have let her leave the house unaccompanied.

But then it crossed her mind. What if something had happened to Benjamin?

Was it possible that Virginia was looking for Ellie because she needed her help?

'Virginia?'

The girl had been eying Ellie warily, one eye on Poppy, but hearing her name seemed to spook her and before Ellie could react, she had charged out of the French doors and onto the patio, heading for the gate at the side of the house, her strides long and clumsy as her dress flapped about her ankles.

Ellie raced after her but wasn't quick enough to stop her before she had bolted through the gate and disappeared back towards the Thorne house.

That was obviously where she had made her entrance and

Ellie quickly pulled it shut again, conscious that she didn't want Poppy getting out.

Was there a reason why Virginia had come here?

Ellie was still a little worried about Benjamin. Maybe she should call him and check that he was okay. If he was then it was probably a good idea to let him know that Virginia had been inside the house.

Her phone was upstairs and as she made her way up to the studio, she again wondered what the deal was with Virginia. Maybe, after what had just happened, she deserved to find out.

She saw the word as soon as she entered the room. It was written in the dark plum paint they had bought to go in the bathroom, crudely slapped on the freshly decorated sage wall and dripping down onto the floor.

LEAVE

Virginia had done this. She had broken into and vandalised their home. A whole host of emotions raged in Ellie's gut. Fear of what else the woman might be capable of, shock that she had done this, and anger that it had happened.

Benjamin needed to know about this. His sister might have some kind of illness, but it did not excuse this kind of behaviour.

Ellie snatched up her phone and pulled up his number, annoyed when it rang half a dozen times before cutting into voicemail.

She didn't bother leaving a message, knowing she was annoyed and would likely rant.

It wasn't Benjamin's fault. Yes, he was responsible for his sister and perhaps he needed to control her better, but he couldn't be held accountable for Virginia's actions.

Knowing it would annoy her just looking at the word and its rude instruction, Ellie took half a dozen photographs of the wall, then set about cleaning it up.

Half an hour later, the lettering had been scrubbed away and the wall repainted. Not exactly how she had planned on spending her afternoon, but at least it could no longer annoy her.

She was gathering up her brush and roller, ready to take them downstairs to clean, when there was the creak of a floorboard below her.

Ellie exchanged a glance with Poppy, saw the dog's ears prick up as a low growl rumbled.

It wasn't Ash. She would have heard his car. And she had locked the French doors before coming upstairs. There was no way Virginia was able to get back in the house. At least not without breaking a window, and there had been no sound of shattered glass.

Was it her imagination? It was an old house, filled with groans and creaks.

But even as she tried to convince herself it was nothing, the noise came again. Footsteps this time and they were clear enough for Ellie to know she wasn't imagining it.

She slipped her phone into her pocket, unsure if she should barricade herself in the room, call out to see who was there, or whether to phone Ash or the police.

There was no point in disturbing Ash. He would never get back in time. And the police felt like an over-reaction, plus she couldn't hide up here all afternoon.

Still, she kept one hand on the phone as she picked the hammer up out of the toolbox and stepped cautiously out onto the landing.

'Hello?'

There was no answer.

'Virginia? Is that you?'

Still nothing.

Locking Poppy in her studio, figuring it would be easier to go look herself, Ellie quietly descended the stairs, hoping there was a really innocent explanation for the footsteps.

The hallway was empty, and she did a quick search in all of the rooms, grateful that they currently had very little furniture.

The kitchen was the last room she entered, and she saw it immediately, her stomach dropping.

The cellar door was open.

What the hell?

Unsure if anyone was still down there, Ellie rushed across and closed it before pulling out her phone. Was she over-reacting by calling the police?

Then her eyes landed on the open drawer and the knives that had been removed and arranged on the counter, all neatly laid out.

And she hit 999.

17

Benjamin had spent much of the day trying to think of an excuse to visit Ellie. He had only seen her once since dropping off the apples and she had been with Ash, the pair of them saying a quick hello before disappearing out in Ash's car.

Knowing that Ash would be back at work today, it was the perfect opportunity to check in with her and see how she was, try to subtly gauge how things were in her relationship and whether Ash had been the one to put the mark on her arm.

The problem was that Benjamin couldn't think of a reasonable excuse to drop by unannounced. It wasn't in his nature to impose, and he had already taken round the apples, so could hardly show up with more. But then his problem was solved when he looked at his phone and saw that he had a missed call from Ellie.

This was perfect. He would stop by the house, say he was passing by and wanted to check she was okay.

As he changed into a clean shirt (he had been gardening and didn't want to show up looking a mess) smoothed his hair down and sprayed a little of the aftershave he had been given as part of a leaving gift when he had left the accountancy firm he used to work for, he heard the floorboard creak behind him and tensed. Although the old house was full of creaks and groans, he knew when it was more than that. It seemed he couldn't go anywhere or do anything these days without Virginia watching him.

He glanced in the mirror, tried to keep the irritation out of his voice when he spoke to her. 'I'm just nipping out for a bit. It's a lovely day and I fancy some fresh air, so I thought I'd go for a walk.'

It was, of course, a lie and they both knew that.

Virginia knew that Benjamin never wore aftershave, just as she knew he would never change shirts midway through the day.

His cheeks heated. He was making an effort and they both knew who for.

As he headed down the driveway, relieved to escape Virginia, he worried again about what his sister might potentially do, aware of the damage she could cause.

It made him sick, knowing what she was capable of, and he knew that helping Ellie came with its own risks. He was going to have to be extra careful.

He expected Ellie to be pleased to see him, so was a little taken aback when she opened the door looking flustered, a scowl darkening her face when she saw it was him.

Had she been waiting for someone else?

A tiny coil of jealousy tightened in his gut.

'Benjamin.'

No 'how are you?' or 'it's lovely to see you,' not even a hello. Just his name spoken, in surprise, and quite coolly, he thought. Or was that just his imagination?

Poppy had limped through behind her, tail wagging as she greeted Benjamin with a bark. At least someone was pleased to see him.

'Hello, Ellie.'

'What are you doing here?'

No, it definitely wasn't his imagination. She wasn't happy to see him.

This had him wrong-footed and immediately set him on edge, unease tensing his shoulders. Had Ash been trying to poison her mind? Benjamin had read this about controlling partners and how they tried to remove any perceived threat, wanting to isolate their victim from friends and family.

Ellie had told him she had no family. What if Benjamin was one of her only friends? If Ash cut him off, she could be all alone.

'You called me.' When she didn't react to that, apparently waiting for him to elaborate, he continued. 'I was passing by, so I thought I would find out if everything is okay.'

Ellie gave him a hard stare. 'No, it's not actually. I'm waiting for the police to get here.'

'The police? Why on earth... Has something happened?'

'Virginia was here, Benjamin.'

'What?'

'Virginia, your sister. She was here in my house.'

'She was... what?'

Everything inside Benjamin went cold, icy perspiration licking at his skin. He was aware he was repeating himself, his mouth hanging open in shock, but what Ellie was saying, it couldn't be possible. Or could it?

He had been so careful.

'I don't understand,' he said numbly. 'Virginia has been home in the house with me all day.'

'Well, someone broke in, someone wrote graffiti on my freshly painted wall, and she looked a hell of a lot like your sister. They even had on the same dress.'

'You saw her?'

'Of course I bloody saw her. How do you think I knew it was her?'

Ellie was getting angry now and Benjamin's throat grew thick, tears pricking at his eyes. He had come here as Ellie's friend, wanting to help her, but as always, Virginia had found a way to ruin that. He was so sick and tired of being accountable for her actions.

'I'm sorry, Ellie. Please forgive me. I had no idea that she had snuck out of the house.' He was aware of a tear rolling down his cheek and shame heated his face.

It seemed to thaw her slightly, though, and while he could tell she was still annoyed, there was now sympathy in her eyes as she held the door wide. 'You'd better come in.'

As he followed her inside, he recalled that she'd said she had called the police, and panic set in. He had spent years protecting his out-of-control sister. If they found out the truth about her, about what happened and what she had done, he didn't even want to think about the terrible consequences. Although she had made Benjamin suffer greatly, she was still his responsibility. His cross to bear.

'Have you really called the police over graffiti?' he asked, stepping back when she wheeled on him, the temper in her eyes turning them from sea green to a stormy grey. He quickly held his hands up. 'I'm not condoning what she did. It was wrong and I am appalled that she broke into your house. She's really sick though, Ellie.'

'I wasn't going to call them about the graffiti. It's why I called you. But then I came downstairs and saw this. This is why I called the police.' She led him into the kitchen and pointed to the worktop where the knives were laid out.

'Virginia did that?' Benjamin asked numbly. This was worrying.

'Well, I didn't do it and no one else has been here.'

'Did you tell the police it was her?'

Ellie's eyes narrowed. 'Not yet. I told them someone had broken in. They're sending someone over. Why?'

'Please don't tell them she was here.'

'Are you serious? She broke in, Benjamin. She damaged my property and this...' She trailed off, indicating the knives again. 'This is just bloody creepy. And threatening too. What is the deal with your sister? Is she trying to drive us away?'

'No, no, of course not. She's a sick girl and not of sound mind. It's nothing personal against you.'

'Really? Because this feels personal.' Ellie had her phone out, was holding it up for Benjamin to see.

He stared at the picture of the wall with the crude letters painted on it and had to bite down on his shock. *Oh Virginia. What have you done?*

'I'm sorry, Ellie. I'm so sorry.' Fresh tears dampened his cheeks. 'I will keep a closer eye on her, I will make sure she never comes back here again. But please don't tell the police. She's not well, but she's not dangerous either.'

'Benjamin–'

'If they arrest her or take her in for questioning... well, she's so fragile, it could destroy her.'

'They are on their way. I can't lie to them.'

'I promise this will never happen again. I will help you fix the damage, and I will speak to Virginia's doctor, explain the setback and see if we can change her medication.'

'The damage is fixed. I already took care of it. But that's not the point. She can't–'

'Please Ellie, I'm begging you. She's my sister.' The tears fell harder, and he saw that she was struggling, unsure what to do.

Eventually her expression softened. 'You have to promise me. If she comes back here again or ever pulls any of this kind of shit in the future, I will be reporting her.'

Her use of the crude S-word made Benjamin inwardly cringe. Ellie was a lady and too intelligent for such language. He brushed over it, though, aware she had thrown him a lifeline. 'I promise, I do. Thank you, Ellie. You honestly have no idea how much this means to me.'

She still seemed uncertain as to whether she had done the right thing, but as she put the kettle on, made them both a cup of tea, asking questions about Virginia, which Benjamin did his best to answer, she gradually seemed to calm.

He was there when the police constable arrived, the tension in his neck and shoulders giving him a headache, as the officer asked questions, relaxing only when he heard Ellie tell him she hadn't seen the person who had broken in, and while he could tell she was uncomfortable with the lie, it didn't seem to rouse any suspicion.

He had been careful not to say anything about Ash before the constable left. It was such a delicate situation and one that needed broaching carefully, and he was conscious of staying on Ellie's good side in case she changed her mind and told the police about Virginia. As he got up to leave, though, taking his mug over to the sink, he casually asked about the bruise on her arm. It had faded a little, though was still visible.

'It's fine,' she told him, seeming surprised that he asked, rubbing her hand over it, self-consciously, he thought.

'How did you say you got it again?'

'Oh, I'm such a klutz. I slipped when I was climbing down from the ladder. Ash says I need an idiot-proof suit.' She rolled her eyes.

'That wasn't a very kind thing to say.'

'What?' Ellie stared at him. 'He was joking.'

'Calling someone an idiot isn't very nice though.'

'You should hear the names I call him.' She laughed about it, shrugging it off, which had him wondering if she had become conditioned to being insulted by this man she was in a relationship with.

If Ellie was his, Benjamin would compliment her and treat her with respect at all times. He certainly wouldn't call her an idiot.

He picked his next words carefully. 'I do hope you view me as your friend, Ellie, as well as your neighbour, and that you know if you ever need someone to talk to, I'm a very good listener.'

She looked a little surprised at that, taken aback even. 'Of course we're friends, but there's nothing in particular I need to talk about.'

'Okay, well the offer is there if you change your mind. Sometimes it helps if there are any...' He searched for an appropriate word. 'Difficulties.'

Was that right? From the expression on Ellie's face, possibly not.

'Difficulties?' she repeated. 'What kind of difficulties do you mean?'

Now she had put him on the spot.

'Oh, you know,' he blustered, flapping his hand about.

'Do you mean with Ash?' Her green eyes were wide. 'Because I can assure you there are no difficulties there.'

'Of course not. I just meant in general. Though, of course, if there were any difficulties with him then I would be happy to be a friendly ear.'

'I see.' Ellie gave him a tight smile. 'Well, it was nice of you to stop by.' She ushered him out of the kitchen and back to the front door, holding it open for him. 'Don't forget to speak with Virginia's doctor.'

'I won't.' Benjamin couldn't help but think her last comment was intended as a dig. She hadn't reacted well to his subtle probing. Disappointing, but not unexpected. She was in denial, unable to see how unhealthy her relationship with Ash was.

It made him all the more determined to help her.

She might not welcome his meddling, but in the long term he was certain she would realise it was all in her best interests.

18

Ellie had lied to the police and then she had lied to Ash, and the guilt was eating her up.

Well, okay, technically she hadn't lied to Ash. She just didn't tell him about Virginia breaking into the house.

But the police constable. There was no getting away from it. She had definitely lied to him.

He had asked her outright if she had seen any sign of the intruder or if there was anyone she was suspicious of, and she answered no to both questions.

Benjamin had been so upset, begging her to help him, and making Ellie feel terrible for calling the police on his sister. When he had started crying it had been difficult to stay angry with him and somehow, despite what had happened, she ended up being the one who felt bad.

She had agreed she wouldn't tell, but it had been in the heat of the moment, and by the time the constable arrived, she was already having doubts.

She should have been honest, but Benjamin had still been there, and she had felt the weight of his stare as she answered the officer's questions. It was almost like he was keeping an eye on her to make sure she didn't go back on her word.

She had lied to the police constable and she hadn't told Ash, and she was beginning to think it was a huge mistake. But it was one she wasn't sure she could get out of now.

Okay, she could get in touch with the police again, but would they trust her if she changed her statement? And would she be in trouble for wasting their time?

And if she told Ash, well, she was pretty certain he would be angry that Benjamin had coerced her. Best-case scenario, he would call the police, worst-case, he would go storming round to see Benjamin and Virginia. She knew how hot-headed he could be in the heat of the moment and that could work out badly for everyone.

No, she had made her decision and unfortunately there was no going back on it. She would just have to hope that Benjamin kept to his word and made sure Virginia stayed away.

But still, the knives. She kept thinking back to how they had all been laid out on the worktop and couldn't see how it had been meant as anything other than a threat. Yes, Virginia was unwell, but was she unstable enough to cause harm? And how much control did Benjamin really have over his sister?

And truth was, it wasn't just Virginia who was playing on her mind. Benjamin's forward questioning, digging even, into how things were with Ash, had annoyed Ellie.

Okay, he hadn't actually come out and said it, but it was obvious he was questioning their relationship, which quite frankly was none of his business, and she couldn't help but believe he disapproved of Ash. After the huge favour she had just done Benjamin, it was a shitty move and she decided she might try and cool things with him a little.

Her plan worked initially, but that was because she didn't

hear anything from him for a couple of days then on Thursday she received a text from him asking how she was.

Ellie responded to that with a quick, 'Fine. Very busy', ignoring his follow-up message saying to let him know if there was anything he could do to help.

It was Friday morning when she saw him from one of the upstairs windows approaching the house and quickly stepped away before he looked up and saw her. She cursed when seconds later the door knocker sounded, Poppy went nuts.

She should go downstairs, speak to Benjamin and tell him she was busy, but she really wasn't in the mood for dealing with him.

Problem was, her car was in the driveway, so he would know that she was home.

Of course, that didn't mean she was able to get to the door. For all he knew she could be in the shower. Or maybe she had gone for a walk.

Ellie waited, slowly releasing the breath she had been holding, willing Poppy to shut up, and telling herself she was being stupid. Up until Monday she had been getting on fine with Benjamin and had been pleased they had such a nice neighbour.

Okay, so his sister was a bit creepy. No, scrub that. Virginia was scary as hell. And it had been wrong of Benjamin to persuade Ellie to lie to the police, but if she could move past that, they could get back to the easy friendship that had been developing, couldn't they?

Although she was trying to convince herself they could, she remained rooted to the spot, flinching when the knocker sounded again.

Damn it, Benjamin. Go away.

And then a few moments later her phone started ringing.

Ellie was glad it was on vibrate, though it was still making enough noise, bouncing around on the chest of drawers, that she worried he might hear it.

She waited and she watched, relieved to see him eventually leave, so she could finally stop acting like a fool and get back to work. She remained in the shadows of the room, watching him as he glanced back at the house a couple of times and he seemed a little irritated that she wasn't at home.

Letting out a shaky breath, grateful that she had taken to locking all of the doors since Virginia broke in, she snatched up her phone, saw she had a voicemail. It was him.

She listened to Benjamin as he told her he had stopped by and wanted to check things were okay with her, that he would try and catch up with her later. And she felt terrible.

She should have answered the door.

He was harmless and he had been good to her. She couldn't hold him responsible for what his sister had done, and she couldn't blame him for talking her out of telling the police. Virginia was his flesh and blood. It was only natural he would want to protect her.

Ellie had been the one who had lied to them. That was all on her.

Still, she didn't call him back, and was a little ashamed of the relief she felt when Ash returned home from work earlier than expected, knowing that now the weekend was here, she wouldn't have to face Benjamin alone if he stopped by.

But then Ash had dropped his bombshell.

He had been in a good mood, excited at a big contract he had just landed for his firm, wanting to go out to dinner and celebrate, and his enthusiasm was infectious. He had reserved a table at a restaurant that had been recommended in one of the neighbouring villages and booked a taxi so they could both have a drink.

Ellie knew how hard he had worked and loved seeing him on such a high. She had practically lived in scruffy, paint-splattered clothes since they had moved in, so relished the idea of getting dressed up, and after showering, and applying make-up for the first time in what felt like ages, she took her time deciding what to wear. She settled on a striking coral shift dress and a pair of nude heeled sandals. Then she twisted her naturally wavy hair back into a loose knot to show off the diamond stud earrings that Ash had given her for Christmas.

The appreciative look he gave her when she reached the bottom of the stairs, a sly lopsided smile on his face and a glint in his amber eyes, heated her up inside. They had been so busy with the house, and a night out together was long overdue.

'You look... edible.' He left that last word hanging there.

Ellie laughed as his smile widened to a wicked grin. 'Do I now?'

'Yes, you do.'

He pulled her close, smoothing his palm down her back and cupping it over her arse, kissing her hard on the mouth before trailing hot kisses along her jawline, and everything inside her melted when his mouth moved to her ear, whispering filthy promises of what he wanted to do to her when they returned home after dinner.

It was a warm night, and he was doing nothing to help her cool down.

Poppy chose that moment to interrupt them, trying to nuzzle her way between them with her stuffed bear, whining when they didn't part to give her attention.

Ash released Ellie and she immediately missed his touch, as he bent down to fuss the dog. 'I should let her out for a pee before the cab gets here.'

'Okay, I'll make sure all of the windows are closed.'

They reconvened in the hallway just as Ash's phone rang to confirm the taxi had arrived.

Ellie grabbed her bag. 'Did you lock the back door?'

'Yup. All the windows shut?'

She nodded. 'They are,' she confirmed before leaning down to kiss Poppy on the head. 'You be a good girl. We won't be late. You have the keys?'

'Yeah.' He caught hold of her hand as the front door closed behind them, pulled her close to brush a kiss against her temple, before opening the door of the taxi for her.

As Ellie climbed in, and said hello to the cabbie, she spotted Benjamin at the entrance to the driveway and her heart sank when she realised he held a carrier bag and was heading towards the car.

'Well, if it isn't our favourite neighbour,' Ash muttered sarcastically as he climbed in beside Ellie.

She poked him in the ribs. 'Don't be mean,' she whispered, asking the driver to wait a moment, as she wound down the window. She painted a breezy smile on her face.

'Benjamin, hi.'

'You're heading out.'

'We are.'

'Okay, well I thought I would just stop by. I brought round some more cuttings for you, for the garden.'

'That's very kind of you.' Beside her, Ash let out a sigh that was loud enough to bring heat to Ellie's cheeks and she knocked her knee against his as a warning to cool it. Yes, Benjamin's visits were becoming a little bit irritating, but he wasn't a bad person. He was harmless and he meant well.

'I can come back tomorrow.'

'No, no, it's okay. Just leave them by the front door.'

'Are you sure?' Benjamin glanced around as if checking for plant thieves.

'Yes, I'm sure they'll be perfectly safe there. And thank you.'

'You're welcome.' There was an uncomfortable pause as he hovered, seemed to want the conversation to continue. 'Well, have a nice time,' he said eventually.

'We will,' Ash answered, leaning across Ellie and closing the window.

Feeling a little bad she gave Benjamin a parting smile, as the taxi pulled away.

'He fancies you. You know that, right?'

'What, no he doesn't. He's just lonely.'

'Lonely and clearly horny. I've seen the way he looks at you. He's like a besotted little puppy dog.'

'You shouldn't be so rude to him,' Ellie scolded, ignoring his comment. 'He's harmless.'

'I'm not rude. I think I'm being quite tolerant given that he has a thing for my girlfriend. It's your fault for encouraging him.' There was no malice or jealousy in Ash's tone. He sounded amused.

'I haven't encouraged him.'

Had she?

Okay, so she had called round to thank him after he returned her phone then she had invited him over for dinner, but she was just being neighbourly. She hadn't led him on, plus she was living with Ash, so Benjamin knew she wasn't interested in him that way.

Besides, Ash was winding her up. Benjamin didn't fancy her.

She must have looked worried because he slipped his arm around her now, squeezing her waist as he nuzzled in close. 'I'm only teasing you; you know that, right?'

'So you don't really think he fancies me?'

'Oh, he fancied you.'

That was from the taxi driver, who had remained silent until now.

'I knew it. Cheers, mate!' Ash grinned at Ellie. 'See, I told you.'

~

His bombshell came as they were eating dessert.

Ellie had managed to put thoughts of Benjamin out of her mind, and they had enjoyed a lovely meal, accompanied by a bottle and a half of wine.

Pleasantly relaxed in that mildly tipsy way, she listened as Ash told her about the contract he had secured for a project down in London and how this was potentially huge for his firm.

'I have meetings with them next week to go over everything before we begin.'

'Are they coming up to Norfolk?' Ellie asked, pushing the last piece of chocolate torte around her plate, not sure if she could manage it.

Ash took the decision away from her, spearing it with his fork and stealing it away from her.

'Hey!'

'You've been staring at it for ten minutes.' He laughed, popping it in his mouth. 'You had your chance.' He washed down the mouthful with a sip of wine.

'So, they're going to need me down there next week.'

'For the day or will you need to stay overnight?'

'They need me for the week.'

'The week?' Ellie put down her empty fork. 'So you're gonna commute?'

'No, it'll be easier to stay over.'

'For the whole week?'

She must have sounded horrified at the idea, as he was

studying her now, concern in his eyes. 'That's not a problem, is it? I know we're up to our neck with things in the house, but this is a huge job, Ellie. I can't afford to lose it.'

Bless him, he thought it was about the renovation project, but truth was, after everything that had happened in the last couple of weeks, from learning about the murder, to John Tanner's appearance, then Virginia breaking in, Ellie really didn't want to be there alone.

Of course, she couldn't tell him that, so she simply smiled and tried to be supportive. 'No, of course not.' She reached across the table, taking hold of his hand. 'I'm really proud of you. I know how hard you've worked for this. So when do you have to leave?'

'I figured I'd head down early Monday morning. I'll be back Friday latest. Maybe sooner if we get wrapped up early.'

Despite trying her best to mask it, Ellie must have looked worried, because he linked his fingers with hers and gave her hand a gentle squeeze. 'You're okay, aren't you, about being in the house alone?'

'Yes, of course,' she lied. 'I'll be fine.'

His revelation had knocked her, though, and she was quiet on the taxi ride home.

Her inebriated brain wondered if she could perhaps check into a local hotel for a few nights. Of course, she wouldn't tell Ash she had done it. He would never need to know.

But then she remembered Poppy and that made everything a little more complicated. Sod it. She would stay in the house. She would put on her big girl pants and face her fears. Ash sometimes had to travel with work, and she couldn't be a wimp whenever he went away. Hazelwood Cottage was her home, and she was determined she was going to stop being scared of it.

As the taxi pulled up outside the driveway and Ash settled the fare, Ellie climbed out, staring into the blackness, the only light coming from the car. She wished they had remembered to leave the porch light on, hating coming home to a dark house.

A nearby bark made her jump, her eyes adjusting at the shape bounding towards her.

'Poppy?' How the hell? 'Ash, the dog's outside.'

'What?' He scooped Poppy up when she hurled herself at his feet. 'How did you get out here?'

Of course, she couldn't answer, giving him a delighted face wash instead, pleased to have them home.

He glanced at Ellie and she could see the questions going through his mind, knew they were the same ones she had. Someone had let Poppy out of the house. That meant someone had been inside while they were out.

Her immediate thought was Benjamin. He had seen them leave. But Ellie immediately felt bad. He had done nothing to deserve her sudden distrust.

That left two potential suspects. Virginia and John Tanner.

Both of them scared Ellie half to death.

Ash kept a step in front of her as they approached the front door, realising it was ajar.

He looked at Ellie again, handing her Poppy. 'Wait here.'

'You can't go in there alone. What if someone is still inside?'

He was ignoring her, had already eased the door open, letting himself into the dark hallway and Ellie's heart thumped as she hugged the dog tightly. Then he switched the light on, and she ordered herself to calm down, disobeying his instruction as she followed him through the door.

Poppy wasn't reacting and Ellie took that as a good sign, certain the dog would be growling or barking if there was anyone still in the house. Still, she helped Ash check the whole of the downstairs then accompanied him up to the first floor to check the bedrooms before she allowed herself to relax a little.

'Are you sure you definitely closed all of the windows?' he asked when they were satisfied they were alone in the house.

'Yes. You can see for yourself that none of them are open.'

'Now they're not. But someone could have climbed through then closed it. They left through the front door.'

'I told you I checked them all.' Ellie followed him back downstairs. She set Poppy down as she watched him lock the door, a little irritated that he was doubting her. 'Are you sure that you closed the door properly when we left?' she threw back, knowing full well he had.

Ash shot her a look. 'Touché.'

'So how the hell did they get in, Ash?'

'I'm not sure. But nothing seems to be missing.'

'So they just broke in to let the dog out and leave the front door open.'

'I don't know, Ellie.' He shook his head. 'Look, it's late and I'm tired. I think we should go to bed and sleep on this. We'll try and figure it out in the morning.'

There didn't seem to be anything else they could do so Ellie reluctantly agreed. 'Okay. I'm gonna head upstairs and take off my make-up. Will you let Poppy out again? She might need a wee.'

'Sure.' There was a pause. 'Ellie?'

She turned to look at him. 'Yes?'

'Before I leave on Monday, we'll make sure the house is secure, okay. I can change the locks. I won't leave you until I know you're safe here.'

Ellie nodded, found him a smile. 'Okay.'

But as she headed up to their bedroom, she couldn't help worrying. Someone had been in the house and they had no idea how that person had gained entry. Unless they figured it out, how would they be able to stop them breaking in again?

19

Ellie wasn't answering his calls and she had stopped replying to his text messages, and Benjamin wasn't quite sure what to do.

He could feel her slipping away, and the panic that he had caused this, had driven this wedge between them, had played on his mind all weekend, causing him sleepless nights.

When she left the house with Ash on Friday evening, she had stolen Benjamin's breath. He had never seen Ellie dressed up like that before and she was a beautiful vision in orange, her legs long and shapely in heels and her hair tied back to accentuate the curve of her neck and jawline. It physically pained him, knowing that she belonged to Ash.

After getting no answer when he had stopped by earlier, he had taken some more cuttings from the garden, using them as a ruse for another visit. It had caught him off guard when he saw them getting into a taxi.

Ellie had been polite, though coolly so, he thought, while Ash was his usual rude self. Benjamin guessed he shouldn't expect any more from the uncouth Australian. And they had driven off in the taxi, leaving Benjamin standing in their driveway with his bag of cuttings.

After depositing them on the doorstep, he had returned home, the whole situation troubling him more than he cared to admit.

Ash had Ellie fooled. She was not a shallow woman, but somehow it seemed she had been charmed by him. There was no denying he was a good-looking man but take away his toned physique and his handsome face, and there was only ugliness underneath.

He lacked manners, was aggressive, and Benjamin suspected he was a bully, was certain he had put that bruise on Ellie's arm. Ash didn't deserve her. It was up to Benjamin to show her how a gentleman should really treat a lady. Except he couldn't do that as she wasn't giving him the time of day.

He had messaged her on Saturday morning, saying he hoped she'd had a nice time out, and she had ignored that. So he tried again in the afternoon, this time phrasing his message as a question, asking if she had liked the cuttings and offering to help with planting them.

He had really expected a reply to the second message. It was unlike Ellie to be rude and ignore him, and he had repeatedly refreshed the screen, even worrying that there might be something wrong with his phone.

Not liking to text her again, he had spent a miserable night conjuring up all kinds of scenarios in his head. He worried he had burnt his bridges with Ellie, and she no longer wanted anything to do with him. And then he wondered if Ash had taken her phone and deleted the messages.

That was where his head was at when he tried to call her on Sunday morning. If, as he suspected, his messages had been deleted, he would soon find out by speaking with Ellie.

Except, of course, she didn't answer.

He left a voicemail. A garbled message asking if she had received his texts and asking again about the cuttings. It was embarrassingly bad, but he couldn't take it back. Hopefully she would get it and understand that he was simply worried about her.

When she didn't respond he accepted that he was right about Ash: that the man was controlling every aspect of Ellie's life, including keeping tabs on her phone. Either that or her phone was broken.

What if Ash had seen Benjamin's texts coming through and he had flown into a rage with Ellie, smashing her phone?

That had Benjamin's fear escalating. What if Ellie needed help, but couldn't call anyone? His skin prickled with unease. It would be his fault.

He had to go check. He had to know that she was okay.

As he made his way up the driveway towards the house, he pondered over what excuse he could use to be dropping by. He had already taken apples and then the cuttings, and it was going to start looking ridiculous if he kept showing up bearing gifts.

Deciding that perhaps honesty was the best policy this time – he would admit that he was concerned after Ellie hadn't responded to his messages and just wanted to check that she was okay – he approached the end of the hedge between the two driveways, abruptly halting.

Ash was stood on the doorstep and he was talking to a woman Benjamin didn't recognise.

They appeared to be having a heated discussion, Ash with his hands on his hips and a sullen expression on his face, the woman, whose back was to Benjamin, gesturing angrily with her hands, her red ponytail swinging.

Benjamin took a step back to make certain he was hidden by the hedge. He didn't want to approach the house while they were there, but he was intrigued.

Who was the woman and why was she arguing with Ash? It was clear they knew each other. Benjamin was pleased to see that not every woman fell for Ash's charm.

Was she perhaps a friend of Ellie's and had come to check up on her too? Maybe Benjamin's messages hadn't been the only ones ignored. He wasn't sure if he found that worrying or reassuring.

Ellie's car wasn't in the drive, but that didn't mean anything. What if she was trapped inside the house and Ash wouldn't let her see anyone?

How was Benjamin going to check she was okay? Maybe he should flag down the friend when she left, try to find out what was going on.

Ash had hold of her arm now, was marching her towards the little black sports car parked across the drive.

Benjamin took another step back, scared in case they saw him, almost missed the moment the woman turned to Ash, hands cupping his face as she leant in and kissed him on the mouth.

Shocked at what he was seeing, Benjamin's mouth dropped open. He didn't hear the approaching bicycle and jumped when the cyclist passed him, calling out a cheery, 'Good morning.'

Flustered, he raised his hand to her retreating form, then took another step back. When he peered around the hedge again, Ash and the redhead were no longer locking lips. The redhead was back in her car as Ash disappeared inside the house.

Benjamin quickly retreated as he absorbed this new information. It changed everything. So what he had witnessed was a lovers' tiff. Ellie's boyfriend was cheating on her. Ash really didn't deserve her, but then Benjamin already knew that.

Ellie was going to need his help and he needed to act sooner rather than later.

20

Ellie was dreading her first night alone in the house without Ash. He had left early on Monday morning, pressing a kiss against her lips and telling her to go back to sleep when she tried to get up to see him off.

'I'll be back before you know it,' he'd told her, and she just hoped that was true.

She couldn't get back to sleep after she'd heard his car leave, her mind replaying what had happened on Friday night, knowing that someone had been inside their house.

True to his word, Ash had changed the locks, but even so, she was still uneasy with the idea of being there alone. At first she had been paranoid that John Tanner had been the one who'd broken in, but if she was honest with herself, the most likely suspect was Virginia, given her track record. Of course, she couldn't tell Ash that.

Eventually she threw back the sheet, deciding she might as well get an early start on her own work.

She hadn't taken on any illustration work since moving into the house, wanting a chance to get things straight, but she had received a couple of enquiries that she needed to deal with.

After letting Poppy in the garden for ten minutes and sorting her with some breakfast, she made a coffee and took it upstairs to her studio, firing up her Mac.

One client was dealt with easily by email. The other wanted a call. The call then turned into a Zoom meeting for the following week, which Ellie put into her diary. At least she now had a decent and presentable space to work in, that wouldn't look too bad on camera.

She glanced at her phone; Ash had been gone for a couple of hours now. He had promised to check in with her when he arrived, but there was nothing from him yet.

There was a new text message from Benjamin, though, and her shoulders tensed as she opened it, unease creeping down her spine.

Do you fancy getting together for coffee later?

She knew she was being mean ignoring him, but Ash was right: he had latched on to her. This had Ellie feeling guilty that she had inadvertently led their neighbour on. The problem was, he wasn't taking the hint. And it worried her that if she didn't reply to this message he might show up at the house again.

She left it a little while, making another coffee and ordering some wallpaper samples before responding, keeping it really brief.

Sorry, I'm really busy.

Cool, but not unfriendly. Hopefully he would leave her alone.

No such luck.

Another message pinged back almost immediately. It was as if he had been sitting there waiting for her to reply.

No worries. Maybe tomorrow or we can do later this week if you prefer.

Damn it, Benjamin. Ellie quickly fired another message back.

I have a crazy week. I'm not sure I'll have time.

Again, his reply came back straightaway.

Well, see how things go. You don't want to work too hard. x

Oh crap. He had put a kiss. Ellie ignored that last message, putting her phone on silent. She felt a bit sick.

She tried to lose herself in more wallpaper stripping, turning up the radio and singing along, relieved when she checked her phone again to see there were no more messages from Benjamin. There was just the one from Ash telling her he had arrived safely and would call her later.

The rest of the afternoon and evening passed without incident, Ellie working hard on the house then chilling in the garden for a bit with Poppy. Ash called not long after she had finished eating dinner and as the evening was warm, she poured a glass of white wine, took it outside and sat on the patio as she spoke to him.

'You okay there? You're not getting freaked out being there alone, are you?'

'I'm fine,' Ellie told him, keeping her tone light. 'I have Poppy to keep me company.'

She suspected he knew she was lying. Ash wasn't stupid and he knew that Friday night had left her shaken. At one point he had even talked about cancelling his work trip, but Ellie had persuaded him not to. Yes, she was dreading being there alone, but this was his job, and it was important. She would not let her fears ruin this opportunity for him.

He was in his hotel room, chilling after an afternoon of meetings, and they spoke for an hour before calling it a night. After ending the call, Ellie whistled for Poppy who was mooching around further down the garden and they went inside. She was careful to double-check all of the doors and windows downstairs were securely locked.

Grabbing a bottle of water from the fridge, she switched off the lights and headed upstairs.

In the stifling heat of the bedroom, she was reluctant to open the balcony doors, fearing what might get in, so she brought the fan through from her studio. It wasn't ideal, but it was better than nothing.

Letting Poppy stay on the bed, she turned out the light and prayed for sleep.

It didn't come, the quietness of the house and the countryside, which had been appealing when they had first moved in, now unsettled her. The faint whirring of the fan only added to the ominous silence.

Damn it. The mugginess was oppressive, the fan offering little respite, and Ellie was drenched in sweat. She threw back the sheet to try and get some relief, but she felt all the more vulnerable with no cover. She adjusted it again, so it was partially over her, flipped her pillow and rolled onto her side. Beside her, Poppy whined in protest at the disturbance.

At least one of them was managing to settle.

Staring into the dark, imagining sinister shadows that weren't even there, her mind worked overtime thinking about John Tanner and his family. Wondering what the man was doing back in Corpusty, whether the ghost of his dead wife haunted this house and speculating what may have happened to his daughter.

Damn it, Ellie. Stop!

She was driving herself nuts and she was never going to fall asleep at this rate.

Until tonight, knowing what had happened to Louise Tanner hadn't affected her sleeping pattern. Yes, she was freaked out by what had happened in the house, but with Ash in bed beside her, she hadn't had trouble falling asleep.

Alone it seemed was a different story, and she had another few nights of this to go.

She had to get a grip.

Realising she was just too hot to sleep, she reluctantly got up, unlocking the balcony doors and edging them open just a little.

There was a light breeze, and it was a blessed relief against her hot skin.

Telling herself that Poppy would bark if anyone was outside, Ellie returned to bed, rolled onto her back.

She tried to steady her breathing, focusing as she inhaled deeply through her nose then exhaled through her mouth. With the window open the room was slightly more comfortable now. Gradually her body relaxed, and she could feel the pull of slumber.

It was the crunch against gravel that woke her.

Ellie wasn't sure if she had actually been asleep or almost there, but she was disorientated enough to at first question what the noise was as her eyes shot open.

Beside her Poppy growled, a low warning noise that had Ellie tensing.

She lay in bed, wide awake now, her ears peeled as she listened, one hand on the dog, trying to calm her. When the noise came again, it was louder, clearer, and sounded as if it was directly beneath the bedroom balcony.

Poppy's growls turned to barks then as she bolted off the bed and towards the French doors, nudging them open with her nose so she could get outside.

Ellie hurried after her, her over-active imagination already picturing an intruder climbing up the side of the house to get onto the balcony. She stepped out of the doors, caught hold of Poppy's collar, glad when the dog stopped barking and relieved to see there was no one on their way up to attack her.

The garden was quiet, the lawn immersed in dark shadows. If anyone was down there it would be impossible to see them. The footsteps had stopped now, but that offered little relief. What if the intruder's intention was to get inside the house?

Ash may have changed the locks, but if someone really wanted to get in, they could easily do so by smashing a window.

What if someone was already inside?

And why were they lurking around in the dark? It couldn't be for any good reason. Did they plan to rob her, rape her, kill her?

She thought again of Louise Tanner, lying dead at the foot of the stairs.

Stop it, Ellie.

There was no reason for anyone to be outside though. She lived in the middle of the countryside. It wasn't as if it was someone needed to pass her house to get anywhere.

Could it have been an animal? She considered that. A fox maybe.

But no. The footsteps had distinctively crunched against the gravel, much as a boot would. It had definitely been a person.

Ellie stayed out on the balcony for a moment, the now cool breeze licking at her sweaty skin, as she debated what to do.

She guessed she could call the police.

And tell them what though? That she thought she had heard footsteps outside. That Poppy had barked. She had heard the footsteps, but that wouldn't be enough to make her a priority. That was if they took her seriously. Would they even bother to come out?

And there was no point in calling Ash. He was too far away to be able to help.

She glanced at her phone on the bedside table, knew there was one other possibility.

Benjamin.

She really didn't want to have to call him though, scared it might only encourage him further. And the last thing she wanted was him knowing that Ash was away.

Eventually she took Poppy back inside, locking the doors behind her. She glanced at her phone, spotting it was only just after 1am. She hadn't yet managed any sleep.

Beyond the bedroom door, the dark house loomed.

She couldn't hear any unfamiliar noises, but that meant nothing. She thought back to Friday night, remembering that someone had managed to gain entry to the house while she and Ash had been out.

The memory did nothing to soothe her frazzled nerves and she knew there was no way she would be able to sleep worrying about it.

She glanced around the room wondering if there was anything she could use to block the door, her eyes falling on the ottoman at the foot of the bed. It was heavy, filled with sheets and blankets that she would need to take out in order to move it, but at least if it was in front of the door she would feel safer. And if whoever was outside did manage to get into the house they wouldn't be able to get into the bedroom without waking her.

It took some effort, Poppy watching her from the bed as if Ellie had gone completely mad, but eventually she shifted the ottoman in place.

Satisfied that the room was now as safe as she could make it, she crawled back under the sheet, reaching across to switch on one of the bedside lights, illuminating the room with a warm glow and driving away the shadows. Snuggling up with Poppy, she settled back down against the pillow and closed her eyes. She suspected, though, that it was going to be a long night.

21

I saw her.

She came out on the balcony wearing just a little nightie, looking like one of those tarty women in the mucky magazines Daddy used to keep hidden in the garage, and she stared right at the bushes where I was hiding.

Of course, she couldn't see me. It was too dark to see anything, and I've always been good at keeping out of the way.

I know why she moved here, why she came to live in this house. She's the same as the others. Here to tempt and lead astray.

She pretends to care, to be a nice person, but it's all an act to try and fool us. I know why she's really here. She wants to destroy us. To break up our family.

He is mine, not hers, and I won't let her have him.

He is weaker than me, he doesn't understand that what he is doing is wrong, but it's not his fault. He can't see that it's a trap and he has walked right into it again.

I won't let her hurt him. He deserves better.

He is the only person in my life I have ever truly loved.

He is mine and I will do everything necessary to protect him.

22

Ellie and Ash had hoped that by keeping the cellar door closed, Poppy's fascination with it would wane, but it was still her chosen place to sit whenever she was in the kitchen and wasn't being distracted with food. Her obsession was another concern to Ellie's growing list of things that made her uncomfortable in the house.

Ash had been as blasé as ever, presenting half a dozen rational explanations for why the dog kept going to the door. But none of them particularly rang true to Ellie, who was beginning to get frustrated with having a boyfriend who was such a staunch non-believer in anything otherworldly.

She was still a doubter, she reminded herself as she boiled water for poached eggs early Tuesday morning. Poppy finished her breakfast and immediately moved to her position pressed up against the cellar door, trying to scrape her paws in the gap underneath. Ellie's scepticism was just being tested a whole lot more since moving into this house.

The tiredness wasn't helping with her cranky defeatist attitude. She'd had a bad night's sleep, struggling to relax after hearing the footsteps, and had only managed a couple of hours' slumber. Knowing she had several more restless nights before Ash returned filled her with dread.

Given how tired she was feeling, she decided to take the day off from the house project. She would do a bit of housework then either head into Norwich for a spot of shopping or spend some time in the garden.

She put the radio on as she worked, glancing occasionally at her phone to see if she had any missed calls or messages from Ash. She had neither. Luckily, though, there was nothing from Benjamin either. He finally appeared to be getting the hint.

Poppy followed Ellie around the house, mostly getting under her feet, though she was glad of the company. It was amazing how quickly the retriever was adapting to being on three legs. Stairs were still a bit of an issue, though she could just about manage them now.

Still, Ellie kept an eye on her as she went back downstairs with a basket of laundry, careful to make sure she didn't slip.

After loading the machine, she glanced at the kitchen clock. It wasn't yet midday, but the weather was warm, and she was really tired. She had been working hard on the house, so she deserved a day off.

There were a couple of sunloungers in the basement that she had brought from her old house. She would take one outside with her Kindle and read the Patricia Dixon book she had downloaded weeks ago but had been too busy to start.

Poppy had already positioned herself by the cellar door and Ellie was debating how she was going to get down there without the dog following, when her phone rang.

She pulled it out of her pocket, relieved to see it was Ash, not Benjamin, though surprised he was calling her during the day. 'Hey Ash, everything okay?'

'Yeah, everything's fine. You okay? You sound surprised to hear from me.'

'I am,' Ellie admitted. 'I thought you'd be busy with meetings.'

'We took a break. Thought I'd take an early lunch and give you a quick call. The client wants to take a few of us out to dinner tonight so I won't get a chance to speak to you later.'

'Oh, okay.'

She must have sounded disappointed because he pushed, 'Are you sure everything's okay, Ellie?'

'Yes, I'm just missing you.'

'I miss you, too, but it's not for long. You haven't had any problems since we changed the locks?'

'No, everything is fine.' Ellie kept her tone breezy. Ash didn't need to know that she had barely slept last night, that she had heard footsteps outside. No harm had come of it, so there was little point in distracting him from his work. She didn't want him worrying about her.

They spoke for another twenty minutes until she heard someone in the background tell Ash they were getting ready to reconvene.

'If I get time I'll try and give you a call in the morning, okay?'

'Okay. I love you. Stay safe.'

'I love you too.'

And then he was gone, and Ellie was left with an emptiness inside. After wallowing for a few minutes, she made herself snap out of it. It was only a few days and Ash would be home.

She would get out in the garden, relax with her book, and hopefully her mood would pick up. She just needed to get the sunlounger.

Looking at Poppy still lying in front of the door, she considered her options.

She could move the dog out of the way while she got through the door, but then she would have to keep it closed, and with all the stuff that had been going on there was no way she planned on doing that.

Deciding she would have to come down with her, Ellie scooped her up, opening the door, wrestling to hold on to Poppy who was frantically wriggling in her arms to be put down, as she whined in excitement.

What the hell was she so interested in?

She managed to reach the bottom of the stairs without tripping, putting her down, and watching as Poppy started sniffing around, her nose to the floor and then to the walls, and her tail frantically wagging.

'Why are you so excited? There's nothing down here.'

As the dog ignored her, Ellie hunted for the sunloungers, finding them stood up behind a pile of boxes under the stairs. She managed to pull one out without disturbing anything and decided she would take it upstairs, before coming back down for Poppy, who seemed to be in her element now she was finally in the cellar. Strange dog.

When Ellie returned for her, she was in the space where the old washing machine had stood, fascinated with how the area seemed to smell.

It had to be the scent of the men who had been down here. Barry and his mate. Though would it have seriously lingered for so long?

'Come on, Poppy, let's go back upstairs.'

The dog was scraping at the wall now, whining at Ellie in frustration.

'I don't know what you want, Pops. There's nothing there.'

She was answered with an excited bark.

It was just a wall. Why was she finding it so interesting?

A rectangle of the brickwork was a slightly different colour to the rest of the wall, but that was probably from where the washing machine had been pushed up against it.

Poppy had her nose nudged up against it now, was pushing on it with all her might and Ellie double-blinked when the wall seemed to move back slightly.

Had she imagined it? Were the walls really that unstable down here? If so, that was a worry.

She went over to where the dog was still frantically scraping and pushing.

No, she definitely hadn't imagined it. A large rectangle of bricks had definitely moved.

Had they come loose?

Ellie put her palm on the brickwork, testing how secure the wall was, frightening the life out of herself when she applied some pressure, and the section of the wall pushed back.

What the fuck?

Was it some kind of secret door? From the fraction it was open she was fairly certain there was a room on the other side.

Curious now to see what she had stumbled across, she left Poppy again, running back upstairs to fetch her phone from the kitchen counter. Back in the cellar she used the torch to flash it through the hole, casting light on the other side.

Yes, definitely a room and it looked quite big.

Is this why Poppy had been scraping? Did she somehow know the room was here?

Ellie slipped her phone in her pocket and pushed at the wall again. It moved further back, creating a gap big enough to poke her head through. As she reached for her phone, and shone the torch again, Poppy barged past her, disappearing into the room.

Shit.

'Poppy, come back.'

Her request fell on deaf ears, as the dog was on a mission.

Ellie really didn't want to go in the room by herself. Intrigued enough as she was to discover it, she had planned to wait for Ash before exploring further. But Poppy had just put paid to that plan. She couldn't leave her down here.

She pushed the stone door back as far as she could, creating a gap wide enough that, on hands and knees, she was able to crawl through.

'Poppy?'

The dog didn't react and there was no sound to indicate she was close by. Flashing the torch around the room, Ellie saw it was empty. Then she spotted the doorway on the far wall and her heart sunk.

How far back did it lead and where the hell had the dog gone?

Reluctantly she pulled herself through the gap, finding herself in darkness on the other side. The only light came from the cellar room she had been in.

'Poppy?'

The dog wasn't responding, and Ellie's panic grew. What if she couldn't find her and Poppy became lost or trapped down here? Tentatively she approached the doorway on the far wall.

Was it simply another room or was it a passageway that led further away from the house?

Whatever it was, this place hadn't been on the plans they had seen when they bought the house. They had known the property had a cellar, but this...? Was it even theirs?

A stupid question as it couldn't belong to anyone else.

So who had built it and who had put in the secret doorway?

Had it always been here?

Ellie flashed her torch into the doorway, found it led into a tunnel, and her heart sank.

This wasn't good.

'POPPY!' When there was no response, she made a pathetic attempt at whistling – Ash so much better at doing it than she was – and called again. 'POPPY!'

She heard a faint bark, far enough away to realise the tunnel led for quite some distance.

'Bloody hell, Poppy.'

There was a better torch in the toolbox upstairs, but no time to get it. Ellie had already hit the dog with her car, was responsible for the fact she now walked on three legs; she couldn't lose her now. Holding her phone ahead as a guide, she tentatively stepped into the narrow corridor, wishing to hell Poppy would reappear.

She had a phobia of tight spaces and rats, tried to keep her breathing even so she didn't have a panic attack about the former, while praying she didn't run into the latter.

Whatever this place was, it was far away from the bright, warm August day she had left behind and even though she was walking in a straight line, with each step she took, the greater the fear was that she would become trapped or not be able to find her way back.

She tried to remember how much charge she had on her phone before realising that she probably didn't even have a signal down here, so if she ran into trouble she wouldn't be able to call anyone anyway.

Knowing that had the fear clamping her heart, squeezing tightly.

Ash was away for another few days and she had no planned visitors. If she became lost or trapped down here, no one would know to look for her.

Fuck.

The anxiety bubbled now, through the tightness that

clogged in her throat and chest, a cold sweat beading on her skin, partly from the cool, damp, musty air, partly because she was more than a little bit scared down here, and a waft of sickness passed over her.

She couldn't be here. But also she couldn't leave Poppy. She would never be able to forgive herself. *Damn it.*

'POPPY!' She could hear the panic rising in her voice, told herself to get a grip, taking a moment to draw deep steady breaths.

If only she hadn't taken Poppy down into the cellar.

It was too late now though. The deed had been done and she had to find the dog. She could do it. It was just a straight narrow tunnel, and it had to come to an end at some point.

She forced herself to move forward. Told herself that when she had caught up with Poppy, she would take her back to the house, block up the entrance to the tunnel and they would never ever come back down here again. At least not without Ash.

And to be honest, if Ash wanted to explore, he could come down here on his own. Maybe bring Pete with him.

The tunnel became narrower, tighter, and Ellie tried to ignore that the stone walls were now brushing against her arms and she was having to duck slightly to avoid hitting her head on the roof. Surely this meant that it would be coming to an end soon? Poppy couldn't be too far up ahead.

She called the dog again, heard a faint whining. She still sounded far away, and Ellie's heart sank. She tried to distract herself with the rewards she would treat herself to, once this was over; a long hot shower to wash away the grime and clamminess she could feel clinging to her skin, lunch in the garden enjoying the warmth of the sun.

She was thankful when the tunnel opened out again, this time becoming much wider.

That moment of relief, though, was quickly replaced with

fresh panic when she saw a crossroads up ahead, realising that the tunnel veered off in different directions.

What the fuck was this place? A network of underground passages that led directly from their house. Had it always been here since the property was first built or had someone added it? And what purpose did it serve?

She reached the crossroads, flashed her phone torch in both directions, though the beam wasn't strong enough to show her much.

'POPPY!'

A bark came from ahead and, knowing that the retriever hadn't headed off down one of the new tunnels, Ellie released the breath she hadn't realised she was holding.

Thank fuck.

She pushed ahead. The passageway she was in was now wide enough for her to pick up her pace, though she tried not to move too fast. She couldn't see the ground properly and didn't want to trip. If she hurt herself...

No, best not to think about that.

She called Poppy again, gave a silent thank you that this time when the dog barked, she sounded closer.

Stay where you are, Poppy, please.

A few moments later, the phone torch picked up the little dog. She had finally reached a dead end and was scraping at the wall.

Except as Ellie got closer, she realised it wasn't a wall. It was some kind of door. A big piece of metal with a handle, almost like a door to a walk-in freezer.

Not sure she wanted to know what was beyond it, Ellie caught up to Poppy, managing to catch hold of her collar and scooping her up.

'You scared the life out of me,' she scolded, though honestly at this point she didn't care. She was just happy she had found the dog, even though her heart was still racing.

Now she just had to get back to the house. That was easy enough, right?

But as she turned, flashed her torch back in the direction from which she had just come, the light flickered and died, plunging her into darkness.

23

Shit, shit, shit.

Ellie tapped frantically at her phone, but there was nothing.

In her arms, Poppy wriggled and whined, and she fought to hold on to the dog as she slipped her phone into her pocket, scared she might drop it, and aware she needed her free hand to help navigate.

She was in pitch blackness, though, and realised she was going to have a nightmare finding her way back. How long had she been down here? Five minutes? It was going to take at least twice that amount of time without a light, and of course, she couldn't let go of Poppy, who was going to slow her down further.

The need to give in to panic was overwhelming, her breath coming fast now as terror clawed its way into her throat. She couldn't wait here to be found because no one knew she was down here. That meant she had to help herself.

Think, Ellie. Think, damn it.

There was the door behind her, the one that Poppy had been scraping at. Did it lead to another room or was it a way out?

Wary as she was of wandering further away from the house, she had to check. If it led above ground it would save her having to find her way back through the tunnel.

Clinging onto Poppy, she felt for the wall, slowly turning herself around and carefully stepping forward, her free arm stretched out as she reached for the door.

Her fingers touched the smooth surface, and she worked her way across the metal searching for the handle, gripping hold of it when she found it and trying to pull it back towards her.

It didn't budge

Damn it.

She ignored the sting of disappointment, yanking again, harder, scaring herself when the door this time released suddenly and flew back with ease.

She let out a yelp and Poppy barked in excitement, wriggling again.

'Okay, okay, keep still, please.' She tried to calm the dog, and then herself, as she was met with more darkness.

What was this, another room?

She reached out again, expecting to find a doorway, surprised when she found it was blocked. Another smooth surface. A second door? She pressed against it, felt it ease back slightly. Faint light spilt into the tunnel.

Not a door, but something was blocking the entrance. She pushed again, felt it shift and could definitely see light.

She found herself peering into a room. This one was lined with floor-to-ceiling bookshelves.

Ellie eased her way through the gap, still wrestling with the struggling Poppy, who was even more frantic to be released now they were on the other side of the door. She glanced around the room, realised that the door to the tunnel had been blocked by a bookcase.

This was some kind of library. There was a desk in the

middle of the room with a big leather chair and light filtering through from a domed skylight.

What the hell is this?

She was tempted to call out but had no idea where she was or if the place was even occupied. It was best to find a way out and fast. Spotting a spiral staircase on the opposite wall, she quickly crossed the room and climbed it. At the top of the stairs she found herself in what looked like a storage room. A rack on the floor was filled with wellington boots and there were anoraks hanging on pegs on the wall.

Did someone live here?

There was a doorway straight ahead and a steep staircase to the left. Ellie tried the door first, frustrated when she found it locked.

In her arms, Poppy squirmed again and let out a whimper.

'Shh.' Ellie stroked her soft ears.

Until now, the dog had been blessedly quiet. Ellie really didn't want her alerting anyone to their presence. She didn't want to be caught trespassing. Just needed to find a way out.

The stairs appeared to be their only option and Ellie climbed them cautiously, now very much aware she was in someone's private space.

If she was caught, she would just have to hold her hands up and explain what had happened, but honestly, she would rather not be in that situation.

At the top of the stairs, she found herself on a tiny landing, a door in front of her, and she opened it hesitantly, surprised to find herself in a much wider hallway with several rooms leading off. Large brass chandeliers hung from the ceiling and the paintings on the walls looked expensive. This was definitely someone's home and there was only one nearby property, certainly, that she was aware of.

Benjamin's.

Did the tunnel link the two houses? And if so, was Benjamin aware it was there?

The fact that there was a bookcase blocking the door suggested he knew. In which case it was something he should really have mentioned. It wasn't as if he hadn't had plenty of opportunity.

Unless, of course, he assumed Ellie and Ash already knew about it. She supposed it was the estate agent who should have flagged it up. Another black mark against Jeremy Fox.

Knowing that it probably was the Thorne residence should have made Ellie feel a little bit easier. Benjamin would understand if she explained what had happened.

Given that she had been trying to cool things with him and had gone out of her way to avoid him over the last few days, she would rather not run into him if she had a choice.

Whispering to Poppy to stay quiet, even though the puppy didn't understand a word she was saying, she crossed the landing, hating that the plush red carpeted floor creaked in places, worried that she would be heard. She could see another staircase ahead and, if she was right, it was the main one that led down to the front door.

Hopefully Benjamin was outside gardening and as for Virginia... Well, Ellie hoped she wouldn't see any sign of her. She remembered Benjamin saying his sister liked to paint and that he had set an easel up for her in the conservatory. With any luck, she would be in there.

Most of the doors leading off the landing were shut, but one was open, and Ellie couldn't help but glance inside as she passed, pausing when she saw the pretty pink room and the dozen or so dolls that were neatly lined up on the ottoman at the foot of the bed.

The dolls looked expensive, all beautifully dressed and their faces delicately painted, eyes all staring at her, as though judging her for being in the house uninvited.

As she took a step closer, wondering if this was Virginia's room, Poppy started whining again, this time seeming more agitated.

'Shh, hush, baby. We're going now.'

The whining turned to low growling as the floor creaked loudly behind Ellie and she froze, hearing the distinct sound of footsteps. Turning back in the direction from which she had come, she spotted Virginia.

The girl was standing at the end of the hallway, close to the door that Ellie had come through, and she was staring at them. Same dress, same cloud of scruffy curls, same thick glasses. Something glinted in her hand and Ellie's gaze dropped. Scissors.

Everything inside her went cold and she took a step back.

'I wasn't snooping. We got lost.'

Virginia's hand with the scissors started swinging back and forth.

They were dressmaking scissors; Ellie was pretty sure. The blade long and sharp. Poppy was still growling, growing agitated, and she backed up another step.

'We're going now.'

She didn't wait for Virginia to react to that, was fairly certain she wouldn't anyway. At least, not verbally. Turning on shaking legs, she hurried the rest of the way to the staircase, making her way down the steps quickly, keeping everything crossed that she didn't bump into Benjamin, though if she did she no longer cared. All she wanted was to get the hell away from his creepy sister.

She crossed the hallway to the front door, wishing Poppy, who had gone from growling back to whining, would shut up.

She knew the dog was picking up on her own distress, and that was probably what was unsettling her.

She tried the door, cursing when it didn't open, and fumbled with the bolt using her one free hand, her fingers shaking. Another creak came on the stairs behind her, but Ellie didn't look round, her only focus on getting out of the house. Virginia was crazy, first leaving the knives arranged on the worktop, now standing there holding a pair of scissors.

Benjamin had said his sister wasn't dangerous, but Ellie wasn't so sure.

The knob was slick in her hand when she tried it again, and she could have sobbed with relief when the door opened. She quickly stepped outside, and as she turned to pull the door closed behind her, she caught a glimpse of Virginia on the stairs, watching.

Keeping a tight grip on Poppy, she hurried down the driveway, her heart thumping, not stopping until she reached her own front door.

At which point she realised that the house was locked, her keys inside.

Fuck! Seriously.

Ellie let out a frustrated GRRR, raking the fingers of her free hand back through her hair and fighting the urge to give in to a tantrum of tears.

Poppy twisted in her arms, licking at her cheek, and she clutched at the puppy tightly.

Think, Ellie. Focus.

She had been keeping the downstairs doors and windows locked during the day, ever since Virginia's intrusion, but the bedroom window was open. Would one of the ladders in the shed reach it?

She made her way round to the back garden, thankful to put the wriggling Poppy down and give her arms a rest. While Poppy chased around after a butterfly, Ellie went into the shed and fetched the tallest of the ladders, taking it over to the house.

It didn't quite reach the bedroom window, but it was just tall enough to allow her to get onto the balcony. She glanced at the brickwork. There was about a six-foot gap between the balcony and the open window and a narrow ledge between the two. Would it be safe to walk along?

She wasn't a fan of heights and if she slipped onto the patio below she would likely break something, but other than going back to the Thorne house and finding Benjamin to help her or returning through the tunnel (neither of which she fancied doing) did she have a choice?

Her house and car keys were locked inside, and she had a dead phone. She was screwed.

Trying not to debate over it too much, she did the easy part, climbing up onto the balcony. From there she eyed the ledge. It looked stable enough, jutting out maybe about half a foot. She would have to hold on to the trellis. Would it support her weight?

Glancing at the ground below, she wasn't sure she was brave enough, and she played for time, trying to get in through the French doors. Without smashing the glass, though, there was no way she was getting inside.

She tried to view that as a bonus. If she couldn't get in then hopefully no one else could either.

It didn't help her situation right now, though, and she realised that if she wanted to get back into the house she was going to have to climb across to the open window.

Sucking in a deep breath, she climbed over the edge, tentatively putting one foot on the ledge, while clinging onto the balcony wall for dear life.

Don't look down.

She didn't, though her nerves were on edge as she reached

one hand for the trellis. She tugged on it, relieved when it didn't budge. Still, she had to psych herself up before she dared let go of the balcony, her stomach dropping as she took the leap of faith that the trellis would support her full weight. She stood, nose against wall for a moment, not sure if she was brave enough to move, her legs shaking so badly, she was scared she was going to topple right off the ledge. It wasn't wide enough to fully support her feet, and her heels were hanging precariously over the edge.

You can do this, Ellie. It's just a few steps to the window.

Hesitantly, she shuffled a couple of steps, almost had a panic attack when she realised the balcony was now out of reach as well and she was fully reliant on the ledge and the trellis.

From somewhere behind her, Poppy barked.

For fuck's sake, don't look. Ignore her. Keep moving.

She shuffled a little bit further, could feel the sun beating down on her bare shoulders. Sweat was beading on her forehead and top lip, and she longed to wipe it away, but didn't dare.

The whole time she kept expecting the trellis to give, knew there was no way she would remain balanced on the ledge if that happened.

She paused for a moment, drew another deep breath, took another couple of steps, and when she looked at the window, she was relieved to see it was almost in touching distance.

Those last few steps were achieved on the promise of a large glass of wine once she was inside, and her relief as she finally pulled herself through the window was immeasurable.

As she landed on the soft carpet, her legs still shaking, she sunk to the floor, needing a moment to gather herself.

So much had happened since she had gone into the cellar to get the sunlounger and her scrambled brain was struggling to process it all.

Remembering that the entrance to the tunnel was still open spurred her into action. She had access to the tunnel, but so did Benjamin and Virginia. While it was a stretch trying to imagine Benjamin in his pressed shirt and trousers down in the tunnel, she wouldn't put anything past his sister. There was no way she wanted Virginia being able to get in the house.

It occurred to her that it might have happened on Friday night. There had been no visible sign of a break-in. Had Virginia used the tunnel to get into the house while Ellie and Ash were out?

The idea was more than a little creepy.

Back down in the cellar she pushed the section of fake wall back into place, glancing around for something heavy to put in front of it. There wasn't much down there, though, not now the washing machine had gone, and she cursed herself for selling it.

Some of hers and Ash's belongings were still boxed up and under the stairs, so in the end she dragged a couple of the heavier ones across, pushing them against the wall. It wasn't perfect, but it would certainly make it more difficult to gain entry.

Upstairs in the kitchen, she closed the door, wishing that the cellar was lockable. When Ash returned she would get him to put a latch on the door. Hell. She was going to make him brick up the wall in the cellar.

For now she dragged the low sideboard through from the lounge, wedging it in front of the door. Again it wasn't a perfect solution, but with it there she felt that little bit safer.

After letting Poppy in from the garden, she locked the French doors again, glanced at the clock, saw it was still only half three, thought, *Fuck it*, and poured that well-earned promised glass of wine.

Taking it upstairs, she plugged her dead phone into the charger then stripped out of her manky clothes and indulged in a hot shower, trying to relieve some of the tension knots in her back and shoulders.

Back in the bedroom, wrapped in a big fluffy towel and feeling human again as she sipped at her wine, she knew she had to talk to Ash. This couldn't wait until he came home.

Remembering he was in a meeting, she sent him a quick message.

Can you call me when you get this? I really need to talk to you.

She had just pressed send when a loud banging on the front door made her jump.

Ellie froze, her mind conjuring up an image of Virginia standing on the doorstep with her scissors. Or John Tanner.

Shit. She really didn't want to answer it.

Instead, she crept through to the window in the front bedroom, tried to see who it was.

There was no car outside. It had to be Virginia or Benjamin.

Another loud knock and she flinched, taking a step back when Benjamin moved into view. He glanced up at the window and she froze. Could he see her?

If so, he gave no indication, trying the door once more before giving up and going back out of the driveway.

He hadn't looked happy. Had Virginia told him that Ellie had found the tunnel, that she had been in their house uninvited?

Her phone started ringing from the bedroom. *Ash.*

Quickly she ran through to answer it, needing to speak to him, to tell him everything that had happened.

She snatched it up, dropping it on the bed as if it had burnt her when she saw Benjamin's name on the screen.

As soon as his call went to voicemail he started ringing again.

Ellie watched his name lighting up the screen as he rang

another four times before he finally gave up, instead leaving her a message.

She couldn't bring herself to listen to it. Instead, she finished her wine, and, feeling sick, she curled up in a ball on the bed, still wrapped in her towel, and waited for Ash to call her back.

24

Benjamin was beside himself with worry about Ellie.

They hadn't spoken properly in days and she had been ignoring his calls and messages or giving brief replies fobbing him off. Initially he had blamed Ash, assuming he had control of Ellie's phone or was telling her what to say, but Ash wasn't there now, just as he hadn't come home last night.

Ellie was in the house alone and when Benjamin had tried to contact her, she had ignored him. She had even refused to answer the door to him.

He thought he may have seen her in the shadows of the bedroom window as he had left the house, watching him. If so, she knew what she was doing.

At first he was hurt, but then that hurt turned to concern and fear for Ellie.

He recalled what he had read about toxic relationships, how the abuser conditions their victim into believing they are the ones at fault, and suddenly it all made sense. Ash had brainwashed her.

This was so much worse than he had initially thought, and he wasn't quite sure what he should do to help. Did he give Ellie space and hope she would come to her senses or did he try to help her?

He thought back to Naomi, remembering how he had got it wrong with her. He had wanted so badly to help her, but he had failed her.

Now history seemed to be repeating itself and it was stressing him out.

This time he had to make the right decisions. He couldn't let anything happen to Ellie. She had become far too important to him.

25

Ash never called.

Ellie had remained on the bed, refreshing her phone periodically, willing it to ring, not wanting to disturb him by calling when she knew he was busy, but hoping he would find five minutes for her at some point. Eventually she had dozed off.

When she awoke she was shocked to see it was twilight. She guessed that the previous night's lack of sleep must have caught up with her.

She immediately checked her phone again. Still nothing from Ash. Just Benjamin's voicemail notification sitting there taunting her.

Poppy was on the floor by the bed and realising Ellie was awake, she let out a whimper.

Shit! She had forgotten to feed her.

She apologised to the puppy as she hurriedly slipped on sleep shorts and a vest top, figuring there was no point in getting fully dressed. Taking her empty wine glass and fully charged phone downstairs, she closed all the blinds and curtains. She didn't like thinking of who might be outside looking in. She fed the dog and poured a fresh glass of wine before tapping Ash's name into her phone.

Yes, he was busy with this work's dinner thing, but he had ignored her message from earlier and this was important. She needed to talk to him.

Irritation hummed through her when her call went to voicemail and she left a brief message reiterating that she needed to speak with him urgently.

Why is he avoiding me?

She supposed she should eat, but the stress of the day had taken her appetite. Hunting in the fridge, she put together a small plate of crackers, cheese and olives and took it through to the living room with her wine and phone.

Flooding the room with light, she turned on the TV, tried to lose herself in reruns of *Friends*, not sure her addled brain could focus on anything more complicated. The sounds of the show and the alcohol in her glass eventually helped her to relax a little, made her even wonder if perhaps she was over-reacting. But still she was uneasy.

Virginia had been in the house at least once, possibly twice, and that was a concern given her disturbing behaviour. Setting knives out on the counter... that was not normal. And okay, Ellie had been trespassing in her house, but the way Virginia had stood there waving a pair of scissors had scared the crap out of her.

Plus, it still bothered her; Benjamin must know about the tunnel, and probably was aware that his sister used it, so why hadn't he ever mentioned it before? Ellie glanced at her phone and the voicemail that she hadn't listened to. He had seemed agitated when he had stopped by the house earlier. Was he angry with Ellie because she had discovered the tunnel?

Tempted as she was, she wouldn't listen to his voicemail

tonight. It would put her on edge again and she was already going to have a difficult enough job getting to sleep tonight.

Maybe she should just stay on the sofa, keep the TV on for company.

It wasn't the most comfortable place to sleep, but it was better than the quietness of the bedroom.

Deciding it was a good idea, she went upstairs for her pillow and duvet, a confused Poppy hot on her trail, tail wagging in excitement as she tried to figure out what this new game was.

Ellie gave her some dog treats then grabbed the bottle of wine from the fridge, taking it back through to her temporary bedroom. It was a warm night, so she settled herself down on top of the duvet, topped up her wine glass again, then snuggled back into the pillow, smiling as on-screen Joey gave Ross advice on how to pull up his leather trousers.

She watched a few more episodes of the show, finishing her wine, her tired eyes struggling to stay open, and eventually she drifted off to sleep.

With the TV still playing, she didn't at first hear the sound coming from the kitchen. It was Poppy barking that woke her, and it took a second to realise that she was on the sofa and to remember why she'd decided to sleep there.

She was wide awake now, her shoulders tensing. Poppy wouldn't be barking at nothing. Sitting up, she glanced around the room. Couldn't see any sign of the dog.

Where was she?

Unwilling to call out, just in case anyone was in the house, she got to her feet and crept across the living room towards the barking.

Poppy was just inside the kitchen door and she was growling as Ellie approached, her focus on the cellar door.

It was shut, thank God, but then Ellie realised that the unit she had pushed up against it had shifted several inches forward.

She swallowed hard, knew there was no way it had moved by itself.

Had Virginia tried to get in the house?

She rushed over on trembling legs, pushed the heavy unit back against the door.

Really, she should go check the cellar, but it was the middle of the night, and she wasn't that brave. The sideboard would have to do.

She'd had enough though; her frazzled nerves couldn't take any more of this. In the morning she was going to pack a few things and go stay with Pete and Roxanne until Ash returned. She didn't want to spend another night in the house alone.

For tonight though, she would barricade herself in the living room. She could push the sofa she was sleeping on up against the door. If Virginia managed to get up from the cellar again, at least she wouldn't be able to get into the living room.

Ellie wasn't sure if the girl meant her any harm or not, but she wasn't willing to take the risk.

As she was already up, she drank a glass of water then went for a pee, leaving all of the rooms flooded with light.

Poppy was in the hallway when she returned, and she still seemed agitated, whimpering as she paced between the kitchen and the living room.

'Come on, Pops. Let's try and go back to sleep.'

Ellie beckoned her as she stepped back into her makeshift bedroom, but the puppy seemed reluctant to go with her. She didn't like the idea of leaving her in the hallway, just in case Virginia did return. 'Poppy. Come on.'

Instead of doing as she was told, the dog started growling again, which had Ellie's nerves immediately on edge, and she jumped when the growls turned to ferocious barks.

But there was another sound. A creak of a floorboard, and she froze, realising it had come from behind her.

Before she could react, a hand clamped over her mouth, yanking her backwards, and her legs flailed as she lost her footing, tried to fight whoever had hold of her.

The last thing she felt was a sharp stab of pain in her neck, and then everything faded to black.

PART II

AFTER

26

Knowing she had hidden from him, refusing to answer the door, Benjamin had decided the best way forward was to give Ellie some space. He was quite certain that she wouldn't react well if he tried to approach her at the moment, so he kept himself busy tending to his summer flowers. Eventually, he would have to explain that he was going to help her whether she wanted him to or not.

It was Ash Brady who told him about her disappearance, paying a visit to the house late on Wednesday evening. Benjamin learnt that he had been away with business, and his absence hadn't been because of a fight as he had originally assumed. Ash had returned early when he couldn't get hold of Ellie, and Benjamin's heart had raced as the other man explained Ellie had been trying to call him Tuesday evening saying she needed to speak to him urgently, but that when he had tried to get hold of her the following morning, she hadn't answered.

Benjamin's expression had been one of shock when Ash had told him he had arrived home to find Poppy on her own, going frantic, no sign of Ellie, and her phone missing.

'Have you seen her?' he had demanded, the accusatory tone clear in his voice.

'No, I haven't.' Benjamin was aware he sounded defensive, but he really didn't appreciate the insinuation. Still, he guessed it paid for him to be as honest as possible at this point. 'I stopped by the house yesterday afternoon, but Ellie didn't answer the door. I tried to call her too, but she ignored it.'

'But you know she was there?' Ash was staring at him, seeming agitated, and Benjamin was aware of heat creeping into his cheeks.

'I saw her at the bedroom window,' he admitted. 'At least I think I did. That's when I decided it was best to give her some space.'

Ash scrubbed his hands over his face. He looked tired. 'Her car's there, so she left with someone, either voluntarily or against her will.' He looked at Benjamin again, studying him. 'And her cash card and driver's licence are still in her purse.'

'When did you last speak to her?'

'Tuesday morning. And you say you saw her yesterday afternoon?'

'Well, I thought I had, but now you have me doubting myself.' Benjamin's gut twisted. This whole situation was reminding him of what had happened with Naomi. 'I think you need to call the police,' he advised. 'Do you want to come inside? We can call them from here if you like.'

Ash shook his head. 'I'm gonna go back to the house. In case she comes home, or I hear from her. I'll call them from there.'

'If there's anything I can do...'

'If you remember anything at all, please let me know.'

'Of course.'

'Thanks, Ben.' Ash caught himself. 'Jamin,' he added.

Benjamin watched him go. He had looked haunted. But was

he really worried about his girlfriend and the fact she had disappeared, or was it all an act? Just what was going on there?

He closed the door, scrubbed his own hands over his face as he considered Ash's revelation, and he thought of Ellie, worrying about her. He wanted to help her, he really did, but perhaps he should have done things differently. If he had just gone back to the house that Tuesday afternoon and insisted she talk to him... No, he couldn't think that way. Everything he had done to try and help her was with the very best of intentions.

He would not let himself feel guilty.

He thought again of Naomi. He still blamed himself for failing her. He would not let the same thing happen with Ellie. He was not to blame.

John Tanner had dark secrets and eventually they had been revealed.

Benjamin suspected Ash had secrets too. And just like with John, he was determined to expose them.

True to his word, Ash called the police on Wednesday evening and reported his girlfriend as missing.

As Benjamin expected, they paid a visit to him, too, and he tried to help them with their enquiries, though wasn't sure anything he said was going to be of use. He told them about the friendship he had formed with Ellie, but how she had closed herself off in the days leading up to her disappearance.

He thought back to when he had stopped by the house on Tuesday afternoon. He had been sure he had seen Ellie at the bedroom window at the time, but now he wasn't so certain.

'Maybe I imagined it,' he told the two police constables.

Feeling it was his duty, he also mentioned his concerns

about Ash to them and was pleased when they gave him their assurance that they would look into the points he had raised. Benjamin knew that Ash was hiding something, just as he had known that he was bad news for Ellie. If Ash had done anything to her, he was going to make sure he didn't go unpunished.

27

I like it when the night falls. When the shadows fill the hallways and everything is silent, except perhaps the haunting sound of a hooting owl.

The witching hour, that is what they call it. It is a time for hunters and watchers and for all the dark things to come out of hiding.

It's when I am supposed to be asleep in bed, but often I am awake and restless. This is my time. When there is no one around to tell me what to do. I can move freely. I am alive.

My favourite place is in the darkness. It's where I can truly be me.

Except, I am no longer alone.

I have never been good at sharing. People, places, things. If I claim something, I want it to be mine, and mine alone.

And I will do anything necessary to make it happen.

28

When Ellie had first awoken, she thought she was still in her dream, back in the tunnel and chasing after Poppy, the darkness consuming her as the little dog led her through a warren of tunnels. She was running blindly, getting further away from the house with each step and knew it would be impossible to find her way back. In the distance she could hear what sounded like a tap dripping. Was that where Poppy was heading, towards the source of the water? Ellie knew somehow she had to find her before she reached it. Unable to see where she was going, she caught the toe of her trainer on something and stumbled forward, arms flailing as she tried and failed to stop herself from falling.

But then she had been jolted back to consciousness, could feel the warmth of a blanket tucked under her chin, and the softness of the pillow her head was resting against. She wasn't lost, she had been dreaming. A nightmare. But it was over now, and she was safe.

Her first emotion was relief and she sighed deeply, breathing in the heady smell of petrol. As her sleep-addled brain tried to figure out where it was, wondering if it could explain the throbbing headache that had started behind her temples, she heard the tap dripping again, the one from her dream, and it shocked her fully awake.

Her eyes opened, blinking rapidly at the unfamiliar surroundings. The ceiling above her was lower than the one in the bedroom and much darker, shadows flickering over it. It was still night, almost black, though light was coming from somewhere.

She wasn't in the house, of that much she was sure, so where the hell was she?

Sitting up too quickly, the blanket falling from her shoulders, the throbbing in her head turned to a pounding, and for a moment she thought she was going to vomit.

She tried to take a moment, but panic and confusion about where she was had her heart thumping in her chest. Although she wasn't sure what was going on, she could sense this wasn't good and that she was in some kind of trouble. Blurred memories of being in the house, sleeping on the sofa because she was scared being there all alone came back to her, and then that awful realisation that someone was in the house, of someone grabbing hold of her, had bile rising in her throat.

Whoever had attacked her had brought her here. She needed to leave now.

But even as she was pushing back the covers, still frantically glancing around, the true horror of where she was began to dawn. The stone walls, the ceiling. It all looked so familiar because she was certain she had been here before. If she was right, she was somewhere in the tunnel that linked the houses.

A different part though, as this space was wider, and bathed in an eerie glow. Lamps perhaps. That would explain the petrol smell. She looked for the source.

And it was in that moment that she spotted the bars.

The panic bubbled over now as she pushed herself from the

bed, stumbling towards them. Something caught on her foot, and she tripped, landing hard on her knees, her ankle twisting behind her.

Ellie cried out, taking gulps of the stale, petrol-fumed air as waves of pain washed over her. Breathing deeply, she managed to turn herself, so she was sitting on her bum. She had cut both knees, but her focus wasn't on the dripping blood. It was on the heavy cuff she was wearing on her right ankle. She yanked on the chain attached, realised it was concreted into the ground. Just enough slack for her to move to the end of the bed, but not enough to get out of the door of this cell she was in.

Someone had done this to her. Someone had broken into the house, knocked her unconscious and brought her here, locking her in a cell and chaining her up like an animal.

As the comprehension of that started to sink in, so did the uncontrollable shaking and the rising panic. Why was she here? What were they going to do to her?

She clawed at the cuff and yanked hard on the chain, yelling out in frustration, realising there was no way she was going to free herself without a bolt cutter or a key.

As her voice echoed around the cell, around this cave-like room she was in, she wondered, was she being watched?

She tried to pull herself up, though it wasn't easy as she could not roll on to her knees, with the chain also hampering her movements. She winced as it cut into her ankle.

Holding onto the bed, she fought the nausea and eventually clambered to her feet. This time she was mindful of the chain, especially as she struggled to put her foot on the floor, pain shooting up her calf. She had definitely twisted or sprained it. She limped gingerly towards the edge of the cell, realised that if she approached to the left of the door, she had just enough slack to reach the bars. She grabbed hold of them, tried to rattle them loose, but they held fast. Instead, she pressed her face against the bars, peering through them.

'Hello?' Her voice echoed again. She could hear the tremor of fear in her tone, and it made her feel so alone. 'Who are you?'

She waited, listened, but there was just her breathing and the drip, drip, drip of the tap.

'What do you want from me?'

Still there was nothing.

She tried to calm herself, drawing in more deep breaths, hating the nausea that came with each one. The petrol smell had to be from the lamps. Lamp oil or paraffin she guessed. She could see them placed around the floor. Three of them. And the way they cast shadows over the walls of her prison was creepy as hell. She kept seeing movement and it was making her paranoid of who might be watching her.

Without the lamps, though, it would be pitch black in this hellhole and that would definitely be worse. At least with them she could see her surroundings.

She studied them now, knew she had to somehow find her own way out of this. No one was coming for her, no one knew she was here. She could only save herself.

From what she could see there was a tunnel leading off the far wall. There didn't appear to be any doors preventing access, which meant if she could get to it, she could probably find her way out. Or at least she could if it wasn't for this stupid chain and these stupid damn bars that were caging her.

The futility of her situation hit hard, and she tried to rattle the bars again, giving in to the urge to scream.

Of course, there was no one to scream for. Ash was miles away and wouldn't be back for days, and Benjamin and Virginia had access to this tunnel. Had one of them done this to her?

Virginia had seen her in the Thorne house, but did she have the strength to drag Ellie down here?

But that left Benjamin and despite everything that had happened, she didn't think he had it in him.

Yes, he had become a little bit annoying, but he was a good person with a kind heart. She wouldn't believe him capable of doing this to her.

There was one more possibility and her blood ran cold at the thought of John Tanner in her house. His daughter Naomi had disappeared. What if her father had brought her down here?

Was Naomi still down here?

Ellie screamed again, pulling at the bars. 'Let me out of here? Please!' She continued screaming, for all the good it would do, until her throat was raw, then her screams turning into choking sobs.

No one came and eventually, frustrated and broken, she retreated to the bed, perching on the edge as she wiped at her eyes.

She was starting to calm down, rational thoughts returning, when she remembered Poppy. The dog had been in the house with her, and she would be going frantic all alone. Who was going to feed her, let her in the garden? And then another even worse thought occurred to her. What if whoever had attacked Ellie had hurt the puppy?

Fresh tears fell as she thought of Poppy alone in the house. Not understanding what was going on. Possibly hurt or worse. And Ellie couldn't get to her. Couldn't explain.

Who the fuck is responsible for imprisoning me down here?

Twin emotions raged through her, fear and anger causing her whole body to shake. It wasn't just the terror of her situation, though, she realised. It was cold down here and she was still wearing just her sleep shorts and vest. No bra and her feet bare. Her state of undress made her feel even more helpless.

She glanced at the blanket covering the bed, snatching it up and wrapping it around herself, her teeth now chattering, from both the adrenaline and the cool temperature.

Focus, Ellie. You need to figure out a way to get out of here.

She didn't have her phone. At least she didn't think she did. She was certain it had been in the pocket of her shorts, and it wasn't there now. Whoever had taken her was unlikely to have left it with her. Not that it would have done her much good anyway, as she was unlikely to get a signal down here.

Was there anything she could use to try and break the cuff off?

She glanced around the cell, for the first time spotting the two boxes and the bucket on the other side of the bed. She leant across the mattress and pulled the first box towards her, saw it was filled with food. She spotted cereal bars, fruit, and biscuits on the top with plenty more underneath. There were water bottles in the box too. Maybe there would be cutlery that she could use.

Before checking, she glanced in the second box, realising this one had some of her clothes in it. She pulled out a couple of T-shirts and a jumper, a pair of jeans and her old joggers. Beneath them were half a dozen pairs of knickers and two of her bras. She picked up the items, repulsed at the idea that whoever had brought her down here had gone through her underwear drawer.

Along with the food box, the clothing suggested that the plan was to keep her locked in this cage for an extended period. While a tiny part of her was reassured that whoever had kidnapped her wasn't planning to kill her if they had brought her food and clothes, she couldn't help but worry what else they had in store for her. They had gone to the trouble to imprison her down here. Did they intend to torture or rape her?

Whatever their motive, it wasn't going to be good.

She peered in the bucket, wanted to throw up when she

realised its purpose. It contained two toilet rolls, a pack of baby wipes, and a small torch.

Seriously, this was supposed to be her toilet?

Ellie glanced around the dark cave cell again, swiping at fresh tears as she understood that whoever had done this hadn't randomly attacked her. They had gone to a lot of trouble.

She climbed off the bed, grabbed hold of the bars again, shaking them in frustration. 'HELP ME! SOMEBODY PLEASE HELP ME! I'M TRAPPED DOWN HERE!'

She waited and she sobbed, and she shouted out again, even though she knew it was futile.

Eventually she sunk to the floor, still gripping at the bars, drawing her bloody knees up to her chest, then letting go to hug herself tightly. As she rocked herself back and forth, the shock of her predicament sending tremors through her body, she knew she was wasting her breath.

No one was coming.

29

With no watch, phone or window to tell her if it was day or night, and no idea how long she had been unconscious for, it was impossible for Ellie to know how long she had been trapped in the cell.

Was Ash still away with work? Had he tried to get hold of her?

Ellie recalled the message and the voicemail she had left him. He hadn't responded to either, which was unusual for him, especially since she had told him it was urgent.

And Poppy. She was still frantic about the dog, desperate to know if she was okay.

If whoever had put her in this cell would just show themselves, she could ask these questions. They cared enough to leave her clothes and food and she was clinging to that. It suggested they wouldn't want to hurt her. If she could speak to them she could try to reason with them, couldn't she?

She gingerly pulled herself up from the floor, trying to ignore her stinging knees and her bladder that was aching with the urge to pee. The thought of going to the toilet in the bucket when she had no privacy (even though she doubted anyone was down there watching) was mortifying and she had put it off for as long as she could. She was pretty sure she was alone but she couldn't be certain, and the idea of peeing in front of an audience was humiliating. She really did need to go though, and it was getting to the point where it was either peeing in the bucket or her knickers.

Realising she had no choice, she pulled the bucket towards the end of the bed, removing the contents, then yanked down her shorts. As she squatted, her face flamed at the thought someone she didn't know might be watching her doing this most basic of functions.

Afterwards, disgusted, she pushed the bucket as far away from the bed as she could get it.

What she would give for a shower right now. Even a simple wash. Instead, she used one of the baby wipes to clean her hands then another to try and wash the grime off her face, before climbing onto the bed.

Shivering from the cold she grabbed her jumper and slipped it on, wishing she could put on her joggers too. Her captor had brought them down here, along with the jeans, but she was unsure how she was expected to get them on when she had the cuff around her ankle. Instead, she made do with the blanket, wrapping it over the lower half of her body, before pulling the food box towards her and trying to heave it up onto the bed. It was really heavy, the water bottles weighing it down, so she removed those and tried again, this time lifting it easily, and emptied the contents onto the mattress, sifting through them.

As well as the fruit, biscuits and cereal bars, there were other stock cupboard items in the box; bread, jam (though nothing to spread it with, she noted) a packet of scones, and a few chocolate bars, plus a bag of tomatoes and a couple of tins of baked beans. Nothing much of any substance. Was she really expected to live off this?

And what if some of the food had been tampered with?

She wouldn't touch anything that wasn't sealed she decided. Not that she had much appetite anyway. Being kidnapped and locked in a cell had taken care of that.

The only thing in the box that she could possibly use were the tins of baked beans. Maybe she could do something with the sharp lids? As she debated the idea, she eyed the water bottles, realising she was really thirsty. There were six of them and all looked unopened. Grabbing one, she twisted the cap, relieved when she heard the seal break. The water had to be safe.

She took a test sip first anyway, swigging it around in her mouth for a few seconds, then when it tasted normal she gulped furiously from the bottle, some of it spilling down her chin and onto her jumper. As she wiped at her mouth she realised that a third of the bottle had already gone and she panicked.

How long was this food and water supposed to last her?

She replaced the cap, put the bottle back on the floor, her mind going into overdrive.

What if she ran out of food and water? She needed to eke out what she had, make it last.

While she was eager to get the tin lids off the baked beans so she had some kind of weapon, she couldn't afford to waste them. The fact the box was down here suggested she was on her own, that whoever had taken her had no plans to come see her any time soon. Were these meagre supplies supposed to last her for a week or longer?

Which, of course, raised the question of why she had been kidnapped.

Why take her and lock her in a cell, only to leave her there?

She had assumed her attacker's motive was to hurt or kill her, but now it occurred to Ellie for the first time, that perhaps this was financially driven.

Although she wasn't rich by any means, she did have some

savings, the sad result of losing both parents young. Was her captor looking for a ransom? It would certainly explain why she had been left down here with food rations. And that changed things. Virginia Thorne and John Tanner were unlikely to have a financial motivation, neither would Benjamin, which suggested someone else was involved.

Did Ash know she was missing? Had her abductor contacted him asking for money? He would be able to access her accounts, so he shouldn't have a problem getting whatever was needed.

As she put the food items back in the box, and placed it back on the floor, her mind wandered to the Tanner family and Naomi's disappearance. No one had ever learnt what had happened to her and gossip would be rife when people found out that someone else had vanished from the house.

It was almost too coincidental to not be connected. Unless it had been intended to look that way. Ellie didn't like the doubt that was niggling in the back of her mind.

Ash had sworn he hadn't known about the history of the house before they had moved in.

He had been telling the truth, hadn't he?

No, she trusted him implicitly. Enough that he had access to all of her bank accounts. She loved him and he loved her. He would never do anything to hurt her. They had bought a house together, at some point would get married and probably have kids too. He was her forever and she trusted him enough that she had set up a will before moving in with him. If anything happened to her, he got everything.

But that had been her idea, not his.

The life insurance policy had been his idea, though, and he had been the one to persuade Ellie that they should go for a higher amount.

No, she was scared and confused. This situation she was in was making her irrational.

Ash was the one person in this world she loved and trusted unconditionally. To even consider that he would betray her was ridiculous.

Did he really go away with work though? You couldn't get hold of him, remember?

Stop it!

She couldn't, wouldn't believe he was involved.

Unsettled by her train of thought, she lay back on the mattress, rolling onto her side. She pulled up the blanket, so it was covering her, a literal safety blanket against whatever was outside the cell, and she tried to draw her knees up to her chest, needing the comfort of huddling into a ball. The chain crudely stopped her, reminding her just how helpless her situation was.

Squeezing her eyes shut and trying to ignore the tears that were leaking from them, she prayed for sleep. Prayed for an escape from this nightmare.

30

She doesn't know that I can see her. That I have been watching her from the shadows.

I felt her fear when she first woke up, could hear the panic in her voice when she called out for help. She tried to figure out a way to escape, pulling at the cuff on her ankle. She won't break free, though, no matter how hard she tries.

The others didn't and neither will she.

She thinks she is going to find a way out, but no one knows about this place. The others couldn't escape, and Ellie will be no different.

It will probably take a few days to break her, for her to realise that no one is coming, and she is trapped. When she understands that, once her dignity has been stripped away, that is when she will become more obedient.

But obedience is not the same as love or respect and a cage cannot change someone like Ellie.

She doesn't deserve this chance. The others didn't either. That is why I am watching her closely.

I press the tip of my finger against the blade in my hand, feel it cut into my flesh and release the sweet burst of pain.

Ellie never should have come here. She got in the way, and I will have to take care of her. She is another one who isn't worthy and when the time comes, I am going to make her go away.

31

Don't fuck this up. Don't fuck this up.

Those were the words running through Ashton Brady's head the first time he had laid eyes on Ellie Summers.

He had paid an impromptu visit to his best friend, Pete, had already screwed up because Roxanne, Pete's she-devil of a wife, had greeted him with a mouthful of venom for daring to interrupt the precious dinner thing she had going on.

Pete had managed to calm her down, inviting Ash to join them, and taking him through to where the others were eating. That was when he had first seen Ellie. She was talking to a man sat opposite her, laughing politely at something he had said then she had turned her head at the footsteps and her eyes had locked with Ash's. Wide glittering eyes and a warm smile that dimpled her cheeks, and it was like he had been sucker-punched in the gut.

He had taken a seat beside her, wanting, no, needing to know who she was and to get to know her better, and luckily for him, the feeling appeared mutual. As they talked, Ellie's pretty laugh sent a delicious shiver through him, her intoxicating perfume jangling his senses, and her eyes (at first he had thought they were blue, but up close he could see they were a sea green) focused on him, only him; he knew he had walked off a cliff.

He was a flirt. There was no denying that. He serial-dated, never got serious, and had a terrible reputation with women. But that was because none of them had mattered. Until now. Ellie was different. Straightaway he knew that.

His mum had told him it would happen like this. That one day the right person would waltz into his life, and it would change everything. At the time he had been amused by her words, certain no woman would ever have that effect over him. He was happy just jogging along doing his own thing. But turns out she was right, as meeting Ellie changed everything.

Of course, there was the whole problem to get past of her being Roxanne's friend. It was a given that Roxanne would do everything she could to warn Ellie off. And she didn't waste any time trying either, pulling Ellie to one side for a private chat before she left.

Ash wasn't deterred and figured he had scored a coup when he persuaded Ellie to give him her number before she got into her taxi. He came up to Norwich to see her the next weekend, considered their date a success when they spent much of the day laughing and by the time he returned home, he was more than a little bit smitten with Ellie Summers.

For the first year of their relationship, they took it steady, living in different cities, content to spend weekends together as they learnt more about each other. Both approached it with a fair amount of caution, aware this was more than a casual fling, because neither of them wanted to fuck it up. But after that rainy week trapped together in a tiny cottage in Scotland, a situation that was going to either make or break them, Ash knew he had to have more.

Moving into Hazelwood Cottage with the girl he intended to eventually marry and start a family with should have been the happiest time of his life. But just a few short weeks after they had exchanged contracts, Ellie had vanished, and, not that things could get any worse, Ash knew the police were suspecting foul play and viewing him as their number one suspect.

It didn't help his case that Ellie had a sizeable bank balance, that the pair of them had taken out life insurance before buying the house, or that Ellie had recently changed her will, leaving everything to Ash.

They always look close to home. That was what Pete had told him after Ash had spent much of the day in the police station answering questions.

It was true, he knew that, but while they wasted their time focusing on him, Ellie could be in trouble or worse. He hadn't been arrested and he had attended the station voluntarily, but even so, that didn't help the situation and back home he was going insane trying to figure out where the hell she had disappeared to.

She wouldn't have walked out. He was certain of that. They sometimes disagreed and occasionally had fights, but nothing major, nothing that caused a rift between them. They were both quick to temper but quick to forgive, that was how Ellie had once described them, and she was right.

Ash had been raised to realise life was too short to hold on to anger. It was one of the reasons he and Ellie worked so well together.

So if she hadn't left of her own accord, that meant someone had taken her.

But who?

Nothing had been disturbed in the house. The doors were all locked and there was no sign of forced entry. Ellie's bag with her purse and credit cards, plus her keys, had all been left behind. Nothing was missing from the house and her car was parked in the drive.

She had slept, or had been sleeping, in the living room, judging by the duvet and pillow on the sofa. The TV had been playing when Ash had returned home and there had been an empty bottle of wine on the floor. Was there a reason for that? Had something happened that had made her scared to sleep upstairs? And why had she dragged the living room sideboard through into the kitchen?

Poppy had been alone and upset, barking like crazy before Ash had even stepped foot in the house, the stench of her pee and shit filling the hallway. She had been hungry, too, her bowl empty and her water dish almost empty.

Ellie would not have just left her. He was convinced of that. She loved the dog.

No, Ash was convinced she had been taken, refused to believe she was dead, and he was certain the puppy had seen who was responsible. In the days following Ellie's disappearance, he had spent hours with Poppy, the one living connection he still had, talking to her, desperate for answers that he knew she couldn't give him.

He knew Pete thought he was going crazy, even though he tried his best to be sympathetic, while Roxanne had sneered at him. She was playing the 'best friend' role with aplomb, making pointed digs that Ash might be responsible for Ellie's disappearance, and annoyed with Pete for standing by him.

'Do you need us to go pick up some bits and bobs from the supermarket?' Pete asked now, sniffing dubiously at the milk he had just taken out of the fridge. He was making coffee for himself, Ash and Roxanne, who had been dragged along today as part of Pete's mission to check in with Ash every day.

Roxanne couldn't have looked less like she wanted to be there. 'He has a car for God's sake,' he heard her mutter to Pete. 'We're not his housekeepers.'

'I'll go later, mate. It will get me out of the house.' Of course,

Ash would do no such thing. He couldn't give a flying fuck about having a stocked fridge or if the milk was off. All he cared about was finding Ellie.

His friend was worried, though, he got that, and it was why he hadn't yet chewed Pete's head off. Ash hadn't shaved in days and was wearing the same tatty T-shirt and joggers he'd had on during yesterday's visit, and he knew Pete was concerned by his unkempt appearance and the fact the house was turning into a tip. Unlike his judgemental wife, who had been a crap friend to Ellie, and was now trying to twist her disappearance to make herself look better.

The two-faced bitch.

He scowled at her now, aware she was looking at him like something she'd scraped off the bottom of her ridiculously high, high-heeled shoe, her red hair sleek and shiny (had he ever seen a strand of it out of place?) and her pale face perfectly made up. Thank God Ellie wasn't high-maintenance. She seldom wore make-up and didn't care if someone saw her in her old decorating clothes, her hair tied back and covered in paint splatters.

Fuck, I miss her.

'If you've got something to say to me, Roxanne, then spit it out,' he snapped.

He saw the warning look Pete shot his wife, wanting her to rein it in, though honestly, Ash would rather she just came out and said what she was thinking. It would give him an excuse to rip back at her, tell her a few home truths, and maybe it was time the truth came out. Yes, he would get caught up in the fallout, but honestly he was sick of the guilt he had been carrying all these years.

She pursed her ruby lips, and he could see the debate in her eyes. Although they had never had the conversation, she was convinced she had his silence because of his friendship with Pete. Had she misjudged that?

Ash was normally measured in his response to things and tended to ignore Roxanne's existence as much as he could, but emotions were running high with Ellie missing. He knew she was wondering how far it was wise to push him.

'I just think you need to start accepting some responsibility here, Ashton,' she eventually told him.

'Responsibility for what exactly, Roxanne?'

'Well, you're moping around in this...' She gestured around the messy kitchen, rolling her eyes dramatically. 'This ramshackle place, looking like a slob and feeling sorry for yourself. You're the one who dragged Ellie out here, convincing her it was a good idea to move to the back arse of nowhere.'

'I didn't drag her anywhere. You know full well that she wanted to move here as much as I did.'

'She didn't know about the house, though, did she?'

'Roxy!' Pete warned.

Roxanne shot her husband a look before turning her glare back on Ash. 'She would have had a different view if you had been upfront with her and told her what had happened here. Do you know how hard it's been, keeping your secret from my best friend? Having to lie to her and pretend I didn't know?'

'Your best friend?' Ash gave a bitter laugh. 'I like how you've upgraded yourself. You've hardly been a good friend to her. Ellie's been getting sick to death of your negativity and lack of support.'

'No she hasn't.'

'Yes, she bloody has. And you know damn well why I didn't tell her about the house. We had already exchanged when I found out. You really think I would have moved her here without telling her I had known sooner?'

He thought back to the day he had learnt about the Tanner

family and the history of the property. Couldn't help thinking at the time that it had been too good to be true, getting the house for the price they had, and kicking himself for not investigating further before they had put in an offer.

Though seriously, who the hell thought to ask if any murders had ever happened in the place you were buying?

Pete had been with him at the time. They had headed over to take some measurements ahead of moving in, the contracts already exchanged. It was purely by chance that they had run into a nosy local, Nigel, Ash recalled his name was, who was eager to tell them all about John Tanner and his unfortunate family.

Ash had cursed on the drive back to Pete's, knowing that Ellie was going to freak out. It didn't bother him living in a place with a violent past, but Ellie was different, and this was going to upset her. He had spoken with their solicitor and tried to find out what their options were. He learnt that it was going to cost them more than they could afford if they pulled out at this stage, and that had left him with an awful dilemma. Did he tell Ellie the truth and move her into the house when he knew she was going to hate living there or did he lie to her?

Well, technically it wasn't a lie. He just wouldn't be telling her what had happened.

But damn it. He really didn't want to start keeping secrets from her. She was so excited about the house, though, and the idea of ruining that for her... well, he really didn't want to do that either.

He had been talking it over with Pete, trying to figure out what to do, and neither of them had heard Roxanne come in. By the time they realised, it was too late and she had heard everything.

Pete had made her promise that she wouldn't say anything to Ellie, having decided with Ash it was best to keep her in the dark, and she had agreed. How typical of Roxanne to throw it back in his face.

Of course, he had ended up lying to Ellie. When she had found out about the Tanners and confronted him, he hadn't owned up to knowing. But the lie had gone too far by then and emotions were running high. It would achieve nothing to confess that he had known all along.

Still that lie ate him up now. It didn't change anything about her disappearance, but he hated that he hadn't been truthful with her.

The Tanner thing had bugged her, played on her mind, and Ellie had even become paranoid enough that she started believing she had seen John Tanner.

Ash was pretty certain it was her mind playing tricks, that it was someone who looked similar, but he had mentioned it to the police anyway. To be honest, he was clutching at anything that might lead to Ellie's whereabouts at this point.

'She was worried about being here,' Roxanne told him now. 'But you just left her all alone, swanning off to London.'

'I was working. I have a fucking job to do, if you remember.'

'If you hadn't left her though, she wouldn't be missing, would she, Ash?'

Her vicious words and spiteful smile were the tipping point. He had managed to remain reasonably calm up until now.

'Get out.'

'Excuse me?'

'I said, get out.' Ash spat the words at her, and her eyes widened, her expression shocked. 'You're not welcome here anymore.'

'Ash, mate.'

Ash glanced at Pete, saw the dilemma on his best friend's face. This was his wife, but he also knew what she was like, and that she had really overstepped a line.

'Get her out of here, Pete. I know she's your wife, but if she doesn't get out of my house, I will throw her out myself.'

'Come on, Roxy. Time to go.'

Roxanne's mouth flapped open and shut as she gawped at Pete. 'You're seriously going to let him talk to me like that?'

Ash took a step towards her and realising he was being serious, she pushed her chair back, getting up abruptly, shaking off Pete's hand when he tried to guide her towards the door.

'I was just speaking the truth,' she snapped as a parting shot before storming out into the hallway.

'I'm sorry, man,' Pete offered him, with a shrug of his shoulders. 'You know how she is.'

It was an excuse he used all too often for Roxanne and it was getting tired.

Ash shook his head. 'Just go, okay.'

'I'll check in with you later. See if there's any news.'

Ash remained silent at that. Ellie had been missing for almost four days now and there were no clues to her whereabouts. He didn't see how the situation was going to change later today.

After he had heard the car leave he went back in the kitchen, Poppy hot on his heels, took a couple of sips of the coffee Pete had made, then dumped all three mugs in the sink.

Poppy had settled herself against the cellar door, her favourite spot, and was watching him the whole time through big brown eyes, as though fearful he might disappear, too, if she let him out of her sight.

Feeling bad for the dog, Ash took her into the garden and threw the ball for her, watched her hopping around after it. She was recovering from the accident much faster than expected and Trevor had been pleased with her progress during their last check-up.

The appointment coming up in a week was a bitter reminder

that Ellie probably wouldn't be there and the well of emotion hit him fast. Leaving Poppy to play, he went back inside, needing a moment.

Where the fuck are you, Ellie?

She wouldn't just leave.

Ash knew the police believed she was dead, whether it was through foul play or by her own hand, they were still uncertain. They hadn't actually come out and said it, but he knew what they were thinking, just as he knew he was top of their suspect list.

Of course, he was innocent, just as he was certain Ellie wouldn't take her own life. No, there had to be another explanation for her disappearance, and he knew in his gut that she was still alive. He just had to figure out where the hell she was.

32

Ellie glanced at the food box, her belly rumbling and wondered if she dared eat anything. She really had no idea how long she had been down here now, but guessed it was at least a day, maybe longer. At first she hadn't had any appetite, had just been sick with shock, but she guessed her body needed to function and if she was going to keep up her strength, she needed to feed it.

She plucked out a banana and the scones, figuring she should start with the things that were most perishable, checking the plastic packaging on the scones to ensure it was still completely sealed. She also grabbed the beans, wanting the tin lid. She peeled it back, licking the juice off and hiding it under her pillow. It wasn't much, but it was better than nothing. With no cutlery, she had to use her hands, and she realised just how hungry she actually was as she scooped the cold beans into her mouth. Licking her fingers clean, she put the discarded tin to one side then picked at the scone, though the bread was so dry, she struggled to swallow each bite.

A shuffling sound came from somewhere in the distance,

cutting through the silence and she froze, dropping the scone in her lap. Was someone there?

'Hello?'

She was trembling.

Although she had been desperate to know who was holding her prisoner down here, now she was about to come face to face with them, she wasn't so sure she wanted to know. What if they had come down here to hurt her or worse?

'Please. What do you want from me?' Her voice cracked on the last word. She wanted badly to be brave, but she was so damn frightened.

There was no answer. Just the awful ongoing silence broken by the intermittent dripping. Was that something moving in the shadows? The paraffin in the lamps was burning low, making it more difficult to see. She was dreading the oil running out and plunging her into darkness, though she guessed that would happen as she had been left with a torch.

'If you want money, I can get it for you. Just please let me go.' Ellie held her breath and waited. Still there was nothing.

Had she imagined it? She had been down here for long enough now, much of the time on the edge of hysteria. It was quite possible that she was starting to lose her mind. She remained still, staring into the shadows, scared to look away in case she saw the movement again, but as the minutes ticked by, she became more convinced that she was hearing things.

Although her stomach still grumbled, she couldn't bring herself to eat any more of the scone, was certain she wouldn't be able to keep it down. Instead, she threw it back in the box, along with the banana, and took a few sips of water to soothe her dry throat.

Still shaking, she huddled back down under the blanket and cried herself to sleep.

~

In the dream she was back in her own bed and Ash was beside her, his fingers tangled in her hair. This was good Ash. Sexy, funny and dependable Ash who loved her as much as she loved him, and she knew he would never do anything to hurt her.

But, as she drifted towards consciousness, the scratchy blanket tickling against her, she smelt the awful petrol fumes of the lamps, heard the monotonous drip, drip, drip, and her heart plummeted as she realised the nightmare was real and she was still in the prison cell.

Squeezing her eyes shut, trying to return to the dream, she felt movement on the pillow behind her, realised that something was touching her hair, their fingers stroking gently through the strands, and she froze.

Someone was in the cell with her.

She tried to keep as still as possible even as her heart nearly thumped its way out of her chest. Who was it and what did they want? She needed to look, but she was too scared.

Fresh tears leaked out of her eyes as the stroking became more aggressive. She heard heavy breathing, the fingers forming a fist in her hair and pulling hard.

Ellie screamed, tried to pull away, but then the fingers were gone, and she was rolling over, could see the figure scurrying to the open door of the cell.

Virginia.

'Wait. Please!' She pushed back the blanket, tried to go after the girl, but she wasn't quick enough, and then the chain was halting her movement, jerking her to a stop, as she fell forward, landing again on her bruised knees. She heard the door shut and the click of the lock.

'Please let me out of here. Please!'

Virginia stared at her through the bars, her head dipped and her hair falling so far forward, it almost covered her thick glasses.

'Please. Why are you doing this to me?'

There was no answer, but Ellie swore she saw her lips curve into a smile.

Then Virginia was stepping away, heading back to the tunnel, and Ellie was screaming after her to come back, knowing that she wouldn't.

The girl paused before stepping into the tunnel, raising her hand and giving Ellie a childlike wave. And then she was gone.

33

Ash had been checking Ellie's social media and email accounts frequently since she had disappeared. At first he had been riddled with guilt, snooping through her private things, but as his concern for her grew, he knew he had to do it and that he wouldn't forgive himself if he missed anything.

Luckily it was easy for him to check. Ellie was not one for secrets and didn't even have a lock on her phone. She often asked Ash to read her texts to her if she was preoccupied, and all of her accounts were logged in on her MacBook.

With her phone missing, the MacBook became his lifeline and he had spent hours scouring everything, trying to find clues to her disappearance.

Ellie had Facebook, Instagram and Twitter, though didn't post much on any of the platforms, other than to her business pages. She kept in touch with a handful of people on Messenger and Ash had contacted everyone she had been messaging with over the last couple of months. No one had heard from her, and they all seemed shocked that she had abruptly vanished.

Her email account didn't throw up any clues either. He had been hesitant about contacting her clients, not wanting to jeopardise any work she had lined up in case she did suddenly reappear, but as the weekend rolled into Monday, each day making that possibility seem less likely, he went through the motions.

He could see she had been speaking with a couple of clients via email a few days before her disappearance and that was where he started, wondering if the proof she had been at her desk working after Ash had left for his works trip would be enough to convince the police he wasn't responsible.

Of course, they would probably say he could have sent the emails pretending to be her. No, he needed something more concrete to prove his innocence.

He got hold of one client easily, though it led nowhere. The other he left a message for to call back.

After taking a break to make coffee and put in a quick call to his boss, telling him he was taking the rest of the week off, he went back upstairs to Ellie's studio and spent an hour rooting through all of her paperwork, looking for any kind of clue. It was a thankless task though, and, frustrated, he logged back into her Facebook account, clicking on to her profile photo.

It was one that had been taken of the two of them at Ash's work's Christmas party, Ellie looking gorgeous in a deep-blue dress, her hair scooped up and diamonds glinting at her earlobes. He had his arm round her, and she was leaning into him, and they were both smiling at the camera, happy, carefree, with the future ahead of them. The photo would have been taken not long after they had decided to start house-hunting, just a few months before they viewed Hazelwood Cottage for the first time.

He could remember how she had smelt that night, of fresh peaches and clean linen, the warm subtle spicy scent of her perfume adding a seductive edge, and how she had tasted of the prosecco she had been drinking when he had kissed her in the taxi on the way home.

Finding the album of photos she had uploaded of their rainy week in Scotland, he flicked through them, pausing when he reached the one he had snapped of her wearing his T-shirt, with bed hair and lust-heavy eyes. It was the same one he had as his phone screensaver. No one looking at the photo would know it, but it had been taken after they had enjoyed a lazy and indulgent afternoon in bed. Ellie had the munchies and he had fixed mugs of tea and a huge plate of buttered toast for them to snack on.

Clicking on the like on the photo, he recognised the name, Benjamin Thorne.

He hadn't even realised Ellie was friends with their neighbour on Facebook and it irritated him a little that the man was looking in on such a personal memory.

Of course, it was Ellie who had put the picture up, though, for everyone to see, he reminded himself. And he shouldn't be annoyed with Benjamin. Although the guy was a bit strange and clearly had a soft spot for Ellie, he had been nothing but good to Ash over the last few days, seeming upset by her disappearance and checking in on him a couple of times to see if there was any news or if there was anything he could do.

Ash had wrongly judged him, and he felt bad about that. He recalled the first time he had met Benjamin, when he had been good enough to return Ellie's phone. He had answered the door to him in a foul mood, having just got off a call with one of his junior colleagues whose head he had bitten off for losing a huge contract. He hadn't been particularly hospitable, and Benjamin had seemed half afraid of him, no doubt having heard Ash in full flow.

Not a great way to endear yourself to the new neighbours.

Putting thoughts of Benjamin to one side, he continued scrolling through the photos.

There were so many little memories of Ellie lingering in his mind. Her bubble of laughter whenever she was excited about something, the little hmm noise she made, catching in the back of her throat, whenever he nibbled on that sweet spot of her neck, just below her ear, that drove her crazy. The way her eyes reflected her emotions, from bright glittering green when she was happy, to the colour of a dark stormy sea when he had pissed her off.

He had taken all of those things for granted and now he was terrified he wouldn't get to experience them again. And these memories of her, would they fade with time? The idea of one day not being able to recall her scent or her taste, or the way she sounded, it was enough to drive him insane. He couldn't lose that.

His phone rang, snapping him out of his thoughts, and he took a moment, scrubbing his hands over his face and gathering himself, before answering, not recognising the number and hoping for a brief second it was going to be Ellie.

Of course, it wasn't. Deep down he knew it wouldn't be, but still, disappointment coursed through him at the unfamiliar male voice.

At first he assumed it was the police, and his tone was a little abrupt, but then he realised it was the other client Ellie had dealt with last week.

The man didn't offer much in the way of sympathy over Ellie's disappearance, if anything seeming a little put out that she wasn't there. 'She agreed to a Zoom meeting when we spoke on the phone,' he grumbled. 'It's supposed to be in the morning!'

Ash was about to reply with a sarcastic comment, his temper

bubbling over at the client's lack of understanding, when the relevance of his words hit him.

'You talked to her on the phone?'

'Yes, last week. This is rather inconvenient. I'm going to have to reschedule everything.'

As the man rambled, Ash blocked him out. If he had spoken to Ellie last week, it would have been after he had left for London. As much of an arsehole he might be, this guy was proof that Ellie had been alive and well when Ash left to go to London.

After ending the call, he got in contact with the police. This new information didn't help him find Ellie, but it was a relief to at least have an alibi. Ash wasn't foolish enough to believe he was completely off their radar, but at least it should push him down their suspect list and perhaps make them start exploring other avenues more closely.

He WhatsApped Pete and told him the news, wishing he could see Roxanne's face when she found out.

No, scrub that, he didn't want to see her irritating face, period.

The news left him feeling fractionally lighter and gave him a much-needed kick up the backside. Speaking with the client and knowing that Ellie had been actively seeking work reaffirmed his belief that she wouldn't have taken her own life.

That meant either some fucker had taken her unwillingly or something had happened to make her leave home without any of her things. He was determined he was going to get to the bottom of it but given there was no sign of a break-in, he was now even more convinced that she was alive.

At some point she was going to come home, and he didn't want her walking into a shit-tip. He would tidy the house then he would sort himself out, have a shower and a shave, put on some clean clothes.

Downstairs in the kitchen he went through the stack of dirty crockery that had been accumulating then took the sunlounger that had been propped up against the wall back down into the cellar. Ellie must have brought it upstairs with plans to go into the garden.

He thought he had closed the door behind him, swore at himself when he found Poppy beside him. She'd had no trouble getting herself down the stairs, though, and was scraping at the boxes where the old washing machine had stood.

Ash had spotted them when he'd first come home and was searching the house for Ellie and he hadn't paid too much attention to the fact she had moved some of the stuff they had stored under the stairs. Now though, especially with Poppy so fascinated as she sniffed and whined, he took a closer look.

There was nothing much of interest in the first box, stacked high with paperbacks they didn't yet have the storage space for. He pushed it out of the way to get to the second box, found it was again filled with books. Maybe Ellie had been looking for something to read.

He closed the box, started to push it back towards the wall, heard a clatter as it hit something, the small object shooting across the floor.

As Ash stared, Poppy started barking, her tail wagging madly.

It was Ellie's phone.

Heartbeat quickening, he snatched it up.

Yes, definitely Ellie's, the screen cracked though, and there was no power when he tried to switch it on. What the hell was it doing down here behind the boxes?

He glanced frantically around the cellar, searching for her, even though he logically knew there was nowhere she could be down here.

He had to get her phone on, see if it gave any clue to her whereabouts.

Upstairs he found her charger, plugged it in, swearing when he realised it didn't have a flat battery. It was actually broken.

Would her SIM fit in his phone?

He tried, relieved when it worked. Sitting on the bed he went through her calls and messages. Nothing unusual there. She had tried to get hold of him a few times and he felt a stab of guilt, because he hadn't answered.

Not that he could have. He had forgotten his phone when he left the client's office, having plugged it in to charge it and he hadn't realised that Ellie was trying to get hold of him until he was able to get it back the following morning.

Other than the missed calls and WhatsApps to him, she had spoken to her client, and exchanged texts and calls with Benjamin and a couple of friends.

Everything seemed normal. Nothing to alert any concern.

But then he clicked into her photos and saw the pictures of the wall in her studio, the word written in dripping paint. LEAVE.

What the fuck?

And he knew for certain that Ellie was in trouble.

34

She has been down here now for nearly a week, and she hasn't moved much in the last three days. I guess she is probably worried about the batteries dying in her torch, as she only turns it on when she needs to use the toilet or eat.

The lamps went out a while ago and she has been in the darkness, the smell of paraffin replaced with the stench of her bucket.

She must be broken by now, must realise that no one is coming for her, as she has stopped calling out for help.

Sometimes I can hear her breathing, other times there is the sound of her crying, but mostly, other than the occasional clink of her chain and the drip from the faulty pipe, there is just silence.

I took a risk that day going inside her cell, but I wanted to get close, to see what this one was like. I touched her hair while she slept, and it felt so soft and silky. Not at all like mine. Untameable. That's what Benjamin used to call it when he would urge me to sit still so he could brush it for me. He said it was a good word to describe me, too.

You're an untameable child, Virginia.

I'm a big girl now and I brush my own hair, but mine will never be soft and silky like Ellie's, though I imagine hers is now a mess as she no longer has access to the fancy shampoos I saw in her bathroom cupboard, and it hasn't been brushed in days.

She won't be the same person now that she was six days ago. Being down here, losing all hope, it does that to you.

But she doesn't have to worry. Soon it will be over.

35

Ash saw red as soon as he listened to the voicemail.

He supposed he should have called the police, but the SIM card to Ellie's phone was his only real link to her and there was no way he wanted them taking it from him.

He had read all of her recent texts, seen the photos of the word painted on her studio wall threatening them, telling them to leave. Why the hell hadn't she said anything about it to him? Then he had listened to her voicemail.

Benjamin's voice was still rattling in his ears after he had ended the call.

We need to talk, Ellie.

I'm worried about you.

Why are you ignoring me?

You can't keep avoiding me.

I'm sorry about what Virginia did.

Please just call me back.

We have a connection.

Let me help you.

Ten minutes later Ash was hammering on the man's door,

having convinced himself that Benjamin knew more about Ellie's disappearance than he was letting on.

He knew Benjamin had a soft spot for his girlfriend and that Ellie had been a little freaked out when it had been pointed out to her. She was always so good with the waifs and strays of the world, taking everyone at face value. But sometimes that came with a price, as men like Benjamin didn't seem to know how to take no for an answer. Or certainly it would seem that way from his texts and voicemail.

And he was sorry about what Virginia did? Which was what exactly?

Ash knew little about Benjamin's sister, other than that she was unwell. Benjamin hadn't elaborated much the night he had come to dinner, though Ash suspected she was more than a little unbalanced. He knew she was prone to tantrums and that Benjamin was her legal guardian.

Something was bloody fishy about this family. He should have trusted his first instinct where Benjamin was concerned, and he was kicking himself for giving the man the benefit of the doubt, thinking he had misjudged him.

His knocking went unanswered, and it appeared neither Benjamin nor his crazy sister were home. Stepping back from the house though, Ash could see there were windows open upstairs. Benjamin didn't seem the type to go out without locking up.

He tried knocking again then when he still didn't get an answer, he went round to the back of the house. Ellie had mentioned that their neighbour was a keen gardener. Maybe that was where he was.

He found Benjamin pruning a rose shrub on the back patio. The conservatory doors were wide open and classical music was playing loudly.

Approaching a man who was holding garden shears and

who hadn't heard he had a visitor over the sound of the music perhaps wasn't Ash's smartest move, but he was angry and not thinking straight.

'Where the fuck is she?'

Benjamin swung round in shock, eyes bug wide behind his glasses as Ash quickly stepped back to avoid being stabbed.

'Ashton. Sorry, I didn't see you there.'

'Drop the friendly neighbour act, Ben. I found Ellie's phone and I'm pretty certain that you and your wacko sister know more about what's happened than you're letting on.'

'I have no idea what you mean.'

'Bullshit.'

'Look, something's obviously upset you, so why don't I make some tea and we can sit down and talk about it.'

Ash pulled his phone out of his pocket, that still had Ellie's SIM in it, and held it in front of Benjamin's face. 'I listened to your voicemail. It sounds to me like you were stalking her.'

'I was not!' Benjamin spluttered, his face turning purple. 'Ellie is my friend.'

'*Why are you ignoring me? You can't keep avoiding me.* That doesn't sound like a friendship. It sounds like harassment. And you have a connection? Seriously? What the fuck, Ben!'

'It's Benjamin.'

'Where's my girlfriend?'

'I don't know. And I think perhaps you'd better leave.'

'Oh, I'm not going anywhere until I get some answers.' Ash took a menacing step forward when Benjamin retreated towards the house. 'What did Virginia do?'

'What? She didn't do anything.'

'That's not what you said in your voicemail. You said you were sorry about what she did.'

'Oh that.' Benjamin waved a dismissive hand. 'Ellie popped round to see us, and Virginia wouldn't open the door to her. She gets shy like that sometimes.' His eyes were darting all over the place, a sure sign that he was lying.

'I don't believe you.'

'What? Why? I'm telling you the truth. Now I really think you should leave. I know you're upset about Ellie, and I really wish I could help and give you answers, but I honestly don't know anything that will help you.'

Benjamin was almost inside the conservatory now, Ash just a couple of steps away.

'I want to see Virginia. Was she the one who painted "Leave" on Ellie's studio wall?'

'What? I have no idea what you're talking about.'

'Really? I don't believe you. Where's Virginia?'

'You can't talk to her. She's resting.'

'I don't care. You keep making excuses for her. Something's not right here. I want to see her now. You can either get her down here or I'll go in and find her myself.'

'You can't do that. You don't have permission to come inside my house.' Benjamin sounded panicked.

When Ash took another step towards him, he held his hand up to stop him. 'Okay, okay. I'll call her. Virginia? Can you come downstairs, please?'

Benjamin watched Ash closely while they waited for his sister to respond, as if fearing Ash might suddenly try to barge his way past him into the house.

It was tempting. Freaking bloody family.

When there was no answer, he called again, this time an edge of frustration to his voice. 'Virginia, please. This is important. Can you come downstairs now?'

She continued to ignore him, and Benjamin offered Ash a shrug. 'I'm sorry, she's very stubborn.'

'That's not my problem.'

Benjamin heaved out a frustrated sigh. 'Look, wait here. I'll go and get her. If she's being like this she's going to be in a bad mood though, so don't say I haven't warned you.' Shaking his head he stepped inside the conservatory.

Ash rolled his eyes. 'I honestly don't care. Just go get her.' He scrubbed his palm over his unshaven jaw, turned on his heel to pace the patio while he waited, and let out an irritated sigh. The click of a latch had his head snapping back.

Benjamin peered through the glass of the closed doors, a smug look on his face, though his expression turned to one of alarm when Ash flew at the door, trying to get in.

The fucker had locked them, though it didn't stop him rattling them, getting a glimmer of satisfaction when Benjamin took a couple of worried steps back.

'Unlock these fucking doors now.'

Benjamin was ignoring him. He had his phone out of his pocket. 'I'm calling the police. I suggest you get off my property, Mr Brady, before they get here.'

Ash was too wound up to take any notice of the threat, rattling the French doors again, before circling the house, trying to find another way in, which is how he found himself sitting in the back of a police car later on that afternoon.

'Mr Thorne has decided not to take this any further,' the police constable who was driving him the short distance back to Hazelwood Cottage told him, his tone suggesting that Ash should be grateful.

He wasn't.

'Instead of warning me, you should be back there finding out what the hell he's done to Ellie.'

'We have no proof that he's done anything to Miss Summers.'

'You don't think that voicemail he left her is suspicious?'

'Mr Thorne is as distraught about her disappearance as you are,' PC Saunders told him, avoiding the question.

'Of course he is,' Ash muttered as much to himself. He was annoyed that he had lost his temper, pissed off that the constables had taken Ellie's SIM card, and frustrated that the smug bastard living next door seemed to continually come up smelling of roses.

'I need you to stay away from the Thorne residence. Leave us to do our job. Next time you might not be so lucky, and Mr Thorne will want to take things further.'

'Are you going to speak with his sister?' Ash asked, ignoring him.

'My colleague is talking with Mr Thorne right now. I'm sure he will speak with Miss Thorne before he leaves.'

'You saw the photos Ellie took. You need to ask Virginia Thorne about them.'

'You have no proof she is responsible.'

'Well, Virginia's the bat-shit crazy one in the house. Though to be honest, I'm starting to think Ben's not all the ticket.'

'Mr Brady, I would suggest you don't make baseless accusations.'

'They are our only neighbours and they're bloody strange. I hardly think they're baseless. Don't you think it's a little odd that Naomi Tanner vanished while living next door to Benjamin Thorne and now so has Ellie? It's a little coincidental, don't you think?'

'Naomi Tanner disappeared five years ago. I very much doubt your girlfriend's disappearance is in any way related.'

There was no point in arguing. The copper wasn't listening to him, and Ash was just getting himself more worked up.

Benjamin Thorne knew what had happened to Ellie; he was certain of it. And somehow he was going to prove it.

36

'I really am sorry to drag you out here over this,' Benjamin apologised for the third time as he cleared away the teacups. 'I know you must be very busy and don't really have time for neighbour disputes.'

'It's no bother, Mr Thorne. Just doing our job.'

'I've never seen Mr Brady like that. I guess the worry about Ellie must be taking its toll. He has quite a temper on him when he gets angry. It was rather frightening.'

'You were right to call us. PC Saunders has taken him home and will make sure he cools off.'

Benjamin hesitated, wondering how much more he should say. 'I mentioned to your colleagues, after Ellie first disappeared, that I was a little worried about her. She had bruises on her, and I was concerned that Mr Brady was responsible.'

PC Wilton nodded, jotting in his notepad, though didn't comment on it. 'You said you were close with Miss Summers?'

'We are friends. I'm not sure that her boyfriend approves though.'

'But you had fallen out?' When Benjamin hesitated, needing

a moment to gather his thoughts, the PC pushed. 'Your voicemail asked her to stop avoiding you.'

Although he wanted to deny it, didn't want to admit to the hiccup in his friendship with Ellie, honesty was probably the way forward at this point.

'A couple of days before she vanished, I confronted Ellie about her relationship with Ashton. I was concerned about her. Unfortunately she didn't react well.'

PC Wilton seemed to consider that, making a few further notes. 'Have you ever seen him behave violently towards her?'

'No, but I could tell she was worried. I picked up on things.'

'Can you elaborate?'

'Well, there were the bruises I told you about and I've heard him yelling at her before. I think he is quite controlling.'

Benjamin wanted to add that there were so many similarities to what had happened with John and Naomi Tanner. Yes, they had been father and daughter, not a couple like Ellie and Ash, but both were toxic relationships. It perhaps wasn't best to draw comparisons though. Besides, his statement about Naomi Tanner's disappearance and what he knew about her father would be on file if the constable wanted to look.

'In your voicemail, you also mentioned that you were sorry for what Virginia had done. Virginia is your sister, correct?'

'She is.'

'Can you tell me what you were apologising for? What your sister did to Ellie?'

Benjamin repeated the same lie he had told Ash, the words rolling easily off his tongue now. He hated the dishonesty, but he couldn't have PC Wilton finding out what she had done.

'Is Virginia in the house now?'

It was an innocent enough question, but one that had the collar of his shirt tightening and he struggled to breath normally. 'She is upstairs resting.'

'Could she spare us five minutes?'

'My... my sister isn't well, PC Wilton. I'd rather she wasn't disturbed.'

The constable seemed to consider that then smiled. 'Well, perhaps we could nip upstairs then. I just have a couple of questions for her.'

The ticking of the clock on the mantle was a little too loud, the room a little too warm, and a flustered heat was creeping into Benjamin's cheeks. 'I'd really rather–'

'It will just take a second.'

Wilton asked the question so affably, as if it was no big deal, and Benjamin wondered if he would feel the same way once he knew the truth.

'Of course,' he agreed stiffly. 'If you want to follow me.'

This wasn't good. He knew Virginia was in one of her moods because he had come downstairs this morning to find the box of cornflakes tipped over the kitchen floor, lying in a puddle of milk, much to the delight of Miss Moneypenny.

She was angry with him, and Benjamin suspected he knew why. He couldn't risk her revealing this side of herself to PC Wilton.

'Do you live around these parts?' he asked, trying to be conversational as they approached the first-floor landing.

He wasn't really listening as the constable replied, his focus on Virginia's room up ahead.

One time when she had been really angry with him, she had ripped the heads off her dolls and left them all in Benjamin's bed. Some of them he was able to fix, but others had needed to be replaced. He tried not to think about that now, scared at the time of how violent she had become, just as he tried to block from his memory the morning he had gone in to wake her and found the axe lying on her pillow.

'Virginia?' he called out. 'Are you awake?'

Please don't be there.

There was no reply.

'This is her room,' he told Wilton. The door was open, and he led the constable into the pink bedroom, his mouth dropping open at the neatly made bed. He looked at the constable, his eyes widening as he stated the obvious. 'She's not here.'

'Might she be somewhere else in the house?' Wilton asked calmly, the kind smile on his face suggesting this wasn't such a big deal. 'Maybe she's feeling better.'

'She said she was going for a nap.'

'Well, perhaps she changed her mind. I'm sure she won't have gone far.'

'The garden perhaps. She likes it out there.' Benjamin furrowed his brow. 'It was that bloody man. He must have spooked her.'

'Well, why don't we go check. If she's not outside then perhaps you can ask her to call me, or I can always pop back later.'

'Yes, yes. I guess I can do that.'

He let Wilton lead the way downstairs and out into the garden, but he already knew they weren't going to find Virginia.

37

The fridge was just about empty, and Ash knew he was going to have to drag himself out to the supermarket soon and do a proper shop. For now, though, he made do with the local Spar shop, reluctant to stray too far in case Ellie returned.

He knew it was unlikely to happen, but even so, if she did come home he wanted to be there.

It seemed word had spread about her disappearance and people knew who he was. It would also appear that some of the locals had decided he was responsible. An elderly man gawped at him as he got out of the car, making no attempt to look away, and as he crossed the small forecourt a woman with a pram gave him a wide berth, her expression full of suspicion.

Ash scowled at them both.

Inside the store he grabbed a few essentials, pausing by the alcohol section to pick up a couple of bottles of wine.

'I can't believe he's had the nerve to show his face here.'

'Me neither.'

Assuming they were talking about him, he paused, temper rising as he turned the aisle, ready to confront the two women he could hear gossiping.

'John Tanner needs to stay as far away from here as possible.'

What?

'Christine thinks he's staying with his sister. Her daughter, Alison, saw them together when she was leaving the hairdressers.'

'Excuse me.'

Both women turned to look at Ash, eyebrows raised.

'I heard you talking about John Tanner.'

'And?' That was from a blonde woman with heavy make-up and a pinched look on her face.

'I'm Ashton Brady. I recently moved into Hazelwood Cottage, where the Tanners used to live.'

He could tell from their expressions that they already knew that.

'I'm aware of who you are, Mr Brady.' That was from blondie again, who was smiling tightly, while her friend stayed as quiet as a mouse. 'Your wife is missing.'

She left that last word hanging there, cranking up Ash's irritation level. He didn't bother to correct her on his marital status.

'Ellie said she saw Tanner hanging about the house a few days before she disappeared. I need to speak with him.'

The two women exchanged a glance and while they still seemed distrustful, he could see he had piqued their interest. 'I'm not sure how you expect us to help you.'

'You said he's staying with his sister.'

'Oh my, you really were eavesdropping.'

Ash gave the woman a pointed look. 'Maybe you should gossip quieter then.'

Her cheeks reddened at that, and he mentally patted himself on the back.

'We think he's staying with his sister,' the quiet friend suddenly piped up. 'We don't know for sure.'

'Okay. Well, does his sister live here in the village?'

'No, she's in Aylsham.'

'Any chance you have her address?'

Despite wanting to meddle in everyone's business, both women claimed they didn't. Ash suspected they were lying, but didn't push it, knowing that if he was in their position he would be reluctant to give it out as well. They didn't know him and clearly believed he might be responsible for Ellie's disappearance.

He did persuade them to give him the sister's name, though, and back home, a quick Google search told him that Juliet Oxborough ran a dog-walking business. He found her contact number on her Facebook page, called under false pretences claiming to need her services then bundled Poppy in the car to go meet with her.

Juliet opened the door, delighted when she saw the three-legged puppy, but her demeanour quickly changed when she realised Ash's true intentions for being there.

'He's not here and you have no right to show up here at my home like this.'

'I know and I'm sorry, but it's really important I speak with him.'

'Don't you people think he's been through enough? He lost his wife and his daughter, and if that's not enough, he's had to put up with people pointing the finger at him and calling him a monster for years, even though he was never charged with anything.'

'I get that, I really do. It's why I need to speak with him.' Ash offered a smile, hoping to win her over. He knew it was forced though. He hadn't had much to smile about this last hellish week. 'I live at Hazelwood Cottage and Ellie, my girlfriend, has vanished, just like Naomi did. So yes, I get a little of what he's gone through. I'm beside myself with worry about her, I can't sleep, can't think of anything else but finding her. I'm desperate here. Please.'

Juliet's arms remained folded, and her face pulled into a scowl, but her eyes softened slightly. 'How do you think John is going to help you? What happened to Naomi was five years ago.'

'She saw him, you know. Ellie saw your brother at the house. I didn't believe her at the time.'

Juliet's expression tightened. 'I told him to stay away.'

'Well he didn't, and it freaked her out. There were a few things freaking her out though. Not just your brother. Someone broke into the house, though no sign of forced entry, and nothing was taken. They let this one out though.' Ash stroked Poppy's head. 'We found her running about loose. Then there was the graffiti. Someone wrote the word "Leave" on the wall.'

'Look, I'm truly sorry about your girlfriend and about the things that have been happening to you, but this has nothing to do with John or what happened to Louise and Naomi. It's a coincidence.'

'Is it though?'

'What do you mean?'

'How well did John know the neighbours when he lived there?'

'Benjamin Thorne?' Juliet had paled slightly. 'What about him?'

'I don't trust him, and I don't like how he was around Ellie.'

'In what way?'

'It was obvious he had a bit of a crush on her. They started off as friends, but she tried to cool things. He wasn't taking the hint.'

Juliet hesitated, seemed to size Ash up, deciding how much she could trust him. Eventually she held open the door. 'I think you'd better come inside.'

~

She had been lying about John not being there. She left Ash and Poppy to wait in the living room and she went upstairs to talk to her brother.

Ash glanced around the room while he waited, studying the titles on the bookshelves and the photos on the mantle. The room had a homely, lived-in feel and his gut instinct told him that Juliet Oxborough was genuine. As he took a seat on a sofa filled with scattered cushions, all in different shades of blue, settled Poppy on his lap, stroking her soft ears when she whined a little, the new environment with all of its doggy smells making her curious, he wondered about John Tanner.

He had scared Ellie and at the time Ash hadn't even believed her. He was kicking himself for that. Was Tanner really the ogre she had believed him to be though? The locals had cast him in the role of the villain, but no charges had ever been brought. Had he murdered his wife and been responsible for the disappearance of his daughter? Or had he been innocent of the accusations made against him?

It was easier for Ash to sympathise with the man now he had been through a similar experience.

But why had Tanner been at the house? And just a week before Ellie had disappeared. While he wanted to give the man the benefit of the doubt, the timing in itself was suspicious.

Hearing the creak of footsteps on the stairs, Ash stood up, eyes on the door when Juliet walked through, followed by a haggard man with grey close-cropped hair and haunted dark eyes. He was a couple of inches taller than Ash's six-one height, bulkier too, seeming a little too big for the room.

'This is Ashton Brady,' Juliet said, before excusing herself, leaving the two men alone.

Tanner eyed Ash up warily. 'I'm sorry to hear about your girlfriend, but I'm not sure how I can help you.'

'Please just hear me out, okay?'

Tanner nodded, taking a seat in the armchair opposite the sofa, gesturing for Ash to sit down again too. He listened as Ash went over everything, from the break-in, to their neighbours, his expression growing more intense.

'Why were you at the house? Ellie saw you.'

Tanner chewed the inside of his cheek; an anxious habit Ash was learning he had, before fixing him with sad brown eyes. 'Last week was Louise's birthday. I always come and stay with Juliet. Lou's ashes are nearby. I like to go spend some time with her.' He hesitated, rubbing at the back of his neck with a beefy hand. 'I shouldn't have stopped by the house, but there are memories, you know? I had seen it was up for sale, that new people were living there, and I guess I had it in my head that I would knock on the door and say I used to live there. The closer I got though, the more stupid the idea seemed. Lou and I grew up locally, we were friends as kids and dated from the age of sixteen. Our daughter was born there and Hazelwood Cottage was supposed to be our forever home. I'm a pariah around these parts now though. I only come back for the anniversaries. Lou's birthday and Naomi's too. I stay away apart from that.'

It was difficult to doubt the man as he spoke. Ash wasn't foolish enough to blindly believe everything he said, but his voice was steady, his breathing even, and he spoke with an honesty that would be difficult to fake, all the while maintaining eye contact.

If Ash was a betting man, he would say John Tanner had nothing to do with his wife's death or his daughter's disappearance.

'How did you get on with Benjamin Thorne?' he asked now.

He had touched on Ellie's friendship with Benjamin but was curious to know Tanner's views and experiences of the man.

'I didn't like him much if I'm truthful,' Tanner told him now. 'Benjamin Thorne had been a few years behind me at school. Polite enough kid, but a little odd. I didn't know him well, just enough to say hello to. But then we moved in next door to him and his sister. She was odder than him. Sometimes I'd see her in their garden, but she never spoke if you said hello to her. Lou said she was shy. Maybe she was, but I always thought she was a little rude.

'Lou and Naomi had more time for Benjamin. I worked away a lot and I think Lou liked having someone she could call on if she needed help with anything.

'He didn't do me any favours after it happened, tried to make me out to be some sort of monster to the police. Said I used to fight with Lou, and I was violent towards my own daughter. I never laid a hand on that girl. Sure, we disagreed sometimes, she was seventeen, had her mother's strong will and a fiery temper, but I loved the bones of her. She was my flesh and blood, and I would never touch a hair on her pretty head.'

Tanner's lips twisted into something like a grimace, the pain in his eyes clear. 'She's dead, you know. At least that's what I have to believe. I know she didn't run away, and it's been five years. To believe she's still alive and what she might be going through, well... I can't go down that route of thought.'

38

Ellie was beginning to understand how someone could go mad.

Trapped in the darkness with no end in sight, the simple motions of life, such as eating and using the toilet became huge chores. She wanted to keep going, wanted to fight to survive, but she was beginning to wonder what the point was.

If she was going to die down here then wouldn't it be better if she didn't prolong the agony?

She had no idea what Virginia's plans were for her, wondered if the girl even knew herself, and as the minutes slowly ticked into hours, the nightmare never ending, she became more and more convinced that there was nothing to keep going for.

She slept mostly, longing for that escape, though the darkness had started invading her dreams too. She seldom dreamt of Ash now, instead, she was trapped in this eternal hellhole, often screaming herself awake.

During the time of consciousness she tried to cling to memories of him, desperately digging for some kind of hope to make her keep fighting; the first weekend they had spent together when she realised this might just be the start of something; when Ash had announced his intention to move to Norfolk because he didn't want to spend his weekdays away from her; that long rainy week in Scotland when they had spent every moment together, but she still couldn't get enough of him.

She loved how his moods were reflected in the changing colour of his hazel eyes; golden-brown when he was calm, sparked with green when he was annoyed about something, and simmering down to the colour of whisky when things heated up between them. She loved the scent of him when he got out of the shower. She loved how he could tease her out of a mood, always making her laugh when she was trying so hard to be angry with him. How, no matter what he did to it, his hair refused to behave. She loved his ridiculously long lashes and that little crease in his brow that deepened when he was concentrating on something. And she loved how he always supported her, accepting her for exactly who she was. How she never had to pretend when she was around him.

He was going to marry her. He had told her so. Ash wasn't the type of man who made grand sweeping gestures. He was thoughtful and considered and matter-of-fact, just saying things the way they were going to be, and Ellie loved that about him, knew that he never said something unless he stuck by it, that nothing he ever did was shallow or without meaning.

When he told her he was in love with her, she knew it was true, when he said he would never cheat on her she believed him, and when he announced one night when they were curled up on the sofa together that he was going to marry her, that he intended to spend the rest of his life trying to make her happy, it came from the heart.

Knowing that she might never see him again, that she might never get the chance to tell him how important he was to her, was ripping her heart apart. She wanted to scream at Virginia, shake her and make her understand, but the girl never came close to the cell again, or at least if she did, it was while Ellie was asleep.

Ellie could hear her though, her footsteps sometimes moving around the cave, even though she couldn't see her in the darkness. Occasionally she would flash the torch on, try to catch a glimpse of her, but the girl was too quick.

Instead, she clung to Ash and a hope that somehow she would get to see him again. But with each passing moment, that hope began to fade.

39

Ash's conversation with John Tanner had given him a lot to think about and he was now more convinced than ever that the Thornes were involved in Ellie's disappearance, that they had also been behind the break-in and the graffiti.

There was no point in going to the police without hard evidence. Ash had already been warned to stay away from his neighbours and was certain that any accusations he made were likely to be twisted against him.

It seemed Benjamin was good at doing that. The friendship he had formed with Louise and Naomi Tanner appeared similar to the one he had struck up with Ellie. The good neighbour, always on hand to help, gradually inserting himself into the lives of the people next door.

John had said Louise had been the same as Ellie. Grateful at first but becoming a little irritated as time went on. She had also voiced her concerns to him that Benjamin was showing a little more interest in Naomi than was appropriate.

Lingering looks when the teenage girl had been wearing a short skirt or shorts, the occasional touch that could have been innocent enough, but somehow felt out of place, and he had taken to bringing her little gifts, the odd bunch of flowers from his garden then a brooch pin he said he had found when clearing out some of his mother's old things. It had made Louise uncomfortable given he was more than twice Naomi's age.

She had asked Naomi to stay away from him and suggested John have a chat with him when he returned from his business trip. Instead, he had come home to a dead wife and a missing daughter.

He had told the police about Benjamin, of course, and at first they had seemed to take him seriously, speaking with the neighbour and his younger sister. The Thornes had apparently been more than co-operative, inviting the officers in and welcoming them to search the property.

The police had found nothing and, instead, left with their heads filled of stories of what a terrible husband and father John had been.

There was another similarity too. As had been the case with Ash, John had returned from his business trip to a locked house. There was no sign of forced entry, which suggested that Louise had let her killer in.

Alone, all of these little things meant nothing, but put together they began to build a disturbing picture, especially when you looked at connections between Ellie and Naomi's disappearance.

Ash ran his theory about Benjamin past Pete on Tuesday evening, not liking that his friend seemed more concerned about whether he was eating properly.

'I'm going to ask Roxy to go shopping for you on Friday. She's on a day off, so she can drop it round in the afternoon.'

'I don't need Roxanne to go shopping for me. I have a car.'

'And when was the last time you went to the supermarket?'

'I've been going to the Spar shop in the village.' Ash didn't bother to add that his purchases had been mostly of the alcoholic variety.

'That's no good for a weekly grocery shop. She can pick some bits up for you, get that fridge and freezer stocked. I know you're worried about Ellie. We all are. But starving yourself isn't going to help anyone.'

Ash's pleas for Pete to butt out on giving him nutritional advice fell on deaf ears.

He supposed he had a point. He wasn't eating properly, hadn't been to the gym or for a run in over a week. Regardless, he didn't want Roxanne in the house and wished his friend would at least listen to his concerns about Benjamin Thorne.

He ended the call frustrated, fed Poppy (as long as she had food it was fine) then opened one of the bottles of wine he'd picked up at the Spar. Taking his glass upstairs he settled down in Ellie's studio (the place where he seemed to spend most of his time at the moment) checking her emails and social media for any signs, then turning his attention to Benjamin Thorne.

He started with the man's Facebook account, where logged in as Ellie, he was able to view his posts. It didn't take him long to go through everything on Benjamin's profile and immediately he noticed a pattern.

He had posted a handful of times in the period between Ellie and Ash moving into Hazelwood House and Ellie's disappearance – a couple of shared memes and a few rather bland updates, but before that there had been nothing since 2016.

Five years ago.

Ash googled Naomi Tanner, saw that her disappearance and the night her mother had been murdered had been Thursday 19th May. Benjamin's last post had been on Monday 16th May.

He looked through the eighteen friends on his list, saw that both Louise and Naomi were there.

That couldn't be a coincidence.

Curious, he went through the remaining friends. At least half a dozen worked for an accountancy firm, Stobart and Greaves. He recalled Benjamin saying he was self-employed, but had he perhaps worked there once?

Clicking off Facebook, he looked at the Stobart and Greaves website, noting it had a page which featured staff profiles, and each employee had a contact email. Picking a couple of members of the team at random, he emailed saying he was an old friend of Benjamin's and was trying to get hold of him, and he asked if he still worked there.

Knowing he wouldn't get a reply until the morning, he sipped at his wine and typed Benjamin's name into Google. The name was fairly common though, bringing up dozens of different Benjamin Thornes, so he tried adding Norfolk and then Corpusty. There was just the one entry about his neighbour – something about winning a flower competition years back – and there was a grainy photograph of Benjamin shaking hands with one of the judges.

The search with Corpusty did also throw up a few results for Harold Thorne and Ash clicked on the first article, which was a funeral notice. Harold had died in 1996, and was survived by his wife, Daphne, and their two children, Benjamin and Virginia.

The next story was a local unsolved mystery blog. The disappearance of Daphne's younger sister, Imelda Walters. She had been living with the Thornes, having moved in with them after losing her job in the mid-nineties, and had vanished the year prior to Harold's death.

Curiosity increasing, Ash looked up the contact details for the blogger, a guy called Nathan Henderson, and seeing he had a mobile number listed, he gave him a call.

Henderson answered straightaway, seeming thrilled that he had been contacted via his site and Ash quickly learnt he was a true-crime junkie and a bit of a nerd. He couldn't knock him though. The man thoroughly researched the topics he blogged about, and he was more than eager to share the mystery of Imelda Walters.

'She was the irresponsible one in the family,' he explained to Ash in his broad Norwich accent. 'Daphne had married well, but Imelda flitted from job to job, unable to hold one down, was always involved with the wrong men, took too many drugs and never had any money. After their parents died and she didn't have them to bail her out, she turned to her sister. Daphne agreed she could move in with them while she sorted herself out. She helped find her a job and made her go see someone about her addiction, but after about six months of living there she disappeared.'

'It says on your blog that there were conflicting reports about what the family think happened.'

'That's right. It was Harold who called the police. Daphne was certain her sister had done her usual thing and left when the going got tough. All of her things were gone, so there was a lot to support her theory and it's why the police didn't take things too seriously when Harold called them. Imelda had a history of running away from her problems, so it's understandable why they were sceptical that anything sinister had happened.'

'But you don't believe she ran away?'

'I don't.'

Ash rolled Ellie's chair back, put his feet up on her desk and picked up his wine glass again. This was getting interesting. 'How come?'

'Well, for starters she completely disappeared off the radar. Has never been seen again since. That was very out of character for Imelda. She would run away, sometimes not surface for a few weeks, but she was incapable of looking after herself and always returned at some point fishing for a handout.'

'So maybe she ran away, and something happened to her.'

'Or maybe she never left at all.'

'Why would you think that?'

'Daphne had helped her sister get a job in a pub in one of the neighbouring villages. She became friendly with another barmaid who was quite vocal that Imelda wouldn't have run away. She claimed that Imelda was having an affair with Harold and that he had promised her he was going to leave Daphne. Of course, the police asked the Thornes about this, but they both denied it, putting on a united front. Daphne poured scorn on the idea, pointing out that Imelda was prone to fantasies and often had a twisted version of the truth.'

'But you believe her?'

'Debbie, that's the barmaid, she claimed she saw Harold kissing Imelda in his car, after he came to pick her up one night to take her home. She also said Imelda had a locket he had given her, and that the girl was often covered in love bites. According to her, Imelda was head-over-heels in love with Harold and that there was no way she would have left him.'

'Am I able to speak with Debbie?'

'Sorry, mate. She passed away a couple of years ago.'

'But you're convinced she didn't make any of this up?'

'She had nothing to gain and nothing to lose,' Nathan pointed out. 'I spoke to her face to face and believe she was telling the truth.'

Ash was silent for a moment as he considered that. 'So what do you think happened to Imelda?' On his blog, Nathan had presented the facts as he found them but left everything open-ended for his readers to make up their minds. The man had to have an opinion though.

'Honestly? I don't think she ran away. I think someone made her go away.'

'As in forced her to leave?'

'No, as in made her disappear.'

'You think Harold killed her?'

'Possibly, though my money is on Daphne.'

'Really? But Imelda was her sister.'

'And Daphne was despairing of her. Everyone I spoke to told me she was already at her wits' end when Imelda showed up asking for a bailout. She wasn't happy about it and Harold had been the one to talk her into letting her sister stay. I think it's quite possible that if she found out Imelda was having an affair with her husband she might have snapped.'

'And you think Harold knew?'

'I can't be certain. I do know, though, that Imelda disappeared in the November of ninety-five and Harold died in the February of ninety-six of a massive heart attack.'

'You think it was brought on by the stress?'

'Or by his wife perhaps. Maybe it wasn't a heart attack. Maybe Daphne wanted to punish both her sister and her husband.'

That was quite a stretch, to go from a possible cheating husband to a double murder. 'So is this simply just your thoughts or is anything pushing you to that conclusion?' Ash asked.

'It comes from gossip, the people who knew her, but when they're all saying the same thing you have to put some stock in it. They say she had a ruthless streak, that she didn't tolerate fools or those who betrayed her. After Harold's death she became worse, distrustful of everyone. Locked herself and her kids away in that big house mostly shunning the outside world. I think the girl has issues and her brother is a little strange too. Just the two of them there now after Daphne died. Needless to say my request to interview them was turned down.'

Ash thanked Nathan for his time, ending the call with a dozen questions on his mind. Had Daphne Thorne, Benjamin's mother, really been a murderer, or was true-crime junkie, Nathan, jumping to conclusions?

Shutting the Mac down, he picked up his wine glass and took it through to the bedroom, glancing briefly at Ellie's side of the bed, hating that she hadn't slept there in a week, before heading out of the open French doors and onto the balcony.

From his position on the first floor he could see the very top of the Thorne house, the wide chimney set into the dark roof.

Someone inside that house knew what had happened to Ellie and he was determined to find out where she was.

40

Benjamin was quite certain that Ellie wouldn't react well if he tried to approach her until she'd had time to adjust to her situation. Plus, of course, it was safer if he didn't, so he had kept himself busy with the garden, keeping his mind off the difficult conversation he would inevitably have to have with her. In time he knew she would realise that he was right, but for the first few days he understood that she wouldn't see it that way, and so it was best to leave her be.

Of course, he hadn't planned to leave things quite so long, but bloody Ashton Brady had been like a dog with a bone, and he had been forced to call the police out, which had unfortunately made things awkward.

He hummed to himself as he put together the tray. His mother had always said the way to win people over was through their stomach. Ellie was going to be angry with him initially, but hopefully a hot breakfast and a pot of freshly brewed tea would help win her over.

As he made his way along the dark passageway, carefully balancing the tray in one hand, the beam of his powerful torch lighting the path ahead, he tried to push aside his guilt.

He hadn't planned to leave her in dark and hoped she wouldn't resent him too much for it.

No, he shouldn't feel guilty, he reminded himself. He was the one who was trying to help her.

It was all her boyfriend's fault. It was because of Ash that she had been alone down here for a week, and that Benjamin had been forced to go to these lengths in the first place.

She was asleep when he reached the cell, or at least he assumed she was, her back was towards him, and she was curled up under the blanket. The chain to her cuff was pulled taut from where she had tried to draw her leg up and he felt another pinch of guilt, knowing it couldn't be comfortable for her. But the chain was a regrettable necessity.

Placing the tray on the ground, he spent a couple of minutes sorting the paraffin lamps. As the cave room basked again in a warm glow, he heard her stir behind him, the bed creaking and the rattle of the chain slackening as she sat up.

'Benjamin?'

When he turned to face her, he could see her bewilderment, but knew it would quickly turn to anger.

'You need to help me. Your sister locked me down here.'

His sister? Why would Ellie think Virginia had locked her down here? It must be the stress of this new situation. She was getting herself confused.

Ellie was out of bed now and had approached the bars and he could see that she didn't look well, her skin pale, even in the flamelight, and her eyes dark and sunken. Her bare knees were crusted with dirt and blood. 'Please, Benjamin, help me.'

Her pleading tore at him, but he knew he had to be strong. 'I'm sorry, I can't do that, Elisabeth.' He tested her full name, liking how it sounded. It was more graceful than Ellie and suited her much better.

'What do you mean? Why can't you?' Her eyes were wide

with shock and he realised she actually had believed he was going to let her out.

'I brought you some breakfast,' he told her, fussing with the tray, unable to meet her look of horror as his perceived betrayal sunk in. 'I thought you might enjoy a hot meal. I have made a pot of tea too.'

She didn't say anything as he approached the cell, balancing the tray again in one hand as he fished for the keys, and he tried not to screw his nose up in disdain as he smelt the contents of the bucket he had left for her.

Fresh guilt swamped him. He shouldn't have left her all this time with that stench. Though seriously what was he supposed to have done?

Ash had a lot to answer for.

Ellie... no, Elisabeth he corrected himself, stood silently watching him as he unlocked the door and stepped inside. As he went to place the tray down on the bed though, she suddenly flew at him, shocking the life out him and causing him to almost drop it.

He jerked back, stepping just out of her reach, relieved that she was wearing the ankle cuff.

'LET ME OUT OF HERE!'

He winced at her words. Yes, she was definitely angry. She had a wild look about her, her hair unkempt and her face a little thin. He needed to get her eating. None of this would have any benefit if she starved herself.

He glanced at the tray, a little annoyed that she had caused him to spill some of the tea. He had taken considerable effort in putting this first meal together for her, the boiled eggs in little plastic cups and the buttered toast cut into soldiers so she could dunk the strips in the yolks. He had folded a spoon in a proper napkin, given her one of his mother's favourite teacups, and even picked a yellow rose from the garden, which he had laid on the plate, to give it all a finishing touch.

'Why are you doing this to me?' She spoke the words more calmly, but there was still a flash of temper in her eyes, and Benjamin didn't doubt she would try and attack him again if she was given the chance.

'I'm trying to help you, Elisabeth.'

'Help me? How? By locking me in a prison cell in the dark and making me go to the toilet in a bucket? How is that possibly helping me?'

'You don't understand, not yet, but you will. You just have to give it time. Give me time. That man is too inside your head at the moment.'

'What man? What the hell are you talking about?'

'He's been manipulating you. You can't trust him.'

'Are you talking about Ash?'

'He's not good for you.'

'Why the hell would you say that? I love Ash. And my relationship with him is none of your business.' She was getting defensive, still blinkered by the control Ash had wielded over her. It was a classic sign of the toxic nature of their relationship.

'You think you love him because that is what he has conditioned you to believe. I know what it's really like for you though. You don't have to pretend with me.'

'I'm not pretending. I do love him. I'm crazy about him.'

'He controls you; he doesn't respect you, and I know he is jealous of our friendship.'

Elisabeth burst out laughing. It sounded a little hysterical. 'You think he is jealous of *you*?'

The words were spoken nastily, and Benjamin tried to shrug them off, even though they hurt. She was lashing out, didn't mean them. 'He wants to keep you isolated, doesn't want you having other people in your life, because that way he can get into your head easier. I understand about toxic relationships, Elisabeth.'

'My name is Ellie!'

'I have read about them, and I know how they work,' Benjamin continued, ignoring her. 'Ash is manipulating you, but you can't see it.'

'No he isn't!'

'I know he hits you.'

'What?'

'I've seen the bruises. I know you're embarrassed by them. You don't have to be afraid of me. You can talk to me about what has happened. About the things he has done to you. I only want to help you.'

'Help me? By locking me in a prison cell? By chaining me up like a dog? Tell me, Benjamin, how the fuck are you possibly helping me?' She spat the words at him, furious.

It was still early days and he had expected this reaction, but still he hoped to get through to her. Or at least calm her down a little. 'I know you're angry with me at the moment and you don't understand why any of this is necessary, but you have to trust me. I promise you that one day you will thank me for rescuing you from that man.'

'Trust you? You're not right in the head. Ash has never hit me.' Elisabeth's eyes widened, looking at him like she thought he was the crazy one. He understood now that they had a lot of work to do. He hadn't realised quite how brainwashed she was.

'I've seen the bruises. You can deny it all you want.'

'We've been doing up a house. It's physical work and I bruise easily. I already told you that.'

'The bruise on your arm is–'

'You mean this?' She held her arm up to him. The mark had mostly faded now, but even after all this time, it was still visible. 'I told you what happened. I fell off the ladder. You have seriously locked me up down here because you're suspicious of a bruise on my arm? You're fucking insane!'

'He's cheating on you.' Benjamin blurted the words out without thinking, but she was getting angry again and he needed to calm her down so he could give her the breakfast before everything got cold.

That revelation had her reeling and for a moment she looked lost for words. 'No he's not,' she managed eventually.

'I saw him kissing a red-haired lady.'

'You're lying.' Although she snapped the words at him, she didn't sound convinced and he suspected she knew who the woman was.

He took the tiny opening and tried to widen it. 'I would never lie to you, Elisabeth. I would never hurt you or betray you. I only want to help you, to make you understand what he's really like.'

'Stop calling me Elisabeth! My name is Ellie.'

Benjamin breathed in deeply through his nose, aware the edge of his temper was fraying and needing a moment. He didn't want to get angry with her, that would... it would set things back, but she was testing his patience. He had gone to all this trouble to cook her a nice breakfast and she was ruining it. She had always been so lovely and gentle before and it was hard seeing this side to her. Of course she was going to be upset at first, but he had really hoped that once he had explained to her that she had nothing to be afraid of, that everything he was doing was for her benefit, she would listen to reason.

'I don't want to fight with you, Elisabeth.' He made a point of saying her full name firmly this time. 'We can do this the easy way or the hard way. While you are angry with me you are staying in this cell. If you become a little more reasonable then we can negotiate on that. Now I came down here to bring you a warm meal and I had hoped you might be more grateful. If you don't want it, I can take it back upstairs.'

When she didn't react, just stared at him, her arms folded, he took a tentative step forward. 'I am going to place the tray on the bed. Don't think about doing anything silly. I don't have the key to the cuff on me, so you can't get out. If you try to hurt me you will be trapped down here, and you really don't want that. You might not like it or appreciate it right now, but you need me.'

Benjamin kept his eyes on her as he set the tray down. She glanced at the contents but didn't say anything.

'Now, unfortunately everything is probably a little bit cold now, but why don't you tuck in, and I will go and empty your bucket.'

Elisabeth didn't move, her eyes back on him now. 'Let me go. Please.'

'I can't do that.' Benjamin reached for the bucket, wrinkling up his nose at the smell. He quickly carried it outside, pushing the door back with his elbow, the lock catching. 'Eat your breakfast. I'll be back in ten minutes.'

Ignoring him, she grabbed hold of the bars. 'You can do it. I know you're not a bad person. I just want to go home. Please.'

Her voice broke on the last word and Benjamin's shoulders tensed. He didn't like it when they got upset. Although the anger irritated him, in some ways it was easier to deal with.

He didn't look at her again, taking the bucket away to deal with.

When he returned she was sitting sullenly on the bed next to the tray of food. 'Here you go, all nice and clean for you,' he told her, trying to keep his voice cheerful as he unlocked the cell door.

'I want to go home.' She repeated the last words she had spoken, this time, though, much firmer and there was no 'please' at the end.

'I already told you that's not possible, Elisabeth. The sooner you accept that, the sooner we can move on.' He put the bucket down, started to turn to face her as something smacked hard against his forehead. He heard the smashing of china and looked down to see one of his mother's lovely teacups lying in pieces on the floor.

Fury raged inside him, the heat of it burning his cheeks. 'Look what you've done!'

He glanced at the tray, saw that she hadn't touched any of the food he had prepared for her, and the anger choked him a little tighter. She was testing him, and he reminded himself that he couldn't afford to become emotional or lose his temper. He had to stay in control.

'You didn't eat your breakfast.'

'I don't want your stupid food.'

An egg cup, the egg still inside it, followed the teacup, knocking against his clean shirt.

'Elisabeth! Stop it.'

'IT'S ELLIE!'

This time it was the pot of tea, the water catching his trousers, the teapot breaking as it hit the floor. He was going to have to go and get a brush and dustpan to clear this mess up.

Seething, he stormed out of the cell, heard the clink of her chain as she got up from the bed. As he turned to pull the door closed, she scowled at him through the bars.

'What's your plan, *Ben*?' She made a point of emphasising his name the way he had just done to her. 'You can't just keep me down here indefinitely. People will be looking for me. You say you want to help me, but how is this helping me? Keeping me prisoner? You're forcing me to use a bucket as my toilet, I can't even properly get dressed because of this stupid bloody cuff, and I haven't been able to shower or even have a wash in God knows how long. You think Ash is abusive towards me? You're the abuser. I don't want your help and I don't need it. I despise you.'

Benjamin could feel a vein throbbing in his neck, and he fought to hold on to his temper.

This wasn't working out quite as he had planned.

He locked the door and pocketed the key before pushing his face up against the bars. 'I would think about your attitude towards me very carefully if I was you. I can make this easy for you or I can make it very difficult.'

'Why, what are you going to do, Ben? Send your creepy sister down here to try and scare me again?'

What? That had him hesitating. It was the second time she had mentioned Virginia. 'She doesn't know you're here.'

'Yes she does. I told you. She's been down here. She was even in the cell when I woke up one time. I think you should focus on looking after her, rather than kidnapping someone who doesn't want your help. Because you know that's what you've done, right? You're forcing me to be here against my will.'

Benjamin wasn't listening to the rest of what she was saying. How was it possible that his sister knew about this place? They had always kept it from her.

If she had been down here and she knew about Elisabeth, that really wasn't good at all. Elisabeth was supposed to be safe.

But if Virginia knew about this place then that changed everything.

He had brought Elisabeth here to save her from Ash, but now it looked like he might also have to protect her from his sister too.

41

Joyce Cuthbert was the longest serving employee at Stobart and Greaves. Thirty-seven years and six months she told Ash, even though he never asked, which meant she knew everyone who had worked there, including Benjamin Thorne.

She had started on a YTS training scheme as an administration clerk. 'But I worked my way up the ladder,' she proudly told him, and she was now Mr Stobart's personal assistant, one of the most sought-after positions in the company. During the conversation he also learnt that Mr Greaves assistant was called Flora, that the woman wasn't a patch on Joyce, that Joyce prided herself on running an orderly office and Mr Stobart would never cope without her if she took early retirement... Oh, and that she had a soft spot for the men of the office, while, from her comments it seemed, she took a rather more critical stance with her female colleagues. He also discovered that she had a loose tongue and liked a good gossip.

She hadn't replied to his message until Friday. Ash had already heard from the other employee he had emailed, who had apologised, saying he didn't know Benjamin Thorne, so he wasn't holding out a lot of hope that Joyce Cuthbert would be able to help. He had started to explore other avenues, though all so far had led to dead ends. He was still convinced that Benjamin was the key to Ellie's disappearance and was trying to find out everything he could about the Thorne family history.

It turned out Joyce's delay in responding had been because she had been off sick, but she was back now and full of energy, and after pinging back and forth half a dozen messages, Ash gathered that although she had been fond of Benjamin, it appeared he had left under a bit of a black cloud. That was what prompted Ash to call her.

She had been delighted when he had and he quickly realised that perhaps it hadn't been his smartest move as, once in actual conversation, Joyce loved to waffle. Still, the forty minutes spent on the phone with her (did the woman have any actual work to do?) was worth it, as she remembered Benjamin Thorne well, and while she might have a soft spot for men in general, Benjamin, it appeared, had been one of her favourites.

'Such a nice young man. Always so polite and considerate. He would regularly stop by my office just to say hello and check in with me that I was okay.'

'Are you still in contact with him at all?'

'He still sends me a Christmas card, but I haven't actually spoken with him since he left. I assume he still lives with his sister in Corpusty. His family were quite wealthy, you know, but Benjamin never had any of those airs and graces you sometimes get with these rich people. You know how some of them can be a bit snooty, like they think they're better than you. He wasn't like that. He was a nice boy.'

'Have you ever met his sister, Virginia?'

'A few times. Bit of a strange girl. Nothing like him at all. She would sometimes be with him if he stopped by to pick up a file. He used to do that a lot. Would take work home with him. He took a lot of pride in his work, you know.'

'Strange how?' Ash asked, gently guiding her back onto topic.

'Well, she never had anything to say for herself. He told me she was shy, and I think she had something wrong with her. In my mind though, that's no excuse for rudeness.'

'You said Benjamin no longer works there. You must have been sad to see him leave.'

'Oh I was. It was all such a terrible shame.'

Joyce had touched on this "terrible shame" in her initial email, and he was curious to know what she meant. 'How come?' he asked now, keeping his tone casual.

'Well, it was that girl who worked here. Little stirrer. She got him into trouble.'

'Who was that?'

'Alicia, her name was. I can't remember her last name. She was only here for a few months, but she caused no end of bother.'

'For Benjamin?'

'Well, mostly. I could tell she was a troublemaker, though, as soon as I laid eyes on her. I know her sort.'

'What did she do to Benjamin?'

'Is that an Australian accent you have? How have I only just noticed that? I'm normally good at spotting accents. I've always wanted to go to Australia, you know. I'd like to go to that opera house. I'd love to cuddle a koala too. I bet you've cuddled loads of them, haven't you?'

She was off topic again and Ash bit down on his frustration, reminded himself to be patient. 'They're not keen on being held.'

'Aren't they? That's a shame.'

'You were saying about this Alicia girl and what she did to Benjamin?'

'Oh yes, I was. Vile girl. She led that poor man on and then accused him of all sorts of nasty business.'

'Really?' Ash reminded himself that Joyce was a big Benjamin fan, so tried not to sound too eager. 'That sounds terrible,' he added, wanting to keep her on side.

'As I say, I could spot her type as soon as I met her. Poor Benjamin though, he thought they were friends. He used to bring her pastries from the bakery down the road and he was always asking after her. She was quick to take advantage of his kindness, but what she did to him was plain nasty.'

'Why, what did she do?'

'Well, Benjamin had invited her round for dinner. She had this on-off boyfriend and things were going through a rocky patch again. It was getting annoying if I am honest, affecting her work performance... not that it was great in the first place. I had dropped a few hints to Mr Stobart that he should let her go, but he's another one who always wants to give people an extra chance. Very generous in nature, but he's supposed to be running a business and you can't think with your heart. Now if I was in charge I would–'

'You said Benjamin invited her round for dinner?'

'I... um... yes, he did.' Thankfully the reminder pulled Joyce back on track. 'He was another one always trying to help people. Too nice for his own good. Alicia had been using him as a shoulder to cry on and he offered to have her round for dinner, try and cheer her up. That was a huge mistake though. She started spreading all sorts of nasty rumours about him after that.'

Ash's heartbeat quickened. 'What kind of rumours?'

'She said he had made advances on her. Sexual advances. And that he tried to stop her from leaving the house, locking her in one of the rooms. Poor Benjamin, he was devastated. That boy was so upset he was in tears.'

Ash's irritation level cranked up a notch. He wanted to ask her why she was so quick to believe Benjamin and doubt Alicia. How had Joyce known for certain that the girl hadn't been telling the truth? He didn't want her to clam up, though, until he had found out everything. 'What happened after that?' he asked, trying to keep his tone neutral.

'It was awful. There had to be this whole investigation. Absolutely ridiculous if you ask me. These young girls, they get away with dressing like tarts and leading men on, then they cause all of this fuss. All Benjamin did was show that harlot some kindness and in return she dragged his name through the mud.'

'How long ago did this happen?'

'Well, it must be at least seven or eight years ago.'

'And does Alicia still work there?'

'No, she left a few months after.'

'So was Benjamin sacked?'

'No, thank goodness. It was Alicia's word against his, and I think Mr Stobart and Mr Greaves knew well enough who to trust. The thing is, she had tarnished his reputation by then. I know there were whispers and some of the other girls were giving him a wide berth. Benjamin was so uncomfortable with it all he decided to go of his own accord.'

Figuring he had gained as much relevant information as he could, Ash wrapped things up as quickly, ending the call, and turned to Google again in an attempt to find Alicia.

He didn't hold out a lot of hope with just her first name, but a combination of that with the company name did bring up old photos from a team-building day and there was a group shot that named the employees taking part. Ash spotted Benjamin straightaway. Looking at the names below the picture, Alicia Hewson was standing to the right of him.

Ash studied her. A slim blonde girl, not dissimilar in looks to

Ellie. Of course, in this photo she was much younger. Maybe nineteen or twenty. And what age would Benjamin have been seven years ago? Maybe late thirties? Nearly twice her age.

In the photo he had his hand resting on Alicia's shoulder. Proprietarily.

He really needed to find Alicia and get her version of events.

More googling and he learnt that there was an Alicia Hewson working as a mortgage broker in Norwich. The name wasn't that common, so chances were, it had to be the same girl, didn't it?

There was a mobile number and Ash called it (no messing around with emails this time) and when Alicia answered, he cut straight to the chase.

Initially she went silent, and he was certain she was going to hang up on him, though her reaction told him he had the right girl, but then she quietly informed him that the incident was in her past and she had no interest in dragging it up again. She sounded like she was working herself to a close and this time he was in no doubt that the call was about to end.

Desperate, he told her about Ellie.

'Please just hear me out. This isn't what you think. I live in Corpusty, next door to Benjamin Thorne. My girlfriend has gone missing, and I'm convinced he is somehow involved. Don't hang up on me, please. I'm at my wits' end and I honestly have nowhere else to turn. If you know something about him, anything that might help me find Ellie, you have to tell me.'

There was another long pause, as Alicia seemed to consider. Eventually she spoke. 'There's a Costa Coffee down at Riverside.'

'I know it.'

'Can you get there, say in an hour?'

'I can.'

Ash agreed to her terms that he would arrive and get a table outside then call her so she could decide if she was comfortable approaching him.

He understood her concerns and knew that if it was Ellie in Alicia's place, he would want her to take similar precautions.

After giving Poppy ten minutes in the garden, he locked up, grabbed his car keys and let himself out of the front door, heart sinking when he spotted Roxanne's sporty little Mazda pulling into the drive.

Fuck! He had forgotten arguing with Pete about his wife doing a food shop for him.

She had the radio blaring, sunglasses on, and a big smile painted on her lips as she pulled to a halt beside him. The last time Ash had seen her was when he had thrown her out of the house, but Roxanne would have glossed over that. She was good at choosing what she wanted to remember and what was best to discard.

'Hello, stranger,' she shouted over the music, far too cheerfully for someone whose alleged best friend was missing. Thankfully the music went off along with the engine, though then she was getting out of the car, which was a delay Ash couldn't afford to deal with.

'I told Pete you didn't need to stop by,' he told her tersely. Roxanne might have moved past their argument, but he hadn't. The things she had said about Ellie and how Ash had let her down had been unnecessarily cruel and still stung.

'Oh, don't be silly. Forget the other day. You know what I'm like when I get in one of my moods.'

Yes, he knew only too well. Roxanne had two moods when it came to him. She was either rude and stuck-up around him, treating him like he was the scum of the earth, or she was sweetness and light, and honestly, Ash preferred the former, because at least he knew where he stood. Whereas right now his guard was up as he knew exactly what to expect when she was like this.

'I thought rather than me picking you up random things, we could go food shopping together,' she told him now.

'I can't.'

'Oh don't be silly. It will stop you mooching around this house in a bad mood. Life goes on, Ash.'

The temptation to slap her burned his palm. Of course, he never would. He had never hit a woman in his life and he had no intention of starting. But seriously, what a shitty thing to say.

He bit down on the retort he was about to give her; aware the clock was ticking. He couldn't afford to miss Alicia. 'I really can't, I'm on my way out,' he told her instead, keeping his tone purposely flat.

'Where?'

He levelled her a look. 'That's none of your business.'

As he went to push past her, she caught hold of his arm. 'Come on, Ashton. Don't be like this. Let me look after you.'

She tried to pull him into an embrace, pouting when he pushed her away.

No, he wasn't falling for that trick again. Last time she had tried that he had found her mouth pressed against his and had to forcibly push her away.

'Will you just fucking stop it!' he snapped. 'I've honestly had enough, Roxanne. I'm in love with Ellie and Pete is my best friend.'

'That didn't stop you once,' she spat. 'I wonder what he would think if he knew what his best friend was really like?'

'Why don't you tell him then?' Ash challenged, enjoying the look of shock on Roxanne's face. 'Or maybe it's time I did.'

'You wouldn't dare.' But all of a sudden she wasn't sounding too sure.

He was sick of this, sick of knowing he had once been a

shitty friend to Pete, sick of keeping it a secret and sick of having to fight off Roxanne who thought things should continue.

It had been one foolish drunken encounter that was years in the past, long before Pete and Roxanne had tied the knot, but Ash would never forgive himself for betraying his best friend, or for keeping it from Ellie, even though he hadn't known her at the time.

He had been off-his-face drunk and Roxanne... well, he was quite certain she had known what she was doing when she let herself into his hotel room.

Ash had never told Pete the truth about that night. Was overcome with guilt that he had let his best friend go on to marry a woman who was willing to cheat on him. Not that Ash and Roxanne had actually had sex. No, he had stopped it before that point, insisting she leave.

She had alternated between hitting on him and hating him ever since. But then he had met Ellie and her jealousy had meant she mostly hated him.

He had never threatened to tell Pete before, and Roxanne had seemed convinced she had his silence. But not any longer. Ash was done and the relief at realising that was immeasurable.

He would talk to Pete, let him know the truth about his wife, and hope there was a way to save their friendship. And if– no, *when* he got Ellie back, he wouldn't have to dread those moments when he and Roxanne were alone together and she tried to throw herself at him. No more worrying in case Ellie walked in and caught her in action, thinking the worst that he might be cheating on her.

'I need to go.'

'Ash, you have to promise me you won't tell Pete.'

Ignoring her, he shook her off again, clicked his keys at his car.

'Ashton!' Roxanne was sounding desperate now. 'This is my

marriage. Don't you dare try to ruin it.' She was still making demands when he shut the door, turning on the engine. And then he was pulling past her, leaving her standing on the driveway, and on his way to meet Alicia Hewson.

And hopefully getting one step closer to finding out what the hell had happened to Ellie.

42

Ellie had been down to two crusts of bread and the apples, having tried to eke out the food she had been left with for as long as possible, when she finally decided to cave. After her confrontation with Benjamin, he had still brought her lunch, a sandwich which she had been desperate to eat, but she hadn't wanted to give him the satisfaction. She refused to look at him or answer his questions, forcing herself to leave the food, and he had eventually returned for the plate, muttering in annoyance. She considered it a small victory, even though her belly was rumbling uncomfortably.

After that he had left her alone and, although she had no concept of time, she was fairly certain enough of it had passed to know he wasn't bringing her any dinner.

Her mind had been reeling as she tried to come to terms with the fact that he was the one who had locked her down here, and for what? To detox her from Ash? To keep her for himself? The idea made her shudder. She had honestly thought Benjamin was a good, kind person and she had trusted him, felt safe around him. How could he do this to her?

And what was his long-term plan? Was he ever going to let

her go or did he intend to keep her chained up down here forever?

That couldn't happen. She wouldn't let it.

Ash must be back from his work trip by now and would know she was missing. Had he called the police? He would be going out of his mind with worry, she was sure of it. Benjamin might have tried to trick her into believing something was going on between Ash and Roxanne, but she wouldn't fall for it. Ash loved her. She had to hold on to that.

And if he had called the police, had they questioned Benjamin? Would they even think to?

No one knew he was a threat. He had seemed like such a harmless and pleasant man. An upstanding member of the community. If someone had told Ellie a couple of weeks ago that he had a prison cell built in the basement under his home, she would never have believed them. And Ash, he hadn't been a fan, but mostly because he thought the man was dull and a little odd. He would never think him capable of this.

Benjamin and Virginia must have been using the tunnel to access the cellar. How long had that been going on? Knowing that they could have been creeping about in her house while she was in the shower or sleeping made her feel sick.

Had they done this with the previous occupants? Hidden in the shadows, spying on them, and making threats to them to leave?

Her mind had gone back to the Tanner family. She had been so convinced that John Tanner had been guilty of murdering his wife, probably his daughter, too, but what if it had been one of the Thornes?

Had Benjamin or his sister murdered Louise Tanner? John said he had been away on a business trip, the same as Ash had been. Louise and Naomi would have been home alone and vulnerable.

Had he taken Naomi and locked her up in this cell?

She had simply vanished five years ago, and no one had ever found her. Ellie knew most people suspected her father had killed her and hidden her body, but what if she had been trapped down here? And if so, where was she now?

Had Benjamin murdered her?

The fact he had a cell beneath the houses with a bed in it and a chain concreted into the floor, suggested this was more than a simple crush on Ellie. He had done this before.

That sudden realisation had terrified her and when the trembling started, so did a fresh wave of tears, her breathing becoming erratic as she gulped for air.

Pull yourself together. No one is coming to rescue you. You need to help yourself.

Benjamin was a monster, but no one knew. He had done this before and got away with it, so why would this time be any different?

It took a while to calm herself down, the tears finally subsiding, though her breathing was still a little jerky, eventually giving way to a bout of hiccups. The water would get rid of them, but she was trying to ration it, not knowing when – if – Benjamin would return.

Was that what had happened to Naomi? Had she made him angry? Had he let her starve to death?

Don't think about it.

She had realised she needed to focus. No one else could help her and that meant she had to help herself. So far she had been hostile and aggressive with Benjamin, and he had told her that while she was angry with him, she would be staying in the cell. Did that mean that eventually he would let her come up into the main house?

If that happened she would have more opportunity to escape.

She knew she needed to get this cuff off her ankle and get out of this cell, and unfortunately the only way to do that was going to be by biting down on her hatred for him and allowing him to believe she was being co-operative.

Could she manage to do that?

What seemed like hours dragged by and she was beginning to believe that he wasn't coming back again. Alone with her thoughts and that awful dripping sound, she honestly thought she was starting to go insane.

A couple of times she had looked up and was convinced she saw Virginia watching her, but honestly, had she really or was her mind beginning to play tricks on her?

When she eventually heard the footsteps, she wondered if she was imagining them too, but then they became louder, more decisive and in the burning flicker of the lamps, she saw Benjamin approaching the cell.

This was her chance. She had to be docile. Had to let him think that she was coming round to his way of thinking and that she would be compliant.

She smelt the food before she spotted the tray, her starving belly pathetically grateful. Even if she wasn't going to play ball, she wasn't sure she had the willpower to turn it away again.

As he unlocked the cell door, stepping inside, she shifted to a sitting position and watched him as he fussed with the tray.

'Now are you going to be a good girl today, Elisabeth?'

His use of her birth name had made her skin crawl. She had never been Elisabeth. Her parents had died when she was barely out of nappies and she had been raised by her maternal free-spirited grandmother. To Bee (never Barbara) she was Ellie and the shortened name had stuck.

Although she couldn't bring herself to respond to his question, she wasn't hostile to him either, trying to arrange her face in a neutral expression as he had approached the bed and set down the tray.

Scrambled eggs on toast. This time there was no pot, but there was a mug of tea. As her stomach growled appreciatively, she could have cried with relief. Instead, she swallowed the rising ball of emotion and forced herself to say, 'Thank you.'

He seemed pleased with that, watching as she picked up the plastic cutlery he had provided, and took the first mouthful. It was so good. Hot food was already such an alien concept to her, and she had to force herself to slow down, not wanting to appear too eager.

'Let me go take care of your potty,' he told her, picking up the bucket, and she had almost spat out the mouthful she was chewing on, struggling to bite down on her rising temper.

Your potty? He was treating her like she was a baby and reliant on him to look after her.

Which, she guessed she was.

The thought of that made her want to scream, but she was well aware that screaming wouldn't get her out of here, so, aware her body desperately needed to be fed, she continued to eat the food, even though she was no longer enjoying it.

She decided she would play his twisted little game and wait for an opportunity to make her escape.

'You enjoy your breakfast and I'll be back in a few minutes,' he told her, a little too jauntily. He acted like she was okay with this. I mean, seriously, how the fuck was she supposed to be okay? That's what she wanted to ask him, but instead, she docilely watched him step out of the cell, closing the door.

'Wait!' Her own voice sounded croaky and foreign to her, weak too, and that shocked her. If she was going to escape she needed to build up her strength.

'Yes, Elisabeth?'

'Could you bring me some socks? My feet are freezing. Please.'

She had forced that last word out, knew manners were important to him. *Locking someone in a cage is fine, but mind your Ps and Qs, eh, Benjamin?*

He cocked his head on one side, studying her for a moment, but she could tell he was pleased that she had asked and that she had done so politely.

'Let me see what I can do about that.'

Ellie had been given the socks and was so pathetically grateful to have warm feet again. And the upside of trying to keep Benjamin on side meant that she was getting three warm meals a day, the lamps stayed lit, and her bucket was cleaned daily.

Much as she had wanted to starve herself initially, it served no purpose other than to piss Benjamin off, and it did nothing to help her escape. Plus, of course, the meals were now helping her keep track of her days. While she had no idea how long she had been held prisoner down here, breakfast, lunch and dinner were at least giving her an idea of what time it was.

The flipside was that now she was in his eyes 'coming around', he was also spending more time in the cell with her. While that was irritating, she tried to remind herself that it was also good. She needed to befriend him again. Persuade him that he could trust her enough to let her come upstairs into the house. She had memorised the route that led up from the library onto the first-floor landing, remembering where the main staircase was and knew the exit points; front door, kitchen door, and the French doors at the back of the house.

All she needed was a couple of seconds. Break free, run for the exit. Once she was outside she would run hell for leather down the driveway, hope Ash was home, and if he wasn't, then get out into the lane, try to find somewhere to hide until she heard a passing car.

During their time together in the cell, she didn't say too much, careful about being tripped up, so she let Benjamin do most of the talking, but made a point to thank him – for the socks and for her meals – and nodded where she felt it was appropriate.

He had mentioned again that if she behaved he could consider letting her out of the cell and she clung to the hope that it would happen in the not-too-distant future.

Her chance finally came three days later, when Benjamin brought her breakfast and she gently pushed about how dirty she was feeling. She reminded him that she hadn't had a proper wash or shower since being in the cell. It was no word of a lie. She was filthy and disgusted by her own stench.

He slowly nodded, assessing her as he considered her point. 'If I let you have a shower, you have to promise me you won't try anything silly.'

Ellie's heart thumped. 'I promise. I just want to feel clean.'

'Okay, stay here and finish your breakfast. I'll be back in a bit.'

Like she could go anywhere!

She watched him leave. Was he really going to let her out of this cell? Butterflies swarmed in the pit of her stomach, and she struggled to manage the egg and toast she had just put in her mouth.

This could be her only chance and she needed to be careful about how she took it. She did as asked, clearing the plate, and was compliantly waiting for him, sat on the edge of the bed, when he eventually returned.

'Okay, I have sorted everything out,' he told her, going round the side of the bed and picking up her box of clothes. 'Come on then.'

As Ellie got up, he set the box down on the mattress, she assumed to let her out of the ankle cuff, horrified when he produced a pair of handcuffs. 'Wrists out,' he instructed, his tone far too cheerful for a man who was holding someone captive in a cell under his house.

'You don't have to put those on me. I promised I wouldn't run away.'

'And I want to believe you, Elisabeth. I really do. But we need to build trust and it has to be earnt. Now wrists out, please.'

She bit down on her frustration, resisting the urge to slap him or scream in his face. Neither would help her and reacting badly would only set back the progress she had made over the last few days. She was a fool to think he would have made things so easy for her.

Reluctantly she held her hands out, wincing at the click as the cuffs locked.

As Benjamin bent down to fuss with the ankle cuff, she considered kneeing him in the face and trying to make a run for it the second she was free. It was a risky move though, as she wasn't entirely sure of how to get back to the main passage, plus being in the dark with her wrists cuffed would slow her down.

No, her best bet was to wait until they were in the main house.

Once her ankle was released, he picked up the box again and linked his free arm through hers, guiding her out of the cell, his torch lighting up the path ahead. Ellie tried to pay attention to the route they were taking, left, then after a minute, left again, though she was struggling to keep up. Her ankle was still hurting from where she twisted it and she realised that if the opportunity came to run, she was going to struggle.

Eventually they reached the door that led through the bookcase and into the library. Benjamin switched off the torch as Ellie blinked rapidly, trying to adjust her eyes to the light. She was still doing that as he led her to the spiral staircase. She struggled a little with the steps, thanks to her ankle and her swimming vision, the cuffs meaning she had nothing to hold on to other than Benjamin, but then they were heading up the steep staircase and through the door onto the landing.

Ellie's heart was pounding. Freedom was so close.

'You can use my bathroom,' Benjamin told her, pushing her through a door and into a large pale-blue room with a high ceiling and dominated by a wooden sleigh bed. The space was sparsely furnished and lacked personality, the bed made with military precision and a pair of pyjamas folded neatly and lying on the throw that covered the bottom of the sheet. There were no knick-knacks, no little touches to give the place personality, and the blue décor made it feel cold, despite the blazing sun beaming through the window.

Ellie stared at the outside view longingly, desperate to feel that sun on her skin, not realising until she heard the turn of the key that Benjamin had locked the door.

Her heart sunk further, realising he had just blocked off her escape route.

'Come this way.' He guided her over to the bathroom, opening the door for her and pushing her inside. 'Okay, so I have left towels for you on the hamper, there's a toothbrush and some paste on the sink, and here are your things.' He put the box down on the toilet seat. 'Take your time, but don't try anything silly. This is that first step towards building trust. If you are respectful of that then I can start letting you use the shower on a more frequent basis. Do I have your word you will behave, Elisabeth?'

Ellie nodded, glancing round the small room, noting there was no window.

'I didn't hear you. Do I have your word?'

'Yes.'

'Good girl. Now turn to face me.'

She did as asked, relieved when he removed the cuffs.

'Thank you.' She forced the word out, even managing a small smile for him, and noted that he looked pleased at that.

'Enjoy your shower. I'll be back in a bit.'

Then he was closing the door and she heard another click as he locked her inside.

Quickly she checked over everything in the bathroom, dismayed that he seemed to have pre-empted her every move. The bathroom cabinet was empty and even the lid to the cistern had been removed. There was nothing she could use as a weapon.

He was starting to trust her, though, and had said this could be a more frequent thing. Frustrating as it was, she might have to bide her time and wait for a better opportunity.

She turned on the shower, slipping out of her filthy clothes as she waited for the water to heat up. Under the hot spray she wept tears of relief at finally being able to clean herself, and then she plotted.

While she was locked in the cell she was helpless. That's why she needed to keep gaining Benjamin's trust. The more times he let her into the house, the better the chance she would have to escape. He might be taking every possible precaution with her at the moment, but eventually his guard would slip as he came to trust her. And when it did, she would be ready and waiting.

43

Would Ash really tell Pete the truth and, if he did, who would Pete believe?

Those were the two questions playing on Roxanne Walker's mind as she watched Ash pull out of the driveway and she considered how best to handle the situation.

She had always been so convinced she had Ash's silence, knew how far he went back with Pete and how important their friendship was, but with Ellie missing, Ash had become grumpy and irrational, and most worrying of all, unpredictable.

If he told Pete what had happened all those years ago, he was also going to tell him that Roxanne took every opportunity to rekindle things between them, which okay, maybe she did, but Pete, love him as she might, wasn't the most exciting man to be married to, while Ash had always hit a solid ten on her radar.

Pete thought she hated his best friend, and yes, that was true, but only out of frustration. Then of course, when Ash had hooked up with Ellie it had made things so much worse.

Roxanne was used to getting what she wanted. Pete was a safe bet, but she would have dumped him in a second if Ash had been interested.

Now, if he told, she stood to lose everything, and there was no way she was going to let that happen.

So her options were, call Pete and confess before Ash got there, spin things and make out it was Ash who had hit on her and tell her husband he had continued to do so over the years (which wouldn't be that great a stretch, given Ash's reputation for having a roaming eye. At least he had before he met Ellie) or sit tight, do nothing, and hope Ash was calling her bluff.

Eventually she decided on a halfway house, calling Pete from the car and telling him how rude his friend had been, refusing her help, and how she had driven all the way out to Corpusty for nothing. At least that should get Pete's back up sufficiently for if Ash did call.

'You know he's not in a good place, Roxy. He's worried sick about Ellie.'

Yes, Roxanne was perfectly aware of that. Though what exactly was so special about Ellie, she wasn't quite sure. Ash had never been one for settling down and it still shocked her that the one woman to tame him had been Ellie. Sure, she was pretty enough, in an understated way, and she could be a laugh, but she didn't exactly go out of her way to take care of her appearance. If it was a special occasion she would make an effort, but mostly she wore her hair pulled back in a scruffy ponytail, her face make-up free, and Roxanne despaired of her wardrobe. Even her jewellery choices were awful, she thought, recalling the ugly hippy bracelet Ellie always wore. She was nice enough in a bland way, but she didn't exactly turn heads.

'That isn't an excuse to treat his friends badly.' She pouted.

'I know, but you need to cut him some slack. You do like to wind him up and I'm not sure that's the best idea at the moment. Put yourself in his position and imagine how you would feel if I had gone missing.'

Roxanne huffed at that, livid that he was taking Ash's side

already. It didn't bode well if Ash blabbed. Pete was her husband, and he was supposed to support her and have her back, not his best friend's. She told him so and pointed out that he could go missing for all she cared.

'I'll talk to him,' Pete said, eventually backing down. 'But please just go pick up some shopping for him. Even if it's the basics. He's not eating properly, and I'm worried about him. I know what he's like. He's going to obsess over Ellie and not focus on anything else.'

Although she wasn't happy about it, Roxanne eventually agreed. Doing this favour for Pete would hopefully put her in good stead if Ash did say anything.

She went to the supermarket, bought fifty quid's worth of groceries, then drove back to Corpusty, scowling when she pulled into the driveway of Hazelwood Cottage and saw that Ash's car still wasn't back.

Where the hell had he gone to?

She found the spare key on her ring that Pete had given her, just in case Ash hadn't been about, and unlocked the front door. Barking immediately came from the other side and, as she pushed it open, the three-legged dog came charging into the hallway, tail wagging.

'Oh God, it's you. No, don't jump up.'

Roxanne pushed the dog away, not wanting to get her white, tightly-cropped trousers dirty. They were the ones that showed off her toned arse and thighs, and she had hoped that teamed with her tight little black vest top and skyscraper heels, they might attract Ash's attention. That had been a waste of time though.

The dog followed her back outside, dancing around her as she pulled the bags out of the boot of her sports car, lugging them into the kitchen. She emptied the contents onto the table, throwing the bags away, then took a picture of everything she had bought. Maybe she would WhatsApp it to Pete with the caption, 'Happy now?'

From somewhere upstairs there was a loud creak then what sounded like footsteps. Her gaze shot up to the ceiling as the sound grew closer. It was overhead now and yes, definitely someone was moving about.

Ellie?

It had to be her. Ash was still out.

Was she playing some kind of game? Had she faked her disappearance? Did Ash know?

Unsure what the reason was, but quite certain she was about to solve the mystery of why Ellie had vanished, she headed for the stairs, resisting the urge to call out. If Ellie was upstairs, she didn't want to let on that she was about to be found out.

As she approached the landing, a girl stepped out of one of the rooms. Taller, bulkier than Ellie, with long drab hair and the ugliest, most shapeless dress Roxanne had ever seen. Her eyes were hidden behind bottle-bottom glasses, but Roxanne guessed they were panicked, as her mouth had dropped open.

'Who the hell are you?'

Then it was happening fast. The girl charging at her... no, past her, clearly making her escape, and in that moment of shock, Roxanne was losing her footing, tottering on the top step then losing her balance, falling.

She hit her head against the wall, lost consciousness before she reached the bottom. She wasn't aware of the dog barking or the girl approaching, circling her as she looked down with curiosity. She held a pair of scissors, the tip pointing downwards, and as she studied the woman on the floor, she opened and closed them. Snip, snip, snip.

'Oops.'

44

I have always liked the pretty things.

The roses in the garden and the dolls that sit at the end of my bed.

Maybe it's because mother called me an ugly child. She said I was broken inside and out.

She never understood though.

Nothing is perfect. Anything that is pretty on the outside, will have ugliness within. Sometimes you have to dig deep enough to find the ugly stuff.

Dolls and flowers are easy. They hold still. People though, not so much.

This one is the prettiest I have seen, with her smooth, milky skin and long lashes. At first I thought the fall down the stairs had killed her. That's why there was no harm in me taking her. A life-sized doll to play with. And I didn't have to feel guilty. She had fallen. This one wasn't my fault.

I would paint her, I decided, and so I had placed her on one of the heavy dining chairs in the conservatory before going upstairs for my sewing kit. I needed her eyes open.

When I returned to the room she was no longer there. Then

I spotted her crawling across the floor, trying to make it to the open French doors.

She wasn't dead and that realisation made me panic. I grabbed one of the heavy candlesticks from the table, smashing it over her head, my heartbeat slowly returning to normal as she slumped to the floor again.

This time I would be more careful, I told myself and I fetched rope from the garage, securing her to the chair. This was better. If she woke again, she wouldn't be able to wriggle about so much.

Her hair was so pretty, the colour of flames, but she wore it tied back. I would pull it loose, I decided, but after I had fixed her face.

I threaded my needle with white thread, before poking it through her left eyelid, pulling it up and securing it to the skin beneath her eyebrow. One stitch, two stitch, three stitch. I counted to myself as I repeated the process, a dozen stitches in place before I tied off the knot.

That was better. Her eye was open wide now, showing off her beautiful sapphire-blue iris.

I repeated the process with her right eye then stepped back to admire her. She really was so very lovely.

Should I do her mouth too? She wore blood-red lipstick, which I liked very much, and I didn't want the thread to ruin that. If she woke again though, I would need her mouth to be still.

Glancing in the basket, I spotted the red cotton and rethreaded my needle.

By the time I had finished she was almost perfect.

Maybe just a little bit of colour was needed on that pale skin. I selected a rosy-pink paint, let my brush glide over her cheekbones, then I loosened her hair, let it fall over her shoulders.

There. Now she was perfect.

I was midway through painting her when she awoke again. At first I didn't realise, as her eyes were already open, but the strangled groan and the thrashing against the ropes alerted me as she jerked against the chair.

I ignored her, continued with my work, humming to myself. This was my best painting yet. I was sure of it.

Finally I was finished, and I turned the canvas to show her, smiling.

I think she was trying to tell me she liked it, but it was only coming out as a grunt.

Picking up my scissors, I approached her chair. I had my painting of her while she was pretty.

Now, though, it was time to find out what she was like on the inside.

45

Elisabeth was making progress and Benjamin was secretly pleased.

They hadn't got off to a good start and he was beginning to worry that perhaps he had bitten off more than he could chew, that perhaps she was beyond saving, so the last few days had been a revelation.

He had taken a leap of faith in her, trusting her to behave if he let her have a shower and she had obeyed his instructions, not attempting to get away when he had unlocked the bathroom door, nor protesting when he had slipped the handcuffs on her wrists, leading her back down to the library and through the tunnel to her cell. She had even sat on the bed compliantly while he locked on the ankle cuff and had thanked him for letting her use the shower.

It made him glad that he had changed the sheets on the cell bed for her, while she had been in the shower, and had picked a few flowers from the garden, which he had arranged in a plastic vase on the floor of the cell. He had also brought half a dozen paperbacks down from the library for her.

She had been a good girl today and he had decided she deserved to be rewarded. He would let her come up into the house for dinner. It would be easier to talk to her sat around the dinner table, rather than in this cramped cell.

He could make it special for her too. Candles on the table and a nice dessert to follow. Maybe get some of that wine she liked.

He had spent some time outside in the garden, after he had left her cell, losing himself among the flowers. There was always so much work to be done and it was easy for his mind to drift.

When he eventually stopped to look at his watch, he was shocked to see it was already afternoon. If he was going to sort this dinner out then he needed to get cracking.

As he wandered through the French doors into the conservatory he could see someone sat in the chair near Virginia's canvas and he froze, wondering what they were doing in his house.

Red hair, he spotted, and his mind immediately went to the woman he had seen Ash with. The one with whom he was cheating on Elisabeth.

'What are you doing in my home?' he asked stiffly, but before the words were even out of his mouth he noticed the rope and understood that the woman wasn't there voluntarily.

Then he spotted the puddle of blood pooling on the floor.

'Virginia! What the hell have you done?'

He launched forward with jerky steps, taking a sharp intake of breath when he saw the stab wound in the woman's chest, her startled eyes held wide open, and her mouth sewn shut.

'No, no!' He rubbed his hands over his face, muttering to himself under his breath. Where had the redhead come from? Ash and Elisabeth's house? She had to have done.

And what about Ash? Was he home or had Virginia attacked

him too? Benjamin realised he needed to check. And then he would have to clear his sister's mess up.

She was becoming violent again and that wasn't good.

It was also another reason to bring Elisabeth up into the house. If Virginia was on the warpath, then Elisabeth was going to need him to protect her.

46

Ash did as Alicia instructed. After ordering, he sat at a table outside, facing towards the car park, eyes scanning the cars as he called her to let her know he was there.

'Table to the left. Dark hair, grey T-shirt,' he told her.

After a few minutes a woman approached. Older than her picture, and her hair brown, not blonde, but it was definitely her, and as she paused by the table, offering him a hesitant smile, he was struck by her similarity to Ellie.

'Ash?'

It was the wide, almond-shaped eyes, he realised, that reminded him of his girlfriend, though Alicia's were darker. They had similar-shaped faces and she was shorter than Ellie by a good few inches though, thinner too.

Ash remained seated, not wanting to intimidate her with his size. 'Thanks for coming,' he told her, pushing the second coffee towards her. 'I got you a flat white. I wasn't sure what you like.'

'Flat white is fine. Thank you.'

Alicia pulled up a seat and studied him across the table. 'I'm sorry about your girlfriend, though I'm not sure anything I say will be of any help.'

He was trying his best to put her at ease, but he could tell she was anxious. Despite the heat she wore a jumper and kept worrying the ends of the sleeves with her fingers.

'I'm beating my head against a wall here. I promise you, anything you tell me will be helpful.' He offered her what he hoped was a genuine smile, even though the action felt forced given he hadn't had much to smile about recently, and took out his wallet, opening it to pull out the battered photo he carried around.

He could show Alicia the one he had on his phone, but although it was personal to him, how could he prove that it wasn't an image he had just taken off the internet? This felt more sincere.

It was one of him and Ellie a few months after they had started dating, taken with a Polaroid camera at the wedding of one of her friends and although it wasn't her favourite picture; she had grumbled that her eyes were half shut and her grin too goofy (because he had made her laugh the second before clicking) it was one of his. Okay, so maybe she didn't look perfect in it, but he didn't need her to be. He wasn't looking at the camera properly either because his attention had been focused on her as they had giggled together like a pair of idiots. That had been the night he realised he was halfway in love with her... no, more than halfway, and that he wanted to spend the rest of his life with her.

Except now she wasn't here, and it hurt like fuck.

'This is her,' he told Alicia now, biting down on the stab of pain the memory had brought. 'We bought our first house together recently, just rescued a little dog. Honestly, if you had asked me two weeks ago, I would have told you my life was pretty much perfect. I was away with work. Ellie has been at home working on the house. When I got back she had just vanished.'

He saw the questions in Alicia's eyes, knew she was wondering if Ellie might have left of her own accord. 'Her car was parked in the drive,' he quickly pointed out before she could voice any suspicions. 'And I found her phone smashed in the basement. She'd been trying to call me that evening, left me a message saying she needed to talk to me. And our dog, Poppy, she wouldn't have just left her without food.'

'I take it the police are looking for her?'

'She's been reported missing, but I don't think they have the first clue where to start looking for her.'

'And you think Benjamin Thorne is somehow involved?' Alicia's lips twisted. 'Have you told the police that?'

Ash gave a bitter laugh. 'Of course. But the problem is I can't prove it.'

'But you're certain he's involved?'

'He had a bit of a thing for Ellie. She thought it was harmless. We both did. But honestly, now I look back, I'm not so sure. We had some odd stuff going on at home as well, before she disappeared.'

'What do you mean "odd stuff"?'

'Someone broke in while we were out, though they didn't steal anything. There was graffiti on the wall telling us to leave. I know he's involved, even if I can't prove it.'

Alicia was silent as she absorbed everything he was telling her. 'It was the same for me,' she said eventually. 'My word against his. And unfortunately most people chose to side with him.'

'Are you comfortable telling me what happened?' Ash kept his tone gentle. He didn't want to spook her or push her too far, but it was important he found out exactly what kind of man Benjamin was.

Her eyes darted to his, wary. 'How much do you already know?'

He had already told her about the conversation with Joyce Cuthbert, though had been quick to add that he hadn't believed the woman's account of things. He picked his words carefully now. 'Not much. I know you went to Benjamin's for dinner. That he made you feel uncomfortable and tried to prevent you leaving.'

'I thought he was my friend. Looking back though, I see that I was a stupid, gullible twenty-year-old. He seemed so nice, and he had time for me, showing me how things worked in the office and answering my questions if I got stuck. We tended to go to lunch at the same time, so were often in the break room together and he was always friendly, chatty. He would ask me stuff and was interested in what I had to say. I realised afterwards that he had probably planned it all that way. None of it was a coincidence.

'I'm sure there were plenty who would say it's my own fault and that I led him on, but honestly, it wasn't like that. He was several years older than me and I guess I saw him as a bit of a father figure.

'Whenever I was having problems with James, my boyfriend at the time, Benjamin was always there to listen and offer advice. When James and I had a big bust-up, I was really upset, and Benjamin invited me over for dinner to cheer me up. I honestly took his offer at face value. A friend trying to cheer up another friend. I had no idea that he saw it as something different.' Alicia paused, reaching into her handbag and pulling out a packet of cigarettes and a lighter. Almost as an afterthought, she glanced up at Ash. 'Do you mind?'

Ash didn't smoke and wasn't a fan of the smell, but he could tell she was finding this difficult and knew she probably needed the cigarette to help calm her nerves. 'No, go ahead.'

'Do you want one?' Alicia offered the pack of Benson and Hedges.

'Not for me, thanks.'

He waited patiently while she lit up, taking a sip of his Americano, appreciating that she twisted her chair, so the smoke wasn't wafting towards him.

'I suppose I should have seen the warning signs when I arrived,' she eventually continued. 'He had gone to a lot of effort for what was supposed to be a simple dinner with a friend. Fancy little nibbles, candles, wine. I had driven, so said I could only have the one glass, and he kept trying to persuade me to stay over. He said there were plenty of guest bedrooms.'

'I take it you said no?' Ash asked.

'Yes. When I said I couldn't stay though, he got a little sulky. That was the first time I felt a little uncomfortable and wondered if I had made a mistake.

'We had dinner. He kept trying to top up my glass and I kept saying no and the conversation turned to James. Benjamin knew we had been having problems and he had always been sympathetic, but that night he started getting aggressive about it, telling me it was time to end the relationship. When I told him I had planned to meet James the following day for lunch, he demanded I cancel.'

Alicia paused, took a long drag of her cigarette.

'What happened next?'

'I'd had enough at this point, and I told him that I was leaving. He got panicky then, begging me to stay, but I already had my coat on. He apologised and I said it was fine, to just forget about it and I would see him at work on Monday. By then I just wanted to go. I used the loo before I left, and it was when I came back out that...'

Ash could tell this was difficult for her, watching as she took another drag of the cigarette, while the fingers of her free hand drummed a pattern on the side of her cup. He didn't say anything, waiting for her to continue in her own time.

'He was waiting for me and completely caught me off guard. Next thing I knew he had grabbed hold of me, and he was pulling me towards the stairs. I tried to fight him off, to get away, but I guess I must have been in shock, and he was stronger than he looked. He dragged me up the stairs and pushed me into one of the bedrooms. He gave me a hard shove and I landed on the floor then I heard the door slam shut, the twist of a key. The bastard had locked me in there.'

Alicia sucked in a breath, looked at Ash. 'I was so scared. I had no idea what he planned to do to me. He started talking to me through the door, saying he was going to help me and that I would one day thank him for this. I begged him to let me out. I screamed at him and threatened him. Eventually I realised he had gone. He had walked away and left me trapped in that room. I tried to force the door open, but it was too heavy. Then I looked at getting out of the window. I didn't have my bag or phone, but my car keys were in my pocket. It was a sheer drop though, and I was scared I might break something. It was too risky.'

'Did he come back?'

'Eventually, yes, though he left me locked in there for a couple of hours. There was a vase on a dressing table. It looked expensive, but it was the only thing I could find to use. When he unlocked the door, he wasn't expecting me to be waiting the other side. He had a tray in his hands, and I was able to catch him off guard. I smashed the vase against his head. Although it didn't knock him unconscious, it slowed him down and I was able to push past him, get down the stairs. I didn't have time to look for my bag. I got straight out of the house and in my car and got the hell out of there.'

'Did you go to the police?'

Alicia looked down at the table now, her expression suggesting she was embarrassed. 'No,' she admitted. 'I should have done, I know. But I was young and stupid and in a panic.

When I got home I called James, told him what happened. He was livid and insisted on driving out to Corpusty with me to get my bag back. It didn't go well. I waited in the car and Benjamin played the innocent when he answered the door, making up some crap about how I had scared the life out of him running out when he was in the kitchen and leaving my stuff behind. James said he didn't believe him, and he got a little aggressive with Benjamin, punching him in the face. It was Benjamin who was threatening to call the police on us in the end. We got the hell out of there.'

So similar to when Ash had confronted him. Even though Benjamin was the one in the wrong, he had still managed to use the police to his advantage.

'So what happened when you went into work?'

'I told one of my colleagues and she insisted I put in a complaint with HR. He countered it though, saying my boyfriend attacked him. It all got messy, work couldn't do much because it had happened off the premises and outside of working hours, and we were both encouraged to drop the matter.' She looked up at him now, her eyes wide and clear, reminding him so much of Ellie. 'I couldn't stay working there, though, having to see his face every day and remembering what he had done.'

Ash mused over what he had learnt on the drive back to Corpusty, thinking about what he already knew about Benjamin Thorne and how this new information fitted in. The man was socially awkward and tried so hard to present this image of a mild-mannered accountant, but what he had done to Alicia Hewson was not normal behaviour.

He had integrated himself into her life, leading her to believe he was an innocent friend, much the same as he had tried to do with Ellie and, judging from the calls and texts to Ellie's phone, and the regular visits to the house before she had disappeared, the stupid little crush he had on her had definitely become more of an obsession.

When he had gone round to confront Benjamin, Ash had been convinced the man had Ellie trapped in his house somewhere, but then Benjamin had called the police. He wouldn't have done something stupid like that unless she wasn't there, which begged the question, what the hell had he done to her and where was she?

She wasn't dead. He refused to believe that. Couldn't believe that.

Back home, he let himself in the house, surprised when he didn't hear the patter of Poppy's paws. She usually ran to greet him, her stuffed teddy in her mouth.

He whistled to her and called out her name, frowning when she didn't respond.

As he started to search the house for her, his phone rang, and he dug inside his pocket for it.

Pete's name flashed on the screen.

'Hey, mate.'

'Ash, is Roxy still with you?'

'No, she left hours ago. I saw her as I was going out and told her not to bother doing any shopping.' The table full of food caught his attention as he stepped into the kitchen. 'Which apparently she ignored.'

'She said she had seen you and you said that. I asked her still to go.' Pete paused. 'So she dropped your shopping off then?'

Ash picked up the four pints of warm milk and the melting bag of frozen salmon. 'She did. And left it all out on the kitchen table. Mate, I'm going to have to bin half of this.'

'So, you don't know what time she left.'

'No, I told you. I'm only just home. Her car's not here and I can't find the bloody dog.'

Ash took the stairs two at a time, concern gnawing at his gut now. Where the fuck was Poppy? 'You don't think Roxanne took her, do you?'

'Why would she take your dog? You know she's not really an animal person.'

'Well, she was here, and now both her and my dog are gone.'

'Trust me. She wouldn't take your dog.'

'So where are they then?'

'I don't know. Roxy's phone is switched off. I've left her half a dozen messages. She was supposed to be home an hour ago to let the electrician in.'

Ash had searched all of the rooms downstairs and up now. Poppy wasn't in the house. As he listened to Pete talk, he crossed through into the bedroom, unlocking the French doors and stepping out onto the balcony, scouring the back garden for the dog. He would go outside and do a thorough search for her, but already suspected he wasn't going to find her.

Poppy would have barked when he called her, he was sure of it.

Ellie had disappeared suddenly and now so had Poppy. As for Roxanne, her car wasn't here, which suggested she had left of her own accord, but even for her, buying a load of perishable food then leaving it out on the table to cook in the warm afternoon sun, was a shitty move. He wasn't sure she would do that.

He glanced towards the end of the garden and the Thorne house, more certain than ever that all of the answers he needed were locked inside.

47

After this morning and being so close to freedom, seeing the sun again, knowing home and Ash were so close, Ellie's mood had plummeted. There were no highs to being trapped in this hellhole of an underground cell, but she was discovering there were continual lows.

She would probably have just the one chance of escape and she needed to be smart about when she took it. So biding her time, not fighting for her freedom had been the sensible thing to do. She kept reminding herself of that. But being led back down here and shackled up again had been harder than she had anticipated.

No one was aware of this network of underground tunnels and rooms, and the only two people who knew she was here were Benjamin and his sister. Virginia was bat-shit crazy, and even scarier than her brother. That meant Ellie's fate rested entirely in Benjamin's hands.

If anything happened to him, she would be trapped down here to slowly starve to death. The thought made her shudder.

She had wanted to sleep, to shut her nightmare out, but that had been impossible. The tunnels, usually so silent other than that steady drip that she was certain was slowly driving her mad, had been filled with sounds that had her paranoia going into overdrive.

She wasn't alone after all, but that offered no comfort. Someone was down here with her, and she sensed whatever was going on, it wasn't good. The shuffling of footsteps, the flicker of movement in the shadows. Was it Virginia? The girl frightened the hell out of Ellie, and she felt she was caught in a trap, waiting for a predator to attack.

Then a short while later, after the footsteps had disappeared, she had heard what sounded like an animal.

Scurrying footsteps and sniffing. What the fuck was it?

Rats? It was the only thing she could think that would possibly be down here, though whatever it was sounded bigger.

She lay on the narrow bed, listening to the noise, scared that whatever it was might find her, as the animal (it had to be an animal) sounded like it was coming closer then moved further away again.

It was the whining that eventually gave it away and had her heartbeat racing, and she sat up abruptly, peering into the shadows.

A dog.

'Poppy?' Her voice was not much more than a whisper, her tone tentative, as she was scared of alerting Virginia or Benjamin, though laced with hope. If Poppy was back in the tunnels, did that mean Ash was with her? Had he discovered the entrance in the cellar?'

She called out again, this time louder.

For a moment she heard nothing and was beginning to wonder if she was hallucinating, but then there was the scamper of feet and more whining, followed by a bark, as Poppy hopped into the cellar room, her tail thumping in delight when she spotted Ellie.

'Oh my God, Poppy, it *is* you.' Ellie was off the bed, approaching the bars, almost forgetting again that she was wearing the ankle cuff. She managed to steady herself just in time, grabbing hold of the bars for balance. 'Poppy, come here, girl.'

She reached out with both hands, stroking the dog's head and tickling her ears the second she was close enough, as frustrated as Poppy when she whined, wanting the bars out of the way so she could pick her up.

'Is Ash with you?'

The puppy whined in return, recognising his name.

'Ash?'

Fuck it. No, she didn't want to alert Benjamin or Virginia, but if he had found the door and tunnels, she needed to let him know where she was.

'ASH? Can you hear me? Please help me. I'm trapped.'

Ellie waited a moment, but there was no response.

If Ash hadn't found the door in the cellar then how the hell did Poppy get down here?

She called out again, panicked when Poppy started to move away. With the bars between them it was impossible to keep the dog with her and she was scared that she might leave and get lost down here.

Ash had to be down here somewhere. Maybe this network of tunnels was even bigger than she realised. Or Poppy had somehow got in the cellar and through the door without his help.

Knowing she couldn't force the dog to stay with her and aware it might put her in danger if Benjamin discovered her, Ellie tried to think of a message Poppy could deliver to Ash if she found her way back to him.

It was a long shot. Poppy was hardly a three-legged Lassie, but if Ellie could try and get a note under her collar. For which she would need a piece of notepaper and a pen. She had neither.

Could she put something on the dog's collar Ash would recognise? She glanced round the cell looking for anything she might be able to use. Her clothing, underwear? It was too risky. If Poppy ran into Benjamin...

Poppy whined and tried to move again, and Ellie hushed her, glancing at her wrist as she stroked the dog's head. The bracelet that she always wore. It was just a cheap beaded one, hippy in style. Ash teased her about it, but she never removed it. It had been a gift from her grandmother, just a few short months before she had passed away. She could tie it around Poppy's collar. If Ash saw it he would know for certain that Ellie was in trouble.

Trying to keep Poppy distracted, she managed to work the knot loose, slipping the bracelet off, before knotting it around the dog's collar. If Poppy disappeared now and found Ash, he would see the bracelet, but if she stayed here and Benjamin found her, he hopefully wouldn't spot it.

She sat with the dog for a while, though eventually got cramp in her leg from the uncomfortable position she had to sit in. As soon as she got up to stretch her legs, Poppy got up also.

Ellie didn't try to stop her leaving this time, knew with the bars between them there was no way she could make her stay, and tears leaked as she watched the blackness swallow the little dog up.

Please let her find Ash.

Knowing there was nothing she could do but wait and hope, she lay back down on the bed and closed her eyes.

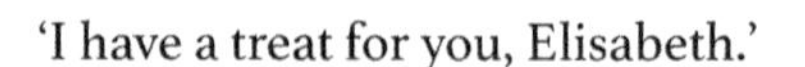

'I have a treat for you, Elisabeth.'

Ellie must have fallen asleep, but she woke now, hearing Benjamin's voice, and remembered Poppy's visit, immediately on edge as she wondered where the dog was.

'Elisabeth?'

She kept her eyes squeezed shut, really not up for having to be civil and make small talk with him, as she pretended to give a shit about his fucked-up plans for her. Hopefully he would just go away.

No such luck.

She heard the cell door unlocking. 'Wake up, sleepyhead. I said I have a treat for you.'

Biting down on her anger and growing hatred towards him, she forced a neutral expression on her face and rolled over, propping herself up on her elbow. 'Sorry, I was out of it.'

'Well I hope you're feeling refreshed because I thought rather than eat down here, you might like to come upstairs and have dinner with me this evening.'

Ellie's mood immediately lifted, and her heartbeat quickened as hope stirred in her gut, mixed with a lick of nervous excitement. Not at the idea of having dinner with Benjamin. She would rather stick pins in her eyes. But he was going to let her upstairs again. Was this it? Was tonight going to be her chance to escape?

He was waiting for her reaction, like a nervous schoolboy asking her out on a date, which cranked her revulsion level up a notch, and despite her new-found hope, she still struggled to force the smile onto her face.

'I would really like that. Thank you.'

'I thought you might.' He seemed pleased with her response, reaching into his pocket and producing the handcuffs.

Ellie held her wrists out willingly before he asked, earning herself a beaming smile. He honestly looked like a proud parent whose child had just been praised by their teacher. 'I was so pleased with how well you behaved earlier. I know you're not going to let me down tonight, are you?'

'I promise I won't.' She made herself beam back, as nausea swirled in the back of her throat, and she thought about how she would like to punch his stupid smug face.

Bide your time, Ellie.

Freed from the ankle cuff, she let Benjamin lead her from the cell, hoping Poppy didn't choose to make an appearance. She was unsure how Benjamin would react if he saw the dog, though she had a feeling it wouldn't go well.

There was no sign of her, though, and Ellie was keeping everything crossed the dog had found her way back to Ash. At least Benjamin was wittering on, excitedly telling her about his planned dinner, so if there were any suspect noises he wouldn't notice.

'I thought I would make a nice beef Wellington. I have some vegetables straight from the garden.'

He hadn't cooked the food yet?

Ellie had assumed that he had brought her up from the cell because it was time to eat. If he was going to be distracted with cooking, would it give her a chance to escape?

She found out her answer to that a short while later when he led her into the kitchen, telling her to sit down at the table.

'I thought you could keep me company while I cook.'

'I can help if you like. Maybe peel the vegetables?' It would relieve the monotony and more importantly give her access to a sharp object.

Benjamin studied her for a moment, as though reading her thoughts, suspicion clear on his face. 'I invited you to dinner. It wouldn't be right to make you help cook it,' he said, tightly.

'You're not asking. I'm offering.'

'Thank you, but I can manage myself.'

Her suggestion must have put his guard up because he

opened the door to a tall cupboard, reaching inside for a coil of rope.

Ellie watched him warily as he approached the table. 'What's that for?'

'Just a precaution. Lift your arms up, please.'

'I'm already wearing handcuffs. You don't need the rope.'

'And I want to trust you, Elisabeth. I really do, but if I'm going to cook you a nice dinner, I need to be able to concentrate. I can't risk you sneaking off.'

'I wouldn't do that,' Ellie lied.

He wasn't listening, already wrapping the rope around her waist and securing it to the slats at the back of the chair. 'There, that's better.' He stepped back and admired his handiwork. 'Is that comfortable?'

'Not really.'

'Well, it won't be for long. Now, shall we have some music?' He fiddled with the dial on an old-fashioned radio that sat on the far end of the counter. She wriggled against the rope, tried to see if there was any slack. Of course there wasn't. He had done this before and wasn't stupid. Although her wrists were cuffed in front of her, she couldn't get to the knots at the back of the chair.

Damn it!

Classical music filled the room and Benjamin turned, a grin on his face as he waved his arms about like he was conducting an orchestra. 'Ah, Brahms. One of my favourites. Now, before I start preparing dinner, would you like a nice cup of tea?'

What Ellie actually wanted was to get the hell out of there. She was struggling not to show her frustration at this latest setback, wondering how the hell she was going to get away from him. He was staring at her, though, and she suspected she had already raised his suspicions when she offered to help with dinner. 'That would be lovely. Thank you.'

As he turned to put the kettle on, the smile fell from her face again. She was tied to a chair in the kitchen of a madman who was dancing around the room to classical music and offering her 'nice' refreshments as if this was all the most normal thing in the world.

And where the hell was his crazy sister? Benjamin was in the throes of making what seemed to be a romantic dinner for two. Was Virginia not going to eat with them?

She asked the question as she tried to drink the tea he had made her, the task made difficult by the handcuffs.

He didn't answer for a moment and at first she wasn't sure if he had heard her.

'Virginia's in bed. She hasn't been feeling well today,' he said eventually. 'I'll take her a tray up before we eat.'

'Oh, okay.'

He stopped what he was doing and turned to face her. 'Tonight's about you and me, Elisabeth. It's better that Virginia isn't there. I want us to get to know each other better and I don't want her to spoil things.'

He gave her a creepy smile and Ellie tried to shift on her chair, uncomfortable with how he was holding the knife.

'You'd like that, wouldn't you, the chance to get to know each other better?'

No.

'Of course.' She forced a smile.

'Good.'

Seeming satisfied with her answer, Benjamin started chopping the vegetables, and Ellie used the opportunity, while he was distracted, to try and free herself from the chair again. She attempted to relax, knowing that getting herself worked up wasn't going to help. Her mind, though, was still working furiously as she watched him work, as she tried to figure out a way to escape.

Eventually, the dish was prepared and in the oven, and he

turned to face her. 'There, that shouldn't take long now. I expect you're hungry.'

Keep playing along with him. 'I'm looking forward to it.'

'Just enough time for another surprise.'

Oh God, what now. At least he had come over to the chair now and was untying the rope.

Relieved to be able to move, Ellie let out an exaggerated breath, noting that Benjamin blatantly ignored it. Instead, he looked annoyed. 'Well, aren't you excited to know what it is?' he asked huffily.

'Yes, of course I am.'

'Good, because I think you're going to really like this one.'

48

She let him lead her out of the kitchen and back up the stairs, across the landing, past the closed door of Virginia's room, to one of the bedrooms that looked like it hadn't been redecorated since the 1970s.

'Mother's room,' Benjamin told her proudly.

Ellie looked around her, at the dresser neatly organised with a jewellery box, brushes, and perfume bottles, the gaudy floral wallpaper, and the large four-poster bed with thick velvet drapes... Oh God, the bed. That wasn't his surprise, was it? He didn't think he was going to have sex with her, did he, in his mother's bed?

Ellie was doing her best to fake a lot of things, but there was a limit. She couldn't fake that.

'Do you want to see your surprise?'

No. 'What is it?'

Benjamin stepped past her to the large, heavy oak wardrobe, opening the door. Every instinct in Ellie's body was telling her to run. She had the cuffs on, but the door was open, and she might be able to get a few seconds' precious head start on him.

If he caught her though – and there was a good chance he would – that would be it. He would lose the trust in her that she had been gradually building up. She wouldn't get another chance and it would have all been for nothing.

Her relief when he pulled a dress out of the wardrobe, holding it proudly before her, was immense, though she was wondering what the fuck he was going to ask her.

'This was Mother's favourite dress. I am going to let you wear it for our dinner.'

Shit, seriously? Ellie studied the cream chiffon evening gown with its long billowing cuffed sleeves and floaty skirt. Definitely vintage, 1970s she would guess, and way too formal for a simple dinner. It wasn't ugly but she really didn't want to wear a dead woman's dress.

'This is lovely, Benjamin, but I think it's a dress that should be saved for special occasions.'

'Is tonight not a special occasion?'

'I didn't mean it like that.' *Damn it.* He was pouting now like he was a spoilt toddler and she'd just stolen his ice cream. 'Of course tonight is special, but this dress is so delicate and lovely, and you said it was your mother's favourite. I wouldn't feel comfortable eating dinner in it. What if I accidentally spilt something on it?'

'You won't, and I want you to wear it.'

'It might not fit.'

'It will.' His face was set like stone, and she could see there was no arguing with him. 'You can change in my bathroom again.'

It was a repeat of when he had let her have a shower earlier, as he led her across the hallway to his own bedroom, closing the door and turning the key, then removing Ellie's handcuffs, before locking her in the bathroom with the dress.

She touched the delicate fabric, annoyed her fingers were trembling. This whole set-up and Benjamin's behaviour was scaring the hell out of her. He had seemed such a rational person when she had first met him and she thought back to the day when the two men had turned up to collect the washing machine, how at the time she had been grateful that he had been there. She had actually felt safe with him there. What a joke.

She really didn't want to put on the dress, but understood she had no choice, and after stripping down to her underwear, she pulled the gown off the hanger.

'Are you nearly finished?'

Benjamin's voice made her jump. He was obviously waiting for her the other side of the door. She didn't like the closeness, feeling vulnerable in just her knickers and bra, aware he could unlock the door at any point.

'Two minutes,' she told him, hurriedly stepping into the dress and pushing her arms into the long floaty sleeves. The dress had a low-cut bodice that was embroidered with delicate flowers then sheer voile fabric leading up to the lacy collar, where she fastened it around her neck before fumbling with the buttons on the wrist cuffs. She reached for the zip at the back of the dress, managing to pull it up over the small of her back before it became stuck.

'Are you ready? Can I unlock the door?'

'Not yet.'

Frantically, Ellie tugged on the zip, her face burning and sweat pooling under her arms. It wouldn't budge though.

Damn it.

Benjamin didn't ask again. Instead, she heard the twist of the key in the lock, looking up wide-eyed and panicked as he pushed open the door.

'I told you I'm not finished.'

'What's the hold-up, Elisabeth?'

'The zip is stuck.'

'Well I can help with that, silly.'

'It's okay, I can do it. I just need another minute.'

'I told you I will help. But first, wrists out.'

When Ellie continued to tug at the zip, ignoring him, he tutted loudly. 'Elisabeth, I said wrists out, now!'

Reluctantly she did as told.

'Good girl,' he said, praising her, locking on the cuffs, and she winced at the patronising words, wanting to spit in his face. It wasn't a good idea though.

'Right, turn around and let's look at this zip.'

She did as asked, squeezing her eyes shut when she felt his cool fingers brush against her bare back.

'Oh, yes, this is caught on the fabric. I think you would have struggled to do it yourself. Hold still.'

Ellie didn't really have a choice, hating every second of having him in her personal space. Eventually the zip pulled free, and she breathed a sigh of relief as he fastened her into the dress.

'There you go. Now turn around. Let me have a look at you.' When she obliged, a beam spread across his face. 'Oh, you look just perfect. Here, come on, there's a full-length mirror in Mother's room. You can see.'

He guided her back across the hallway, acting like an excited child, as Ellie tried not to trip over the hem of the dress as she was forced to keep up with him. Positioned in front of the free-standing oval mirror, she barely recognised herself, her face so pale, no doubt from being locked away underground, with dark bruises under her eyes, and her dull blonde hair hanging limply around her shoulders. The dress was a fraction too big for her, probably because she had lost weight, and the cream colour against her sallow skin made her look like a ghost.

Because that was what she had become, what he had made her; a ghost of her former self, and she hated him for it. The wave of emotion hit suddenly, catching her off guard, and she burst into tears.

'Elisabeth? What's wrong?' Benjamin looked distraught as he fussed around her. 'I thought this would make you happy. It was supposed to be a nice surprise.'

She couldn't answer him for a moment, overwhelmed by the realisation that he had taken everything from her, and scared she would never find her way out of this nightmare.

Don't think like that. You have to keep trying.

'Elisabeth, will you stop crying and look at me please?' He had his petulant voice on, reminding her of all the hard work she had done over the last few days to try and win his trust. 'What is wrong with you? Do you not like my mother's dress?'

She needed to pull this round and couldn't afford for him to lock her down in the cell again. Raising her cuffed hands to her face, she swiped at the tears, sniffing. 'I'm sorry. I do. It's not that.'

'Then what's wrong? Is it him?'

He didn't have to say Ash's name for her to realise who he was referring to and the jealousy in his tone made her grimace.

'No, no, it's not.'

'He's no good for you, Elisabeth. I've told you that. I really thought you had started to see sense and were over him.'

'It's your mother.' Ellie blurted the words, aware she needed to distract him from thinking about Ash and get him back on side.

Benjamin narrowed his eyes in suspicion. 'What about my mother?'

'I was looking at myself wearing her dress and seeing how

important it was to you, and it made me realise just how much you loved her and must miss her.'

The words rolled straight from her mouth, with no time to think them through, and she licked her dry lips wondering if he would buy the lie.

His brown eyes lingered on her for a moment, bulging behind his glasses, his expression unreadable, and Ellie's face flamed. *Please let him believe me.*

Eventually he nodded, his features softening. 'I do miss her. I miss her terribly. That's why it's so important for me that you wear her dress. She would have liked you, Elisabeth, and she would have wanted you to wear it, now you are part of the family.'

What? He was fucking deluded.

'I would have liked to have known her.'

He seemed pleased by that. This was good. Somehow she had managed to keep him on side.

'Come and sit down at the dresser,' he instructed, pulling Ellie by her cuffs, so she didn't have a choice. He pushed her down onto the stool and selected a hairbrush. She watched him in the reflection as he began to stroke it over her hair, trying to keep her expression neutral, even though her skin was crawling at the touch of the brush.

Don't fuck up again.

'Mother was always more the head of our family than Father was. He was a weak man. That's what Mother said. He lacked discipline and had a roaming eye.'

'What happened to your father?'

'He died.'

Ellie knew that. Benjamin had seldom mentioned his dad in their conversations though, and on the few occasions he had, it was in the past tense. 'It was just you, your mum and your sister for quite a while, wasn't it?' she pushed, trying a different approach. 'I guess he must have died quite young.'

'He was fifty-eight. I was twenty at the time, so Mother needed me to become the man of the house.'

'That's really young. Was he ill?'

Benjamin was working the brush more vigorously over her hair now and Ellie winced. 'You're being very nosy, Elisabeth. Why all these questions about my family? Have I been asking you about yours?'

'I'm trying to make conversation. You have...' She paused, stopped herself from using the word "forced", certain it wouldn't go down well. 'You want me to be a part of your life here and I am wearing your mother's dress. In order to do that, I'm asking questions to try and fit in.'

Benjamin didn't answer for a moment, and she looked at his reflection in the mirror, saw the hard look of concentration on his face as he continued to brush, each stroke getting harder and harder.

'Benjamin? Benjamin?' She tried to pull away and he twisted his fist in her hair, pulling tightly. 'Ouch! Benjamin. You're hurting me.' She spoke the words loudly, finally breaking through his trance.

He stopped brushing, looking back at her reflection, his expression softening as he loosened his grip.

'I'm sorry. Father died of a heart attack. It's difficult for me to talk about.'

'I understand. I'm sorry I asked.'

He leaned over Ellie to put the hairbrush back on the dresser and she caught the faint whiff of stale sweat and some kind of peppery aftershave that smelt out of date, and partially masked it. The combined scents were revolting.

'There, now don't you look beautiful.' Benjamin placed his hands on her shoulders and leaned forward to rest his chin on the top of her head as he studied her reflection, and she shuddered at the touch. 'Perfect for our dinner.'

Smile, damn it. She knew that's what he was waiting for, but it was a struggle to curve her lips. Instead, she said with as much sincerity as she could fake, 'I'm looking forward to it.'

49

They ate in the formal dining room at the front of the house. It was seldom used these days. After his mother had passed, Benjamin and Virginia had tended to eat in the domed conservatory, where it was less stuffy and more relaxed.

That's what he had planned, thinking Elisabeth would appreciate the view of the gardens.

But Virginia had put paid to that. Although he had removed the body of the woman she had killed, there were still bloodstains on the floor that he needed to take care of. Fetching the woman's car, which he had found parked outside Hazelwood Cottage, and hiding it in the garage had already taken precious time and he didn't want to delay his dinner plans further.

The dining room was dominated by a polished mahogany table that had been in the family for years, with a huge candelabra ceiling light above it, while the walls were filled with family portraits.

Benjamin had been pleased when Elisabeth noticed them, explaining how his mother had commissioned them from an artist friend. Looking at her now, as she sat there in the shadowy room, the only light coming from the candles he had lit, and the scrap of setting sun that filtered through the partly drawn heavy velvet curtains at the front window, he thought she looked beautiful. His mother's dress was perfect on her. In fact, this whole evening was perfect: the company, the nice dinner. He hoped they could do it together more often.

'More wine?' he asked, noticing her glass was getting empty.

'Thank you.'

She waited for him to get up and come round to where she was sitting to pour the wine for her. Not that she had any choice. He had tied her to the chair again, reminding her that it was still early days and that the trust he had talked about still needed to be built further. While he wanted to believe her when she said she wouldn't try to escape, it was just too big a risk, especially when he needed to go back and forth to the kitchen. With the rope in place, it meant he could relax more, and they could enjoy their evening together.

She held up her glass for him and he felt a twinge of guilt again at the handcuffs. She hadn't been happy that he had refused to remove them, and he knew it made eating and drinking more of a chore for her.

Maybe if she behaved tonight, he might consider a compromise next time.

'Are you going to have some more too?' she asked when he placed the bottle back on the table.

'I really shouldn't. I'm not a big drinker.' It was the truth, he only drank on occasion, and the one glass he'd had was already making him feel a little light-headed.

'Oh go on, please. I don't like drinking alone.'

She gave him such a beseeching look, he found it difficult to disappoint her. 'Okay, I guess one more glass wouldn't hurt.'

He had served salmon soufflé for starter (yes, it wasn't just the one course, this was a special dinner) and they were now eating the beef Wellington he had cooked.

He wanted to say Elisabeth was enjoying it, but he had noted she was mostly pushing the food around her plate. Benjamin had asked her a couple of times if she was enjoying her meal and she told him she was, taking another small bite, but still he wasn't sure.

He noticed her looking at the portraits again. 'Is that your mother and father in the centre pictures?'

'Yes. I love this painting of Mother. She was so beautiful.'

He waited for Elisabeth to comment, hoping she would agree.

'She was, and your dad looked like a nice man.'

It was meant as a compliment, but Benjamin was aware of the anger rising. 'He was weak.' He spat the words. Couldn't help himself.

He had told her all of this upstairs in the bedroom. Had she forgotten already?

'I'm sure he had his good points,' she said quietly, spearing a piece of carrot with her fork and putting it in her mouth. He could hear the disapproval in her tone.

'It wasn't really a heart attack. I lied.'

'Sorry?'

Benjamin hadn't meant to blurt that out, but he found himself wanting Elisabeth to know the truth. Maybe then she might understand. He stared up at the portrait of his father and frowned. 'A heart attack. That's what Mother wanted people to believe.'

'What happened to him?'

'She poisoned him.'

Elisabeth didn't respond to that other than with a sharp intake of breath. She set her fork down and the clink of metal against the plate was enough to draw his attention back to her.

'You need to know these things,' he told her, unable to keep the anger out of his voice. 'At first I thought I should protect you, but if you're going to be a part of this family then you need to know the truth. All of it.'

'What happened?'

'Mother hated Father. She always called him lazy and useless, said he had no backbone. Things were worse after her sister, Aunty Imelda, came to live with us. She took a fancy to him and although they thought they were being discreet, everyone knew they were at it.'

He had her attention now. She was staring at him silently, waiting for him to continue, to air his family's dirty laundry.

'Mother laughed and said she was welcome to him, but I know it was hurtful for her. Insulting too. She had Virginia to deal with and it wasn't fair Father shirking his responsibilities like that. And then there was her reputation. She had taken Aunty Imelda in, put a roof over her head and tried to help her, and she was being made to look foolish.

'One day she'd had enough. Father had gone away on a business trip and Aunty Imelda had conveniently gone to visit a friend. We knew they were sneaking off together for a dirty weekend. That was when Mother knew she could take no more.'

Benjamin thought back to the conversation he'd had with his mother. It was the day she had asked him to step up and be a man, he remembered proudly.

Elisabeth took a gulp of her wine. Her eyes were wide, a little in shock he suspected, as she waited for him to continue. Now he had started though, the words came flooding out. He wanted her to know everything.

'At first she just wanted to punish Aunty Imelda. Although she hated Father for what he had done, her sister had betrayed her kindness. Mother had taken her in, and this was how she had been thanked. Death would be too kind for her.

'No one used the tunnels anymore. Hazelwood Cottage was no longer in the family and Father had boarded the entrance up.

It was the perfect place to imprison Aunty Imelda and make sure she suffered for her betrayal.

'They've been there since the houses were built, you know,' he said, deciding to give her a bit of history about them. 'Originally it was just a servants' tunnel linking the houses. My grandfather adapted and extended them at the beginning of the Second World War, though, so they could be used as an air-raid shelter. Isn't that fascinating? So much history.'

Elisabeth nodded in agreement, though she still didn't say anything as she waited for him to continue.

'There was no cell down there at the time. Of course, no one had needed one of those.

'We made do with a large dog crate. It was quite cramped and uncomfortable, but then it was supposed to be a punishment. It wasn't difficult to get her down there. One day while Father was at work, Mother showed Aunty Imelda the tunnels. I was waiting down there for them, and we overpowered her easily. Once we had her locked in the cage we packed all of her things up and brought them down to the tunnel.

'Father was distraught when he thought she had left. He wouldn't believe it. He even called the police. No one knew where she was though. Mother and I kept her like our pet. We would take it in turns to go down and feed her. One meal a day, always the scraps, and in a dog bowl. That's all Mother said she deserved. We wanted her to suffer.

'And it would have been okay, we could have carried on, but Father just wouldn't let her disappearance drop. He kept on and on and on about it, and he was badgering the police too. Eventually Mother knew she had to silence him.'

He thought back to her special plants and how Mother kept sneaking bits of them into Father's food.

'After he died she paid one last visit to Aunty Imelda, to let her know what she had done then she told me to board up the entrance again.'

'You left her down there to die?' Elisabeth looked disgusted, which had his hackles going up.

'Don't look at me like that. You have no idea what Aunty Imelda did to our family.'

Tears were rolling down her cheeks now. Not the reaction he had expected, and his surprise at that turned to temper. 'You're judging me!' He flung his napkin down in annoyance. 'I have cooked you this lovely meal, allowed you to join me, let you wear my mother's favourite dress and tried to open up to you, and this is how you repay me.'

'I'm not judging you; I promise.'

'Then why are you acting like this?'

'Because you're scaring me, Benjamin. You said there was no cell down there before. Why is there now?'

'I don't understand what you're getting at.' He was aware he was behaving a little petulantly, but he was so annoyed with her for ruining everything. 'Explain please.'

Her voice dropped to barely a whisper. 'Did you build that cell for me? Or have there been others?'

Benjamin bit the inside of his cheek, aware the colour was draining from his face, though his pout remained. He wasn't ready to talk about this bit.

'Did you put Naomi Tanner in there?' When he remained silent, she pushed further. 'Did you kill her mother?'

He stared at her across the table as emotions warred inside him. 'Finish eating your dinner, Elisabeth,' he told her eventually. 'You've ruined a nice evening. I'm not sure if you deserve dessert.' He picked up his empty plate and started to leave the table.

'Please, Benjamin. You said you want me to be a part of your family and you want me to know everything. Yes, some of it is difficult to hear, but I promise I am trying to understand. If you want this to work then you have to be honest with me. No secrets.'

His shoulders tensed and he was going to ignore her, but her words touched him. She wanted to make this work. That relief burst a dam, the long-hidden guilt flooding out as he remembered back to that night and how he had crept through the tunnel, going to Naomi.

'Yes and yes. I didn't mean to hurt Louise. That is one of my biggest regrets. She was supposed to be out. I had gone there to see Naomi. I wanted to help her, to try and get her away from her father. He's a bad man, you know.'

He truly had only wanted to help, but what came next had nearly destroyed him. Emotion clogged his words as they came spilling out. 'Louise surprised me. She had heard me, and she came to investigate. She caught me off guard and we struggled.' It was all so clear in his mind as he replayed it. The shock on Louise's face as she recognised him and his own horror that he had been caught in the house. But what happened next was far worse. 'I didn't realise she had a knife. It was an accident.'

Benjamin was crying now, too, the tears pouring down his cheeks.

'Naomi saw what I did. She was hysterical.'

Those first few days in the cell, she had cried non-stop, begging for him to free her. And each time he had gone to her, to try and offer her comfort, she had recoiled in horror, trembling and screaming, seeming convinced he was going to hurt her. It had made him feel like he was a monster.

'What happened to Naomi? Where is she?'

The tears fell harder now as he remembered. 'I can't say.'

'Benjamin. I need to know.'

'Please, Elisabeth, finish your dinner. You can't know.'

'You can tell me.' Her voice cracked then. 'Please!'

It was that last word that undid him. His shoulders slumping as he put his plate back down on the table. 'I tried to keep her safe. I promise, I really did. I thought she could come to no harm here, but I had to go out and...'

He trailed off, sinking to the floor, putting his hands over his face as he tried to block out the memory.

It had all been going so well. Naomi had been frightened of him at first, but she was also docile. Although Benjamin had been forced to keep her in the cell during the ongoing investigation, he had tried to spend as much time with her as possible and she had quickly learnt he was friend, not foe. He had finally decided it was safe to bring her up into the house, had even allowed her to start sleeping there, too, but then that awful day had happened.

He had to go out and she simply didn't understand that he couldn't leave her free to wander round the house. They had been getting on so well until that point, and it had been a regrettable setback.

She had slapped him before he managed to restrain her, tying her to the chair in the bedroom, and he had left home with the imprint on his cheek, wanting to cry. The anger, the accusations, the threats and the violence. He had never seen that side of her before and honestly it scared him, made him fear for her and for them as a family.

Did she not understand how much he loved her? That he would do, and indeed had done, anything and everything for her? If he could have cancelled his plans he would have. He would have spent the day reassuring her and trying to make things right. He would have taken the time to show her just how much he cared about her. Instead, when he left, she was locked in the bedroom, and he had no idea what her mood would be like when he returned. Would she still be mad, unwilling to listen to reason, or would she have calmed down enough for them to have a civil conversation?

He never got the chance to find out.

When he returned home he found Naomi sat in the chair in front of the dresser, her head slumped forward and blood soaking through the ropes holding her in place.

Anger, panic and despair had blinded him as he rushed to her, slipping in the puddle of red pooling on the rug beneath her, and a howl of anguish had ripped through him as he cupped her cold cheeks, raising her head to look into sightless eyes.

She was gone.

'What happened to Naomi?' Elisabeth's whisper brought him back to the present. 'Benjamin, please.'

It was his baby sister, his flesh and blood, the one he loved most had been his undoing.

She had stood there, her figure silhouetted in the doorway, the knife in her hand still red with blood.

Benjamin scrubbed his palms over his face and peered up at Elisabeth red-eyed. It had been the day he had truly learnt what his sister was capable of.

'It was Virginia. She stabbed her. Oh, Elisabeth, she killed my Naomi.'

50

After Benjamin left the room, Ellie drew in a shaky breath, needing a moment to get her wits about her. She glanced at the portraits on the wall. They had been bothering her since she had set foot in the room and, as she sat there wearing Benjamin's mother's dress, it had felt as though all four sets of eyes were watching her take part in this bizarre seventies-style dinner party for two.

Benjamin and Virginia were in the paintings on either end; Benjamin, who must have only been in his late teens, sombre and a little pompous, his hair slicked back and brown eyes staring at the artist, Virginia just a young girl, her wild hair tamed, and minus her glasses, a blank look on her face. The two middle pictures were of Benjamin's parents. Killer and victim. Neither of them was smiling.

All of Benjamin's revelations had been terrible and learning what he and his mother had done to his aunt had shocked her to the core but knowing he had then taken it a step further, killing Louise Tanner and kidnapping her daughter, that his psycho sister had then murdered Naomi in cold blood, scared her most of all.

Ellie now knew all of the terrible Thorne family secrets, so there was no way Benjamin planned to ever let her go, which meant that unless she could escape, she was trapped here with him and Virginia. She honestly wasn't sure which sibling frightened her the most.

Under the chiffon gown, her heart thumped uncomfortably, the collar of the dress tight around her neck, feeling like it was suffocating her.

After admitting the truth that Virginia had killed Naomi, Benjamin had sat on the floor and sobbed, leaving Ellie helplessly watching him. She had tried to get his attention a couple of times, but it seemed that for now he had zoned out, forgetting she was there.

The wine probably hadn't helped. Ellie knew he didn't really like alcohol and had purposely goaded him into drinking more than he was used to, hoping if she got him a little drunk, it might be easier to escape. Instead, it seemed she had pushed him towards a breakdown.

As subtly as possible she had tested the ropes tying her to the chair. Four loops; two around her waist that were attached to the splats at the back, while the other two crossed over her thighs and went under the seat. There was no way to reach the knots at the back with her hands cuffed in front of her, and the rope around her waist was secured too tightly to give her any wiggle room, but the loops crossing her legs were slightly looser.

He had used just the one piece of rope, so if she could get out of the lower loops, it would hopefully give enough slack to free herself from the rest of the restraints. Was there any way of pushing them down over her legs and wiggling her feet free? The dress was chiffon, and she was barefoot. It may require some manoeuvring, but she was fairly flexible and thought it might be possible.

Her opportunity to try came when Benjamin eventually picked himself up from the floor. Without sparing her a glance (she actually wondered if he had forgotten she was there) he left the room. Ellie waited a few moments, worried in case he returned. She was positioned with her back to the door and facing the front window. If she didn't hear his approach she was screwed.

Eventually, she decided it was now or never.

As she pulled tentatively on the lowest rope, she felt it tighten the loop above. That was good. Pushing the rope down her thighs, she managed to get it touching her knees. Not quite far enough.

Pressing herself back into the chair, she pulled again, gained a little more give, and had a second attempt.

This time she managed to pull the rope over her knees and drew up her left leg, hoping to pull it through the gap. She was almost there when the sound of footsteps coming from behind stopped her. She quickly pulled the rope back into place, putting her foot back on the floor, and was waiting patiently when Benjamin walked back into the room.

Damn!

His eyes and nose were red from crying and for a moment she didn't think he was going to acknowledge her. He started to clear the table, focusing on his task, and she stayed quiet, watching him warily. As he finished, arms loaded with plates and cutlery, his eyes met hers though.

'I'm going to go and put the finishing touches to the dessert', he told her.

Ellie nodded. He hadn't said anything more about Naomi or Virginia, so she wouldn't either.

Instead, she waited until he was gone before making her third attempt to free herself from the chair.

She managed to get the rope over her left knee then with a bit of a struggle over her right. The slack now gone, the other ropes were pulled uncomfortably tight as she tried to draw up her legs to pull the loop down her calves and over her feet. The chair wobbled as she fought to get her left foot through and she froze, panicked for a moment that she was going to topple back.

You're so close. Keep going.

Her heart was thumping furiously, sweat beading on her forehead and beneath the dress. If Benjamin came back and caught her trying to escape... No, she couldn't think about that.

Get free from the rope then get the hell out of the house before he realises.

She tried again, had to force her foot into an uncomfortable position, but finally pulled it through the loop. Foolishly, she had thought getting her other foot free would be easier, and she had to bite into her lip to keep from crying out when the remaining loops tightened painfully as she tried to find extra slack.

Grimacing, she forced her foot through the gap, heaving out a sigh of relief. Already the other loops were looser, and she pushed down the second wrap of rope, heartened when she managed to step out of it easily.

Tilting the chair first forward then back, she managed to free the legs of the rope and knew she now just had to pull free from the two loops holding her against the chair back.

She sucked in another breath, her focus on the window and the partially drawn curtains as she told herself it was just the easy bit left and slipped free from the first loop. She was about to work on the last tie, when she spotted movement outside the window, realising someone was approaching the house.

Ash.

She caught a glimpse of him as he passed the window and

forgetting there was still a rope holding her loosely to the chair, tried to get up.

The clatter of the wood as she fell forward, his name on her lips, coincided with the door knocker rapping loudly, the sound carrying through the house. Frantically, Ellie pulled herself free from the last of her bonds and tried to scream his name again.

As she did so an arm banded around her waist, dragging her up from the floor, and a hand clamped over her mouth.

'Shh.'

Benjamin. She recognised that vile peppery scent of the gone-off aftershave.

Frantically she shook her head, trying to break free as he dragged her across the room, blowing the candles out as they went. Over by the window, though standing far enough back that the shadows absorbed them, she could see Ash and the angry expression on his face as he knocked on the door again.

Did he realise she was inside? She had to alert him.

She tried again to shake off Benjamin, using her elbows and feet to punch and kick at him, this time biting into the flesh of his hand. She heard him wince, but he held on tight, his palm smothering her screams. And then Ash was stepping back, glancing up at the house, but shaking his head as he turned and headed back down the driveway.

No, he can't leave me!

Ellie continued to fight against Benjamin, but with her wrists still cuffed he had an unfair advantage and eventually her muffled cries for Ash turned to sobs.

Benjamin sunk to the floor, pulling her down with him, letting out an audible sigh of relief.

He knew as well as she did that it had been a close call and could have gone either way.

As she struggled against him, choking for air now as her tears fell harder, he removed his hand from her mouth, though twisted his fingers in her hair, turning her head so she had no choice but to look at him.

This was it. It had been her one chance and she had blown it. He was angry with her now and the trust had been broken. She could see it in the coldness of his eyes and in the tightness at the corners of his scowling mouth.

'You've been a bad girl, Elisabeth,' he hissed eventually. 'I trusted you. You promised me you wouldn't try to escape.'

She should protest and try and win that trust back, but she honestly didn't have it in her.

'Do you have nothing to say for yourself? No apology for me?'

Something inside her snapped at his words. She was not a child, not his toy. This probably wouldn't end well for her now, but she refused to go down without a fight.

Her eyes were still wet, her breathing a little erratic, but she stared at him defiantly and managed to twist her lips into a smirk, before spitting in his face. 'Fuck you!'

The look of shock on his face was worth it, as was the slap against her cheek when it came.

But then he was dragging her to her feet again, pulling her out of the room by her hair, and she was struggling not to cry out with the pain.

'Bad girls need to be punished,' he told her, a cruelty in his tone that she hadn't heard before.

Whatever he was going to do to her, she knew it wasn't good and she bit down on her terror, promised herself she wouldn't beg.

A thump came from behind them, and Benjamin's head shot round, just as Miss Moneypenny charged down the stairs.

Ellie seized the moment of distraction, throwing herself against him and knocking him into the side table. When he momentarily loosened his grip, she swung her hands up, catching him on the side of the face with the metal of the cuffs.

It wasn't enough to really hurt him, but it gave her a precious second to break free of his grasp.

Not looking back to see how close he was behind her, she ran.

51

Going back to the Thorne house when the police had warned him to stay away hadn't been Ash's smartest move, but his temper had fuelled him, and he had been ready to use his fists to make Benjamin talk if necessary.

Probably a good job there had been no answer. Whether that was because Benjamin was out or hiding from him, he wasn't sure. He had thought he heard noises from inside, so probably the latter. If creepy Ben had seen him, he would call the police again. Ash figured he would find out if he had soon enough. At least this time he couldn't accuse him of anything other than knocking on the door.

Ellie was missing and now Roxanne and Poppy had disappeared too. While it was possible there was a rational explanation with Roxanne and Poppy, talking to Alicia Hewson had only further convinced him that Benjamin had done something to Ellie. He needed to be smart about this though. Beating the shit out of his neighbour would only get him in trouble. There had to be another way.

He had spoken with Pete again as he walked back to the

house, learnt he had called all of Roxanne's friends and family, and no one had heard from her.

'Do you think there's another bloke?' Pete questioned. 'Maybe she's having an affair.'

Ash winced at the stab of guilt, reminding himself that he hadn't actually slept with Roxanne and that even though he felt completely shitty about what had happened all those years ago, it mostly wasn't his fault. 'No, mate. I don't.'

'I'm going to give her another hour to come home then I'm calling the police.'

Had Roxanne taken Poppy as revenge at Ash or had something more sinister happened to them? If Benjamin was behind their disappearance, what would be the motive? He had developed something of an obsession with Ellie, same as he had with Alicia Hewson. And according to John Tanner, with Naomi. But Benjamin didn't know Roxanne and it didn't explain what had happened to Poppy. None of it made any sense.

Maybe Ash should go back under the cover of darkness? If the freaky Thornes were in bed, it would make it easier to sneak around.

Musing over the idea, he let himself in the house, immediately catching a whiff of the rotting groceries. He needed to deal with those before they stank the whole place out. He went into the kitchen and grabbed a bin bag from under the sink, throwing out the perishables then packing away what could be salvaged.

He had just about finished when he heard what sounded like faint barking.

Poppy?

He paused for a moment, began to wonder if it was wishful thinking when there was just silence, but then the noise came again. Definitely barking and it was coming from somewhere below.

The cellar.

He glanced at the closed door. Had Roxanne shut the dog down there?

No. Roxanne could be catty, thoughtless and self-absorbed, but she wasn't unnecessarily cruel. Ash opened the cellar door, surprised when the dog didn't immediately react.

'Poppy?'

For another moment there was nothing then came a faint muffled barking again. And scraping. It was definitely coming from the cellar, but where the hell was she?

Ash flicked on the light, calling her again as he descended the stairs. 'Poppy, where are you, girl?'

He whistled loudly, heard another bark. It was coming from over where Ellie had moved the boxes of books. From where he had found her phone. And he immediately noticed the boxes were pushed away from the wall again.

What the fuck?

He remembered moving them back into place when he had picked up her phone.

Had Roxanne come down here? There was absolutely no reason for why she would, but still, what other explanation was there?

More barking and scraping, followed by a pitiful whine, had him looking behind the boxes at the wall and he immediately noticed the brickwork didn't match. It was a false wall.

That wasn't on the plans.

'Poppy?' Another bark and he could tell she was excited now he was closer. She was definitely behind there. What was it? Another room? Ellie's phone had been in the cellar. Was she trapped in there too? He pushed the wall, heart catching when it moved back.

Why the fuck hadn't he paid more attention to the cellar when he found her phone?

Truthfully, he knew the washing machine had been there when they moved in, then the boxes. He simply hadn't considered looking behind them. And why would he? It was just a wall.

But if Ellie was on the other side and she was hurt or worse, he would never forgive himself.

Poppy's barking was louder now as the wall pushed back further then she was bounding out of the blackness, jumping into his arms and licking at his face, her tail wagging frantically.

'How the hell did you get in there?' Ash held her close for a moment, scratching behind her ears and rubbing his hand up and down her back, before putting her down. Thrilled as he was to see her, he was worried about finding Ellie.

He peered into the dark hole, getting out his phone and flashing the light into the space. A room that looked like it had never been used... and was that a doorway on the other side?

It was bigger than he expected and if he was going in there to go look for Ellie he would need a proper torch.

Turning his attention back to Poppy, he glanced over her, making sure she was okay and not hurt at all. He would take her upstairs and give her some food and water, then grab the torch. Running his hand down her head and over her collar as he talked to her, giving her plenty of fuss, his fingers caught onto something. He looked closely at the colourful beads, immediately recognising them.

Ellie's bracelet.

Whatever this place was, he was now certain she was in there, and he didn't intend to rest until he had found her.

52

Ellie didn't stop to look behind her, knowing Benjamin was almost in touching distance. Instead, she focused simply on getting out of the house.

Down the hallway, into the kitchen, trying the back door and finding it locked, then through into the conservatory. The room was in shadows, the shutters all down, and she barely registered the easel with the crudely drawn portrait, didn't notice the puddle of red on the floor until she had stepped in it and felt the stickiness on her toes. She started to slip, managed to right herself and charged for the closed doors, rattling them in frustration when she realised they, too, were locked.

A thump and a grunt came from behind her and as she turned to flee, she realised Benjamin hadn't been so lucky with the blood and had lost his balance.

As he picked himself up, she bolted back out of the conservatory and into the kitchen, could hear he was already on his feet again and coming after her. She paused to grab the handle of the largest saucepan on the Aga, holding it with both cuffed hands, and slammed it hard into the side of his head as he made a grab for her.

The blow had him stumbling, and a second one to his face, knocked him down. He yowled in pain, clutching at his nose with both hands, and Ellie gave him a final whack for good measure.

Dropping the pan, she ran back out into the hallway to the front door.

Also locked. Damn it.

Into the dining room again and over to the window. She tried to open it, realised it needed a key. Had he done this purposely? Locking all of the doors and windows so she couldn't escape?

She couldn't even use a chair to smash the glass, as she wasn't sure she could break through the wooden panelling, and there was no way she could fit through the gap as it was.

She needed to find a way out, but he was already getting to his feet and there simply wasn't the time. Instead, she fled for the stairs.

The long landing of doors greeted her, and she struggled to unscramble her panicked brain as she tried to figure out where the hell she could go.

There would be no escape from up here, so she needed to find a place to hide.

Not Benjamin's room or his mother's. She knew neither offered any safe space. And the door at the end of the landing would lead back down into the library, where there would be no way out except for into the tunnel. No way was she going back down there.

She hurriedly tried a few of the closed doors, dismayed to find them all locked, saw only one room that had the door ajar.

Virginia's.

She couldn't go in there. The girl was scary as fuck and even more dangerous than Benjamin. She would only be putting herself in a more perilous situation.

Why was Virginia's door open anyway? She was supposed to

be in bed. The door had been closed earlier. Was she up and about, and creeping the hallways? Did Ellie have both Thorne siblings to contend with?

As she edged closer to the room, trying the door next to Virginia's then opposite, finding both locked, she heard Benjamin's voice, scolding.

'Elisabeth, you'd better get downstairs right now. If I have to come up there after you, you'll be in serious trouble.'

Fuck!

He sounded like he was talking to a child, which might be laughable in any other situation, but the tone of his voice chilled her.

She peered into Virginia's room, saw the bed was empty. It hadn't even been slept in; the covers pulled up neatly over the pillow.

Was she even here?

The tray with the plate of food Benjamin had taken up to her sat untouched on the bedside table, which was odd. He had told Ellie that Virginia had been tucking into the meal when he had left her.

Why would he lie about that?

Easing the door open further, she stepped into the room. A quick glance round showed her it was empty.

While she didn't like the idea of being in Virginia's room, it was the best of very few options right now, and if Benjamin thought his sister was asleep, hopefully he wouldn't think to look for Ellie in here.

She pushed the door closed, frantically looking for somewhere she could hide. The wardrobe looked too small and there was no bathroom. The only other furniture was a dresser similar to the one in Benjamin's mother's room. There was an identical set of hairbrushes and Virginia's thick-lensed glasses.

Could the girl see without them? She had to be close and that was a worry.

Ellie went to the window, wondering if the drop to the ground was doable, biting down on a frustrated sob when she realised it was locked.

It seemed that since kidnapping her, Benjamin had gone out of his way to turn the house into a prison.

She glanced at the bed. Getting underneath it was a possibility.

Then she looked up, spotting the loft hatch. There was a handle on the door. Could she get up there? It would be a safer bet than under the bed and she was certain he would be less likely to look for her up there.

Pulling the hatch open, she reached for the ladder attachment, the climb up made difficult with her wrists cuffed together, and her legs shaking as she heard the boom of Benjamin's voice again.

'Your choice, Elisabeth. Here I come.'

Although the door slightly muffled his words, they were loud enough for her to hear them, and he sounded angry.

She could not let him catch her again.

What if he locked her back down in the tunnel then boarded it up? Like he had done to his Aunt Imelda. The idea of being trapped down there to slowly die terrified her.

She scrambled into the loft, managed, though with some difficulty, to pull the ladder up and close the hatch, immersing herself in darkness. Every single part of her trembled as she sat by the door, her heart thumping, and barely daring to breath, as she listened to his footsteps growing closer, a couple of doors opening and slamming shut (his bedroom and his mother's room she guessed) and then him calling her name again.

Would he go down to the library, assume that was where she had gone?

The footsteps and the yelling became fainter. If he thought she had gone into the tunnel she could try and make her escape. Would she be able to use a chair to break a window?

Or if not, was there a phone in the house? She could alert the police.

She held her breath. Waited.

Seconds ticked by with no sound from him. Still she waited, tried to pluck up courage.

Do it, now.

Her fingers fumbled in the darkness, finding the loft hatch handle. She was about to open it when she heard the creak of a floorboard below and froze.

Was it Benjamin? Or had Virginia returned to her room?

Shit.

She was trying to work out what the hell to do, when the decision was taken away from her, as the hatch opened, light spilling through. Biting down on her scream, she scrambled back from the hatch.

The attic was now filled with shadows, and she could see her surroundings. There was a whole wall of boxes stacked behind her and she managed to roll onto her knees so she could use her cuffed hands to help pull herself behind them.

Hearing footsteps on the ladder, she peered out from a gap between the boxes, saw Benjamin's head as he climbed up through the hatch. He reached out to pull a cord and a bare ceiling bulb filled the space towards the far end of the attic with light.

Behind the boxes, Ellie didn't dare move. Although she was still mostly in darkness, she was terrified he would spot her. She watched as he closed the hatch, before heading across the loft towards the light.

Did he think that's where she was?

Glancing at the hatch, she wondered if she dare risk trying to get down. She had to get the door open, though, without alerting him and the cuffs were going to make climbing down the ladder more difficult. Instead, she waited and watched.

She could see his back and saw he had stopped by a chair.

'I hope you are looking after the new girl.'

Who the hell was he talking to? Was someone else up here? Ellie hadn't heard any sound from them.

'You wanted her, so she's your responsibility to look after now. Do you understand?'

There was no answer and Ellie wondered if he was holding someone else prisoner?

Curiosity nudging at the edges of her fear, she peered over the box. She could see Benjamin's profile now and that he was facing a chair. It didn't look like a person he was addressing though. Was he talking to a doll?

But then he moved, giving her a better angle, and her hand flew to her mouth to stop herself from screaming.

Not just one chair. There were three. Benjamin's body was still blocking one, but she could now see that what she had thought were dolls were actually decaying skeletons.

Both were wearing long dresses, the holes where their eyes and mouths had been making it appear as if they were grimacing at his words.

What the hell had he done?

'I asked you a question. Do you understand?'

He had dead people in his attic, and he was talking to them, waiting for them to answer.

Ellie now knew with absolute certainty that if he caught her again she was going to die in this house, that she would end up like these women.

Was one of them Naomi Tanner?

It was impossible to tell, but she suspected so. She had no idea who the other girl was though.

As she tried to figure out how the hell she was going to get away, she watched Benjamin shake his head in annoyance, turning on his heel, and at that moment was given a view of the third occupied chair and the person sitting on it.

This one wasn't wearing a dress and Ellie recognised the outfit and red hair straightaway. She balled the hand covering her mouth into a fist and bit down on it, fighting the urge to completely break down.

Don't scream. Don't scream. You can't let him know you're here.

Roxanne. What had he done to her?

Her friend's eyes were wide open, but she wasn't moving, slumped in the chair and soaked in blood. Almost certainly dead. As Ellie blinked back tears, she spotted the crude thread pulling Roxanne's lips together, realised there was more thread on top of her eyes.

That's why they're open.

For a moment she thought she was going to be sick.

Why did he have Roxanne here and what the fuck had he done to her?

And then an awful thought occurred to her

What if he was planning on attacking Ash and Pete too?

Benjamin was obsessed with her. Was he removing the people in her life he saw as a threat? Ash would be top of that list.

Oh God, oh God, oh God.

She didn't want to watch this grotesque spectacle any longer, but she also couldn't bring herself to tear her eyes away. Instead, she remained hidden behind the boxes, shaking uncontrollably and willing herself to hold it together, wishing she could find a way out of this nightmare.

'I don't feel well,' Benjamin announced to the corpses. 'I think I'm having one of my turns. I need to go lie down.'

Yes, do that.

He was clearly bat-shit crazy, because, if there was one blessing, it seemed he had temporarily forgotten about Ellie, but as she watched him walk back to the loft hatch, he stumbled a couple of times, seeming a little disorientated, and she noticed his eyes were glazed over.

He opened the hatch door and pulled the light cord, and she saw his head disappear down through the hole, plunging her again into darkness.

She stayed where she was for a few moments, knowing she needed to give him time to go and lie down. She wasn't sure where he planned to do that, whether it was in his bedroom or maybe downstairs, so she would have to be really careful not to make any noise.

This was her one big chance to get away and she couldn't afford to blow it.

53

Benjamin wasn't feeling well at all. His head was throbbing, and his coordination was off, and he had a terrible sense of desolation.

It always started like this. He could be in the house or working in the garden and suddenly he would be hit by all these peculiar sensations that would consume him, leaving him exhausted and faint.

As he made his way into his bedroom, he knew he was supposed to be doing something, but he couldn't think what. He would worry about it later. Right now he needed to rest.

He didn't even make it to the bed this time, collapsing on to the floor, a sense of loss and grief overwhelming him, then pulling him under, and his last cohesive thought, before the darkness took hold, was of Virginia.

54

Minutes ticked by. At least Ellie assumed they did. They felt more like hours, but she had to know it was safe for her to leave. Eventually she eased the hatch door open, peering down into Virginia's bedroom, relieved to see it empty and her door closed.

Letting down the ladder as quietly as possible, she negotiated the rungs, found it harder going down with cuffed wrists than she had going up. Once the ladder had been folded away and the hatch shut, she crept towards the door, the hard wood cool under her bare feet, and slowly opened it. Her mouth was dry, her head, neck and shoulders thumping with tension, as she peered out, saw the landing was clear.

Where was he? Had he gone into his bedroom?

The door was still open.

Ellie's focus remained on the hallway, as she kept a lookout for him, pulling the door wider and leaving the room. She was about to tiptoe across to the stairs, when Benjamin stepped out of his bedroom, and she froze.

There was an awful deer caught in headlights moment where she couldn't move, as she waited for him to look in her direction, but then he glanced away from her, towards the doorway that led down to the library and she managed to get her legs to work, backtracking into Virginia's room.

She quietly closed the door, glanced at the loft hatch again, but wasn't sure there was time.

That left the bed and dropping to the floor, she pulled herself underneath it, holding her breath as the bedroom door eased open again and she saw his shoes as he entered the room.

Shit, her dress was sticking out.

She couldn't reach it with her wrists cuffed together, so instead, she rolled herself further under the bed and tried to tuck it under her using her legs.

She watched as he approached the wardrobe, heard hangers scraping against the rail.

What the hell was he doing? He had said he was going to rest.

Her heart was racing as he moved towards where she was hiding, then there was a creak as the mattress dipped and he sat down on the edge of the bed.

Did he know she was underneath him?

Ellie tried to pull herself further away, terrified he was going to reach down and grab her.

'Bad, bad Benjamin.' He was talking to himself, the words barely more than a whisper, but in the silence of the room, she could hear every word.

'He really is a naughty boy.'

His voice was almost childlike and his tone sing-song as he appeared to scold himself.

Sane Benjamin was scary, but this new side of him was far more frightening. At least sane Benjamin had appeared to be in control. Now he appeared to be unravelling and she had no idea what he might be capable of.

She watched as he took off his shoes then peeled off his

socks, set them to one side.

What was he doing?

Oh God. Please don't let him go to sleep in here.

Another creak of the mattress as he got up. Was he going? *Please go.* Or was he going to get down on his hands and knees and look under the bed?

The urge to squeeze her eyes shut, block everything out, was overwhelming, but she knew she had to stay alert.

She heard his belt unbuckling then a zip. Moments later his trousers were falling around his ankles.

Shit, shit, shit. He was getting undressed. Why the fuck was he getting undressed?

It was so hot and stuffy under the bed and sweat was beading on her forehead and dripping onto her eyelids. She didn't dare move though. Barely dared to breathe.

The shuffle of more clothes, whether he was taking them off or putting them on she wasn't certain, but then there was the sound of another zip and fabric fell around his ankles.

Was that a dress? Why had he put on a dress?

Ellie tried to twist her head to get a better view, saw him open one of the drawers in the dresser and pull something out.

Hair.

Human hair?

It looked like Virginia's.

Why the fuck did he have his sister's hair? What had he done to her?

And then she realised it was a wig.

As he sat down at the dresser, she managed to manoeuvre herself into a slightly better position, giving her a clear view, and as she watched him fuss in the mirror as he pulled the hairpiece on, it dawned on her that he was wearing Virginia's dress.

Virginia's dress, Virginia's hair and now he was picking up Virginia's glasses.

Before he slipped them on, he stared at his reflection and his gaze dropped, as if he was looking at the bed, a creepy smile on his face.

Fuck. Could he see her?

But then the glasses were on, the transformation complete, and he was up from the stool, wringing his hands together as Ellie had seen Virginia do, almost skipping as he left the room, leaving her reeling as she processed what she had just seen.

Virginia Thorne. Benjamin's sister.

Ellie had only ever seen her at a distance, finding it strange how the girl never spoke, how she hadn't shown up for dinner or when Ellie had been in the house with Benjamin.

He spoke about Virginia, but she was never there. At least never there when he was.

Because it was impossible for him to be in two places at once.

But if Benjamin was Virginia, then where the hell was his sister? Did he even have one or had he made her up?

She thought of the skeletons upstairs.

Had he killed his own sister?

Ellie needed to find a way out of the house and she needed to call the police.

But where was Benjamin? He had disappeared out of the room, but had he gone downstairs or was he waiting for her?

She hesitated, too afraid to rush, listened for any movement. At first there was nothing, but then she was certain she heard footsteps on the landing, and was that counting?

'Twelve, thirteen, fourteen, fifteen, sixteen...'

Benjamin's voice was a soft whisper that was gradually getting louder.

'Nineteen, twenty.'

Why the fuck was he counting? What was he doing?

Silence then, and Ellie rubbed her trembling hands over her

face, every one of her nerves on edge.

'Coming, ready or not.' His voice was high and childlike.

What?

The creak of the floorboard warned her he was back in the room, and she turned her head, saw his feet just inches from her face. Ugly, large pale feet with hairy toes, the skirt of the dress brushing over them. She didn't have time to react as he dropped to the floor.

'Found you, Elisabeth.'

A hand clamped around her ankle, shocking the hell out of her, and then he was dragging her out from under the bed.

Ellie screamed, catching hold of the bed leg and clinging on for dear life. He was too strong, though, and when she refused to let go, the bed started scraping along the floor with her.

They reached a stalemate at the bedroom door as the bed became wedged. He had hold of both ankles now and she frantically tried to shake him off.

'Let go of me, please.'

There was no reasoning with this version of Benjamin though. She could see no trace of the man she had known and was quite certain he wasn't in there right now.

She tried a different approach, making her voice softer, more pleading.

'Virginia, please don't hurt me. I know you don't want to.'

Benjamin cocked his head on one side, studying her for a moment. Through the thick glasses, the scruffy hair falling around his face, she couldn't read his expression. Didn't even recognise him.

Was she getting through to this side of him? To Virginia?

He knelt down, still keeping hold of her ankles, as if wanting a closer look at her, but then to her horror he let go, clambering on top of her so his weight was pinning her to the floor. Leaning in close, he sniffed at her hair, the wiry strands of the wig brushing against her cheek, and she tried not to gag, as she breathed in his stale peppery stench.

'Please, Virginia. Please help me. I just want to go home.'

Her voice cracked, a tear escaping, and Benjamin eased back, stroking his fingers across her cheek and back into her hair. Although his touch make her skin crawl, she tried not to react. 'Please,' she repeated.

'Your hair is so soft and pretty.'

'Please let me go.'

'NO!'

When the slap came it caught her off guard and Ellie flinched, her cheek stinging.

'You're just another one of those tarts.' Benjamin's voice was shrill and effeminate, his tone laced with anger. 'Leading him on. Making him obsessed with you. Pretty on the outside and ugly on the inside.' He twisted her hair in his fingers and pulled hard, making her cry out in pain.

'Please. I want to go home.'

'No, no, no!' He sounded like a child having a tantrum, his bottom lip sticking out. 'You're mine now. Mother told me that tarts need to be dealt with.'

There was a pause as he studied her, his eyes huge behind the thick lenses. 'Why are you wearing her dress? Who gave you permission?'

'Benjamin made me put it on. He–'

'LIAR!'

Another slap stung her cheek, then a third and a fourth.

Ellie let go of the bed leg, putting her hands up to try and shield herself from the blows.

'Please! Stop!'

She didn't have time to react to what happened next, as Benjamin caught hold of her cuffed wrists, dragging her up with him as he got to his feet, and the next thing she knew he had hoisted her into the air and over his shoulder, carrying her from the room and across the landing.

Ellie screamed and pummelled at his back, but he took no notice, and then they were in his mother's room, and she was flat on her back in the middle of the four-poster bed.

As she pulled herself up, Benjamin reached into the dresser drawer and pulled out a pair of scissors.

The same scissors she realised that Virginia had been carrying the day Ellie had found her way up from the tunnel.

For a moment she thought he was going to stab her with them, but then he was holding her down with one hand and using the other to work the scissors, as they sliced into the material.

'Get it off! Get her dress off, now!' he was yelling at Ellie in that high-pitched childish voice.

As he ripped at the gown, she kicked out, managed to catch his chin, heard the satisfying crunch of his teeth bashing together before he stumbled back.

Ellie didn't waste a second. She pushed herself off the bed and ran out of the room.

He caught up to her quickly though, grabbing hold of her hair and swinging her around, and there was another tussle as she fought to pull herself free, this time adding a knee to his crotch for good measure.

When he yelped and let go, she fled down the landing, realising a moment too late that she was heading the wrong way to the staircase.

She glanced at Benjamin, knew she had bought herself a few precious seconds, but didn't have long. No way was she going to chance running past him, and that left just one escape route.

Down into the library.

And she realised, fear in the pit of her belly, back into the tunnel.

55

The tart has got herself cornered.

There is only one place for her to go now and that's back to her cell. She is mine now.

How dare she wear Mother's favourite dress.

I know all about her type. I remember Auntie Imelda. She was the first tart that came to the house. Mother had to take care of her and now she's gone, it's my job.

I used to sneak into the tunnels and watch Mother and Benjamin. They didn't know I was there, didn't realise I even knew about the tunnels.

There is no rush as I go after this one. I took care of that last tart he brought here; the one he had left tied to the chair in his bedroom, and I will take care of this one too. It will be fun. Before she closes the door to go down the stairs into the library, she glances back at me, and I can see the fear in her eyes.

I still have the scissors in my hand, and I hold them up so she can see, snipping them against the air, and I laugh.

'Run and hide,' I tell her. 'I'm coming for you, ready or not.'

56

With the door behind the bookcase closed, Ellie was in complete darkness, and she stumbled her way along the tunnel, holding on to the wall and jumping at every little sound she made, aware that Benjamin would soon be close behind her.

And, of course, he knew the tunnels. How the fuck was she going to get away from him?

Keep following the wall. It will lead you back to the house.

It would, but it was a hell of a distance in the pitch black. She recalled the crossroads, too, that she had to pass, where the tunnel forked off in different directions. It was disorientating in the darkness. What if she took the wrong one? Worse still. What if she ended up back at the cell?

Don't think like that. You will find your way back. You have to.

If Benjamin didn't catch her first.

Benjamin who was dressed up as his dead fucking sister.

At least, Ellie assumed she was dead. There was no sign of the real Virginia anywhere in the house. Except perhaps up in the attic.

Don't think about that.

She couldn't help it though, knew that what she had seen would be burned onto her brain for a long time to come. She recalled the two skeletons and Roxanne with her grotesquely stitched face and soaked in blood, a stab of grief piercing through her. Her friend had plenty of faults, but she hadn't deserved what had happened to her.

As Ellie stumbled forward, the cold stony floor rough against the soles of her bare feet, uncomfortable and exhausted, it was tempting to give up. She had tried to get away, but it was no good, she simply couldn't do this. It was that reminder of the attic, though, and what awaited her if Benjamin caught her, that spurred her on.

As did the sound of the tunnel door opening behind her.

It was too close. She had thought she was further along the tunnel than this.

The open door spilt faint light onto the path ahead and Ellie let go of the wall, picking up her pace. If she could see ahead then Benjamin would be able to see her. There was nowhere to hide.

As the crunch of footsteps sounded behind her, far too close for comfort, her foot caught in the long billowing skirt of the dress, and unable to use her hands to balance herself, she landed on her cuffed wrists, crying out in pain.

Get up.

Her knees throbbed, and she thought she might have twisted her wrist. Still, she pushed herself up, tried to climb to her feet.

'I can see you.' The creepy voice echoed around the passageway, followed by a bubble of childish laughter.

Move.

Ellie was trying. Back on her feet, she held the dress skirt higher, so she didn't trip over it again, and ran forward. The sliver of light was growing fainter, the blackness waiting for her.

In the distance far ahead, another voice echoed. This one much further away.

'Ellie?'

Someone else was down here and the voice was familiar. She barely dared hope.

Was it really him?

'Ash?' As she screamed his name, a hand clamped down on her shoulder, yanking her back off her feet. Ellie stumbled again, this time though, arms caught her before she fell.

'Gotcha!'

As the arms banded around her waist, lifting her, she pounded at them with her cuffed wrists, kicking out with her bare feet.

'Ash. I'm here. Help me! Please!'

She wriggled in Benjamin's arms, trying to free herself, but he held her easily, seeming amused by her struggles. As she begged and pleaded with him to let her go, he ignored her, marching straight ahead into the darkness.

He was no longer in there, she remembered. She was with Virginia now.

And Virginia liked to do very bad things.

57

'Ellie?'

Ash was sure he had heard her calling his name or was that just wishful thinking?

Moments later though, he heard the yelling, realised it was definitely Ellie and it sounded like she was in trouble. His heart raced as he ran towards her voice; his relief at realising she was alive, though, was coupled with fear at the level of distress in her tone.

'Ellie? Where are you?' Initially she had sounded close by, but now it seemed her screams were getting further away.

Just how deep were these tunnels? She could be anywhere.

'Ellie?' Frustrated, he shone his torch around the tunnel, glad he wasn't claustrophobic. The dark stone walls were narrow in places and the ceiling low enough that he had to keep his head bent forward.

Had she been trapped down here all this time?

And how? Had she wandered into the tunnels and become lost or had someone brought her down here?

It was difficult to gauge his direction, but Ash was pretty certain he was heading towards the Thorne house. Which would add up with his theory that Benjamin was involved in Ellie's disappearance. And in all honesty, it would make sense. She was level-headed and he really couldn't see her being foolish enough to go exploring a network of deserted tunnels by herself.

Like you.

He pushed that thought to one side. This was different. If Ellie was in trouble he had to find her.

Still, it had him wondering, should he have brought Poppy back down here?

The puppy had found Ellie before, and she had her bracelet tied to her collar. Would she be able to find her again?

It was too late though. He didn't have time to go back for her and he needed to find Ellie and now.

But where the fuck was she?

He reached a fork in the tunnel, shone his torch both ways, deliberating which one to take, and yelled her name again. At first there was nothing, then he heard a faint scream down the left-hand tunnel and headed in that direction, picking up his pace.

The screaming was getting louder, which meant he was getting closer, and he ran towards it, spotting the flicker of light on the wall up ahead as the tunnel opened out.

He saw the cage first, was thinking *What the fuck*, when he spotted the two women, both wearing long dresses, one pinning the other to a bed, a pair of scissors in her hand.

The woman being attacked turned her head slightly and he caught her profile.

Ellie.

Ash didn't even think, charging into the cell and grabbing hold of her attacker, pulling her off Ellie, surprised by the woman's strength. He had a grip on her hand holding the scissors and managed to twist her round so she was facing him, baulking in surprise when the woman's hair slipped back on her head, and dropped to the floor.

Even with the thick glasses on, he recognised Benjamin, his next-door neighbour.

Why the fuck was he dressed up like this and why had he tried to stab Ellie?

The moment of shock had him hesitating and Benjamin wrenched his hand free, raising the scissors and stabbing them down at Ash's chest. Ash managed to grab his hand again, trying to force it back, but the point of the scissors was already pressing against his T-shirt.

'Leave him alone.' The growl came from Ellie. She was standing on the bed, her hair glowing a silver blonde in the fiery lamplight, her face gaunt and pale and her eyes shadowed, ethereal in the long white dress, as she grabbed Benjamin from behind in a headlock.

Ash spotted that she was wearing handcuffs and that she had managed to get the connecting chain around Benjamin's neck and was pulling tightly. As Benjamin choked, his eyes magnified behind the thick glasses, he dropped the scissors, trying to clutch at the chain to free himself. Shaking frantically from side to side, the glasses slipped down his face and his eyes were bug wide as he tried to throw Ellie off, but she clung on tightly.

Ash punched him hard in the stomach, once, then twice, then gave him a smack on the nose for good measure, heard a satisfying crack. The man went limp in Ellie's grip.

She let him drop to the floor, looked up at Ash and burst into tears.

58

At first Ellie struggled to believe that Ash was with her, and her nightmare was finally over, but then he had hold of her, kept whispering to her how sorry he was for going away on his trip and leaving her alone, telling her how Poppy had alerted him to the tunnel, and he was hugging her so tightly to him that she could barely breathe. It was as though he was scared that if he let her go she wouldn't be there.

There would be time to reassure him later that it wasn't his fault and to tell him that Benjamin was both crazy and obsessed, that no matter what they did, it was unlikely they could have stopped him. He had wanted Ellie and if he hadn't taken her that night, he would have simply waited for another opportunity. For now, though, she breathed in Ash's clean, familiar scent and held on, realising that she had almost given up hope of ever seeing him again.

She had so much to tell him, but now wasn't the time. Now they had to take care of Benjamin and ensure he never hurt anyone ever again.

As she eventually eased back from his embrace he scowled

down at their neighbour's unconscious body on the floor of the cell.

'I want to kill him for whatever he's put you through over the last two weeks.' He said it with conviction, his voice close to breaking, and Ellie realised that while she had suffered, he had too. She also suspected that if she asked him to, he would end Benjamin's life right now.

She wouldn't let him do that though. Benjamin Thorne had already taken too much from them. They would not have his blood on their hands.

But prison would be too kind for him.

She looked solemnly at Ash. 'I have a better idea.'

'Go on.'

Did he suspect what she was going to suggest? If so he didn't say, but neither did he react with surprise when she told him. He simply gave her a brief nod to confirm he was on board with her plan.

59

Much later, after the police had been called, after their many questions, after the doctor had checked Ellie over, and after they had been allowed to go home, Ash and Ellie finally crawled into bed, with Poppy in her usual spot down near the footboard.

It had been a toss-up who was the most pleased to see the other. Poppy's tail wagging madly as she leapt up at Ellie with surprising grace, given that she only had three legs, while Ellie had showered her with hugs and kisses.

Ash still had questions and, lying in bed facing each other, Ellie had answered them as best she could, swiping at fresh tears as she relived her nightmare.

He had his hand on her leg, running his palm gently up and down her thigh, aware that he had barely stopped touching her since he had found her, and he knew it was because he was frightened that if he let go, she might evaporate.

'I want to move. I can't stay here,' she told him when he eventually fell quiet.

He nodded at that, had realised it was coming, and truthfully, he wanted to leave as well. This place now held too many bad memories and he would not make Ellie live in a home where she felt unsafe. 'We can go anywhere you want. As soon as you're ready we'll get the estate agents round.'

'Somewhere busier, newer, more than one neighbour, and I don't want a cellar.'

'Okay.'

'Do you think Pete is going to be all right?'

Ash thought now of his friend. While he had been reunited with Ellie tonight, Pete had lost his wife. The police and his parents were with him, and Ash had spoken with him briefly on the phone, knew at the moment he was still in shock, and that he was going to need his friends over the coming weeks and months.

'He will be. It's going to take time though.'

'We'll be there for him.'

'Yeah, we will.'

Just as Pete had been there for him, even though Ash realised he hadn't been particularly appreciative of it.

He toyed with telling Ellie the truth about Roxanne. It was not the right time though. The woman hadn't yet been dead twenty-four hours and Ellie had already dealt with enough. He would tell her though, eventually. He didn't want any secrets between them going forward.

Would he ever tell Pete? He was still undecided on that, though his initial thoughts were that tarnishing Roxanne's name at this point would help no one. Pete deserved to hold on to fond memories and Ash did not want to be the one to take those from him.

Instead he would endeavour to be a good friend and support him as best as he could.

As for Ellie, being apart from her had made him realise what he had almost lost. She had always been the one for him, but he would be lying if he didn't admit that he had started taking her for granted.

The bond they shared was stronger now. Tonight had reinforced their commitment to one another, and he knew that what lied between them would be taken to the grave.

~

They moved out the next day.

After a restless night for both of them, one that had been disturbed by Ellie's nightmares, staying wasn't a choice.

She hated feeling weak and that was what this place now made her. She wanted to be strong again, she told Ash as he had held her and comforted her, wiping away her tears, and the following morning she found them a dog-friendly hotel, while Ash made calls to three estate agents.

The house wasn't going to be an easy sell, they both knew that. It still needed a lot of work and people were going to be put off by the history. Chances were, they would have to cut their losses and start afresh.

While Ellie focused her days searching for a suitable rental, Ash returned to the house to tidy things up and get the place ready for viewings.

The police kept them updated with their investigation over the following weeks.

Ellie now knew that the two skeletons that had been found in the attic with Roxanne had been identified as Naomi Tanner and Virginia Thorne. Benjamin was suspected of murdering all three women, as well as kidnapping Ellie, and a manhunt was underway for him, as he had fled the scene after holding Ellie captive in his house for two weeks.

That was the one little detail they had decided to hold back from the police.

The tunnels.

They had made sure both entrances were closed by the time they called the police from inside Benjamin's house, telling the investigating officers that Ellie had mostly been locked in the attic.

'Is it done?' she asked Ash when he returned later that day.

He nodded, going to her, and she let him hold her, knowing he needed it as much as she did. Away from the house, away from Benjamin Thorne, she was slowly recovering, getting stronger each day, but they would always be stronger together.

'It's all blocked up. No one can get in. Or out.'

'Good.'

She couldn't let the house go on the market, knowing that a new buyer would be vulnerable, like she and Ash had been. The Tanners too.

John Tanner now had closure and Ellie and Ash had a fresh start, plus a guilt-free conscience.

Well, apart from Benjamin.

But they had done the right thing there, she was sure of it. They had made sure he would never be able to hurt anyone ever again.

60

Time alone gave Benjamin plenty to think about.

He thought of Elisabeth and how she had betrayed him, about Naomi and even Alicia too. Women he had tried to help, but none of them would let him.

And he thought about Virginia, knowing that she had done this to him.

When he had first awoken with a bad headache and covered in bruises, he had been shocked to find he was wearing his sister's dress, fear coursing through his veins when he realised he was inside the cell and the door was closed.

He had the key. He must have the key. He always kept it in his pocket.

But of course, he was wearing the damn dress. There was no key and he was trapped.

He had called for his sister, pleading and begging for her to let him out, growing angry when she ignored him.

She was punishing him, he understood that.

Five years ago he had reacted in anger when he had discovered Naomi's body, learnt that Virginia had killed her. He hadn't meant to hurt his baby sister, he loved her, and he was supposed to protect her, but he had been so upset and he didn't even realise that he had his hands around her throat, that he was squeezing.

Much later, when she was motionless on the floor and his anger had subsided, he had completely lost it. Virginia had taken Naomi's life and he had taken Virginia's.

Now he really was all alone.

Calling the police hadn't been an option. He couldn't let them know about Naomi and he couldn't let them take Virginia from him. He had failed her, and he had failed Mother, but Virginia belonged here with him. Naomi too.

They were his responsibility.

He had tried so hard to look after them and keeping up the tricky pretence to outsiders that Virginia was still alive, while silently grieving her, was one of the hardest things he'd ever had to do.

Of course, his difficult sister hadn't forgiven him. Nothing he ever did for her would be enough.

Benjamin had never believed in ghosts. You died and that was it, but Virginia had soon proven him wrong, leaving him warning signs that she was watching him. Angry words on the canvas he kept up in the conservatory, smashed plates on the floor, the axe on her pillow and the dolls' heads in his bed.

She was haunting him, punishing him for what he had done to her, and for daring to bring new women into the house. She had to be.

There was no other explanation for the signs of her that kept appearing in the house.

And now she had locked him down here to punish him.

The light from the lamps was fading, the oil running low, and the flickering shadows would soon turn to darkness. Knowing there was nothing he could do, that he was trapped, his head started to throb, and his frustration grew. He yelled to

Virginia again, this time rattling the bars, panic rising when he was met only with silence.

He couldn't be down here. He had responsibilities. The stale air and this tiny restrictive cage, it was disorientating him, the pounding in his head becoming worse.

He should know not to become overexerted. He would have to lie down now until it passed.

Falling back on the small bed, the darkness consumed him as soon as his head hit the pillow.

EPILOGUE

It is pitch black when I wake and I realise I am still in the tunnel, though I am lying down. I must be on the bed in the cell. I don't remember drifting off. Did I sleepwalk? I hope I haven't creased my dress too much.

Then it starts to come back to me, I was playing a game with one of Benjamin's tarts. I had chased her down into the tunnel and I was trying to catch her so I could punish her.

I wonder where she is as I sit up now and rub my sleepy eyes.

Where are my glasses?

I reach around for them, finally finding them on the floor, and slip them on before getting up, walking to the edge of the cell, and peering out into the darkness.

I bet she is hiding from me, waiting for me to find her, to punish her. I grip hold of the bars of the cell and call out her name.

'Ellie. Here I come, ready or not.'

THE END

ACKNOWLEDGEMENTS

As with every book I write, there are a few people I need to mention.

Firstly, to my brilliant editor, Clare Law, who is so good at her job she makes mine easy. Thank you for being a pleasure to work with.

To Fred Freeman and Betsy Reavley, who are the best bosses, and the rest of the lovely supportive Bloodhound team, Tara, Abbie, Maria, and of course, not forgetting my fab mate, Heather, who came up with the title for this book when I was struggling.

Not so much police procedural in this one, but I still had questions for my sister, DC Holly Beevis, which she answered patiently. And thanks also to Alex Brady of Minors & Brady and my mate, Hannah Spearman (former kick-arse estate agent) who both helped answer my rather disturbing questions about how murders affect house sales.

To the Beevis clan who (mostly) leave me alone when I am trying to write, and to Ellie and Lola, my cantankerous old lady pussycats, for being patient about late dinners when the writing takes over.

And for my good friend, Josephine Bilton, who has been a beta reader for me from the start. Back in February, Jo became a grandmother (for the third time) to little George Ashton John Tyrell. Ashton Brady is a tribute to George.

To Dan Scottow, Val Dickenson, Daniella Curry, Stuart and Dee Beharrie, and all of the other brilliant supportive friends I have, I love and appreciate you all.

Finally to Nathan Moss and Patricia Dixon, fellow writers and good friends, who along with Heather, are there to bounce ideas off on a daily basis. Your friendship and advice makes living this crazy dream so much fun.

A NOTE FROM THE PUBLISHER

Thank you for reading this book. If you enjoyed it please do consider leaving a review on Amazon to help others find it too.

We hate typos. All of our books have been rigorously edited and proofread, but sometimes mistakes do slip through. If you have spotted a typo, please do let us know and we can get it amended within hours.

info@bloodhoundbooks.com

Printed in Great Britain
by Amazon